MARIA'S ODYSSEY

To all the doctors, nurses and medics at BMC with gratitude

Tommy

MARIA'S ODYSSEY

Sonny Nairn

Copyright © 2022 Sonny Nairn

The moral right of the author has been asserted.

Apart from any fair dealing for the purposes of research or private study, or criticism or review, as permitted under the Copyright, Designs and Patents Act 1988, this publication may only be reproduced, stored or transmitted, in any form or by any means, with the prior permission in writing of the publishers, or in the case of reprographic reproduction in accordance with the terms of licences issued by the Copyright Licensing Agency. Enquiries concerning reproduction outside those terms should be sent to the publishers.

This is a work of fiction. Names, characters, businesses, places, events and incidents are either the products of the author's imagination or used in a fictitious manner. Any resemblance to actual persons, living or dead, or actual events is purely coincidental.

Matador
Unit E2 Airfield Business Park,
Harrison Road, Market Harborough,
Leicestershire. LE16 7UL
Tel: 0116 279 2299
Email: books@troubador.co.uk
Web: www.troubador.co.uk/matador
Twitter: @matadorbooks

ISBN 978 1803130 699

British Library Cataloguing in Publication Data.
A catalogue record for this book is available from the British Library.

Printed and bound in the UK by TJ Books LTD, Padstow, Cornwall
Typeset in 11pt Minion Pro by Troubador Publishing Ltd, Leicester, UK

Matador is an imprint of Troubador Publishing Ltd

For Gwen

Odyssey;

Noun,
A long and eventful or adventurous journey or experience

'Luis, you are the one person in my life outside of the ring of corruption and deceit that has been my life for some time, and I didn't want to contaminate you.'

Maria

To all my family and friends who supported and encouraged me in realising my ambition in writing this novel, and bring it to publishing.
I love you all
Many thanks

ONE

PENGE, SOUTH LONDON

NOVEMBER 2015

Travelling had been her life for many years, tending to follow the sun as far as possible. She stayed in the best hotels in prime locations, and enjoyed the good life; eating at the top table. *La dolce vita*

Maria, born in Spain and now in her thirties, was acutely aware of the circumstances that brought her to this place, but it was the bigger picture that puzzled her. How could she, who had been doing so well in the material sense, have slipped so far down the social scale? she wondered, 'Where did I go so far adrift?' she muttered under her breath. Certainly, there had been key moments she could identify when things got out of control and ended badly; she could recall those easily enough. Perhaps it was simply a build up over time, an accumulation of problems that got her here.

Riddled with guilt on many levels, Maria could not work out how best to free herself from those feelings.

Her closest friend, Janet Higgingbottom, a health-care professional, had enrolled her into a programme of recovery, but it was early days. She had suggested to Maria that she should take it easy and not try to tackle too much at once. Janet made it clear that there were many reasons as to why she had arrived at this point in her life and that guilt was just one of many emotions that they would be working on. As she looked out the window, the wind and incessant rain blew rubbish around in the street below, adding to her foul mood. She missed the sunshine and warmth of home.

Her flat was in Penge, South London, small but sufficient for her needs. As it was situated over a small convenience shop, she did not have to travel far for shopping, which suited her as she didn't have a car, and the public transport system was unfamiliar to Maria.

Janet would remind her that this austere period was the price she had to pay for her sobriety. Although constrained, she had choices and freedom from the whims of others. She emphasised that providing Maria worked the programme, her life was bound to improve; her mind and body would recover.

She had taken Janet's word on trust and so far it had paid dividends. The promise of further improvement to her quality of life drove her on; she believed in Janet's prediction that this new way of life would eventually bring her peace of mind. All she had to do was stay away from that first drink one day at a time, work the programme and she would gain freedom from fear and insecurity. That would be her mantra. But she would never have expected such wonderful news.

Sitting and procrastinating, she realised she must take action; Janet had drummed that into her head:

'Don't sit around idly worrying. Get up and do something, anything. Easy does it but do it.'

The faint aroma of spicy food wafted up from the flat below, temporarily distracting her, but she picked up her phone and called Janet, only to be connected to voicemail.

Arvind, her landlord, lived below with his wife Meera, and two girls, Devya age three and Isna five. Maria got on well with all the family and loved having the girls come up to visit. On her bad days, they would bring joy and laughter to the house. At times, they had been an emotional lifesaver, lifting her mood. She wondered if she would ever be able to get her life back and have children of her own.

Along with the aroma of Indian cuisine, which often permeated the building, soft sitar music created a peaceful ambience throughout. On her good days, she really appreciated this new-found simplicity of life; it was still an alien concept, as her life was generally all action.

The walls in Maria's flat were painted magnolia on woodchip paper. The floor was covered by a beige carpet upon which her bed-settee of faux leather rested. The settee was clean but old, with much patina.

When together, they shared English and Hindi, and all enjoyed learning new words. Maria, apart from Spanish, spoke fluent Italian and French, with some German. They loved these sessions learning from each other. She felt safe and warm, and frequently reminded herself of that. She had shelter and love but she admitted in truth that at times she was desperate for a drink.

She knew she would have to do some work on the weather and how badly it affected her; it filled her with dread. It was as if the rain was not ordinary rain but rather a curse for her wrongdoings, such was her guilt.

Powerful emotions gripped her the cold physically and mentally penetrated her very being. A lonely cold right down inside her; it scared her. Maria knew she had to act and shift this feeling, which had always led her to drink. She must deal with it and not let it fester. She called Janet once more.

'Hi, Janet, Mags here. How's it going?

'Yeah, well, you know, I'm busy-busy for sure but not complaining I knew I would be letting myself in for extra work in the new post. How about you?'

'Been pretty good for some while now. Trying my hardest to work the programme with being positive, then, I get down and have doubts. Today is not good.'

'Any idea what's going on? Anything specific or just general stuff?' Janet asked.

'Well, it's sort of more of the same, Jan, I really struggle with the British weather. I feel the cold more than I expected. My mood changes and I get low. Then I miss home and one thing leads to another, I get really down and want to take it all away with a drink. Can we just meet up if you can get free for a bit? Just a chat might help,   face to face. Speak Spanish and maybe cuss a little, like we Spanish girls enjoy.'

'Okay, Mags, *buen dia, chica,* (Good morning) I'm on my way. I've got some literature for you which should help.

Do you need me to get anything for you? I'm calling at the supermarket on my way.'

'No, thanks, Jan got quite a bit from Arv yesterday. So handy and they're such lovely people, gentle and spiritual. Just need a good chat and sort a few things out in my head.'

'Cool, Mags, be over in about an hour after my shop. Don't need much myself.' Janet reassured her; *only she* called Maria, Mags!

Maria felt a little better right away; Janet would be coming, so she made an Americano coffee from her machine and decided to move away from the window to the settee in front of the TV and coal-effect electric fire.

The TV news displayed 10.00. 25.11.2015; the only bit of good news. It gave her a great sense of achievement; she had completed her minimum forty days treatment plan so hoped Janet would have some further good news for her about future treatment options.

The remainder of the news depressed her and she switched over to watch a *Homes Abroad* programme showing a young couple viewing an apartment in Lanzarote, and as she watched, warmth began to reach her inner soul. Maria felt warmer inside and out and less afraid.

The Canary Islands were familiar to Maria, particularly Lanzarote, she had a soft spot but with certain reservations for that island.

The whiteness of the buildings, the blue of the sea and sky, the palms and bougainvillea in the gardens, took her right back there. That was a place of comfort, where, as she watched, she ached with all her might to be; she shed a tear.

The beautiful location with year around sunshine and the good life, but in truth, for Maria, confused memories muddled with a lot of sangria and cava. As she watched the TV, she drifted off into memories of her time there.

The English weather carried on unabated and South London did not offer much for which she felt she should be grateful. With no job and dwindling resources, the foul weather just about capped it off.

The heat from the electric fire and the warmness of the Canarian scene on TV softened her mood; she drifted off momentarily into sleep.

It did not last too long, as she was jolted back to reality with loud banging on the front door. Jumping up, she thrust the window open. The cold wind blasted right in her face as she hollered out. 'Hang on, Jan I'll chuck down the keys.'

'Hurry up, I've been waiting for half an hour down here, freezing to death. Where you been?' Jan shouted back.

Maria fumbled with the keys, which she'd left in her front door, and hurriedly tidied up the coffee table littered with travel magazines and English and Spanish newspapers, finally throwing down the keys in a plastic bag to the street below.

'I'm so sorry, Jan I must have dozed off, erm... I'm sorry.'

Janet interrupted, 'Don't worry, Mags. I'm kidding. I only just arrived, really. Stop worrying, I'm here now Mag just get this down you, café latte and hot bagels. Joe's Corner Cafe didn't have smoked salmon. Butter will do but you might want to pop the bagels in the microwave Jan suggested?

'Oh, you're such an angel, Jan. Don't know what I'd do without you' Maria replied, her voice a little shaky.

'Do you want to tell me what it's all about, Mags?'

'Well, I really thought I was doing so well, one day at a time, then the TV news was so bleak with all the warring and famine all over the globe and now they're talking about some disease or other spreading worldwide It set me right back, Jan.'

'Okay here's what we're doing right now. Pop the bagels in the microwave for thirty seconds, get lashings of butter on them, while they're hot and let's get the coffees down us before they get cold,' Jan said in a firm, controlling voice.

Maria felt much warmer from the fire and the food as they sat and chatted about the possibility of Maria perhaps finding some light, undemanding work to get her out of the flat, and also to provide a little income.

'Mags, we can look at that some other time. It's just important that you place that somewhere in your mind and do a little work on what you could do. But for the moment, let's keep it simple and one day at a time. Let's see what's going on for you, where your head's at. Are you managing to get to your meetings?' Janet enquired.

'Erm...not really, the weather is so miserable I don't fancy going out, especially at night and not having a car. The buses are so unpredictable.' Maria mumbled.

'Right, that didn't take too long. Skipping your meetings for all the wrong reasons is never going to work for you, kiddo. Sitting around feeling sorry for yourself won't cut it either.

'How about the little acronym you've been learning as a check on what's going on with your emotions…been checking Mags?

HALT?' Jan asked in a curt way.

'Jan, erm… I can't actually remember what you're talking about, to be honest. The whole thing just seems so complicated some days, I'll never get the hang of it,' she said.

'Okay, let's not push it too hard, as you're obviously struggling with remembering, which is common at your stage of recovery. So let's have a refresher It's not rare, and although you need to be easy on yourself, you need to be tough on your addiction.'

Maria sat upright, and asked. 'Would you like another drink? Tea or coffee? I've got some appetisers in the fridge, Jan.'

'Mags, I love you so much. I'm desperate for you to *get* the programme. See, what you did there is classic avoidance. Doesn't make you a bad person, love, but it's those little things we have to work on.'

'Jan, you know they talk about sponsors at the meetings, would you be my sponsor?' Maria softly asked.

'Well, I'm not jumping in to rescue you, Mags, that doesn't work. So many people in your past have tried and failed at that. At this point, it's early days and we need to get a few basics ironed out. I want to see a bit more commitment from you. I'm already sponsoring two other people but I'm prepared to consider it. Can we leave it there and get some more meetings under your belt? When was the last time you used?'

'Three months coming up soon. Got the exact date in my journal if you want it, Jan?'

'Mags, that's great, honey. You and a few others never would have believed you could do forty meetings in forty days. You're just brilliant, but you're still at the beginning of your journey. We need to keep momentum.

'There's a meeting in Croydon at eight. I'll pick you up at seven thirty and we'll go together. Meantime, read your literature. Keep a little notebook, and of course use your journal. That will help to monitor your good days and not such good days. I'll give some more thought to the sponsorship thing, and let you know a bit later. See you tomorrow night. Let's say the serenity prayer and I'll get back to work,' said Jan.

They prayed together.

As she set off, Janet called in on Arv to have a chat, only to discover today they were celebrating Diwali. Arv was wearing a beautiful traditional orange robe, and with his neatly trimmed beard reminded Janet of her guru.

He greeted her as he *pranaamed*; '*Namaste, Jai guru.*'

Janet responded in kind; '*Jai guru.*'

The air was fused with wonderful Indian food being prepared, and Meera quickly appeared to offer greetings and food. Sadly, Janet had to get back to work, but Meera was not taking no for an answer, quickly filling a bag with samosas and pakoras for Janet's lunch.

'Where's Maria today? Haven't seen her for a couple of days. Is she well? she enquired.

Janet replied, 'She's fed up with the weather. I would have stayed longer but I have to get back to work in Dartford.'

'She must come down for sharing food. We have so much, she's more than welcome. Sorry you can't stay, but we understand you have patients to see.'

As soon as Janet had gone, Meera went up the stairs and knocked on Maria's door. It was a while before she answered.

'Oh, darling, whatever is the matter?' Meera put her arms around her to console her.

'I'm sorry,' Maria burbled out, 'It's all so miserable and scary. I'm not coping well, Would you like to come in for a cuppa?'

'Well, thanks for the offer of the tea, you're very kind, but we're having food to celebrate Diwali downstairs. You really must come down, please. Jan's gone to work with a bag of goodies. Come down as soon as you're ready. The kids would love to see you.'

Getting herself together, Maria put on a bright yellow sweater and a pair of white slacks and joined the family in the back room of the shop. Arvind didn't want to close, as he didn't have anyone else to help out; he was in and out of the shop serving and eating.

Maria mixed with the family very easily; it came naturally to her, coming from a background of family traditions in Spain. There was a small shrine in one corner of the room with incense and candles burning. Raised in a Catholic family, Maria had recently become drawn to checking out other spiritual and philosophical ideologies.

Janet had introduced her to her guru, so she knew some of the rituals in the Hindu religion. 'Would you mind if I lit a candle for my *abuela*, my grandmother?' Maria asked.

Having received approval, she put the palms of her hands together and pranaamed, and bowed as a mark of respect to the pictures on the shrine. The children very excitedly grabbed a hand each and escorted Maria back to her seat.

She felt an overwhelming sense of peace, and realised she had missed that feeling for a very long time. They all sat a while in this peace, Meera softly played the harmonium, and quietly chanted with the children; Arv made an effort to be with them but had to run the shop, popping back and forth through the dividing curtain.

There was an amazing array of wonderful Gujarati vegetarian food, so exotic. Maria's experience of Indian food was very limited, so she sampled a little of everything; the *gulab jamun* sweetmeats surprised and delighted her.

'Wow, they're something else,' she exclaimed excitedly to the children, who giggled with her. It was all such a treat for her; she felt transported to another world if only for a short while.

She felt very privileged to be in this moment, as she shared with this family. She had often heard the music from the flat below; now she saw for the first time from where it emanated: this wonderful family.

Arvind told Maria a little more about their religion, in particular, the teaching of the guru, in a way that she found deeply interesting; not a preaching or proselytising way, just

'This is our way for the whole family.' Arvind's extended family visited occasionally, although Maria had never met them, only glimpsed them from her window. At such times, she felt sad and missed her own family. A seasoned traveller, Maria had met many people from various races and sampled food of many countries, but this had been special.

A realisation came to her that food was not just for fuel for the day, flavoured to feed the senses, but there may be a spiritual quality to the preparation and eating. She said her farewells to the family and returned to her flat conscious that Janet would be around if needed.

*

Totally at peace with herself once back in her flat Maria dozed off in an unusually deep sleep, only for it to be broken by the arrival of Janet. She had been looking forward to Janet picking her up for the meeting in Croydon. She arrived and in her inimitable fashion casually commented on the improvement and then dropped a bombshell. 'I've got to say your latest blood counts are amazing. Everything is in good order, great improvement. Remind me, how long have we been back in the UK, Maggs?'

'Well, you know, I've completed just over forty days. Couple of months maybe. Not sure.'

'Oh yeah, that figures. Are you seeing anyone at present?' Janet asked.

'No, definitely not. What's that all about, Jan? What's up What's going on with all the questions?' Maria angrily replied.

'Well, I should have called you earlier, but I wanted to give you the news personally. By the way, Maggs, did you know you're pregnant?' Janet asked.

'What? What are you saying? Don't be stupid. What are you saying? You're kidding me, yeah?'

'Not kidding, Maggs. God's honest truth.' Janet said.

'Pregnant! Oh my God, I'm going to have a baby, Oh my God. I can't believe that. I know I've had some morning sickness but thought that was the medication. I must get hold of Luis and *mama*. What news! Jan, my life is turning around for sure. It's wonderful. I can't believe it, I'm going to be a *mama*.' Maria finally came to terms with the news.

The pair spent the rest of the day chatting about the baby. Was it a boy or a girl? Nothing really changed as far as her treatment plan was concerned. She had not been using alcohol or any illicit substances. She agreed to immediately come right off prescribed medication for fear of damaging the baby. It was all good, just spread the word, they agreed.

'It must have been that wonderful afternoon in the Cantabrian hills with Luis when he proposed to me. What a wonderful memory to hold. I'll get right onto him once we're finished here Janet, and of course, dear *mama* and *papa*.'

TWO

CANTABRIA

SUMMER 2000

On the whole growing up in northern Spain, for Maria was a happy time. A lovely part of the world, good school friends and a great environment. She enjoyed northern Spain, the regional variations along that rugged coastline, the aliveness and energy of the place. From Asturias, Galicia and Cantabria, to the Basque Country, subtle differences in language, dialect, expressions, food and drink. They were all Spanish but with their unique identities.

She believed this was where her soul belonged; she was born in Santa Maria del Mar, a stunningly beautiful medieval village which had remained almost intact for centuries. That very sense of preservation was very important to those who lived there. Massive dahlias adorned every available space on walls, balconies and terraces; the colours highlighted by the contrast with the sandstone buildings dating back centuries.

She would happily help out planting, with a sense of duty, when not in school. It made her feel proud of her village. Her favourite little holiday job, however, was helping out her Uncle Bernado in his cake shop.

His family had farmed here for generations. Their prize-winning herd of cows produced wonderful rich full-cream milk, famous in the region, along with the cheeses made from it. His mother, Eugenie, with this milk, cream from their cows and eggs from their hens made the most wonderful cake, which was sold out front of the shop. It was in every way home produce at its very best.

Maria frequently reflected on this part of her life, it brought her great happiness tinged with sadness, missing it as she did with frequent regularity. In her mind's eye, she could see the women sitting on their doorsteps preparing vegetables or knitting, almost in a meditative manner, only looking up occasionally to acknowledge a passer-by with a smile.

Grandma (*abuela*) told great stories of days gone by when her daughter Benita (Beni) would wash clothes with other mums in the communal well in the middle of the square. Stories were shared and gossip abounded, but they generally never bothered with world issues, just local issues, and let the menfolk worry about the bigger picture. The men worked the land, some fished, but the retired (*jubilados*) played dominos and waited until the sun had gone down before tending their gardens; everyone grew their own vegetables.

Abuela and Beni sadly had other memories of '*el Guerre Civile*', (the Civil War). Horror stories which

Maria confessed to never having really taken on board, but realised that at some point she would have to.

As it was clearly such an important part of the family history, she felt duty-bound to fill in some of the blanks in the story, and time was running out, the longer she delayed.

Mama with *papa* Claudio, (an excellent chef), ran the small Café El Reunion in Santa Maria, a picturesque seaside fishing village not far from Santander.

Maria had grown up with many friends, the closest of whom was Janet Higgingbottom. A little younger than Maria and born to English parents in a village in the foothills of Los Picos Europa, she held strong social views and was always up for a discussion about social injustice. They were the best of friends.

Her home with her parents was located in a stunning mountain range, full of wonderful flora and fauna. Wild animals had free range in this wilderness of tranquillity. Her parents settled in the region some years ago, and now ran a *posada* (guest house) on the slopes of a picturesque hillside.

Beni and Claudio made a comfortable living from their restaurant, frequented by both locals and tourists alike. The excellent reputation of the restaurant had gained entries in a number of tourist publications.

The restaurant was blue and white, with tables both inside and out and many references to the sea. Seashell and portholes with rope work adorned the walls, along with artwork from local artists. A large water tank containing live lobsters and fish, guaranteed fresh produce every time.

Outside, there was an old rowing boat painted blue and white, full of dahlias. With tables overlooking the harbour, it was almost too popular at times, as the locals liked to get down there early morning for a coffee, a smoke, a bit of a read and a chat. Beni, however, had devised skills at moving them on to make room for the more profitable lunch trade.

Most of the extended family lived around the Cantabria area, having moved northward, back in the bad old days of the Spanish Civil War, a fact that would never be far from the minds of her parents and *abuela*.

A rich and fertile part of the country with natural abundance, it presented plentiful opportunities for living off the sea and the land. Maria's family had farmed, there for many years; raised sheep, goats and cattle, providing high-quality meat, fish and *tetilla*, a speciality cheese, unique to the area.

Many English-speaking tourists visited, and Maria was always quick to engage with them to enhance her knowledge of the wider world beyond the confines of Cantabria. She spoke very good English and being fully conversant in both languages, she was able to acquire nuances and idiosyncrasies from Janet.

However, what she most wanted to hear about was life in other countries such as America, Australia, Canada and European cities. She would latch on to them and draw as much as she could from them before they travelled on. She loved their tales and envied them; one day, she knew she would be leaving to explore such places.

The 'old boys' drinking in the café Reunion, played cards and talked of football in the main, with little interest in *la corrida*. However, Beni had a brother Ignacio, an aspiring matador who was killed by fascists back in the day. It was a taboo subject.

The Civil War cropped up at some point on a daily basis. Maria, was not aware of the horrors inflicted in that war. It may have been mentioned in school but it never registered with her.

Rather, she would go out fishing with uncle (*tio*) Pedro in his boat, catching the most amazing fish; he often let her handle the boat, which she did with ease and competence. She loved tio Pedro, his boat and the sea.

Occasionally, she would shop with her friends or *mama* in Santander, but Maria even as a child was never interested in clothes and fashion. She was never particularly interested in boys either and got something of a reputation for being a bit of a 'tomboy.'

A local lad, Javier, had been very keen on her and on occasion would invite her for nine holes of golf. He aspired to become a golf professional. Although their relationship had been fairly serious for a while on and off in a tempestuous way, Javi's goal was set on golf and Maria would have to settle for second place.

*

On completion of her high school education, Maria went on to graduate in travel and humanities from Santander University. It was whilst studying at uni. with its frequent parties, that she began to get quite a taste for the local Ria Baixas, a fine wine. There were times when she missed lessons as a result of her drinking.

Few of her university friends left to find work abroad, tending to stay local. Life in general had always been quite comfortable in terms of working the land and finding a local job. The parents reinforced that "stay at home" culture. Get a local job, marry a local boy or girl, go to church, have children and get buried in the local church.

However, Maria's head had been turned by visiting tourists from far-flung destinations. Few of her family ever travelled far; perhaps a holiday in France or Italy but they were not great explorers. Her father, Claudio, always reminded Maria; 'Why would we want to go to all these fancy places, Rome, Paris, Milan or London, when we've got everything here? Spanish culture is the greatest in the world. We have many famous artists, poets, sculptors and some of the finest buildings, both old and new, in the world.

Beni's experience of travelling with Claudio, she explained to Maria; 'The only time we went away from Spain together was to Greece, and your father complained from the start to the finish of the trip. He hated flying, felt sick and got a headache. Said the boat crossing to the islands was too full of people talking different languages he couldn't understand, and as for the food, he said he could cook better himself.'

'On the subject of ancient temples, villas and baths, his comment was classic, stating that he was fed up with them… this is two thousand years old… that is two thousand years old… I want to see something new, like the buildings in Valencia… No, I would never go away with your father again, Maria.'

This point of view was certainly not unique within her family; folks in the village were fairly inward-looking in general. The internet was available and brought the outside world into village life for those who could be bothered to master the technology.

Everyone now had a washing machine; the well in the centre of the village consigned to the tourists as a photo opportunity.

Loving every aspect and anecdote about the place which was her very heritage, Maria still had itchy feet and was keen to move on.

The mention of other European cities and indeed the allure of the U.S.A. for some reason particularly filled her with a sense of excitement and anticipation.

Ready to venture forth, she decided to move to pastures new, but in the full knowledge that she must return to fill in jigsaw pieces that comprised her life. Perhaps she thought her friends would advise on how to go about it. She would leave but she must also return.

THREE

DECISIONS

JUNE 2015

There was in Maria's mind an idea or even a dream of travel, mainly based on others' experiences, the media, and her memories of family holidays in the sunny south. She wanted to construct a plan of sorts and needed to talk with Janet, who was always on the move.

She loved her family deeply and felt the whole project would have to be managed with sensitivity. She was afraid her leaving would somehow be seen as an act of betrayal.

Mama and *papa* were content, with no future plans for travel. Comfortable in their belief that their lives' had been rich enough, they had experienced their fair share of toil, strife, joy and tragedy.

They gained great comfort in their Catholic upbringing and religious observance, although freely admitting there were times during the war when they felt abandoned by God. The collaboration between the church and the fascists during that time to them was irreconcilable. Their faith had been seriously challenged and it was some time before they were able to recover their former sense of devotion.

Attending mass on Sunday almost without fail, they had no concept of, or interest in, other religious practices. Their church of St Andrew was literally right on the beach. Decorated in the best Spanish Catholic tradition, it was a place of refuge and offered the family a feeling of continuity; the cemetery was opposite, just across the other side of the coastal road.

Whilst not a fervent follower of the faith, Maria loved that place. The smell of burning candle wax and incense with the beautiful stained glass windows was an immersive experience. Over the years, she had attended many weddings, baptisms and of course funerals, which she felt went on for too long, especially if mass was included.

During quiet moments of prayer, the sound of the waves from the sea could be heard, and her dream as a small child was to marry there.

But not today, she thought, as she planned her exit. Leaving would not be met with approval by most of her friends, neighbours and, for sure, family.

Timing would be critical to avoid offending the sensibilities of family and friends. Perhaps she would introduce the subject by suggesting that she planned to move on a short-term contract offered to her to expand her knowledge of a new profession and gain experience in the world of travel. She had worked as a Saturday girl in a travel shop in Santander, so that plan was a possibility for six months or so.

With her university degree under her belt and her multi-lingual skills, she felt confident in applying for a position in a travel agency in Madrid. That not only sounded like a plausible cover story, it might also be a workable plan in reality.

Maria had very few people in the village in whom she felt she could confide. Janet, being the exception, had already been approached and was, in principle, in favour of Maria's intentions to move on. She had herself spent a considerable amount of time away from home and managed the process without hindrance. Sadly for Maria at this crucial time she was away in England so was unavailable to offer face-to-face advice.

That only really left some of the students she had befriended in university, a lively bunch and far more confident than she.

*

It was at one of their regular reunions that Maria broached the subject, and was greatly relieved to discover that in general they were widely in agreement with the idea, apart from Pablo, who had an easy going lifestyle supported by his family's wealth. He could come and go as he pleased, with no financial incentives to find paid work.

Most of the others felt the need to experience the world beyond the confines of northern Spain. José had an offer of an apprenticeship with an advertising company in Santander so he was fixed up; Luisa had been working on a casual basis in childcare and would possibly take a postgrad course with that in mind.

The group, who called themselves *Los supervientos* (The Survivors), met once a month in Pepitos, a tapas bar in the centre of Santander close to the main theatre area.

The *plaza de toros* was still in existence, with a category two status, and although support for *la corrida* had waned considerably in recent years, it still had a following of devoted fans.

Maria had only recently heard from her family about her late Uncle Ignacio being a matador and thought that she might like to know more about him. She considered making some time to check out the museum for any trace of Ignacio Garcia

She had never been to *la corrida*, but watching it on TV, she found herself strangely attracted to the spectacle. There was, she felt a certain mystique to the whole affair; the costumes, rituals, music and of course the skills of the *toreadors*.

She had seen pictures of Ignacio resplendent in his *suit of lights*; handsome, he cut a dashing figure.

However, tonight in Pepitos would not be a good time. The bar, very old and historic was located just off the Plaza Major; a haunt for many a student, young or old over many years. A magnet for anyone looking for a fun time with good food wine, and, at the weekends, live music with flamenco dancing.

The place was so full of clutter. A noisy affair, the floor littered, as usual, with tissues discarded by the tapas-eaters; the walls with pictures of well-known celebrities from the world of *la corrida*, movies, stage, but with footballers in prominence.

Jamon hung from the brass rail over the bar. Lottery tickets stuck on walls with a poster advertising the Corrida Caso de Cuarto Caminos, (the bullring).

Maria was getting quite drunk as she turned to her friend Luisa, and raised her voice to be heard.

'Have you ever thought about how disgustingly dirty this place is? I'll bet it's not seen a lick of paint for a hundred years. It would drive my mother insane.'

Luisa replied 'That's the charm of the place. It's been like this probably for hundreds of years, never really noticed the décor. The food is good and the wine is plentiful and the atmosphere is unbelievable, just take it all in, *chica,* a sort of complete package of Spanish culture at its best, almost a *gestalt* moment, if you will.'

Maria had trouble to be heard, let alone understand what Luisa was going on about. Luisa continued.

'It's a bit like, you know, when you are at a flamenco evening, the dance, the music, voices and rhythms all just magically combine together, It's *duende.* The whole experience is like that, to my mind.'

The music had not even started, but the noise levels were already not conducive to conversation at any level. Maria responded with,

'Luisa, I'm sorry but I have no idea what you're talking about. *Gestalt, duende*, you've lost me. I just wanted to have a chat and maybe get some advice from my old friends.'

'Well, sorry if I'm boring you, thought you'd be more

in touch with your Spanishness in a place like this.' Luisa responded, a little gruffly.

'Look Luisa I'm as Spanish as anyone in here, so don't give me that stuff, and I'm not impressed with your highbrow psychobabble.' Maria slurped out with a mouthful of red wine dribbling down her blouse.

Luisa could not resist a dig, as she saw Maria was pretty drunk. 'Well you're top of the class for drinking and making a fool of yourself tonight, Maria.' Luisa reacted with even more anger and indignation.

Pablo, who had been drinking with the others in the group, strolled over just at that moment, unaware of the spat the girls were having.

'Whoops,' he said just as Maria slurped. 'Well, Maria, you don't seem to have slowed down on your drinking since we last met. In fact with the greatest respect, you seem to be drinking even more.' He had to shout to be heard over the intense noise in the place.

She angrily shouted back at him, sliding forward towards him, she almost fell from her stool.

'And who the hell do you think you are, little posh money-bags, mummy's boy? You know how to knock it back.'

The others heard this above the noise and looked over as Luisa verbally went back into the fray. 'Maria your drinking has actually got out of control you're a menace when you come out for a drink. We never know what's coming next. You need to get help chica.'

'Hey, hey now, guys, let's not get too carried away here. It's just a friendly get-together.' Pablo said, just as Maria staggered to her feet, and, crying, rushed towards the toilets, trying in vain to cover her mouth as she threw up. It was a mess.

The bar erupted with jeering; just what they needed to enliven the proceedings before the flamenco. Luisa had spotted the oncoming disaster and trying to catch up with Maria, only added to the confusion by partially jamming in the door frame with her.

Wild cheering ensued!

A young man arrived with a bucket and mop, firing a quick 'Well done, *chica*' at Maria. He expertly cleared the mess, clearly a routine with which he was very familiar.

The pair did their best to clean Maria up enough for her to make a reappearance in the bar. Luisa tried to comfort her as she sat on the toilet with her pants round her ankles, when a drunken man staggered into the toilet to great applause from his buddies in the bar.

'For goodness sake, can't you see it's occupied you stupid drunken idiot? Get out,' Luisa screamed at him.

'*Lo siento*,' (I'm sorry) the man replied as he bounced off the door frame back into the bar, to even more wild cheering and applause.

Back at their table, with some semblance of normality, Pablo arrived with a San Pellegrino mineral water with ice and lemon. '*Lo siento, chica*.' He gave Maria the drink, and put his arms around her.

Luisa tried to console her. 'C'mon, girl, we're all friends here, Pablo only means the best for you. He wouldn't harm a fly, you know that. I know this is not the right time to be discussing this stuff, but it's the only time we get together and we've all noticed you're drinking a lot these days. If it's something we can help with you know we will.'

By this time. the group had got together in a huddle of sorts and were in broad agreement; *they all wanted to help but no one had any idea how they could proceed.*

The waiter arrived, asking if all was well. *'Todo bien aqui, amigos?'*

Pablo assured him all was well and wondered why it was so raucous in the bar this night? It turned out it was the local supporters of Racing Santander Football Club, having just won a local derby match.

After some negotiation, the group were able to offer Maria reassurances, combining a fair amount of skilled restoration with mascara and tissues. She started to feel a little better and very shakily offered a few words of apology. They graciously admitted, 'Well, it's happened to us all.'

But really? thought Luisa.

The only real issue now was how was Maria getting home? The group surreptitiously chatted amongst themselves to decide the best option.

'Maria how did you get here tonight? Did you drive?' Luisa enquired.

'Erm… um I'm not sure.' Fumbling in her handbag for car keys, she found none.

'No, I must have come on the bus, as I expected to be over the legal limit.' she replied, giggling. 'Think I probably am.' They agreed.

Pablo, who had been close-by Maria came in with an offer. 'That's okay, I'll drive you home, Maria, if you'll let me.'

'Would you really, after all the horrible things I said to you?' Maria replied.

Pablo responded. 'Of course, but only on the condition that if you're going to chuck up again, give me plenty of warning so I've got time to open the door.' They all laughed at that, and the atmosphere lightened up considerably.

It was settled and after a few convivial drinks, they began to break up the party. Pablo did not drink alcohol, a fact that had never been an issue for the group all the time they were at uni but his abstinence had always irritated Maria.

Driving Maria home to her parents' Pablo tried to make polite conversation in an attempt to keep her mind stimulated, keep her awake. Gradually, her head cleared a little, so he planned on getting her on her feet to walk into her parents' house. The car ride was only about an hour and Pablo lived about thirty minutes further on.

Pablo opened with. 'We don't see one another very often these days, Maria, not since we were at uni together.'

'Well, we didn't really see a great deal of one another before that.' Maria answered. Pablo realised it was going to be hard work having this conversation, but he plodded on with inane talk.

They discussed life post-uni and work-related issues, but Pablo unashamedly admitted he had not got a job of any description.

'My dad would like me to work in the city, but I could not work in an office all day.' He said.

Maria told Pablo of her ambition to move away, and travel. She explained that was what she wanted to discuss at the tapas bar with the group but now realised it had not been a good idea.

She continued. 'I feel that life is too cosy. I want to get away and experience the world away from the north. I lack confidence and know I always have. I found that drink gave me 'Dutch courage' at first, but now it doesn't work and I just seem to get further into trouble with it. The opposite is happening to me now, I have no real drive and feel dependent on it and have no idea which way to turn.'

'Wow, I had no idea that things were so bad for you. I always saw you as the smart one in the group, full of confidence and ambition. You always got the best grades, and I imagined you would go far. I'm so surprised at what you're telling me. Have you discussed this with other people, Maria?'

'No, never in fact, I can't believe I've blurted that much out. I must feel safe with you, I guess. I know by now I need help but don't know where to get it,' she said.

'Well, I'm no expert but after uni I did a course on psychology, which with other social and economic problems looked at addictions. One of the key elements in the first stage was admitting there was a problem. Perhaps you could be at that stage on the bigger spectrum. Admittance?'

'I had no idea what happened to you after uni Pablo.' Maria changed the subject.

'Well, *papa* got fed up with me hanging around all day, golfing, fishing and hunting, with no sense of purpose. He suggested I go back to uni, turned out to be a brilliant idea.

I loved the course and the knowledge I gained from it. Still haven't got a job as yet but keeps *papa* happy.'

By this time, they had arrived home at Maria's house. The parents were in bed so she was happy not to have a confrontation at the late hour. Maria had a feeling of relief. For the first time, she had admitted she had a problem with alcohol and to her amazement shared it with another person. Pablo of all people, someone with whom she had never spent a great deal of time. He kissed her, wished her a good night and drove home.

*

The following morning, Maria was unable to enjoy breakfast with her parents, as she felt sick.

Mama asked, 'Darling, are you feeling unwell? You haven't touched your breakfast. Perhaps a little coffee and croissant, sweetie?'

'No, *mama*, I don't feel hungry at the moment, maybe later, thanks,' she replied, but *mama* spotted her shaking hands. 'I may have picked up a bug or something, feels like flu.'

Mama was just about to suggest paracetamol when Maria quickly jumped up from the table and rushed to her room, where she promptly threw up into the washbasin.

Papa, who had remained silent up until now, said 'She's drinking too much. Did you see how she shakes? Her whole body shakes and now she's upstairs chucking up. That's drinking too much. She's got a hangover, or worse.'

In her room, Maria took a quick shot of vodka, brushed her teeth for all she was worth and popped in extra-strong mints. She very slowly made her way downstairs, determined to hold down whatever was left in her stomach. *Mama*, quick to her feet, put her arms around her and hugged her. She smelled the vodka and strong mints and felt an overwhelming sense of sympathy for her daughter.

'My darling daughter, I've been worried for some time that something is wrong. Now we know, you must let us help you.'

Papa, still sitting at the table, looked up but did not move. Just watched the two women in his life looking very vulnerable, and wondered how *he* could possibly help.

'*Mama*, you're over reacting. I've just got a bit of a hangover, that's all. I'll be perfectly back to normal within the hour.' But they all knew it was far worse than that.

FOUR

MADRID

JULY 2015

Maria decided to put her plan into place for the move from home. She had deliberately chosen a specific location from where she could see the whole of the village; a hillside covered in wild flowers on the south-side with wildflowers in abundance, cattle munching at the meadow grass and buzzing bees making the most of the perfumed wonderland. The blue of the sky unbroken by any sign of cloud she had taken the precaution to apply her sunscreen and her trusty old broad brimmed hat was firmly in place.

Despite the fact that believed she was making the right decision to leave the village she needed to be one hundred per cent certain. The scene pulled at her heartstrings. *Dear lord give me the strength to do the right thing, show me the way but give me peace above all.* She silently prayed with tears running down her cheeks. The church bells were signalling the celebration of mass so she made her way down the hill to meet her parents with a*buela*. They would be coming out of church soon.

Maria's plan was to tell them she was going to a travel agency in Madrid on a short time replacement; one of the women was taking maternity leave.

*

At first, Madrid seemed to offer all that Maria had been looking for: work opportunities, classy shops, well-dressed Madrilenos strutting their stuff; a vibrant energy of city life. An exciting place of beautiful streets, bars, restaurants; everything that Maria had expected from a major European city.

However, something did not work for her. She could not quite get the hang of the place. For sure, the transition moving from a small village to the big city was huge, but that was not the issue. She coped well with *that* change. Yes, she missed her friends and family, but she developed ways of coping with that. There were plenty of distractions. Cinemas and theatres were brilliant, as were the sports facilities, all of which she took full advantage.

With her experience, gained from working in the travel agency in Santander, Maria soon acquired a reasonably well-paid position with Solano Viajar, a travel agency with a good brisk business record in the best part of town. Maria spoke several languages, a major factor in her ability to communicate in the travel business. The majority of customers coming to the agency were locals,

Madrilenos. She fortunately took a short term lease on a small apartment close to work.

Any French, Italian, English or German customers were usually hived off to Maria; she was more than happy to oblige. The job came easily to her.

An attractive and intelligent woman, she easily made friends and business contacts. Entertaining clients was part of her remit, selling the dream.

Often, her remit would extend to a little dinner or a lunch appointment, which never went amiss.

She was keen to start afresh and put aside her alcohol-induced problems she had in the north. It was early days and she had just begun to make social contacts not work-related.

Considerably reducing her alcohol intake, Maria discovered she could operate at a much more efficient level. So eager was she to make the transition a success, she became almost preoccupied with abstinence.

Reaping the benefits of sobriety, she determined to look after herself and regularly had lunch or dinner in local restaurants. At one such lunch, she met another woman, Leanne, from the office, and after a while they became close friends rather than simply work colleagues.

As time went by, they discovered mutual interests and found they were able to share their joys and sadness.

At dinner one night in the San Marino restaurant in downtown Madrid, the sharing became a little more intense and Maria realised she had a confidante in Leanne. She plucked up courage and opened up about the terrible night she had with her colleagues in Santander.

They had just finished eating starters, *calamares a la Romana* with a carafe of white house wine. Maria finished one glass and declined another, despite the waiter almost insisting she take another.

'You see, Leanne, that's the problem. We are so used to drinking wine at the table, you're considered odd if you refuse.' Maria said.

'Yeah, but if you're going to quit you need to be strong and not care about other people's reactions to your behaviour. Of course, It's not going to be easy but you can't have it both ways. From what you've shared about your drinking, it seems that you are unable to control it, so therefore you need to totally quit. You need to stick around people who don't *booze*. I'm one of the lucky ones. I can take it or leave it.'

'I know you're right, Leanne. I feel you might be good for me. It's probably that old demon hanging over me that's holding me back from fully enjoying living in Madrid. It's not the place. It's me, maybe. I've been thinking of trying Barcelona. What's your thinking on that one, Leanne?'

'Well, now that's weird, Maria. It's not official at work and I certainly haven't told anyone at work as yet, so keep it well and truly under your hat. I've just got a job offer in a "high-end" travel agency in Barcelona.

'Three of us went for interviews. I got confirmation today that I was successful and was hoping to hand in my notice next week. I don't know about the other position, but I'm going down at the weekend to check out the surroundings and the apartment situation. I've seen around the office area and it's very swish.

Maybe we could travel down together and check it out if you're serious about moving there. Keep really quiet about it, though. There are a few right old gossips in the office.'

'Can't believe my luck there, Leanne. I'm game for it. Just tell me where and when. I'm there. Just need to be a bit canny about work as both leaving at the same time looks like we've been poached.'

'Hang on there, girl, getting a bit ahead of yourself. You haven't even seen the place, let alone found a job. That's something else you might want to look at, Maria. You can be very impetuous. But one thing at a time, eh?'

They talked a while, quite excitedly, about the prospect of moving to another big city, new job perhaps, sharing an apartment and Maria making a promise to get her drinking under control.

Their meal, *merluza, corvina a la plancha (fish) con papas fritas* (fried potatoes), simple but well prepared, they declined desert and coffee. The wine bottle sat staring at Maria, but empty, it was of no use whatsoever to her. Maria called the waiter, who had been very attentive towards her throughout the entire evening.

'I hope you had an enjoyable meal. The food was good I see by the empty plates,' resting his hand on Maria's shoulder very gently.

'Is there anything else I can get for you, senorita?'

She gave him a rather knowing smile. '*La cuenta, por favor.*' (The bill.)

He spun around on his heels '*De inmediato*', he quipped.

'He fancies you for sure, Maria. Play your cards right, you're in there, girl.' Leanne said. They decided to 'go Dutch' on the meal, so Leanne gave Maria cash as she proffered her card to the waiter for processing. Leanne discretely got up from the table to leave.

'See you in the morning then. Take care and enjoy the rest of your evening.

The waiter had slipped a note in with the receipt for the meal, but Leanne spotted it. *Room 209 at 9.30 Jose.'*

Maria slipped it into her bag, smiled at the waiter and ran to the door to catch Leanne and called out, 'Leanne, *hasta manana'.* (See you tomorrow.)

'Manana chica' came back through the warm, still, night air. Leanne had gone.

Maria stood in the street collecting her thoughts, excited and apprehensive; she wanted to do this but wondered how this behaviour might conflict with the 'new Maria', the semi-sober Maria. She, who had a very healthy libido, which had not seen any action for some time, decided that it was getting far too complicated. She might as well enjoy herself whilst she still had her looks and the energy.

The hotel was a pretty basic three-star affair; however, the restaurant had a very good reputation, so she reasoned the room would be okay.

If she agreed to the rendezvous there was not sufficient time to go home and freshen up. She felt strangely embarrassed, but knew not why. She was no stranger to impulsively having sex; she really enjoyed the risk and thrill of it.

Maria went back into the restaurant, quickly walking to the foyer, where Jose swiftly handed her the key for room 209.

'*Sube estare vente minutos mas y menos,*' (Give me about twenty minutes or so) Jose whispered, nipping back into the restaurant. Maria thought, twenty minutes… that's time for a shower.

Maria decided to take the stairs, assuming it would be two floors up and wishing to avoid guests in the lift.

Room 209 was a shock. It had clearly been very recently occupied. As she turned to leave, the phone rang. Picking it up Jose was in a hurry to explain.

'It's Jose sorry about the room. I didn't get a chance to clean it. I wasn't expecting you until nine thirty.'

'What's this all about? It's somebody's' room, for goodness, sake.' What's this ? What's this? A bad joke?' she angrily barked at him.

'No, no, *chica.*' Jose insisted. 'It's one of the rooms they let me stay in. It's fine, clean no problem. I just left it in a hurry, a bit untidy. Make yourself comfortable. I'll be up real soon, *chica. Ciao.*'

Maria bought his story… she needed to believe it; she was excited and her hormones were racing, but she was still apprehensive. She took a shower to relax but the thrill and the prospect of sex with a complete stranger was overpowering; all sense of safety was blocked out. As she showered, she could barely wait to be in bed with Jose and her hand strayed down to her crutch, teasing her, but she postponed any further exploration in favour of the real thing.

Drying her hair she sat on the bed to consider her behaviour. This, she thought, was typical of her thrill-seeking. Friends had been telling her about this for ages and had concerns that one day it would go seriously wrong.

'*One day, Maria your drinking will get you into serious trouble.*' She could hear it as she sat there. But she reasoned and tried to rationalise. Even as a child, her reputation as a risk-taker preceded her.

She finished with the soul-searching, poured a vodka tonic with ice and lemon, switched on the TV and slipped under the duvet. As the vodka began to kick in, she felt warm and excited. The door buzzer disturbed her peace. Naked, she got out of bed to let Jose in.

'*Hola chica*. Wow, that's a greeting I wasn't expecting. What a figure! Let me shower and get at you, honey, *una momento*.' Naked, she slipped back under the duvet, now *very* excited. She was bursting with anticipation. Jose, true to his word, was out of the shower and straight under the covers with her; not, however, before she glimpsed his very impressive manhood.

As she sat in bed, Maria looked around the room, cheap regulation hotel in every way; small desk, shower, ensuite, TV and bed. Adequate and clean, she thought, and proffered her drink to Jose. He reluctantly sipped.

'Urhg, what is that?' He asked.

'Vodka tonic, don't you like it then?'

'Disgusting. I'm more a beer and wine man, but I've had enough today anyway,' he said, quite disapprovingly.

For some reason, that statement resonated with her; *I've had enough today*. She was astonished. He was sober, not even tipsy. She realised she never could say, *'I've had enough'.*

They made love; it was pretty ordinary. Jose wore a condom; they both climaxed and sat up in bed. The TV was still on. They commented on the day's news and made further small-talk exchanges.

Maria, clearly very disappointed, began to doubt the wisdom in the whole enterprise. She had always had a very healthy libido and was totally unfulfilled.

'I need another drink, Jose,' she said but no response came back from Jose. Nothing was exchanged for a while, as she poured yet another vodka.

Jose noticed her drink as he turned to Maria. *'Te apetece un porro?'* (Do you fancy a joint?)

Surprised and unsure of exactly what he asked, she replied. 'Sorry did you just ask me if I want a joint.?'

'Yeah could you go a joint? he repeated.

She thought, *well, the drink didn't do much for either of us, what the hell?*

She wanted more sex and hoped that the 'joint' may liven things up a bit. 'Jose, got some smoke then?' she asked.

'Why not? You *skin up* while I fix us a nice drink.' She replied as she fixed herself a vodka tonic, remembering that Jose 'had enough drink for the day.' Thirty minutes later, after wild, heavy love-making, they had been right through the cards; oral, on the dressing table, on all the floor, all fours, they did it all.

Eventually they collapsed on the floor. Exhausted!

They got themselves organised. 'Maria, do you want to stay the night? I've got this room for the week.'

Maria, now completely sated and likening the sex to a workout in the gym, declined.

'No, thanks Jose, that was fun. I've got work in the morning and can't be late. *Muchas gracias y adios, amigo*,' she said as she began dressing. Jose, however, wanted to meet up for another date.

'*No, gracias, Jose, es suficiente...* (enough) *'...gracias y adios.'* She left.

*

Morning brought full Spanish sunshine as Maria stepped out in a smart dark blue two-piece suit with a pale blue silk scarf tastefully arranged around her neck. She decided blue suede three inch heels would be risky, but she had been taking many risks in the last twenty-four hours. She felt impregnable.

The sun hit her eyes like a bolt of lightning, prompting the dropping of the Gucci shades from the top of her head to cover her eyes. Maria actually felt good considering last night's encounter. She had no sense of guilt or remorse; something which usually hit her first thing in the morning.

Her morning coffee Americano and croissant in hand, Maria checked herself out in the lift mirror. 'Looking good girl,' she said to herself. Once at her workstation, she sorted out paperwork for the first part of the day and called Leanne. '*Hola, chica, que tal?*' (How are you?)

'*Muy bien, gracias, es tu?*' Leanne asked.

'Well, can't wait for lunch break to tell you all about last night, Leanne.'

'Yeah, I'll bet, thought you'd go back, cheeky girl. Got some bad news about our weekend away. I can't make it. Something has come up and I need to deal with it, but you should go on your own account, Maria.'

They lunched in a local café, very modern affair, all high gloss, mirrors and stainless steel with white tiled flooring. They perched on high stools at the bar eating a very light lunch. They both checked themselves out in the mirrored wall behind the bar; with a little posturing and obligatory pouting, they confirmed they were a couple of *chicas hermosas* (very cool babes). Both were very aware of their appearance and keeping in shape was important to them. Light lunches and a little workout a couple of times a week worked for them.

Leanne apologised once more for letting Maria down at the last minute, but the good news was she had been in touch with senor Gonzales' secretary and arranged an appointment, subject to her agreement, for Maria to attend an interview at the weekend for the other position in MexTex. It was Friday lunchtime. Maria phoned to confirm the appointment. She thought it showed an amazing amount of goodwill, to interview on the Saturday. Maria would have to get organised in a hurry, booking a train ticket and hotel for the night in Barcelona, but she could do that kind of thing easily.

Leanne, already in possession of a letter of intent for the job offer, would be handing in her notice on Monday; they were moving cautiously, secretly but inexorably towards Barcelona.

The afternoon at work was a challenge for the pair, who were quietly excited at the prospect of the move but although desperate to let their work colleagues know, maintained a strict silence. Maria had spent a lot of her time in the past covering her trails and tracks, ducking and diving, and as such, although excited, she could play the game more easily than Leanne, whose nature was much more one of openness.

They agreed to meet for a short while after work for a chat and a short drink. Leanne plucked up courage to come straight out with it and warned Maria, not to get drunk, as she had a busy day ahead tomorrow.

'By the way How are you and Ferdi getting along, Leanne? Not getting serious, I hope? Could be a fly in the ointment.' Ferdi and Leanne had been in a casual relationship for quite some time.

'Well, it's not serious as far as I'm concerned, but he's pretty keen, and I feel bad about letting him down. Need to play that a day at a time.' They managed to keep the drinking short, and went their separate ways home to their respective apartments.

*

Maria rose early, showered and prepared for her train journey, checking the train tickets, times, and so on. She did not need the possible aggravation of bus travel, so she booked a cab to take her to Atocha train station. She had time to spare. Checking her wardrobe for suitable power apparel, she laid several items on her bed.

After much consideration, she actually chose the dark blue suit already worn this week. She had it sponged and pressed in readiness; she felt comfortable in this outfit. Also importantly, she knew it would still look good after the train journey. With the white silk blouse showing a suggestion of white cuff, the pale blue silk scarf and three-inch heeled dark blue suede shoes, she knew it would be a winner.

Some time ago, Maria's parents had bought her a matching designer set of three travel bags for her first trip away from home. Beautiful light tan leather, they were her proud possessions; the overnight bag was just right.

Arriving at the station, a wonderful collection of buildings, first built around the 1850's, it had all manner of facilities, including Maria's favourite boulangerie patisserie, Pablo.

The smell of the coffee, bakeries, patisseries and chocolates engulfed her; she could stay here for hours, but instead she bought a croissant, *bocadillo* (baguette) with ham, Danish pastry and large latte to go. She comfortably fitted them into her small leather bag.

Sitting on a bench in the main concourse, the sound of the station and the smell which, she recognised, still lingering somewhere in the fabric of the building, of smoke from the bygone days of steam engine locomotives. Glancing at the destination board, her excitement and anticipation increased as Rome, Paris, Lucerne, Nice, St Moritz and Budapest were on offer from various platforms.

'Oh my God, I can't believe what I'm seeing. All those places are available from this station. How can that be?' she asked herself out loud. This would be Maria's first trip of any distance by rail and she was mightily impressed.

The journey time would be approximately three and a half hours. Locating her seat, Maria, once settled, double-checked her necessary paperwork. Letter of introduction for the interview, her CV and proof of identity.

Maria was surprised as to how well she felt, thinking *'I like this new me.'* Vitalised, energetic, with a clear head, and no hangover. She had managed to get benzodiazepine from a doctor friend a couple of days ago, primarily to help with early morning shakes. Constantly checking her hands, she vowed not to succumb to alcohol this day. She really wanted to be able to successfully carry out this part of her plan.

The Spanish countryside literally flashed by at speed with a gentle hum of the powerful motors. A completely new experience and one which she was relishing, with only one problem; There was a faint whiff of disinfectant from the on-board toilet.

The first scheduled stop for the train would be Zaragoza. There, a smartly dressed middle-aged man got on and sat opposite Maria. They exchanged a few everyday pleasantries to pass the time. *Where are you getting off? Where are you heading to?* Just small talk. Maria, canny enough not to give him too much, was more than ready for the almost inevitable question. She could sense it coming.

'Perhaps you would like to dine with me in Barcelona tonight? My wife of some twenty years died a few months ago, finally succumbing to cancer after a long, painful struggle.'

Oh dear, Maria thought, *'this guy's turning the sympathy screws to the limit. I don't even care if it's true or not. I'm not going to meet him any time. I've got work to do and no booze is in my plan.* She turned this over for a very short while, with a cunning plan in mind.

'Oh, what a sad experience that must have been for you to go through all that for such a long time, that's awful,' she managed with her best sad voice.

'You remind me so much of her, in earlier years, of course, a beautiful lady, elegant and sophisticated, as are you. It would mean so much to me if you would give me the immense pleasure of taking you out to dinner.'

Maria almost gulped at this. *What if it's true? Oh my! How can I turn him down?* She needed time, and came up with her toilet escape plan.

'I'm sorry, you must excuse me. I need to powder my nose,' she said, taking off down the corridor. The toilet sign indicated "*ocupado*", so she waited, staring out at the beautiful Spanish countryside flashing by. With her elbows resting on a chrome bar across the large picture window in the corridor, she liked the way she was handling the situation. With a clear head, no alcohol to fuzz her mind. She had purpose, and whether this man was spinning her a yarn or not, she made her decision.

Returning to her seat, Maria smoothed her skirt with the palm of her right hand and her hair with her other hand. Slowly and deliberately, she said.

'I am so sorry about that, I really had to go. Where were we? Ah yes, I am of course very flattered by your offer for dinner and obviously very sad to hear about your dear wife. It must be awful after all those years. What I never explained to you is that I have a business meeting after which I'm meeting my fiancé at our hotel for the night. Just a flying visit really, on quite a tight schedule. Returning to Madrid Sunday night.'

'Oh dear, I'm the one who should apologise for my rudeness and presumptuousness and dumping all that on you. Forgive me, if you will. I hope you and your friend enjoy Barcelona. My very best wishes to you both and I hope you have as loving a friendship as I and my dear wife shared.'

Getting up from his seat, the gentleman leaned forward, took Maria's hand in his own, gently planted a kiss on the back of her hand and left.

She noted the most agreeable scent of a very expensive aftershave or cologne coming from this very cultured and thoroughly pleasant man of advancing years.

This little episode threw Maria into a dilemma; what if the man's story was true? She would never deliberately cause anyone harm, and the thought of that deeply hurt.

She had made the decision to see this whole adventure to Barcelona under her own steam, without alcohol, and was determined to see it through. Maria was now confused, doubting the wisdom of her moves, but so far she was sticking to her guns.

The message over the train conductor's loud speakers announced the arrival at Sants Estacion Barcelona, and advised that the passengers check they had all their possessions and wished everyone a pleasant onward journey.

Alighting from the air-conditioned train, she was immediately hit by the heat, smell and noise of slamming train doors and loudspeakers announcing muffled messages.

Maria's interview was not for another forty-five minutes, so she made her way to the public toilets to freshen up and find coffee.

Travelling by train for Maria had been a new experience. Astonished by the speed of the trains and, the quality of the facilities, both in the station and on the train, she said, 'This was a great start, what a truly amazing place. bring it on, Barca.'

FIVE

THE INTERVIEW

The cab had no air-conditioning, so the open window did nothing for her hair and the heat was very uncomfortable. However, the rather grumpy Middle Eastern driver had no problem finding the office address of MexTex. Without tipping the driver, she picked up her own bags and headed to the office reception. A new construction, it was all very smart and squeaky clean. The high-gloss beautifully tiled entrance hall had a security desk with a uniformed attendant, who on checking her details made a call.

All was confirmed.

'Please take lift number three to the top floor and Senor Gonzales' secretary will meet you there, *senorita.. Buen dia.*' He said.

Checking herself in the tinted mirrored walls of the lift, Maria quietly said, 'You're looking good, babe. You can do this, you're good enough.'

THE INTERVIEW

She stepped out and was greeted by the strange perfumed air-conditioned atmosphere of something between a hair salon and a dentist's waiting room. A very slim, tall, attractive young woman with a skirt which so tight outlining her buttocks; *how did she manage to get that on its far too tight, ok I'm a little jealous.* She thrust her arm forward and welcomed her.

'*Hola, Maria. Bienvenido a MexTex.* My name is Anna Dias. So pleased to meet you. If you would just follow me to the office of Senor Gonzales, he will be with you shortly. Can I get you anything, a drink perhaps?'

The office had a fairly large central section with individual workstations, surrounded by small private offices. Senor Gonzales' office was at the far end of the floor, with a couple of small settees and a coffee table outside. Maria took up the offer of a drink, and waited on a settee outside the glass box office lined with Venetian blinds.

Sipping on an ice-cold ag*ua minerale*, Maria took in everything; she was calm and ready. Anna escorted Maria to a seat in front of Senor Gonzales' desk. He greeted her with a very friendly, warm handshake.

'I'm very pleased to meet you, I've been hearing very good things about you from your friend and colleague Leanne. This other gentleman right here is Gregg Holdsworth, senior partner and my right-hand man and fellow golf bandit. Gregg slowly sort of uncoiled his large fit-looking frame from the armchair and shook Maria by the hand, and with a warm deep American accent greeted her.

'Hi, Maria, I'm Gregg Holdsworth. I try and keep this guy out of trouble on the golf course. Pleased to make your acquaintance, hope we can get you on board.' Maria felt right at home.

She had quickly taken in the surroundings (her speciality); she spotted family pictures, three grown-children – one had graduated – and photos of Senor Gonzales playing golf with famous footballers, but she couldn't recall their names. Models of aircraft on shelves and framed assorted medals. Enough to be going on, she thought.

'Love your office, a lovely mix of contemporary and traditional and wow, what a view.' Maria was right at home.

'But of course you don't have time to look at the view,' she said with a knowing smile.

'Well, maybe the odd glance or two,' he quipped as Gregg chuckled. 'I expect you would like to know about us?' he continued.

'We're a new start-up company dealing in the main with all things travel-related; a high-class travel agency, if you will, but much, much more.

'You may wonder where our name originates, MexTex? Well, I am Mexican, Gregg is practically Texican,' he said, laughing, 'and a great deal of our business emanates from those regions. You will of course be familiar with names of big travel outfits like Phileas Fogg and Kuoni.' Maria nodded in agreement.

'Well, we aim to be able to offer a level of similar service but much more. A truly bespoke service for very exclusive clients to be taken care of by us, from passports and

THE INTERVIEW

medical checks to finances, itineraries, hotels. Everything *Todas*.'

'I can see that would be a wonderful idea, especially geared to selective clients. Everything pertaining to our high-end clients' travel needs, very exclusive. I like that. However we'll have to go some to beat those competitors; top companies' Maria confidently replied.

'So you like the concept, that's a good start, and I'm sure you want to know how that is achieved, yes?' Senor Gonzales affirmed.

'Well, you see all those people out there in the main office at their workstations, they are doing all the work that you currently do. Finding flights, hotels, and transfers, checking those kinds of details. That's the everyday working of the system. Your role will be that of one who requires a higher level of understanding the clients' needs.'

Gregg, who up to this point had said very little, came in with.

'My role within the company, essentially, is to identify potential "high rollers" if you like, and put you and Leanne in contact with them. This will of course not be a nine-to-five job by any means, but one of socialising with your clients, where they are most at ease, perhaps at home or at the club but in their surroundings. It may of course mean very long hours, but the rewards are considerable.'

'Sounds great, I must admit flicking through glossy holiday brochures is beginning to lose its' charm. But I have a real love for travel, and I'm sure I can really convey that to my clients.' Maria said, with great confidence in her voice.

'Well, we've obviously done our research on you, so we know a fair amount about your life-style, family situations, likes and dislikes. Total discretion is required, that is imperative. Our whole business is dependent on that. One slip-up or leak could have the potential to put us right out of business.

'At this point, I will need to be perfectly frank and open with you, Maria. We know that you are a very sociable person who likes to eat and drink well. This position requires that of you. You're smart, dress well, carry yourself well, speak three languages fluently, perfect candidate. There is, however, a but.

'It has been noted that recently your drinking has increased somewhat, with the potential to become out of control. That is something that would not be acceptable at all, and we would have to have assurances that had been dealt with. No question about that.' Gregg demanded.

Maria quietly processed this and, thinking very carefully, hesitated before replying. The men made eye contact but showed no expression. She knew she could not deny it. *How on earth do they know such information?*

Trying to stop her mind from racing away, Maria wondered how difficult Leanne's interview had been, but she must stop drifting and answer. She felt like '"the rabbit caught in the car headlights."' Eventually, holding back any sign of weakness or vulnerability, she said.

'Yes, I am aware that I am drinking a little too much, and I am dealing with it. I have it under control, but I agree I need a little help with it. Perhaps a good doctor may help. Certainly, if I get offered this position, which I dearly would love, that would be my highest priority.'

'Maria would you mind just stepping out for a moment while Gregg and I have a little chat?'

As she sat watching the men through the Venetian blinds, it was excruciating; she had mentally invested so much into this job, she really wanted it big time. They were discussing her future; she could hardly bear it. Fortunately, it did not take them long to call her back into the office.

'Well, Maria, it's been a pleasure to meet you. We both feel you're almost the perfect candidate but for that one issue. We won't keep you in suspense for too long but will get back to you tomorrow with our decision. Thank you for coming in. Will you be staying in Barcelona for a while? It's a wonderful city with lots to see and do. Have you plans for the rest of the day?' Senor Gonzales asked.

Feeling a little shell-shocked by her sudden dismissal from the interview, Maria struggled with a sensible response but eventually came up with.

'Well, tomorrow, I'm travelling back to Madrid, so I'll have a look around before dinner, get an early night and catch a morning train back home.' She could hardly believe she referred to Madrid as home.

'Well, Maria, enjoy your stay and we'll contact you on your cell phone tomorrow. Once again, gracias, adios, hasta manana.' (until tomorrow)

Maria made for the lift, passing the girls in the main office. She was aware of some giggling but ignored them; she felt, however, deflated. She realised her expectations had been too high, rather expecting it would be a shoo-in, but no!

Grabbing her bag from reception, she called for a cab to take her to Pena del Dice, a three star complex of apartments right down by the sea-front, which she had booked online.

*

Her apartment had clearly just been cleaned, as it smelled of vacuumed-up dust and disinfectant. It was on the upper level of a two- storey block facing the sea. Throwing her bag on the bed and kicking off her shoes, Maria felt exhausted and frustrated. Flopping on the bed, she stared at the fan spinning from the ceiling. She had one thought; *'I need a drink.'*

The room was furnished in cheap Formica-type boarding. A TV sat on one top, under which there was… the mini-bar. She was almost transfixed by the glass-fronted mini-bar; it seemed to be calling to her, and desperate as she was, Maria resisted.

Opening the sliding doors to the balcony, she decided on a swim. Children were playing around the complex in the warm sunshine of early evening.

The whole place was looking tired and in need of a complete refurbishment. The sun-loungers had seen better days and the green-painted surrounds of the pool were badly flaking, bits of which stuck to the soles of her feet.

Finding an available sun lounger, she tried to relax and called Leanne, only to be transferred to voicemail. She found herself in new territory, not drinking now for several hours, and although trying to cope with benzodiazepine which she'd acquired from a friend in Madrid, she was beginning to go into withdrawals.

As she was unable to find any relaxation, the playing children were now becoming very irritating and she was getting very angry. The phone rang.

'Hi, Maria, got your message. How did it go?' Leanne enquired.

'Leanne I'll be honest, think it seemed to go well, handled everything well, all very pleasant and amiable, not really sure, but right now I've got a real problem and badly need your help.'

'Anything, Maria, just ask away,' she said.

'Well, the only sticking point was they heard about my drinking.'

Leanne replied. 'Well I hope you don't think I told them it never came up in my interview, and I would never discus anything like that with anyone.'

'No Leanne I didn't think you would do that; I just wonder where they get their information from. I get the sense that they're very powerful guys; well connected. They need to consider that before offering me the position, which is fair enough. I haven't had a drink all day, taken a couple of benzo's and "'clucking'" like mad right now. Don't want to drink in case they call.'

Leanne reassured her. 'Maria, if you have alcohol there, take a little, just enough to take the edge off, but don't take the benzo's. They won't call you tonight, they may even be testing you out tonight, see how you handle the disappointment.'

'Thanks, Leanne. I'll try that. I had the same thoughts about testing me. I would love that job but I'm feeling really sick right now.'

'Maria, sorry to hear that. Get some food, very little alcohol, no benzo's, try and get sleep, get back to me tomorrow. Call me if you need me. Don't forget now, I mean that. Nite nite.'

A plastic ball flew out of the pool and bounced on her head.

'*Oi, pequena molestia, l'impiate*,' (oi little nuisance, clear off) she hollered at the kid in the pool.

The father, bronzed, muscular, with a thick gold chain and crucifix embedded in his hairy chest, came across to apologise to Maria. He sat on an adjacent sun-lounger and clearly made a play for her.

She thought, *that's all I need right now; no, thanks.* and answered him with '*no preocupes, no probelma.*' (Don't worry, no problem.) She grabbed her stuff together and went to her room.

The illuminated glass-fronted mini-bar magnetically drew Maria towards it, and in a matter of seconds she was gulping down a miniature vodka. It was nectar, to Maria's suffering body and mind.

Furthermore, she had permission from Leanne, so there was no guilt attached to her actions. Within half an hour, she was feeling well enough to call a cab to take her out for pizza.

Cabbie Manuel took her to the city centre and as they pulled up outside the Pizza Paradise, she heard jazz music coming from inside.

'*Mucha gracias, Manuel, adios,* and she was in there like lightning, grabbing the first table she saw, ignoring frantic signals from the waiter. Maria sighed a massive exhalation of breath. 'Whoaaah, made it, thank God. *The waiter's ignoring me but that's okay.'*

Eventually, she was eating a margherita pizza with a side salad, and a half carafe of house red wine to the sound of a three-piece jazz band. Relaxed, she asked the waiter about the city tour buses. He explained that he was new to the city, having arrived from Bulgaria just a few weeks previously, but that as far as he knew, they ran up until about eleven, as many people loved to see the city by night.

Equipped with a couple of miniature bottles of vodka and topped up with red wine, Maria was up for the bus trip. She was so grateful for the advice given by Leanne and wondered how she knew how to help, mindful of following her advice by not overdoing it with drink. She determined, however, that the mini-bar did not have her drink of preference, as medication; she had better buy some before returning to the apartment.

The bus tour was a success for Maria; she absolutely loved the city by night, visiting all the well-known tourist destinations; Casa Batlloe, la Sagrada Familia, la Rambla. She lapped it all up, wishing she had someone with whom she could share the experience.

Viewing out from the open top deck of the bus, Maria was sadly becoming more aware of how much she was now dependent on alcohol. She had her physical symptoms sort of in check, by the use of alcohol, but she hated herself for that; her emotional state was fractured.

A young family occupied the seats in front of Maria, having a great time excitedly pointing out the wonderful landmarks. A lovely warm evening; the lights seemed to embrace the city.

The young mother's hand clasping the metal bar of the seat framed her gold wedding ring, seeming like a beacon of married solidarity. It resonated with Maria, afraid that her life was empty and unfulfilled.

She was tempted to take another swig but as she took the bottle from her bag, the young girl turned around to smile at Maria, who froze with guilt; she took her phone out of her bag instead and called Leanne.

'I'm all good, Leanne, being good, took your advice. Ate pizza, a little wine and now having a night-time open-top bus tour of this wonderful city. Wish you were here with me, *chica*.

'I'm so grateful to you, Leanne, for your help. I'm determined not to blow it, just keep topped up and get to bed soon.'

'Wow I'm so impressed with you, girl. Know you can do it. Just get back to your hotel safe and get to bed with no more alcohol. I'll call you in the morning. Nitey nite.'

Maria spotted a 24 hour Carrefour Metro as they drove around the city, so after the tour, headed for a bottle of vodka to take back to the hotel apartment.

Back at the holiday complex, she felt safe once again and after watching a little TV, managed to get off to sleep despite the noisy children in the next apartment.

*

THE INTERVIEW

Morning brought plenty of warm sunshine, early morning bathers in the hotel grounds and beyond in the blue Mediterranean. Maria had a light breakfast of fruit juice, muesli and coffee.

Leanne called to check how Maria was coping, concerned that the shakes would return. She gave the same advice again, having spoken with a former alcoholic boyfriend. Don't try and detox and withdraw while away from your home base. He said he will look at your best options once back home in Madrid.

'Let's wait and talk about the other stuff after the job is settled, girl. Alberto also pointed out that there are many well-meaning people in your life who have tried to help over the years you have been actively using alcohol. Sadly, he said such friends and professionals alike have become embroiled in another psychodynamic known as co-dependency, but he didn't have time to explain how that worked.' Leanne finished.

No sooner had they finished their call than another came in from Anna Dias, Senor Gonzales' secretary, inviting her to come in again and discuss her interview at midday.

Maria stayed calm, giving no indication of her health concerns. Midday gave her enough time to get packed, check out and freshen up for the meeting.

She decided against taking a drink but took a benzodiazepine; she knew that she was dealing with two really sharp men with a great deal of experience of human nature. They would detect the slightest aroma of alcohol despite Maria's best attempts to conceal it, so she knew the tablets were a good bet. She set off again into the fray.

Maria arrived in plenty of time, anxious but quietly confident. She walked purposefully towards Senor Gonzales' office, focussed ahead, not glancing around. Anna invited her once again to be seated outside the office. She imagined that there would be no further business to discuss and that she would be mainly assessed by her ability to bounce back from yesterday's set-back.

'Come on in, Maria take a seat.' Senor Gonzales said in perfect English, which took her back initially but she figured that was part of his game strategy.

'How are you today? Well I hope?'

'Yes, Senor Gonzales, very well. I've had the opportunity to have a good look around your beautiful city.'

'How did you manage that? It's only now midday?'

'Ah well, after I left you yesterday, I went for a lovely meal in the city centre, accompanied by jazz. It was pretty cool, I must say. After that, as I am a tourist after all, I took a night time, open-top bus tour around the city. Wonderful it is indeed.'

'Very enterprising of you to make the most of your time here on such a short visit. Sorry, how rude of me. Did you want some coffee, tea or Juice?' he asked.

'Thank you, no. I'm fine, had a nice breakfast at the hotel, nice little place down by the seafront, Pena del Dice,' she replied.

'Ah yes, I know that place. Friend of mine owns that group of medium-range hotels. Well, I hope you will enjoy the city even more once you come and join us in our enterprise at MexTex. We are in agreement that you are most suitable, so welcome to the company.

'Your contract will be coming out to you later today and we would love you to start with us two weeks from the date on the contract. We already have clients in mind for you, so it's straight in at the coal-face immediately.'

Maria looked at his mouth and heard the words coming from it but was struggling to put it all together as a coherent sentence.

'Thank you so very much. I am obviously delighted and shall eagerly await the mail.' She said rather formally but in full control.

As she ran the gauntlet of the girls in the office, there was a skip in her step. They lightly applauded her; they realised she had got the job. Once again, Maria collected her bags from reception but this time she made for the station, with just about enough time to catch the fast train, only stopping at Zaragoza.

Relaxing in her reclining seat on the train, she could contain herself no longer and called Leanne.

'Hi, *chica* guess what?'

'What?'

'I only got it, that's all.'

'Whoooaa, woop woop that's great,' Leanne fairly screeched down the phone. 'That must have been really hard with you in withdrawals and all. Well done you, girl. I'm so proud of you, Maria.'

The pair continued for some time discussing the interview, what was Gregg all about, the general atmosphere and ambiance of the office, and so on.

It was quite a long conversation, touching on a number of suggested action points for both of them to put into place.

Agreeing that professional advice might be an immediate plan, Leanne said she would contact her former boyfriend, Albert, and see if he could recommend anyone locally to whom she could be referred for a possible treatment plan.

'How is it, Maria, that you have this incredible ability to go into a situation or location with no previous information to assist you and within minutes you have a complete mental picture of the scene. Then put in place a plan of action; but you have not the foggiest idea about how to go about sorting yourself out despite all the advice others trying to help give you?'

In the meantime, they had business to attend to, such as handing in their notice at their current jobs and finding suitable accommodation in Barcelona. Leanne had her job offer in writing, so she would deal with that right away, finally suggesting they had a meal together to celebrate on her return.

The journey continued unremarkably, with Maria reading some lightweight material about Barcelona, interspersed with thirty-minute interval visits to the toilet. A swig of vodka, followed by a spray of strong peppermint mouth freshener, and so the journey went by.

She must have dozed off, as before she knew it, the trains loudspeakers were announcing the train's' arrival in Madrid. Scrambling to get herself and her belongings together, she stumbled onto the platform.

Waiting on the station platform Leanne saw Maria stagger.

'Oh no' she uttered, 'she's drunk again.'

They hugged and kissed; Leanne detected the vodka and mouth spray but said nothing.

Leanne had her car parked in readiness, so they were quickly away from the station and headed to her apartment, in awkward silence.

Neither one wanted to make the first move; there was some mental fencing going on. Eventually. Leanne made the first lunge. At this point, she was deeply uncomfortable, being reminded of her ex-boyfriend, Alberto, who used to behave in a similar manner.

Promising to change, he would stop drinking for a while then relapse. It was painful for Leanne to see this pattern developing in Maria's life. Leanne wondered if she should try and contact Alberto.

'Maria, do you want to have a chat about what happened to you after the interview? Would it help?'

'Not really, same old crap really, Leanne, I'm so stupid. Thought I would celebrate on the train. I was so happy and pleased with myself, I thought I deserved a reward. Same old story. Drink when I'm happy, drink when I'm sad. It's normal for most people but doesn't work for me, don't know why.'

'Well, between us, Maria, we need to get it sorted before you start at your new job. It's a great job, lots of travel, high-class clients, exclusivity and very high salary. Do you have any ideas that might give us a clue as to how best to proceed? How about I try and get in touch with Alberto? I must have his number somewhere.'

'If you think it might help, yeah, go for it. Got nothing to lose. got to do something, as they're talking about giving me a couple of clients right away and I don't even know how to proceed with that.' Maria responded in desperation.

'Leave the drinking bit with me at the moment. We know we can handle clients, albeit really "posh" ones.'

At last, Maria smiled.

SIX

FIRST CLIENT

The following morning, two letters delivered by the concierge dropped on Maria's doormat. One was the job offer, the other a letter of introduction to her first client. Maria was thrown into a mild panic, as she had not even discussed leaving her current job, and now she had to accept the Barcelona job. She knew that she had not planned this properly and got herself in a fix.

'Leanne, come here, please, and help with this decision, please. I'm really stuck, paralysed on deciding, please, Leanne.'

'Calm down, Maria, let's take it in bite-sized-chunks.'

The pair ran through options and came up with the only real solution; one with which neither of them was completely comfortable.

They decided that Leanne would go to work as normal and hand in her notice. Maria would call in sick, saying she had to go into a clinic for a while and therefore felt it was only fair that she resigned with immediate effect. She would write to her boss today for their records, apologising and explaining her change in circumstances.

The other plan was for Maria to get an appointment with a local private doctor for prescribed medication and a treatment plan. She should not drink so that the doctor could assess her physical and mental state.

With all that in place, Maria settled down with a pot of strong coffee and her detailed map of Spain to locate her first client. Something of a relief, she discovered her first client was located just on the outskirts of Madrid.

With the doctor's' appointment at two thirty, she had to take a urine sample, and expect to give a blood sample. The receptionist explained that the doctor would prescribe medication after the result of the tests had been seen, and she could pick the medication up any time after that.

*

Coffee cup in hand, she looked at the Madrid skyline opening with the early-morning sunshine, the multitude of high-rise buildings that had become part of Maria's life in recent times. What a difference a day and a couple of hundred kilometres made. Only yesterday the view at breakfast was the sea, blue sky and swimmers. Her head today was in a different space altogether. Keen to get started, she had the details of her first client.

Pinto, the small town where her client lived, was a mere thirty kilometres away from Madrid. Whilst relieved to some extent, Maria was disappointed by the close proximity to Madrid. She wanted more of an adventure. She loved to travel the thrill of the unknown, and that aspect of her nature was an essential element. She was beginning to understand that was okay provided she could keep it under control.

She called Mr Kennedy, who then answered the phone in a soft Irish brogue of a voice. He was expecting her call and was eager to meet up to discuss details of the trip they would jointly plan. The morning brought a slight drizzle in the air, enough to make the automatic screen wipers come to life but not actually clean the screen; that awkward in-between stage that just smeared.

She was on her way to Pinto, a pretty unremarkable journey that would probably take around an hour and was quite dreary, over very slippery roads that had not seen rain for months. Traffic was busy in the opposite direction with commuters driving into Madrid, but her direction all looked clear enough. She was a little nervous, as this was the first of her clients, but the absence of heavy traffic was working in her favour.

Maria was wearing a pair of light brown trousers, a pale orange high-neck sweater with a white bolero jacket, and flat casual shoes. No power dressing today; she wanted to create an air of casualness, of holiday time.

It was in every sense a dry run, and she felt she must conceal that from her client and present with an air of confidence and efficiency. Armed with her Apple tablet and an A5 notebook in her well-worn leather bag, she felt confident and was raring to go.

Mr Kennedy, dressed in corduroy trousers and a brown check shirt, greeted her on the expansive gravel drive heading up to an enormous old villa. Maria dated it around 1850 Her keen eye took it all in a matter of seconds; she had spotted the walled garden with an archway through to a vegetable garden, tennis courts and what looked like acres of land beyond enormous banks of conifers.

Mr Kennedy thrust his very large hand forward to greet her.

'You must be Maria, I'm Patrick Kennedy and I'm so pleased to meet you. Come on up to the house. There's a wee bit of rain in the air today, or as we say in Ireland, it's a soft day, so it is.'

They went up a wide flight of very old stone steps; Mr Kennedy showed her into the library. Antique furniture and an impressive collection of books confirmed this was a family of some standing.

Despite its grandiosity, Maria thought the room was warm and welcoming. The sort of room that beckoned you to enter in those dark winter days in the north. Days when you might sit by the fire with a small table lamp casting just enough light to read a good book with a glass of your favourite tipple.

Maria just had to share how she felt about the room; it was genuine, not a sales gimmick, and he knew that.

Mr Kennedy happily shared that days like that were not so common in this part of the country, but agreed it was a lovely room.

'So, I'm Patrick Kennedy, me and me extensive family have lived here for many years. Originally, it was me mammy and daddy's house where me and me brothers and sisters grew up. I'm sure you're curious about all of that, most people are, and maybe one day I'll explain. It's a long story. As for now, though, I'd like you to take care of organising a special trip away for me and all those people somewhere nice.'

Maria was shrewd enough to know never to pry, if he wanted to tell her about his life, that was fine.

'Well, sir, I'm Maria and I will be delighted to organise all the details for your trip. Senor Gonzales in Barcelona has given me the very basic details of your requirements, and there are no budgetary limitations. So we can fill in more detail as we proceed.' Maria opened with that much.

'Jeezze, don't tell us you've come all the way from Barcelona to us Kennedy's?' he said. Maria loved his voice; it was new to her.'No, sir at the moment, I'm living nearby in Madrid, but I plan on moving within the next few weeks, but you should have no concerns about continuity. I'll be seeing your trip right through to completion,' she reassured him.

'Ah, well now, that's grand, so it is and in the name of sweet Mary, don't be calling me sir, I won't know who you're talking about, so I won't. Patrick or Pat's fine by me,' he comically replied.

'Well, Patrick, have you any places you would prefer and any you wouldn't like to visit?' Maria enquired.

'Well now, I like the tropics, anywhere warm with clear water and sand. But that's me, you would have to speak with me missus to get a better idea as to what they would like.

'I would not fancy Iran or Kazakhstan, if you know what I mean? It's me parents' sixtieth wedding anniversary, so lots of folks are coming over from all over the globe to a massive party here, which you are very welcome to attend. Then members of me own family, will take Mammy and Daddy away to somewhere really special.

Maria liked Patrick very much and was bursting to know more about how this forty-something man was so wealthy, but she had a vague idea Senor Gonzales would have all the answers. She also realised that she had never really had many, if indeed any, conversations with an Irish person, and was somewhat intrigued by his voice and language, especially the love and affection he showed for family.

At that point, there was a clatter of footfall on the stairs and hallway from younger family members, accompanied by a woman's' voice asking for quiet.

'Well, Patrick, if that's all right, leave it with me and of course I would love to speak with your wife, about her ideas for the trip. I've got some great ideas already, and I've got the time-scale, which is important for booking arrangements, but rest assured we will between us come up with something special for all of you.'

As Maria got up to leave, Patrick said. 'Say hello to Benjamin from me and Daddy he'll be sorry he missed you.'

Maria; 'Sorry, Benjamin?'

'Benjamin Gonzales. They're old pals from way back, been exchanging visits to one another's lodges for years.'

'Ah well, yes, I will, next time I'm in Barcelona,' she replied.

As she was about to climb into her car, the family, or at least some of them, were on the outside stairs waving 'A*dios,* Maria.'

A little more of the mystique was falling into place, the way in which these various men of power were interconnected. Quite simply, they were freemasons. She felt strangely empowered by discovering such information, and chuckled out loud. 'It's Benjamin the freemason. That's the common factor.'

Maria just had enough time to make her doctor's' appointment in Centro Salud, close-by their apartment. She had to see a Dr Hernandes, whose impressive office was on the third floor of the block. He and his young female assistant certainly looked the part in their whites, could have just walked off the 'set' for a TV hospital programme Maria's bloods were checked, along with blood pressure and weight, and Dr Hernandes duly prescribed diazepam, on the proviso that she cut back on her alcohol intake.

Maria paid up and left; she was having a good day and it got even better when, over dinner Leanne told her all had gone well at the office. They ate a rather indifferent ready-made lasagne, washed down with a mediocre red Spanish wine, had coffee, watched TV and dozed off half way through a dreadful film; then it was bed.

*

The following morning, Maria briefly went through her itinerary for the Kennedy's' family trip. Happy with that, she had done many similar holiday packages, and she was comfortable enough to put that aside for a while and check the basic details of client number two. Client number two appeared, at first glance more complicated, and so no further work on that until the next day.

In the meantime, she and Leanne were up for a day out together away from city life. Pinto, as Maria had discovered the previous day, had a park within which was a lake, so they could give it a try. Leanne was very much up for it and the pair quickly got picnics and swimwear together and were off.

Only a short drive and they soon found themselves on the shore of the lake with outstretched blankets and towels. They claimed their territory for the next few hours, weather permitting.

They knew nothing of this park so they were delightfully surprised to find there were boats to hire, a designated swimming area and most importantly, a café selling really good coffee.

'Do you realise' Maria asked, 'this is the first time we've spent any quality time together, Leanne, in all the time we've known each other?'

'Yeah, I suppose it is strange really, as we've managed to get ourselves in and out of some scrapes and survived, but never had a nice tranquil sit, swim, eat and chat together. Sad really, I suppose it's the price we have to pay for living and working in the Big City.' Leanne responded.

'We don't really know much about each other in terms of family and background, and so on.' Maria said.

Leanne came back with. 'Well, I know that you come from the north originally and talk a lot about wishing you were back, but love the Big City Life too much.'

'Well, I know nothing about you, Leanne, apart from your recent life and how you seem to be rescuing me from myself frequently. Where do you hail from?'

'Well, it's a little complicated but not seriously so.' Leanne began. 'I was born in La Linea in the south. My mother is Spanish and my father English. La Linea, as you probably know, is on the frontier between Spain and the British Overseas Territory, as they like to call Gibraltar.

'My grandparents were both British subjects living in Gibraltar. Grandpa served in the British Army during the war and was highly decorated for bravery, a lovely man, I only vaguely remember him. My father was born in Gibraltar. He met my Spanish mother, Lucia, in La Linea and fell in love, resulting in me being born following a 'shotgun wedding.'

Dad eventually came out of the Army with a decent pension, affording them a comfortable lifestyle in a modest flat in Gib. Mum comes and goes in and out of Spain, having friends both sides of the border. That's why I speak the languages and understand the nuances of Englishness. It's served me well in my work.

"I get down there to see them whenever I can, although sometimes the frontier security can be awkward, depending on who's on the gate. I consider myself as a Real Espanola with no identity issues except when England are playing football against Spain, my dad can create a tension, but only in fun.'

'Wow,' exclaimed Maria, 'I feel honoured. Thanks for sharing that with me. I really enjoyed the story and love having such a good friend as you

"I'm having such a good time just want to take it all in and make the most of our time out together. Let's go hire a boat, take a row around the lake and have a coffee when we get back.' Leanne jumped at the suggestion, totally surprised that Maria didn't mention wine or vodka.

Rowing around the lake was fun; the warm sunlight flickered on the water where ducks enjoyed the bread being thrown in by small children. There was a small island that was covered with the most amazing shrubs and small trees and flowers.

'This place is amazing. Do you know the names of any of these trees and flowers, Maria?' Leanne asked.

'Well I know hydrangeas and dahlias as we have those up north but some of these shrubs I have never seen before,' she replied.

'Pretty shameful, I suppose. I should know more. Dad was a keen gardener, but I was too busy chasing boys to be interested in flowers,' Leanne confessed as she lay back on the cushion on her seat, savouring the moment.

'It's pretty shameful how little I know about the countryside. There's a beautiful perfume coming from the bushes on the shore. Do you know what that is Maria? You're more of a country girl?'

'No idea, Leanne. I suppose I'm more of a seaside girl really but that's no excuse either. But I do recognise the smell from the hot deep-fried *churros* coming from that stall on the shore, and wouldn't mind getting into those when we land,' Maria happily confessed.

Checking out a group on shore, she asked Leanne to slow down a little to take a look at some folks on the shore.

'Hey, Leanne, check out those folks over there. I'm sure it's Patrick Kennedy and family having ice cream. I don't want to bump into him. That just wouldn't be right on so many levels. We'll make our way back to the hire kiosk and leave the park if that's okay with you, Leanne?'

They rowed back and picked up their deposit money from the man in the kiosk. They momentarily considered a coffee, until both simultaneously spotted the signage over the door.

KENNEDY'S KORNER

In a hyperactive state of excitement, they quickly gathered up their belongings and ran like a pair of teenagers back to the car park, giggling all the way. The pair collapsed in a breathless heap on the grass. They just laid there for a while, staring at the blue of the sky, giggling, with no idea as to what had brought about that sudden reaction and departure without actually getting the *churros*.

Maria's outstretched hand had met Leanne's; they gently squeezed and remained silent, in the moment. She felt warm and secure, wrapped in love with a powerful sense of wellbeing, which was a very new experience for her. They remained in that state for some time before returning to the car.

The return journey to their apartment was quiet, with just the car radio playing soft, easy classical music. The only conversation was around which restaurant they would eat in later.

They settled for El Gamba Loco, a favourite of the younger folk in town. With a very good reputation for quality seafood, they were fairly confident they would be able to get a nice *bacalao*.

Maria's favourite was *bacalao al pil-pil*, a simple salt cod dish with very thin slices of garlic and olives fried on a hotplate, *a la plancha*, served with fresh warm bread and a glass of cold white wine.

They discussed the day in broad terms, agreed it was a fun, enjoyable day but also a wonderful bonding experience, solidifying their already strong kinship. It would be a lasting memory, they agreed.

Leanne, sensing the opportunity to discuss Maria's drink problem, tentatively noted how little she had consumed throughout the day. There was, however, a strange tension in the air, as neither could predict how the rest of the evening would proceed.

The waiter arrived with a bucket of ice containing the wine and poured a sample for Maria to taste.

'Do you mind us talking about your drinking issues or should we first address whether you think there is a problem or not?'

Maria took the glass and with her nose, tested the bouquet; with a small mouthful, she gently swilled it around the palate before swallowing and answered.

'It's tough really, some days I drink very little. Another day I can't get enough. But it's not a conscious decision. It just kind of happens. It's really hard to explain and I don't really understand myself,' she answered.

They declined a starter, and the main course fish,

arrived with a basket of warm fresh bread; the fish was cooked to perfection, and the wine enjoyed with relish. There was very little conversation, but Leanne thought it might be a good time to gently talk over the basics.

'Today, for example, you hardly touched a drop as far as I could see. By that, I mean I wasn't checking up on you, but do you ever secretly drink out of sight of others?' Leanne asked.

'Yes, I'm afraid, and ashamed to admit that I do. That's on my really bad days when I can't seem to get enough and things go bad very quickly. It's awful,' she replied.

'You need to find a way to perhaps use controlled drinking that works for you and set the limits before it goes badly wrong. My former boyfriend Alberto is something of an expert. I'm not sure where he is now but I believe he works with addictions. I've tried a couple of times to contact him but it goes straight to answerphone. I'll keep at it though.' Leanne said.

'Anyway, we had such a good time today, we need to set aside some time on a regular basis. perhaps once a month would work, wherever we are, just stop what we're doing and catch-up.' Maria suggested.

'How about that strange situation in the park today? That was a hoot. Obviously Mr Kennedy's a very enterprising man, but having been in his house, he didn't get that rich from selling ice cream and hiring out row boats, eh, Leanne, do you think?' Maria asked.

'Don't think so, big money there, but didn't you say his father was friendly with Senor Gonzales? I suspect there's the old pal's' network of freemasonry working again .

Don't know much about them, they help charities but also help themselves in business.

'My dad was invited to join them but declined, always wanted to find his own way in life. What really surprised me, though, I recently discovered there are women in freemasonry, but I don't know of any personally. Apparently goes way back, 1925 or thereabouts, set up in London. Weird if you ask me.'

'How are you getting on with your job, Leanne? Is it what you were expecting? you don't talk much about it.' Maria enquired.

'Yeah, it's okay, very similar to our old job, no great challenges as yet, but personally I'll be a lot happier when we move and get settled into our own place. I am still trying to work out how they are paying me so much money for the amount of work I'm carrying out. It's certainly nothing special. Your stuff is far more complicated. Do you agree?' Leanne asked.

'Yeah, it's strange because I was just getting more familiar with Madrid, having not liked it initially, but I see more to it now. We really do need to be around the hub of the business, though in Barca, despite the fact that a lot of our work can be done, online. It's that personal service that makes us very different,' she concluded.

They paid the bill, including a very nice tip for the excellent service, and made their way back to the apartment. Both felt very satisfied with their day together, having discovered a great deal more about each other, and agreed that they felt re-energised and much more comfortable with each other; a final short nightcap then an early night for them.

SEVEN

THE CAR

The early-morning post delivered by the concierge landed on the doormat with a congratulatory acknowledgement letter from Senor Gonzales for the outstanding work Maria had done with Mr P. Kennedy.

Leanne had already left for work. Unfortunately, she had to travel to Barcelona, but that would be changing soon as they had now found a place to live in Barcelona; a lovely apartment of which they hoped to take tenancy by the end of the following week.

The time had come for Maria to take on her second client. This one appeared very much more complicated. For a start, the location was miles away, in the middle of nowhere. Getting there in itself presented problems for her, and the client was a really wealthy man with firmly held beliefs that may, in theory, conflict with those of Maria.

Time to call Senor Gonzales on this, she decided. He answered.

'Maria, you got my letter. Great work with the Kennedy's. Lovely family. They were delighted with you, personally and very impressed with your holiday plan; well done,' he said.

'Thank you, Senor Gonzales, I must admit I enjoyed visiting the Kennedy family and am so pleased I have put together a wonderful package for the whole family. So I wanted to discuss the next client, who is very far away, and I'm not sure about travel arrangements.'

'You're right, Maria, now is the time. Suffice to say we are offering you a very comprehensive monthly allowance for travel and accommodation. The tenancy agreement on your apartment is all arranged and you can sign the paperwork when next you are in the office. It's up to you to decide how you travel. Initially, you may wish to drive or travel by rail, and in some cases it may be necessary for you to fly. Our clients are all very wealthy, so money is no problem.

'You will have a new car on a lease system through our company You will be able to choose your vehicle. In the meantime, if you decide to drive, hire a decent car, as it's quite a distance.

'Your new client is Don Alonso Ramires, a very wealthy and powerful family, known throughout Estremadura and La Mancha. The family go back centuries, owning vast tracts of land throughout the whole region. You will need to use all of your skills with this family. They will be politeness personified, but at the same time very astute negotiators.

'Skills they have learned from centuries of dealing with the aristocracy, royalty and political giants, fascist dictators even.' Maria.

Stunned with this information, quite taken aback she thought. *I'm wondering why on earth this family would require the services of such a lowly servant as me?* All she could muster in reply was;

'Oh, my gosh, what an undertaking! I hope I'm up for that, *senor* I was a little nervous but now… ?she said timidly.

He came came back with; 'You'll be okay My family have known their family for years. Their 'bark is worse than their bite'. Just be yourself that's your strength. Don't power-dress or try and impress them, that won't work. *'Just be Maria'*. You'll be fine. *Buena suerte.* (good luck) Maria.' he ended.

She poured herself a glass of wine and settled down on the sofa immediately with her laptop, and began her research on the family, and the region. Homework for a couple of hours at the very least; she was soon into the swing of it, thoroughly enjoying the experience of research. Actually, she felt a sense of excitement, not an alcohol- related one but of a natural sense and an inner realisation.

The first thing she discovered was that the destination of her next client may be reached by land, but she would need a decent car; she ruled out flying.

The next dilemma with which Maria was now presented was that, the journey from Madrid would be manageable by road, two hundred odd miles, probably four hours plus, whereas from Barcelona the journey time by car would be around nine hours approximately.

Living in Madrid, the journey would be easier and not so distant as from Barcelona. She would need to get organised quickly, as they had planned to move soon to the new apartment in Barcelona.

Maria made another call to Gonzales on the issue of the car. She was promptly redirected to his secretary, who apparently dealt with such matters. On the clear understanding that the choice was entirely with Maria, she decided to visit the client and interview before moving to Barcelona.

After making a call to Leanne to update her, she confirmed the plan and they agreed that she would be happy to arrange the move into the new apartment.

Maria had already sounded out the local car dealership hire company Pinto Carrera, who could, if required and approved by Senor Gonzales, provide a car of her choice. The one she fancied was in the showroom. A Peugeot 208 sports saloon cabriolet in a golden bronze colour.

Now she had taken the plunge and signed a contract for collection. Trying to get on with the difficult part of planning the details of the journey and her strategy for handling Don Alonso, she could feel the tension building. She had begun working on new ways of defusing situations without alcohol. Janet frequently told her to 'keep it simple.' It was a byword for her, almost a mantra, to try and remember each day.

'Keep it simple Maria.' She repeated the phrase several times but realised right away that she was not practising the principles; she was waiting to collect her car and trying to work out her journey to her new client. Also, studying a little background history on *el don* was emotionally draining her, more than she had expected. Somewhat nervous about the actual driving, she had that lurking in the back of her mind. Fortunately, Leanne had taken charge of the move and although it was a relief, she felt guilty leaving her to deal with that alone.

She actually stopped to consider these points for a while and give herself a bit of a breather. Normally with all that stuff going on in her head, Maria would turn to alcohol, but she desperately resisted and made a strong black coffee with two spoons of sugar, hoping that may stave off the craving for alcohol.

She sat and took stock, and breaking it down to bite-sized chunks, she collected her thoughts for a moment. She remembered the serenity prayer that Janet had given her and muttered it under her breath.

Already with a very quirky idea germinating in her head, Maria felt confident enough to lay aside her plan for providing a holiday proposal to the Ramires family. That was the easy part, but she wanted to develop a strategy for meeting Don Alonso that would be her priority. Her obsessive nature had in the past often resulted in trouble in one form or another, so this taking stock idea was all very new and difficult for her to practise. She sat still and calmly examined the process without acting as yet.

Reading as much as she could, she had become emotionally hooked into the history of Andalucía; the culture, the flamenco, the food, the gypsies and its place in history throughout the Spanish Civil War, Franco (El Caudillo) and World War Two.

She realised that she was taking-in far too much information in her need to impress.

However, this experience awakened another Maria, one who had become stronger in her Spanish identity, with a real connection with her beloved Spain.

Feeling rather ashamed at her ignorance of gypsy culture, its influence on song, dance and food, she wanted to know more.

She until this time, had shown no interest at all in bullfighting, dismissing it as total cruelty; the bull was always to be tortured to the point of death and then murdered. The very word *matador* meant murderer.

With all of this in mind, she pondered her best approach. *How can I possibly engage with someone whose values were totally in opposition to my own,?*

However even as an academic exercise, she realised that she must have a better understanding of the subject if she was to engage with Don Alonso at all. The bigger picture may cause problems, not just for this particular piece of work but for future assignments.

As serious conflict of interests in terms of moral and philosophical beliefs could present challenges that Maria never imagined when she took the job back in Barcelona. She was taking on an assignment to meet someone about whom she actually knew very little, but she had built up a mental picture of a formidable opponent; perhaps a change in mind-set might throw him up in a better light.

With the awareness that she was no longer the Saturday girl in the travel agency but was now in the big league and a serious player, she was very apprehensive and admitted to feeling a little scared. She had become a different person altogether, and she was having doubts about this transformation. She questioned herself; *do I really want to be this different person? Do I like this other person enough to take on her personality?*

Looking around the apartment, she assessed her current situation and tried to imagine where she might be in six months time. Feeling agitated for some reason she could not fathom, she visually checked out the all the familiar trappings of a successful woman about town, but she still felt unfulfilled. 'Everyone's got all that stuff now, big deal,' she said quietly. The apartment, nice as it was, was never going to be warm and cosy like her home in the north.

Then she remembered that Janet had drilled into her, *live your life one day at a time.* She was planning six months ahead and it was all driving her crazy.

Thinking a great deal about home she was aware that whilst she was driven by the need to return home, she was continually moving further away from that destination.

Feelings of melancholy and sadness were always brought about when thinking of home, and they stifled her creativity and strength of purpose. She knew that in order to move on, she had to find another way of dealing with those issues; but she struggled with a solution.

Having spent too much time in the depths of despair the coffee idea was no longer an option. She poured a vodka and tonic and hoped for the best. She sipped her drink and felt instant relief, but as she tweaked the Venetian blind, the landscape view did not inspire, and she felt guilty once more.

'That's the problem, I don't get out in the countryside enough, like the joyful day Leanne and I spent in Pinto by the lake. I need to get outside more often.'

Feeling calmer, Maria decided to pick up on the research of Andalucía and make notes. She had begun making random notes but now wanted them to be recorded in her journal.

She took out the beautiful note-book her mother had given her when she set off on her wanderings. A dark tan leather, very loose kind of folio, tied together with a leather thong.

Back on the sofa, drink in hand, she put the book to her face and caressed it. The smell of the leather evoked other fragrances of home;- the faint perfume of lavender that her mother always wore and the cooking smells of her mother's apron. It was all too much for her; already in a highly emotional state, she simply broke down in floods of tears.

Once recovered, after a short while, she resolved to get busy right away writing up her journal. Some notations had been entered in the book already and she had plenty of rough notes to clean up for entry into the journal. Careful to select an appropriate pencil, she began.

The rest of the day was spent in research and making rough notes, to be followed by neat entries in her lovely journal. Maria felt a real sense of purpose at last.

Totally unaware of the passage of time, she obsessively beavered away reading and writing. Pausing only for the occasional drink of vodka and bowl of potato chips, she missed lunch altogether. She never linked that obsessive behaviour to her obsessive drinking, despite the fact that Janet had told her many times they were related.

Almost at the point of exhaustion, she stopped; physically and emotionally drained, she lay out on the settee and drifted off into deep sleep.

The ringtone on her phone abruptly awakened her; she had no idea how long she had been asleep but the coolness of twilight chilled her bones. She took a swig of vodka and answered her phone.

'*Hola, Maria, como estas?* It's Leanne.'

'Hi, Leanne sorry, I've been so busy writing I just dozed off.'

'What on earth are you writing that makes you so tired girl? *War and Peace* I've been calling for ages.'

'Sorry honey, I'm trying to prepare for my meeting with my new client so doing some homework and making notes,' she replied.

'Oh my gosh, sounds serious. Is this the new Maria?'

'Well, I know I'll feel more in control if I have some basic knowledge about the family and their way of life. Even the region is unfamiliar at the moment. I feel I need to be on the front foot, right from the off,' she explained as she went on to tell Leanne not only about the new client, the location, family history, and so on, but also about the emotional journey on which she had been taken.

Leanne was genuinely very impressed and invited Maria to further share with her at some point. The pair discussed business and the way in which their respective lives had changed in a comparatively short time framework; the car and apartment with the expenses, they were pretty well off these days. The job entailed a lot more than they first expected. Hence, the very high salaries they earned.

Leanne as shrewd as ever, detected that Maria was drinking, but she reasoned that if it was calming her, *I'll just keep quiet, I don't need the aggravation of a tirade from her.*

'Well, listen, my love I'll let you get on. I've got a few things today also, so I'll say goodnight and don't you go over-doing-it and we'll speak in the morning. Nitey nite Maria.'

It was becoming clear to Maria that she must press on and get to a point where she felt comfortable enough to meet up with those folks in Andalucía reasonably free from prejudice.

There were in her mind two main areas of contention;- the wars and the bullfighting. And whilst she had some ideas, she needed more substance.

So to that end she had discovered several books online that seemed to cover those main areas. She spent the next few hours dipping in and out of the array of literature and eventually bought a couple of ebooks she thought may suffice.

Manuel Benitez' (El Cordobes) life story intrigued her. She had never actually heard of him but she quickly got into his life story and was, in a typical Maria fashion, obsessed by him.

She purchased a copy of the ebook and addictively immersed herself in his story.

Taking the bullfight issue first, she needed to be totally objective about it. She learned that there were ranches in Andalucía offering opportunities for tourists to visit and find out more about the whole business of rearing fighting bulls. Perhaps she should do that? After all, she knew that she had a cousin who aspired to be a matador, so perhaps she could muster up a modicum of interest; well, enough anyway to engage with *el don*.

The eBook she hoped might set her on the road to enlightenment regarding bull-rearing and the business of bull fighting. Manuel Benitez had risen from poverty to become one of the most famous and wealthiest men in Spain. That would be enough to get her started.

The book described in vivid detail the extreme poverty in which his family lived. With no money and little food, they eked out a meagre existence feeding on scraps, old potatoes and lentils. Most could barely find enough firewood to burn for warmth.

Manuel, desperate to free himself from this horrendous situation, dreamed of becoming a matador and would go into the fields at night to practise playing the bulls; he risked severe beatings from both the Civil Guard and the ranch owners.

Amazingly, he succeeded and rose to become, *El Cordobes,* receiving iconic status, recognition and vast fortunes. As she uncovered those uncomfortable truths, she knew she must record her version to include her own family and more importantly the impact these recent discoveries were having upon her. She turned to her journal knowing must be recorded.

Life in the cities was even worse where food was so scarce the population resorted to eating practically anything to fill their stomachs, aching from continual painful nagging hunger.

Maria had become totally engrossed, thinking of the comparisons with her own family, especially Grandma (*abuela*). She wondered, would she have resorted to eating cats, dogs, even rats in total despair?

As for the bombings, Maria could not even begin to cope with the horrors, the insanity of both sides bombing each other killing thousands of innocent civilians. She found it impossible to comprehend; the rich thriving whilst ordinary folks starved to death.

The Civil War lasted three years, with volunteers from all over the world coming to Spain to fight against the terrible injustices and murderous activities of the troops against their own people. Maria could make no sense of any of it and wondered how she had never before known about such matters.

Many a time as she made rough notes for transposing into her journal, Maria would have to pause as she became too emotional. As she read such accounts, she was filled with a mixture of sadness and extreme anger; time and again she wrote through a filter of tears masking her eyes.

What had started out as enjoyable, making entries of general interest, had now become hard work. She knew that she must carry on to be true to her family, but she was very uncomfortable about her new discoveries. Feeling that she wanted to pack it all in and go back north to be in the bosom of her family, she struggled onwards.

'How come young people don't know about this horrendous stuff? But perhaps they do and it's only me living in ignorance. Laden with a mountain of guilt for not paying more attention to her family's stories, she ploughed on.

What had become clear to her was that she had only just touched on some of the incredible hardships during the Spanish Civil War and the subsequent Second World War that her family had endured.

To Maria, it all sounded like the American Civil War, of which she had some knowledge; brothers fighting brother, fathers fighting sons, and so on, in a mindless never-ending horror story. At a loss to comprehend and assuage her feelings, she felt sickened with the massive discrepancy between the rich and the poor that had been allowed to continue.

Whilst Franco and his cronies ate off the fat of the land, the peasants were forced to eke out a meagre existence scavenging for scraps just to stay alive. All this new information she recorded in her book; she even named it *El testamento (The Testament)*.

Vowing to return north at the earliest possible opportunity, she promised herself the long-awaited conversation with *Abuela*.

Feeling that her life was going through a sort of metamorphism, she was excited at this prospect, eager for new experiences. Deeply troubled by her recent discoveries, she forced herself onwards. She wrote;-

General Franco, who accorded himself the title El Caudillo (the leader), lived the good life throughout the wars, with his own people being murdered by his troops every day for years. The dreaded Civil Guard with their shiny black hats were feared by all, as they more or less had a free hand to control the population as they pleased. All with the approval of Franco.

Horrified at the realisation that they were quite simply the Spanish equivalent of the Nazi Gestapo in Germany, she became strangely cautious and a little concerned that she, herself, might be under surveillance. However, upon running that by Leanne, she dismissed the notion as paranoia. Maria-was spurred on to learn more.

Realising the importance of this for her family, she had even deeper incentive to get back home as soon as possible and have face-to-face conversations with them. She felt she could not delay much longer. Bitten by the history bug, she concluded that some of this might not be appropriate to discuss with *el don,* who more than likely would be a Francophile.

With time ticking by and the distraction of the journal, she was getting a little behind her schedule; she needed to get back on track, and just at the right moment she received a call informing her that her car was ready for collection. It was time to lay aside the journal and have fun with her new car.

There it sat on the forecourt, resplendent, the metallic gold paintwork gleaming in the warm Spanish sunshine. Maria stood for a while taking it all in waiting for someone to come from the showroom. She slowly made a circuit, touching door handles but not daring to open the car for fear of setting an alarm off.

She had never possessed a new car ever in her life so this to her represented a significant moment. To her it was a badge of honour and trust by her employer. She had feelings of enrichment and empowerment which acted as a balm to all the ugly things she had been reading about.

'You deserve this girl. You've worked hard for it. There's more to come, baby,' she muttered under her breath.

The sliding doors of the showroom opened automatically as she passed; the showroom smelled of new cars, polish and rubber mainly, but also coffee. A very handsome young man in a light blue jacket, designer Jeans and tan-coloured sockless loafers got up from behind one of the desks. He had the appearance of a catwalk model presenting the autumn collection with his ultra-white shirt fashionably unbuttoned, exposing a light tan neck and fine gold chain and crucifix.

Maria's gift of taking in the scene at speed didn't miss anything; she instantly liked this man as he waved the car key fob about in his hand.

'*Hola, senorita como esta?*' he opened with.

Maria had been suffering from cabin fever, and the heavy stuff she had been reading over the last few days had put her in a bad place emotionally. At last, she felt relief as she glanced at his lapel badge; it read *Luis*.

'Hi Luis, you the owner here?' she joked.

'Sadly not yet *senorita pero una dia*.' (Maybe one day.)

They carried on flirting with one another and having fun, much to the amusement of the lads in the showroom.

Maria was having such a good time with the whole scene that she paid little attention to all the whistles and bells with which the car was equipped. All she could manage that made sense was 'How do I put the hood up and down?' This was the limit of her interest in the mechanics. Luis chuckled and pointed out that there was not a great deal of fuel in the tank as the showroom was not allowed to have cars full of petrol for health and safety reasons.

He suggested that he accompany her to the nearest petrol station in order that he could pay for the fuel, to which Maria readily agreed.

Taking hold of the key pad, she fumbled around looking for the usual metal key.

'Well erm ... no *senorita*, It's electronic. There is no key as such You just have the fob on your person or in your bag and the car recognises it. Just push the button. She was in love with the car right away and had very warm sensations for Luis as well.

As they drove to the petrol station top down in the warm sunshine she felt so good inside and thought she might have fallen for Luis. She also had the presence of mind to recall what Janet had told her about her emotional pendulum swings and tried to centre it for a while and avoid an excessive high.

However, by the time they had gassed the car and she had completed her inaugural tour with the car, the pair had agreed on a dinner date. Luis suggested a nearby restaurant, and would pick her up at eight.

On her own with the car, Maria felt so cool. She

couldn't wait to get on the road with it and remembering the way to Pinto, she set off in that general direction.

Driving with the top down in the late-afternoon sunshine, she looked the part; head-scarf, shades on, she turned a few heads at the traffic signals as she meandered through the back roads of Madrid.

With her head working overtime on a hundred and one thoughts, she tried her best to focus and keep it simple, one day at a time, that at some level it may help with her. Perhaps, she thought, the two may work in harmony. Feeling very pleased with bringing these thoughts together, she suddenly realised that she had missed the turn-off to Pinto. She pulled into a lay-by and laughed out loud, very loud;-

'That's it, you silly cow, trying to psychoanalyse yourself and drive at the same time is definitely not "'keeping it simple.'"

Maria just sat there for a while, processing this sudden change in awareness until she got fed up with it. Self-congratulation was not in her psyche. *How*, she thought, *can I feel proud of my achievements and not feel guilty as a consequence?*

She decided not to travel too far on this emotional high. She turned the car around and headed homeward.

However, Maria's self-awareness was undergoing a process of change. Thoughts of those friends who in their own different ways had been trying to help her with her drinking, flooded back. Confused, she tried to remember who said these things, who had advised her.

Well, she thought, *what am I doing with all this stuff going on in my head? I'm supposed to be just enjoying my new car.*

She said aloud. 'I have not had a drink today, not shaking with withdrawals and definitely not getting into the whole Catholic guilt-trip thing about pride.

'I love my car, my job and I'm proud of it, and I've got a dinner date with a handsome Spanish guy,' she shouted out.

Driving on the road back, thoughts re-entered Maria's mind; it was Leanne's former boyfriend Alberto who had made suggestions to her; living one day at a time, staying away from one drink, one day at a time. These phrases came flooding back to her. Perhaps now was the time she should get busy and make changes. It was something of an epiphany moment. Alberto could well be the channel for her to take towards recovery. Alas, the old thinking quickly ensued; '*I'm not drinking today, got no shakes and hot date tonight.*'

*

Back at the apartment, she drove down the ramp into the underground car park, and as she put up the hood, she processed the day. Where had she been? What had she done? What changes could be made? By the time she made the lift. *she had married Luis and had three children and a house in the north, with mama, papa and the grandparents to hand. Luis had his own car dealership and they had a villa in Lanzarote.* 'Shut up head. 'She shouted.

The Janitor heard her and called out. 'Everything all right *senorita?*'

'*Si, Si, senor, todas buen gracias, buenas noches.*' She thanked him and bid him good night.

Confused and amused, she laughed as she arrived at her floor and entered the apartment.

Once in her lounge, her autopilot kicked in and she poured a glass of last night's leftover Rioja, then changed her mind and threw it down the sink. Then it was as if no changes had taken place at all, she poured a vodka and tonic. Glass in in hand, she decided to do a little work on her trip to client number two, Don Alonso. As she sat in front of the computer she realised what she had done subconsciously; she was back on drink mode.

'What is wrong with me? I've just chucked wine down the sink and replaced it with vodka. Why oh why can't I just have a coffee and then work on my story?' she moaned, but there was no way she would pour the vodka down the sink. She took a large swig.

She just sat and felt worse than ever now, full of guilt and shame that she had become so habituated to drinking that she had repeated that scene all her adult life. The story was put on hold for now.

'Please God, wherever you are come to me. Help me to change. I don't know how to do it but help me.' She prayed aloud.

She had always loved travel;- that was one constant in her life. Thinking about that, she assigned to herself the task of planning her proposed route. Not short on travel books and brochures, she opened up *El testament,* and began writing and reading.

The task was pleasurable, imagining some of the places in Spain yet to be discovered. However, a certain sadness overcame her as she realised that a great deal of her time was spent unaccompanied. She loved company; there were times when for one reason or another someone entered her world, for a short while. Generally, though, they were fleeting moments in the broader landscape of her life.

She began to accept the fact that her life was very superficial, with no real depth or meaning;- a thought which affected her deeply. Friendships came and went without any real sense of connectivity with others. She never got to meet others' families or learn of any details about new acquaintances.

Maria opened the pages of an old address book, absolutely full of telephone numbers and names of people whom she could not even remember.

She took another large swig of vodka, and spread a map of Spain on the dining table.

'I've had enough of this soul-searching for today, thank you, Herr Freud. I've got work to get on with,' she said.

With a marker pen, she traced her intended route on the map and made notes from travel books as she went.

The research Maria had undertaken in the last few days had sparked off a latent desire to understand more of the peasants' living conditions now, and how bad it had been in her parent's' time.

Immensely affected by El Cordobes' experience, Maria knew that she must visit his birthplace. The dreadful life his parents had to endure, without choice, and his monumental struggle to free himself forever, even at the risk of death itself, gave her added incentive to visit there. She truly believed it would help her to better understand her own family's struggles.

Simply reading such an account by Manuel Benitez (his real name), filled her with disgust. He recalled his mother working, sewing until the dark enveloped her and she could see no more. They would turn on a single lamp bulb so she could continue working all to earn a few measly *centavos*. The possibility of her *abuela* doing something similar horrified Maria.

In Maria's mind's' eye, she saw *abuela* in the whitewashed one room hovel; whitewashed spotless with pride. She refused to let the authorities take away her self-esteem. She would whitewash others' hovels for a few more *centavos*.

Sitting in the luxurious comfort of her apartment, Maria had herself been struggling with issues of pride and self-esteem. These recent revelations, however, of another era, one in which her family lived, threw into stark relief the appalling conditions which they also would have endured, and how she should have greater appreciation for her own life.

A serious issue of ethics threw her into a head-spin; how, she asked herself, could she in good faith visit Don Alonso, a wealthy landowner? On the face of it, he was possibly another Don Felix, the wealthy land owner in Manuel's life.

Maria had a serious crisis in confidence and an immense ethical dilemma, one which she would have to resolve in advance of leaving Madrid if indeed she were to accept the challenge.

Right on the dot of eight the door bell sounded. She was ready but did not want to appear too eager. On viewing the front door screen, her handsome date came into view, with a big toothy grin.

'*Hola como esta?*' *dama Hermosa.*' Luis addressed her in a rather formal way, which delighted her, being called a lovely lady (*dama*) and not a girl (*chica*). '*Hola hombre guapo,*' she replied. '*Vamo arriba.*' (*Come on up handsome man*).

They always enjoyed these playful exchanges. Luis actually spoke English very well and the pair would be in and out of each language for fun but Maria could lose him with German and French.

Maria pressed the entry phone button to let him in, and with a final check in the mirror, she made minor adjustments, to an imaginary piece of hair.

Luis declined the offer of a pre-dinner drink, as he had the table booked for a quarter past eight. The restaurant, a very popular one, would only hold the reservation for a short while, and he didn't want to be late.

Climbing into Luis' rather cramped red Alpha Romeo sports car, she realised that she had not done this kind of thing for some while. Whilst not wishing to draw attention to her awkwardness, she admitted to herself that she felt a little old.

Luis, ever the gentleman, said, 'Yeah, it's supposed to be a two-seater, but really sensibly, it's a one-setter if you're a golfer. I've had it so long, it's part of me. Trouble is, I'm around cars all day and they don't mean a lot to me. My tough driving days are probably behind me now.' He chuckled. 'Your seat is usually home to my golf bag, and even that's a squeeze.'

THE CAR

'Not much fun in four-inch heels, for sure,' she responded as they drove slowly past El Gamba Loco to find a parking place. Maria did not let on that she had been there before. It was to be Luis' surprise to her. As they they settled down with a couple of aperitifs and checked the menu. Luis apologised 'As you can see, it's mainly seafood. Sorry, I should have checked first with you. They do have meat if you prefer, sorry about that.'

'No, no, that's not a problem, I love seafood. It's perfect. I think I fancy *gazpacho* to go with yummy fresh bread. I've just seen that gentleman's dinner on the next table, and I'm definitely going for the seafood platter to follow.'

Luis suggested the wine. 'Do you have a preference for the wine, Maria? They have a very good cellar here. The house wines are very acceptable. But if you prefer, we can order a local special from the Madrid vineyards.'

She would drink any wine, as long as it had high alcohol content. Nevertheless, she had considerable expertise on the subject of wines in many regions of the world;- knowledge that served her well in this job.

'No, you go ahead and choose Luis. The house white is totally fine with me.' Maria replied as Luis beckoned the waiter to their table. He wished them a good evening and asked what they wanted to order.

The waiter recognised Maria and asked her if she wanted the wonderful *bacalao* again.

An awkward silence ensued as she fumbled around with the menu and enquired about the wine.

'No, not tonight, the *bacalao* was excellent, but my friend and I are trying something different tonight,' she replied.

'I see you're in very nice company tonight, Luis. Is this lovely young lady a new friend?' Luis joked sarcastically, returning with, 'Well, waiter, it's not really any of your business. Just bring us a carafe of your very finest house white if you please.' They all laughed together at the pomposity.

Once over the short awkwardness, they had a very enjoyable meal in a warm, friendly environment. The wine was good the food excellent and over coffee and *licores*, they enjoyed an interesting exchange of ideas and philosophies.

Maria took the opportunity to explain the situation, and the predicament in which she found herself regarding her forthcoming trip. Luis had a fair knowledge of the historical issues with which she was struggling in terms of ethics. Would she be able to carry out her business with people that on the face of it were at the very least unpleasant, and at worst quite despicable?

She admitted that of course over time people change, but there was so much of that period which angered and saddened her that she doubted her professionalism would see her through.

'After all like many others, my forebears had been systematically abused by the regime for years, while the dictatorship flourished,' she posited.

Maria was clearly so hurt that she personalised it to the extent that *she* herself felt abused. Luis actually had considerable knowledge and insight on the subject but that unfortunately did little to improve her dilemma.

She realised she needed to 'lighten-up' or the whole evening would be spoiled.

The food all eaten, the wine all consumed and all the other patrons gone, the waiter presented Luis with the bill and respectfully requested he took the debate elsewhere.

He dropped her off at the apartment block; they pecked each other on the cheek and called it a day. There was no suggestion of a nightcap. She felt very comfortable with Luis; he appeared to understand and was sympathetic without being patronising, a rare quality she thought in her otherwise male-dominated world.

He was a new experience for her, and she hoped her concerns had not spoiled the evening. Certainly, she wished to meet with him again.

Preparing for sleep she sat on the edge of the bed and realised a change was taking place in her life, in a subconscious way. Taking stock of the day, she was not drunk for starters and she had not got into bed with her date. She had a sense of purpose which she had not really previously experienced.

As Maria's head hit the pillow, she felt this was one of the most edifying evenings to date that she had ever spent with a man. Not quite sober, but it was a start, she reasoned. She was happy.

*

Next morning brought storm clouds and high winds lashing the apartment windows; four floors up, Maria-felt exposed and a little nervous. She surprised herself by not running for the vodka bottle but rather made a large cafetiere of coffee, cooked scrambled egg with toasted sourdough bread and phoned Leanne.

'Wow, *chica*, you're firing on all cylinders. What's the difference?' Leanne asked.

She apprised Leanne of her evening with Luis and their subsequent discussion on the subject bothering her, namely *el Don*.

'Oh, don't worry about the bloody Don, how was Luis in bed?' Leanne asked.

'Is that all you think about, sex?' Maria answered.

'It's always right at the top of your agenda girl. Do you mean there is more?'

Maria paused before answering; sadly, she thought Leanne was right. Her usual pattern of behaviour was drink, getting laid and collapsing drunk in someone else's bed somewhere.

'*Hola, chica segues ahi*? Are you still there?' Leanne repeated, as the line had gone quiet.

'Yeah, erm sorry… It's strange really. Met this guy in the car showroom, had a little drive in my new car which was a laugh; out to dinner with a little wine and talked all evening until Pablo chucked us out of the restaurant. He certainly helped me with my dilemma, the struggle I'm having about meeting my next client, Don Alonso. It's not a love job or anything, but we just sort of clicked.' Leanne came in. 'Well, I think I know you well enough, Maria, to know it's not love, but it sounds like infatuation. What's with the alcohol issue at the moment, *chica*?'

'Do you know what? At present, it's not a problem. I don't know why, but I'm not drinking anything like my normal amount. It seems under control. I feel a lot better, and at last I've now got someone else I can share with, apart from you of course my darling Leanne.'

'Do you want to tell me what's really bothering you about meeting this client then honey?' Leanne repeated.

'Leanne the problem is too complicated to discuss like this over the phone. Sorry if I'm sounding rather precious and up my own backside. Goodness only knows we've been through some stuff together and I'd love to share with you, but I've made plans to meet this *don* guy and don't know if I can go through with it,' she explained.

'Okay I respect that, Maria, but I would just say that if you don't go through with the appointment, I imagine your career with MexTex will be over. All these guys are very tricky as we've already found out, lots of 'wheels within wheels' and very serious money. I just hope you make the right decision for you and I hope I've not just made your problem worse.'

'Thanks, Leanne. Let's hope we can have some more days together like we had in Pinto the other day.' Maria finished and hung up.

She spread the map of Spain once more on the dining table and visualised her journey to Palma del Rio, the birthplace of El Cordobes.

She decided to plan the trip on the *hope for the best*, influenced by both Leanne and Luis but each for entirely different reasons.

Luis on the basis that *el Don* may well be a very different gentleman from the one in the book that she had created in her head. After all, he may well be a perfectly philanthropic man doing good works in the community.

Leanne, on the other hand quite simply read the 'riot act' to her. Keep the appointment or look for another job.

With that in mind, she sat and pondered the trip. She pawed the map, which practically covered the entire table, and sipped a glass of chilled white wine spritzer. Genuinely excited at the prospect of the journey, she began adding places of interest to her notepad. She kept *El testamento* close by for inspiration.

Glass in hand, she called home just to tell *mama* about her trip to Cordoba.

'Cordoba? Mama exclaimed, 'why Cordoba? Whatever is in Cordoba for you, Maria?'

'*Mama*, it's my job. I'm visiting there on business. I thought I explained my new business role within my new company *mama*.'

'Well, maybe you did, maybe you didn't. I can't remember much these days, and you always seem to be on the move, it's about time you settled down somewhere and raised a family. You're not getting any younger yourself.

'I've been waiting a long time for grandchildren from you but still no sign.' When are you coming to see me anyway? Where are you now?' *Mama* exploded with questions.

She had expected the barrage of questions; sadly, it was the same theme every time and from her mother's' point of view, it was all perfectly pertinent and relevant. It was always about coming home to the north and settling down with a man and having a family.

Maria would always attempt to placate *mama* with promises which she never fulfilled but this time she meant it. She agreed it was time she came home for a visit. The conversation continued in the same manner as she fended off a further barrage; at last Maria ended the call. She then phoned senor Gonzales to inform him of her plans for travelling to Palma del Rio.

'I feel sure you've got everything covered, Maria. remember what I told you. Just be Maria and don't try and impress, that's your strong hand. By the way, have you been in touch with Alonso yet, because he'll probably be expecting you for dinner on your arrival and an overnight stay, so be at least prepared for that, and wear suitable clothes for dinner. Otherwise, just be smart casual.

'Is everything all well for you in Madrid, Maria? I hear you've got your new car and are moving to Barcelona soon, so we'll probably see more of each other then.

'Yes, everything is fine this end. I love the car and I'm very excited about driving it to Don Alonso's place, then next week moving to Barca.' She finally got in a word as he hung up after wishing her '*buen viaje*' (have a good journey.)

On finishing the call, Maria was reminded of a onetime boyfriend she dated many years ago who mentioned that the best football managers never wanted to hear about injuries occurring to players that was for the trainer to worry about. Good managers simply wanted to know who was available to play; that was all. Gonzales, she knew was the manager.

As Maria enjoyed the map of Spain, she became aware of how little she actually knew about her country. On a broad scale, she more or less knew where the most popular destinations were located but rather ashamedly admitted her ignorance of any detailed knowledge.

Warm thoughts returned to Maria as she was reminded how her new friend Luis clearly had an extensive knowledge of most things Spanish, and was more than happy to show and share in a kind and gentle manner. She liked Luis very much.

EIGHT

LA MANCHA

As far as her trip was concerned, Maria had worked out the distances and expected time the journey would take, with short breaks en route. She noted a few places of interest and possible rest breaks on a separate pad; Aranjuez, Toledo, Cuidad Real, Cordoba and Palma del Rio in total, something around five and a half hours' journey time, give or take.

In the back of her mind she wanted to get as much from the trip as possible and share it with Luis on her return. It was Luis who gave Maria the final push to see the trip through. He suggested that she just take each day at a time and just relax with a '*que sera sera*' mentality.

That was exactly what she needed to hear;- decisiveness. Luis had the ability to keep it simple. She envied that in him, and wondered if he could give her any tips. With that in mind, she packed her bags in readiness for the morning. Smart casual but on the advice of senor Gonzales, a chic cocktail dress and four-inch heels for the dinner tomorrow night.

Maria had over the last few days kept her drinking to a level which she believed was manageable, although there had been several occasions when she had been sorely tempted to *go for it.*

Common sense (which so often had deserted her) told her the prudent course of action would be not to drink and to get an early night to bed; which she managed.

*

Next morning Maria woke early. She made a light breakfast of fruit juice, fresh melon, oat flakes, Greek yoghurt, coffee and toast. As she drew open the blinds with her final coffee in hand, she had a warm glow inside. The sun glowed a mixture of orange and red across the Madrid rooftops. Madrilenas hustled, going about their business. She thought of Luis;- *what time would he be at work?* She called but the phone went to messaging, so she hung up and got herself ready, tidying her breakfast dishes away in the process.

Sitting in the car, she carried out her final checks; paperwork, maps, phone with charger, leather holdall, small leather bag for her daily bits and pieces. All present and correct, she thought:- *she would be all very grown up and sensible today. She would buy food as and when she required, and no picnics today;- she did not want to dirty the car.*

With one final call to Luis, she headed off, disappointed there had been no answer. Her journey, however, would take her literally right past the car showroom, so perhaps she thought she may see him by chance. Traffic was heavy towards the city but light in the direction Maria was heading. This was normal for the morning rush towards the city.

Her phone rang. *'Buen dias, Maria, que tal?'* Luis asked.

Approaching the showroom, she negotiated the traffic and eventually pulled over and answered.

'Hi, Luis, so good to hear from you. I've tried to contact you a couple of times and I'm near the showroom,' she blurted out.

'I know, I can see you from the upstairs office. I'll be right down,' he said.

She pulled onto the forecourt and jumped out of the car, full of energy and very excited. They embraced and kissed to a little light applause from his work colleagues in the showroom; they both responded with a bow and a curtsey.

'I'm so glad you came around, I have something for you for your trip. This is a little blessing for Godspeed.' Luis handed Maria a small black box. Surprised, she very gently opened the lid. It was a silver St Christopher pendant on a chain. Relieved it was not a ring she was delighted. She held it up and with a little tear in her eye, thanked him with an embrace and a kiss on the cheek.

'You may like to hang it on your car mirror for a safe journey and return, and there's something else.'

Luis handed her another package, gift wrapped. She opened it very carefully, as if she wanted to keep the paper.

'The book is the autobiography of Manuel Benitez El Cordobes which I'm sure you will enjoy. It's very informative explaining in some detail the life he experienced, from poverty to fame and fortune.' Clearly overwhelmed, she never let on that she had been reading it online but embraced Luis once again with tears of pure joy.

She placed the book on the passenger seat and hung the pendant on the car mirror; she knew she had better leave immediately, as she was on the verge of tears, so she started the car and slowly drove away without another word. She was reluctantly bound for Cordoba.

Above the noise of the wind blowing through her hair, Maria could just make out Luis as he hollered for her to come back soon, '*Hasta pronto querido.*'

Maria silently wept tears of joy, and sadness, as she shifted through gears in her great new car, heading in the direction of Pinto, and the road to Aranjuez.

Without stopping, she passed through Pinto;- the memories of the wonderful day she shared with Leanne there still remained fresh in her mind. How, she thought, *could I manage in future to string together a few more days of joy, in a more continuous manner?*

For sure, changes were taking place for Maria in her mind, body and, dare she admit it, her soul. A lapsed Catholic, she had not attended mass or made a confession for years. Maria felt the need now to share more of her thoughts and inner emotions with another person she could trust.

Leanne had been brilliant for her for a considerable period of time mainly aiding her recovery from all manner of difficult situations, some of which were serious enough to be actually illegal.

Leanne had been at her side throughout. A fair number of friends and colleagues had also filled that role in Maria's life, but whilst not actually failing to bring about positive outcomes, had in small ways attempted to offer encouragement. However, Alberto had explained to Leanne that paradoxically, without realising it, many of those who tried to help were in fact enabling her to remain stuck. It was a strange dynamic which she never fully understood. *Perhaps I'll get to, meet this Alberto guy face to face.*

Whilst all of this was going on, she drove in and out of Aranjuez without experiencing the delights of the beautiful city known for its' palaces and breath-taking gardens.

She spotted a roadside café and swung rather erratically onto the gravel drive, skidding just shy of a wooden rail protecting the café windows. The handbrake grated into a locked position. Leanne called her back.

'Why oh why, do I have all these crazy thoughts in my head when I'm out driving and supposed to be relaxing? I never seem to have them when I'm sitting on my own, supposedly relaxing in the comfort of my apartment, Leanne?'

Leanne replied sarcastically, 'Oh, hi Maria, thanks for asking. I'm doing just fine, thanks, what's your problem?'

'Why do you think I have a problem? Can't I call you just for a chat without there always being a problem?' Maria retorted angrily.

'Of course, darling whatever you say. Are you having a nice day, off to see client number two, Don Alonso?'

'I'm sorry, Leanne. I didn't mean to be rude. I just get so cross with myself and my behaviour. I can't even blame it on drinking, as I've not had a drink today and won't until I get to el Don.'

Leanne replied. 'I don't pretend to understand but I picked up a lot of ideas from Alberto when we were an item.

'It's about making lifestyle changes, not just quitting drinking and drugging, but dealing with emotions, Maria.

'Alberto uses Gestalt therapy, a holistic way of looking at how we behave. It may be that while you're driving you're distracted to a degree from really feeling your emotions, just focussing on the task of driving. Then they well up later and leave you angry and frustrated, Maria.'

'Oh my gosh, girl, you should have stayed with that guy, you've picked up a lot of stuff from him. Maybe give me his number …yeah?' Maria calmly asked.

She stretched across the passenger seat and reached for her bag. Maria's eyes alighted on the book, still half wrapped, that Luis so thoughtfully bought for her. Warm emotions returned as her anger slowly began to dissipate.

'I've just stopped for a pee and a coffee at some roadside café. I'll get his number when I'm ready, Leanne, honey.'

Maria needed coffee and a comfort break, and grabbed a table by the window so she could see her lovely car. *Oh*, she thought, *that was a hairy bit of parking, close to the barrier. Ah well!*

A couple at the adjacent table, engaged with her in conversation about Aranjuez and the famous musical piece to which the name is attributed. A friendly couple, probably in their sixties, from Devon in England had enjoyed the Palace and the magnificent gardens and recommended she visit at some point. A pleasant interlude she enjoyed before she continued on her way; she felt more relaxed.

Back behind the wheel she felt that she must make the effort to socially integrate more often; simple everyday exchanges that make the world a happier place. Her life did not have to be one of extremes of emotions. *Keep it simple*, she remembered was the word from Alberto.

Back on the road to Toledo, she experienced a new, to her, landscape; one of far horizons and dry, parched tracts of land interspersed with clumps of trees, probably oaks, she guessed. Animals gathered under the trees for shelter from the sun, still scorching this late in the year. Goodness knows she wondered how hot it must be in midsummer.

She could not make out the animals, but she wanted them to be the wild bulls she read about in her book; they were dark in colour. Maria's mind picked out pages from her new book; she saw Manuel as a very young boy playing the bulls illicitly in these fields before getting caught and beaten for his troubles.

With her imagination running free, these new dreams and fantasies were freeing her up from her daily routines. This was fun and she felt alive with her thoughts.

She wanted to further experience this place;- open, dry, with little shelter, a land totally different from her home country in the north. She must, she thought, get closer and feel the dryness and smell this unique dry air.

Turning off the main road, she pulled into a sort of lay-by to check the map, which she favoured over the sat nav.

Her fantasy was temporarily shattered once in the layby. A huge black wheelie- bin with a bright yellow lid confronted her. She saw the funny side of that, but determined to hold on to the fantasy, she plotted a route through the minor roads and lanes. It was not long before all became quite silent, save for the distant faint sound of cattle lowing. Those distant shapes, now clearly visible, were bulls and wild pigs; the sight of which sent a tingle down her spine.

Suddenly she remembered she had a small pair of bird-watching binoculars in the trunk. Focussing on the bulls under the trees the tingling sensation increased. She felt very alive in a serene way.

She imagined Manuel on moonlit nights playing the bulls, honing the skills which would eventually transform his and his family's life forever.

Totally transfixed, she would have wished to stay longer but there was a long road ahead and she needed to keep moving.

The solitude and quiet was eventually broken as a silver Land Cruiser appeared carrying two Stetson-wearing *hombres* on board. They stopped alongside, and without speaking, checked Maria visually before slowly driving off. It was, she felt, very sinister; they were clearly sending a silent warning sign that she was in their territory.

Maria understood that the bulls had to be protected from contamination by others. That was why Manuel had to be stopped. The bulls had to remain totally wild; not even slightly contaminated by human presence.

Like it or loath it, bull-rearing here was a serious business and not to be taken lightly by outsiders. The romantic image of the handsome toreadors risking life and limb for a few moments in the *plaza de toros* was far off at this stage. This was literally grassroots stuff, she thought. She remained for a few moments longer and quietly thanked Luis for the book; she kissed the St Christopher in gratitude.

Time to move on; Maria set a course on the sat nav for the main road to Palma del Rio; time was a little pressing. After a while the sat nav announced the approaching destination, which was confirmed by the sound of *mariachi* music and the loud singing. She never knew the words but had heard it many times at fiestas. She happily joined in with a *'la la la la …'* .The host was clearly celebrating something special.

As she pulled up outside the main gates to the property a man and a woman dressed in great Mexican outfits politely directed her to drive around to the side ,where a sign read A*mple Parking is Available.*   Sitting for a moment, taking in the day and the awareness of her present situation, she simply needed to be still. The scene was somewhat unreal and overwhelming.

Eventually checking in her vanity mirror in the car; yes, it was her, not a dream. A very suntanned version with hair all over the place;-*windswept and interesting*, she thought. A decidedly very happy Maria.

NINE

RANCHERO ALONSO

She put up the car hood and stepped into the extreme heat of late-afternoon Manchego sunshine. Smoothing her skirt and sweeping back her dark hair, she delicately placed her designer sunglasses on top of her head. With a nonchalant swing of her handbag, she approached the entrance to the Hacienda, a little apprehensively.

The extreme heat and dryness of the air smelling very strongly of animals, took her a little by surprise. She had a little difficulty breathing in this dry, arid, dusty atmosphere.

The gatekeepers warmly greeted her, politely asking if she was an invited guest, which she immediately confirmed she was. However, on checking their clipboard list, they could not confirm her as such. There was a slight moment of anxiety as she told them that she had an appointment with Don Alonso, and was unaware that it coincided with a party.

'Ah well, yes I see, let me make a call. I'm sure everything is okay but I need to check. That's my job for today. You see, it's a surprise party for young Sergio. He's thirteen today.'

The confirmation came back and Maria walked through into an enormous courtyard full of people quite literally having a ball. Music, singing and laughter; the place was electric. Maria had never experienced a private birthday party like this in her life. She felt it resembled a public fiesta in a park; such was the scale of the affair.

There were pigs roasting on spits, steaks the size of dinner plates being grilled, lobsters and langoustine; a veritable cornucopia.

Amidst all the clatter and noise, she felt quite alone and conspicuous until someone introduced herself;

'Hello, I'm Pilar, would you like to meet Don Alonso?' she asked as she supported Maria's elbow in her hand. Walking her across the courtyard, she felt as though she was being presented at court. Unsure if she should curtsy, so she did not.

'Alonso, this young lady has just arrived, erm… Maria did you say was your name?' Pilar introduced her.

Suddenly there he was, Don Alonso Ramires, in person. Dressed in a magnificent dark blue Mexican outfit with gold trimming, his sombrero hanging by a cord around his neck; he was impressive. His pearl-handled silver Colt 45 was holstered on his hip. Transfixed she felt as if she was on a movie set..

El don Alonso Ramires, stood erect, snapped his Mexican-booted feet together. bowed very slightly forward in a respectful manner and took Maria's hand in his own, lifted it to his lips and kissed the back of her hand with '*Bienvenida encantadora, dama*.' (Welcome, I'm pleased to meet you lady.)

They briefly talked about her visit, but it was clearly Sergio's day; He was charm personified and made her right at home. He explained that in a moment or two Sergio would get his surprise present following the entertainment.

'Sorry, *senora*, I have something to do right now. I must get on but be sure and catch me later.' He apologised.

Feeling very privileged to be at the event, Maria had a weird thought. *'How old do I look? That's twice in as many days I've been referred to as a lady (dama), not senorita or chica (girl).*

The centre of the courtyard, which was covered by a wooden dance floor, cleared, as folding chairs magically appeared around the perimeter.

A flamenco troupe entered with quite a flourish, ten in number; four guitarists and six dancers,' two of whom were male. The girls' beautiful dresses made a wonderful sound as the voluminous ruffles swished across the floor. They bowed to the audience and sat in the first row of seats.

The clatter and noise faded to a complete silence. Almost eerie; *this was a knowledgeable audience she realised.* Even the young ones were quiet, but an elderly gentleman standing alongside her very softly whispered in her ear, '*Esto seran muy buenos gitanos de Sevilla el major*.'(They are the best gypsy dancers from Seville.)

Maria had already worked out that this group were definitely gypsies, coming from Seville, and they would have to be the best for the Don. Seville was the heartland of flamenco and Maria had some knowledge of the artistic quality of the music.

What then took place was a flamenco show like no other Maria had ever seen. They took the audience to the place of perfection known as *Duende*, when everyone is in perfect harmony, including the audience. It was stupendous. *For a very brief moment, she remembered Louisa on that fateful night in Santander with her group but quickly dismissed it and got into the here and now of the moment.*

Four gypsy girls in the most wonderful dresses and two male dancers in black tight but flared trousers, white shirts and bolero jackets were accompanied by the brilliant guitarists.

Clearly, this knowledgeable audience was stunned. One woman dancer in particular seemed to mesmerise Maria; a heavily built woman full in figure, not young, dressed in a white dress with red polka dots and well beaten-up shoes entranced her, deeply arousing her Spanish soul.

The grace, elegance and suppleness in the way her arms and hands described the emotions of the dance was very special. The manner in which she stamped the floor seemed to Maria to be an act of defiance; *pay attention to my dance or else?'*

'*Ole ole, guapa*' filled the air and no one wanted it to end. However, end it would, as the Don wanted to give Sergio his present.

The flamenco finished to thunderous applause, leading to several encores which gradually faded as the sound of a trumpet fanfare announced the arrival of something special. The audience were familiar with that sound and hushed again.

Maria held her breath, hoping the elderly gentleman adjacent to her had departed. It was pure theatre as the Don proudly strode to centre stage, sombrero firmly placed upon his head. Attractive as he was in this spectacular entrance, he was not the main attraction.

That would be the most magnificent shining black Andalucían horse glistening with sweat being led into the centre. It snorted and whinnied a little, nodding it's head up and down a few times. It's dark, shining wide-open eyes and erect ears signalled it was fully aware of its' importance; the reins were handed to the Don.

A collective gasp once again issued from the crowd. This magnificent animal carried what was clearly a brand-new dark tan leather saddle. Hand crafted with intricate workings, it had a pommel, signifying that this was to be a working horse and not simply a show-piece.

At that point, the man of the day, Sergio, entered to join his father in the centre. They embraced. After a suitable pause whilst both men recovered their emotions, a microphone appeared to be thrust under Sergio's chin. Somewhat overcome with emotion, Sergio could manage but a few words of appreciation. There was not a dry eye at the party. The scene was beyond emotional.

Maria had difficulty believing she was playing a part,

albeit a very minor part, in the family scene, not simply a spectator.

Sergio would naturally have been given a variety of ponies over the years as he grew up in this environment, but this animal was major league. He gently patted its head and was about to kiss its' nose when for some reason, only known to Sergio, he stopped. It apparently was not the right time, yet.

The Don gave Sergio a leg-up. He slowly rode the horse out to a paddock at the rear of the property and expertly performed a few different manoeuvres at various speeds. Guests hurried to catch a photo;- cameras clicked and flashed all around. It was obvious to all that Serge and the animal were 'as one.'

When he eventually dismounted, he held the horse's head, and this time he kissed the nose. This time, the horse lifted its head and neighed its approval.

Maria silently breathed. *'Oh my God I can't believe what I've just witnessed.* 'It was the nearest thing to a real-life fairy tale she had experienced.

As the sun gradually left the sky and the darkness enveloped the scene, flaming torches appeared around the whole area, creating a wonderful mysterious atmosphere. The sheer magnitude of the torches suggested to Maria that money was no object.

Feeling a little awkward, and unsure of her status, she approached the woman she had met on arrival.

'Pilar, sorry to bother you with so much going on, but I don't know anyone here and I'm not sure what I should do. Is there anyone I should speak with?'

She immediately apologised. 'Maria, a thousand apologies, we've both been very rude. My husband of course is totally immersed in our son's birthday, understandable of course but unforgivable. But who exactly are you, Maria?'

She was mortified. Pilar was the Dons' wife, and she had been assuming she was staff. They cleared up this little misunderstanding as a maid came to her and showed her to her room. A nice room very well furnished with all mod cons, located in an annexe to the main building.

The maid, Lola, was friendly; understanding Maria's plight, she immediately became a great help to her. Lola explained the set-up, and knew that Maria was a guest. The room was in a converted stable block, and Pilar said that she was to be told she could stay as long as she wished.'

Lola then proceeded to inform her about the schedule. *'There will be no dinner tonight, as the alfresco banquet replaces the evening dinner. So you need not change clothes unless you wish to. However, tomorrow there will be a banquet in the banquet hall. A formal dress black-tie event for dinner.*

'Tomorrow. Don Alonso and senora Ramires will spend time with you to discuss any plans you may have. There will be plenty of activities tomorrow all of which are available if you're interested. Horse riding, swimming, shooting, golf, bridge; in fact ,a full programme for guests. There's also a comprehensively stocked library and quiet rooms available for writing or contemplation.'

Phew; she and Maria laughed together as she said, 'I think you've done that before, Lola.'

'Yeah I've got that routine down pat for sure, worked in England for a while. But seriously, they asked me to take care of you today, as they've just got so much on today and tomorrow. You've got to come second place I'm afraid.'

Maria, sensing she had someone she could trust, asked a bit more about the family. 'So tell me a little about the family, if you will Lola.'

'Well, you've met the Don and Pilar, then it's Montserrat, nineteen. She's very nice, bit New-Age Hare Krishna, save the whales, and a vegan too. This does not go down too well with all the beef around here.

'Sergio thirteen, birthday boy. He's a chip off the old block for sure. Self-assured and competent without being pushy, nice kid really.

Angelita ten, *mama's* little girl. Spoiled if you ask me very different from the others. Tends to play the helpless card for attention. Don't trust her.'

Well thanks Lola for the 'heads up' very useful indeed

'Keep all this under your hat, for God's sake, or I'm out of here and down the road, never to work in Andalucía again. El Don Alonso Ramires is a very powerful man with connections all the way to the top. Anything else you need, just holler. I'll be happy to oblige. Enjoy your stay, and please, not a word to anyone at any time.'

Maria, loved Lola and her delivery of the family situation; her new best friend, she hoped. She later discovered that Lola had once worked in England for one of the landed gentry and as such was totally familiar with Englishness.

Maria called Luis before her nap; he was delighted to hear from her and apologised for not being able to return her call from earlier in the day. She told him how much she had enjoyed the drive and how deeply it had affected her, in a very positive way. He suggested she get some rest and call back after her nap.

Maria woke around eight, showered, and as she dried herself with an expansive white Turkish towel, she could hear the party going on as more guests arrived for the evening.

She stepped out, checking that she had the room number and key, and wandered around the premises. The annexe was connected to the main building by a covered walkway so she did not have to go out into the now chilled evening air.

After a series of very dimly lit corridors, she arrived at the main body of the house; A hallway of enormous proportions with a staircase that wound upwards .Half tempted to explore, she thought better of it and settled for an imaginary scene of Zorro sword-fighting up and down the stairs.

The walls were panelled in very dark wood, and hung with very old paintings, probably, she imagined of some famous masters or other, but certainly not to her taste. The suits of armour and heraldic shields also did nothing for her; she dismissed it all as clutter. She favoured a minimalist style of living, so this scene to her was a mess.

The cavernous main hallway housed an enormous stone fireplace, to the side of which a very heavy oak door leading into the banqueting hall.

Massive very dark wood, possibly oak; the fireplace from the hallway came right through, obviously to heat both rooms and was used for cooking back in the day.

None of this worked for Maria and feeling quite gloomy, she headed for the *noise* which she rightly discovered was coming from the bar;- she needed a drink.

The bar, noisy and bustling was beautifully designed, with contemporary furniture and fittings. She found a seat by the window looking out on the courtyard, where all the action was taking place.

Waiters, smartly dressed in white jackets and dark trousers, darted very efficiently about the bar and somehow managed to keep on top of the orders. It was not long before she was sipping on her vodka with ice and a slice.

As she sat and relaxed in a very comfortable chair, she reflected on the wonderful full-on day it had been. She looked forward to a short read and a good night's' sleep before another full day tomorrow.

Flicking through the pages of her book, her eyes fixed on the passages where Manuel was playing the bulls by the light of the moon. She had earlier seen those fields; in her mind, she had been right amongst those bulls and was eager to learn more Perhaps tomorrow she would be able.

Darkness had descended;- the air was cooling but was still very oppressive. Most of the families had made for home, leaving the younger folks to enjoy the music and party on through the night.

Suddenly the bar filled up with folks coming inside and more guests arrived. It had quickly become more raucous;- she gave up on reading. Four smartly dressed men entered, one of whom walked over to Maria.

'Excuse me, miss are these seats available?' he enquired.

Maria looked up and could hardly believe her eyes; it was Gregg Holdsworth, her boss at MexTex, the company she now worked for.

'Oh my goodness, Mr Holdsworth!' she exclaimed in shock.

Gregg, also taken aback took a moment or two to recognise Maria. In fact he had trouble remembering her name. Rather embarrassed, he mumbled, eventually coming up with, 'Well, hello. Fancy meeting you here.'

Seats were found;- drinks, were ordered. It was all very convivial as they all sat, drank and chatted for a while, before the men took the hint and decided to break up, leaving Gregg with Maria.

Maria, quite excitedly, despite being tired, regaled Gregg with the events of her very full day. Gregg now fully engaged with her and promised he would introduce her to people tomorrow.

'Montse and Sergio are great company, who I'm sure would be only too happy to talk about local history, including the breeding of bulls for the *corrida*. 'So how long are you planning on staying, Maria?' Gregg asked.

'I'm not sure about that and also not sure how to address you,' she rather coyly replied.

'Don't be silly. Call me Gregg, of course. What a great opportunity to get to know one another. Great surroundings, lovely food and super people.

'I don't think we've really spoken since we offered you the position in the firm, so just relax and enjoy your stay. Alonso won't be in any hurry to kick you out, that's for sure.

'They are just lovely people, great company, perfect hosts and much loved in the community. We've been friends for many years. Tell me about what else is happening. I did hear that you were possibly moving to Barcelona. Any special reason for that, Maria?'

She hesitated, not quite ready to address him as Gregg.

'Well, while we were visiting Barcelona for our interviews, Leanne and I agreed that it seemed somehow a nicer place in which to live than Madrid. Thought it was a vibrant place, full of interest, by the coast, all in all more appealing than Madrid. Also, the office is there, which may be an advantage.'

'Sounds good to me. Tell me, I know your previous job took you to various locations but have you been here before or is it your first time to Andalucía?'

Gregg lifted his hand and made a circle in the air over the table to attract the waiter, who immediately came over.

'Yes, sir, what is your pleasure?' he enquired.

'Maria, what's your tipple today?' which she felt was a somewhat loaded question.

'Today, I'm drinking vodka tonic with ice and a slice,' and deciding to chance her arm, added pointedly, 'Gregg.'

'So what do you make of Andalucía? It can be something of a challenge. There are many positives but also some negatives, but putting the politics and such to one side, do you like what you see so far?' He asked.

'Well, in some respects, I'm reminded of the first trip I made to the Canary Islands in that although Spanish, they were very different from northern Spain. Their culture was different, the dialect different, food and customs different. It was of course Spain but not as I knew it.

'I just wonder how much has changed here compared with other regions in Spain. The north has not changed very much in my lifetime but the Canaries have changed massively, and many did not welcome the changes.'

'Yeah, I get your point. Spain has a lot going for it but I don't believe the ordinary folk get it sometimes.' Gregg, moved on from that conversation rather dismissively, she thought, and ordered more drinks.

'I believe Lonso's got more entertainment for tonight. I just spotted food being taken into the entrance hall. I know he's keeping the banqueting hall closed, as it's being prepared for tomorrow.'

She picked up Gregg's' reference to *Lonso* but assumed that was a personal nickname; she would have to wait to find out how to address Alonso.

However, she also picked up signals from Gregg of a more familiar nature. She was getting tipsy and he spotted that; she liked the flirting and felt very comfortable, as the alcohol was acting faster due to her recent intake reduction.

Several very heavy and massive paella pans wove their way across the courtyard in the direction of the halllway, accompanied by a small army of waiters.

'Ah, here comes the food, as if we've not had enough already today,' piped up Gregg. 'Fancy anything at all Maria?'

Totally uninhibited as the drink was taking effect, she was up for some fun and games, and throwing caution to the wind, she said, 'I know what I fancy but I think I'll have some pizza, paella and a bottle of ice-cold prosecco as well. Know what I mean?'

'I know exactly what you mean, Maria. Give me a few moments I will organise our own version of entertainment for the evening. Just stay here, don't move. Let me have the key to your room,' he said, and disappeared with it.

'Aye aye *Capitan*.' She giggled and slurped another mouthful.

After about twenty minutes had elapsed, a waiter returned and discreetly handed a key to Gregg.

'Shall we?' He gracefully escorted Maria across the room and out of the side door of the bar.

Out into the cool night air, Gregg led Maria across another courtyard. There, in the half-light of the night, stood a very old building that looked very much like a chapel.

Gregg produced an enormous iron key with which he opened the solid oak door with a clink and a creak. Maria, very tipsy, could not resist the chance to wisecrack.

'Are we getting married, Gregg?' she quipped. He did not reply but as he opened the door, she was at a loss for words. The room was indeed a former chapel which had been converted to accommodation. It was illuminated entirely by candlelight. The walls were painted yellow, as was all the furniture; the room was dominated by a four poster bed with yellow drapes.

'How about that, girl? What do you think of that? Was that a surprise or not?'

'I'm flabbergasted, Gregg, totally blown away, almost speechless.'

The table had been laid up with pizza and paella, with a bottle of chilled prosecco in the bucket. Maria threw her arms around Gregg's neck and with 'I'm dying for the loo,' dived into the en suite.

The evening passed by with much delicious food, lovely special wines, a minimum of TV watching but a great deal of brilliant sex. This cycle continued through the night until at some point they both fell asleep in each other's arms.

*

Tip-toeing out in the early morning mist, Maria was trying to piece it all together. She had a vague recollection of yesterday's events but large parts were missing.

Sleeping in a chapel was surreal and she struggled with that, and she was getting cold; she retreated to the warmth of the room. Gregg laid there fast asleep, oblivious to the world.

Cold bits of last night's' food lay about the bed, table and floor;- the room smelled of stale food and sweaty bodies.

She picked up a piece of pizza from the floor, made a hasty return to the ensuite and was very sick.

Unable to raise Gregg from his death-like slumber, Maria called the main bar for coffee and Alka-Seltzer.

As she sat there on the edge of the bed, she felt massive pangs of guilt. *'Here we go again, back on the merry-go-*

round, shame and guilt. Why do I do this to myself?' she shouted, waking Gregg.

Gregg very slowly raised his head from the pillow to squint with one eye at his Omega Sea master watch on the side table. Letting out a great yawn and a grunt, he scratched at his hairy chest. Without as much as a greeting, he simply asked in a slow, ponderous tone. 'Are you fit enough to go across for breakfast or would you prefer to have it brought over?'

'Oh, the Kraken awakes. She said. Oh and how are you, Maria, if you can remember my name. Personally, I want to shower and get out of here as soon as possible.' She was angry at her behaviour once more as the guilt ensued, but almost before she could finish her sentence, Maria rushed to the toilet and threw up again.

Whilst she showered, a youngish looking male waiter arrived, bearing the coffee and Alka-Seltzer that Maria had ordered earlier. He placed it on the table with a '*Buena dia*' on his lips a smirk on his face and left. There was enough for two so Gregg helped himself to a coffee and waited for Maria to emerge from the ensuite.

Maria's belongings had been transferred the previous night so she was able to sort out her clothes for the day. She had managed to conceal a small bottle of vodka; she took a quick slug and they went across for breakfast.

Breakfast was a buffet with the most extraordinary array of food on display. Gregg, clearly a man who enjoyed this meal of the day, had a plentiful breakfast, whereas Maria went for the cereal, fruit juice, melon, yoghurt and coffee in the expectation that she may be able to hold it down. She had taken Alka-Seltzer and felt reasonably safe.

As they ate in silence, Gregg could bear it no longer and asked her. 'So how are you feeling now? A little better? Well enough for breakfast anyway?'

She didn't reply but fiddled about with her breakfast, pushing food around the plate but not really enjoying the experience.

The silence continued then Gregg once more came in.

'I'm sorry but I'm missing something here. What's with the silent treatment? I don't get it. Did you not have a great night in a historic building as a guest of Don Alonso Ramires?'

'Sorry, Gregg, but I feel like crap today, not really in the mood for chatting,' she mumbled, with her mouth full of cereal.

'Well, let me know if there's anything I can help with, as we've got things planned for you today involving other people who need to be contacted if you're not up for it. Plus the fact that I thought you had work to do with the family involving planning a trip.'

Maria had somehow forgotten the purpose of her visit to the ranch and Gregg was her boss. She took a sip of coffee and drew herself up to be more erect.

She had been put in her place, and now wondered if she would still be on familiar terms with her boss. Should she still call him Gregg?

Maria stretched her hand out and touched the back of Gregg's hand. 'Sorry, Gregg, how very rude of me, but I need to explain what's going on for me. You already know that I can at times have a problem with alcohol.

'I have been working on the problem and gradually reduced my intake until last night when I blew it. Of course, it's my problem of my own doing, so forgive me and let's get the day off to a better start.'

'Great, so that's cleared the air,' Gregg continued. 'Let's have a verbal lightning tour of the place and family. Last night, we slept in a very old chapel that used to be part of the original sixteenth century manor house, much of which is still standing.

'Accurate records are difficult to verify due to feudal fighting through the centuries. But we do know that the chapel was originally built for a royal duke for private worship, weddings, baptisms and funerals, communion, and so on, and had always been painted yellow, hence the name Limoneria.

'The duke, a very heavy gambler, mainly at the card table, lost a fortune over the years, including much of his property, but managed to hold on to the chapel. He is buried just at the side of the Limoneria.'

'Quite a history;- puts it into perspective, for sure. I imagine the Ramires family history must be very interesting also,' she said.

Gregg cut to the chase at that point with some urgency in his tone. 'May I suggest, Maria, you carry out your work with the family and we meet around lunchtime, as I know that they have plans to show you around. You can always re-visit if necessary.'

Maria strolled around, taking a second look at the place, yesterday, she had been tired from her drive;- it was something of a blur.

She recalled the entrance to the property from the road, a pair of stone columns with no gates; just a demarcation point in the middle of nowhere, with a very long drive ending at the manor house.

The day was very warm, dry and dusty, when Pilar met with Maria and gave he tips on clothes for the day. She had been a very accomplished concert pianist and classical singer before she gave it all up to marry the don and raise a family. Closing the piano lid on the Steinberg grand piano, she turned to Maria. 'You're very welcome to play if you would like to, Maria. It's always a pleasure to hear our guests play,' she said.

'That's very kind of you, Pilar, but sadly I don't play.' Maria replied. Pilar explained how the place was run. It was vast, on a scale unimaginable to Maria. She was always dressed very neat and trim and never wore trousers; always in a skirt or very light, probably size ten, dresses. Her medium-length black hair always looked as though she had just that minute left the hairdresser's; her skin was lightly tanned and very smooth. Maria thought she was truly beautiful. The Limoneria was not mentioned but Maria knew that she was aware of yesterday's nocturnal activities, and she felt embarrassed and guilty once more.

Sergio was in the paddock in his Spanish riding apparel, complete with black sombrero, riding his magnificent horse, steering it at times using only his knees, totally in harmony, horse and man, he was very much *el caballero* Maria loved that. The sight fairly melted her heart;- poetry in motion, she thought.

Pilar suggested coffee, so she and Maria sat and talked some more, when Montserrat joined them. Raised in the traditional Spanish Catholic religion, Montse, (as she preferred to be called) had travelled and experienced other religions and faiths.

The three spoke freely and easily and Maria got the sense that Pilar did not have the opportunity to sit and chat like this, with ordinary folks with no vested interest in the business.

Montse, a free spirit, was very much the antithesis of her mother, who was a pragmatist and ran the household without the aide of, as she saw it, outside influences or divine intervention.

Montse explained about the spiritual path that she was following; it involved daily prayer, meditation and energising exercises, and was founded by an Indian *swami* who took the teachings from his native India to America in 1925. Montse detected right away that Maria suffered a lot of inner turmoil and made some suggestions to her that may alleviate her anxiety.

'*Mama* and *papa* have their own chapel where they pray daily within the manor house and regularly worship at a church in Palma del Rio. Father was not really very keen but sees it as a public relations exercise. Occasionally, we visit the cathedral in the mosque in Cordoba, but that is very much *papa*'s public relations exercise. Perhaps we could visit the mosque together,' she suggested.

Maria admitted, 'I sadly, have to say I know nothing at all about the mosque. I'm in the process of learning so much about Andalucía, as it clearly is a very fascinating place. Should I know more about the mosque?'

'What is your schedule for the rest of today and tomorrow, Maria?' Montse asked.

'Well, I haven't even started my work with you and the family yet, ostensibly the purpose of my visit, so I'm not sure how long I can stay, to be honest.'

'Forget all that stuff, Maria. You and I are going to the mosque today. We'll be back in time for the banquet tonight have no fear. Now, most importantly, are you happy with your sleeping arrangements? We are all aware about last night. The staff don't miss anything and Gregg's reputation precedes him, I'm afraid.'

'Well, Montse I have to say I'm very embarrassed about that. I feel it would be prudent to have my old room back.'

'Okay don't be embarrassed. Leave that with me, Maria. You can move into my room if you prefer and we will use our time together wisely. So get your stuff together and meet me out back in the yard, white Fiat Siecento. Cordoba's only some fifty kilometres from the ranch.'

Maria thought, *that won't take long, the way she drives.* She explained the history of Cordoba as much as was possible in such a short time. She rattled through a potted history as she drove at speed enroute to Cordoba. As she shifted into top gear, she opened with; 'It was once an epicentre of culture and learning with tolerance towards all levels of society and faiths. Christians, Jews and Muslims all getting along fine, sharing their ideas with a common interest in humanity.'

'So what's life like these days? Has it changed much over time?' Maria asked.

'That's a very interesting question and honestly I don't know. Hard to say how the troubles got started, but suffice to say they all started warring with one another, My faith is the only one, pretty simplistic I know, but that's the essence of it.

'Warring and killing, burning books. Muslims in the mosque were murdered and the Christians built a cathedral right in the middle of the mosque, reinforcing the Christian religion as the dominant faith. And that remains to this day.

'Pretty grim stuff I know, but as we all search for our path, it sometimes helps to understand the history of other faiths. How such dramatic changes can alter the status quo, throw peace and calm into a state of chaos, hatred and fear and alter the course of history.'

By this time, Maria's head was in a spin as they arrived and parked up; the dialogue was as frantic as the driving.

They both enjoyed the experience of the mosque, especially Maria with the added input from her new best friend. She tried to imagine the city as it may have been: a wonderful mixture of culture and faiths, living in harmony together, sharing their art, literature and religions.

About an hour passed as the crowds of tourists flocked in, spoiling the atmosphere of the place; they felt a coffee coming on.

In the relaxed atmosphere of the coffee shop, they freely shared quite personal issues.

Montse began to share:- 'Living in such a busy and materially driven household, I need to detach to a great extent. Finding that my formal religious training and practice were not giving me any real sense or the presence of a higher power, I searched outside the home. I would never wish to offend or challenge the family's beliefs but I could not pretend either. It simply did not work for me.

'*Papa* is a powerful man, well respected both in his local community but also in the wider world. A formidable presence to whom people look for advice and guidance. So, challenging him was not an option.

'I use prayer and meditation through the guru for guidance and over time discovered the answers to many issues were revealed to me. That was my major issue, detaching with love from family and being tolerant, allowing them to be themselves in my personal search for self-realisation. It's a daily programme that works for me. How about you, Maria? How do you work out your problems?'

'Well, if I'm truthful, I don't work them out. I run from them. I'm something of a coward. I find that drinking takes the edge off, all my sorrows and woes, but then I'm left with the outfall, so more to deal with than the original problem,' she confessed.

'But then often the problem gets worse after the drinking. Sometimes I will use alcohol to enhance my feelings similar to the way other people use other drugs. Sex is also a big problem for me. I have a very healthy libido, and that also leads me into trouble at times. Get the two together, I'm dynamite or a disaster,' she said laughing.

'Come, there's another church here. I want to show you some priceless icons, a very special place you must see before leaving.' They left the church.

Montse diplomatically just wanted to break up the scene. It had been getting too emotional for both of them. After the church with the icons, they headed back. Driving the *autopista* they were soon back in Montse's room in plenty of time to shower and change for the banquet.

'Maria, don't concern yourself with any details, You're here as my guest and can stay as long as you wish. It goes without saying that you're my guest at the banquet.'

Sharing the room together, they both showered and had girly chats; all perfectly normal and great fun. They giggled a lot and had a laugh about the previous night.

'Gregg's' a bit of a charmer all right, great friend of *papa,* but he's also a bit of a predator. He can be a lot of fun, very intelligent and a great raconteur. Gets invited to give after-dinner talks all the time. He and his friend and business partner Benjamin Gonzales are a right pair together, and when the three of them get together, the outcome is unpredictable to say the least.'

'Of course, Montse, I'm in a difficult situation, as he's my boss. I'm really happy that you took the initiative and moved me out of the Limoneria. I could not have spent another night in there with him, so a big thank you for that. Oops...' she exclaimed as a bottle of vodka fell from her bag.

'Oh dear, that's embarrassing for sure, That's my secret out of the bag, literally,' she coyly admitted.

'Don't worry on my account, Maria. If you want to drink, go ahead. Personally, I don't drink myself, but that's a life-style choice based on my yoga beliefs.

Certainly don't feel embarrassed or inhibited, but please don't drink it like that from the bottle. I'll call for drinks for both of us.'

She picked up the house phone and moments later a waiter carried in a tray with fresh lemonade, tonic water, ice, lemon and vodka.

TEN

THE BANQUET

They looked resplendent in their ball Gowns; Maria in dark blue and Montse in a very pale pink, both with pashminas around their slender necks. Relaxed and calm, they shared a cheers (*salud*), sipped their drinks and looked forward to the evening. Maria felt as though she had stepped once more into another world;- the whole experience was way beyond her wildest dreams.

Arm in arm, they crossed the great hallway into the banqueting hall, as the fire burned in that massive fireplace. Maria gasped as they entered. The Don and Pilar greeted their guests as a glass of champagne was proffered.

'Maria, how are you? I'm so sorry we've rather left you to your own devices, but I hear that the family are taking care of you.' The Don glanced and smiled at Montse in approval.

'Why, yes, I'm having the best time and don't want to interfere with your arrangements. I feel very honoured to be welcomed to your wonderful home,' Maria enthusiastically replied.

'I hear your boss, Gregg has been entertaining you,' he said with a smirk and a wink of his eye. Sadly, that made Maria feel quite cheap.

Montse chipped in very angrily, '*Really?, papa!*'

Maria, although very angry and offended said nothing in response. Controlling her anger, she raised her glass towards him, and in that instant, gambling with being over-familiar, she said 'Salud, Lonso,' and walked by him.

Montse, choking on her drink, spluttered, 'Well done, you, *chica*.'

The whole massive place was illuminated by candlelight. It was stupendous with an enormous cartwheel arrangement hung from the ceiling bearing a circle of candles, and even more running the entire length of the table.

Two young men suddenly appeared, one of whom was Sergio, who escorted Maria to her seat;- the other escorted Montse. She was once more back in the swash-buckling days of the movies.

'Wish *mama* and *papa* could see me now,' she said to Montse.

'Yeah, well, it's typical of my father. It's so over the top but that's how he is and he loves to do this stuff. I just humour him. As long as I don't take it seriously, I'm okay,' Montse replied.

The banquet, catered for by an outside specialist company, provided the most extraordinary eleven-course feast; a wonderful exclusive assortment of fish, fowl and game with the appropriate wines to complement the respective dishes. Sergio was the perfect escort for Maria, who, making most of the opportunity, sounded him out on the bullfighting side of the business.

Live baroque music was played on genuine instruments of that period, befitting the occasion. The grand log fire crackled in harmony with the spit-roasted pig; it was very special and hypnotic.

Sergio, belied his years as he spoke well on a range of subjects, including philosophy and religion. Uncertain about the direction his life should take, he clearly felt very comfortable talking with Maria, sensing she would be non-judgemental. He proudly asserted his very strong identity with Andalucía.

'Is everything all right for you, Maria? Dont let Sergio bore you, as he can go on a bit once he gets started,' Montse intervened.

'Not a bit of it, Montse quite the contrary. I'm the one with all the questions. I appreciate the opportunity to hear from someone so well versed on the culture of the country about which he obviously feels so passionate.'

She thought that Sergio represented the New Spain of modernity, free living and consumerism. He confessed that college studies had opened up his mind to consider such subjects and he welcomed the discourse with Maria.

Although much older than he, she was able to

reciprocate. They both got along just fine, beginning to drop any potential social barriers.

Respectfully, he explained in some detail how the business worked. He had no problem referring to it as such, but was clear that *la corrida* was an art form and the *toreadors* were great artists in every respect. That to him was definitely where business and the art form separated.

'Sergio, I know very little but, very keen to understand bullfighting, I am reading El Cordobe's book, It's truly fascinating but that's my only introduction to the corrida.

'However, it covers much more. It's a very revealing insight into the history of Andalucía in general, and this region where now we sit in almost regal splendour.' Mischievously, she intentionally invited deeper conversation for a much wider debate.

The ploy worked a treat for her, as Sergio picked up the thread.

'Well now,' Sergio started, 'that opens up a whole different can of worms, Maria. The book to which you refer is a good introduction to the history of this region through a particular period of time. How a man, an ordinary man, or boy even, can rise against all the odds and become a great matador adored by millions of people and gain immense wealth and respect.

'From extreme poverty to that, it's incredible. I love that boy,' Sergio very lovingly explained. She felt his emotion and wondered if this was an appropriate time to discuss such matters, over the dinner table. However she reasoned she must grab the opportunity. '*Carpe diem.*'

Montse, who had respectfully let them have their own private conversation, at last came in with, 'You guys seem to be getting along well, plenty to talk about. Not getting too heavy, I hope. After all, it's only meant to be a little light-dinner chat.' She laughed. 'Not *University Challenge*.'

Maria asked Montse, 'so how's your meal? Didn't really think about what you would have, a non-alcoholic veggie option an all?'

'Well the chef is a vegetarian option genius. He, with Lola, whom you've met, worked for a while in England for Lord somebody or other, I'm not very good on all that lineage stuff. But he got used to the veggie options in that family and I have to say has perfected his skills.

'He's prepared a vegetable wellington to die for, such a wonderful selection of veggies, some of which are only available locally. Something I find is peculiar to France and Spain and certainly not something I have found in the UK. You must try some of mine. Think you'll be pleasantly surprised.

'Of course, the dessert menu would always be very special, with exceptional pastries. I do eat cheese and while *manchego* is omnipresent here, local farmers provide their own unique versions' Montse replied.

After a discreet pause, whilst all discussed their various choices for dinner, Maria was keen to engage once again. 'Anyone else in the family vegetarian, Sergio, or just your sister?' she asked.

'She's the odd one out, not just with food but in many other ways also. I think she would like to be a hippy living in Southern California if she had the chance, but as far as I know, she doesn't smoke pot.' They all laughed together.

'Let's not all gang up on Montse, she's lovely,' Maria said, 'but I would love to get more about the socio-economic history of the area from you, Sergio, while I have the chance. Is that okay with you? Just change the subject if you get bored, Sergio. 'My limited enquiries inform me that local folks hereabouts were literally dirt-poor, eking out an existence from the meagre bits and pieces they could salvage from the unforgiving soil, and even dead animals off the streets.

'Water, clean enough to drink, was a luxury, while Franco and his pals were having banquets. Where does that sit with you now, Sergio?' Maria enquired with total conviction, which she was unaware existed within her. Then she thought she may have over-done it and spoiled the occasion.

They all sat back in their seats and pondered this very provocative question.

Sergio, after a pause, eventually took a sip from his mineral water. 'Yes, it's of course something that is at the very heart of the culture of the beautiful country we live in, and which I love dearly.

'It's a total enigma. How could a dictatorship have come about, and be allowed to continue with such violence and aggression for so long? People from all around the world saw the injustice and came to help our cause.

'I have read extensively and written papers on the subject. I am even in the process of writing a book on the subject and although there are numerous books already in existence, I believe mine may have credence in as much as it is written by a young New Spaniard,' Sergio ended.

Maria, completely enamoured with Sergio's account, could only politely applaud.

'Bravo, Sergio, I would like to thank you immensely for such an erudite personal account of your views. I would like to discuss so much more about the bulls but not tonight. It's time for laughter and fun, thank you so much,' Maria finished.

'Maria, are you around tomorrow? perhaps I can answer your questions tomorrow before *la corrida*?' Sergio asked.

She turned to Montse for guidance at that point, who shrugged in away that said, *it's up to you*. 'Tomorrow is good,' she said.

The banquet was a tremendous success, enjoyed immensely by Maria. Tables were cleared, the floor turned into a dance floor and merriment went on for many hours. Too many hours for the girls, who retired to their room; they relaxed as Montse explained her yoga path of daily meditation. Raj Yoga, the king of meditation.

'Maria, you've had a good day today, kept off the booze pretty well, stayed out of trouble.

'Shame *papa* had to say that. He can be a very typical macho man at times. The old boys' network stuff, so boring. Forget them.

'Do you ever spend time at the end of the day reflecting upon what you did and what you might have done differently and that sort of stuff ?' 'No, I can see it works for you but sadly most of my days end with drinking and oblivion. I would dearly love to change that pattern, but I seem to go two paces forward and three back,' she admitted.

'Maria, I'm going to light a candle for meditation, so I

hope it doesn't freak you out. Please do whatever you wish and I'll see you in the morning. *Om shanti, shanti amen.'*

*

Maria was awakened by the sound of church bells which she loved so much. It took her right back home. She drew back the white net curtains and fully opened the French windows to better appreciate the sounds and country smells of the warm southern Spanish air.

Montse was nowhere to be seen, but a note on the bedside table by a picture of her guru, simply said, '*Buenos dias Maria, cada benediction.*(Good morning, every blessing.)

'The perfect start to a lovely day' she whispered in response, and taking her St Christopher from her bag, she knelt and prayed. 'Every blessing to you also. Montse.'

'What a day what a blessing. This is the good life. I want more of this '*buenos dias, gracias, Dios.*' She could hear the sound of distant cattle, goats and chickens and had an awareness of the smell of the land along with the smell of the land. *this was heaven, she thought.*

She stepped out and noticed Montse was sitting a short distance away in meditative posture, so quietly made her way to breakfast. With much to consider today, she tried to prioritise an order of importance. She was guilty about not contacting Luis, so planned on doing so after breakfast. Maria's plan of action to carry out an assessment for a family holiday had been put on the back burner after Montse had suggested it was not a priority.

However that was the purpose of her being here, not for

a vacation but to work. Sergio last night had offered to take her to *la corrida* today at Los Califas in Cordoba. Ah well, she chuckled to herself, make the most of the offers. *Carpe diem*.

Just as she was about to leave the breakfast room, Montse arrived, wearing an orange coloured, very lightweight sari. Maria thought she looked very angelic and jumped up to embrace her, thanking her for the lovely card, and the blessing. They shared coffee and croissant together, and Maria thought she had never felt more peace in her life.

'I am so grateful to be here and with you, Montse. It's as though I have been transported to another world, but I realise I must prioritise and make a plan for the day.'

'Well, if it were me, I would call Luis first of all. That would be my first priority. How are you feeling about Luis? You haven't mentioned a great deal about him, but I notice today you're holding the St Christopher pendant that he gave you before you left Madrid.'

'He's a really nice guy, probably the nicest guy I've met in years, if not ever. He's never even moved-in on me. A kind, gentle man and we really get along. I'm really guilty about not even giving him a call, it's so disrespectful. The worrying thing about it is, Montse, I don't even know why I do these things, I truly believe I should see a shrink,' Maria confessed.

After calling Luis, Maria felt a lot better, she felt she had absolved herself. He said he understood, and it was a great opportunity for him to play golf and catch up with his buddies. In truth, that was all that she had wanted to hear; he was okay about her absence. She had made some preliminary plans for the family trip she was organising, and had sounded those out with Montse.

ELEVEN

LA CORRIDA

It was Sunday and the time for the first bull in the *plaza de torros* was fast approaching; the men were ready as Montse checked with Maria to be sure she was prepared for the experience. She didn't want to influence Maria in any way, but she had decided not to accompany her. Perhaps it would be a once-in-a-lifetime experience she should grab.

She checked her outfit with Montse, and with her approval left with the men. Alonso greeted her warmly and hoped that she would enjoy the experience, and as she climbed into the back of the SUV with another couple of ranch hands, she realised she was a woman alone. Sergio sat in the front of the SUV with the Don

The men talked the whole way about the corrida, the matadors, which ranch would be supplying the bulls, other-matadors; in fact, nothing else was talked about. Maria felt their energy and anticipation; the only woman in the very macho company. Rather than feel intimidated, she felt strangely secure. The journey was short, and on arrival at the *plaza*, they all piled out and left the parking to the ranch hand.

The atmosphere around the arena was electric, with the noise, the smell of animals mixed with smoke from cigars, and food stalls. Ticket touts jostled with the crowd. She felt excited and although very apprehensive, was looking forward to the event.

Once inside, her excitement shifted to another level. She could really smell the animals and clearly hear the horses and the bulls, snorting and grinding against the wooden pens.

Don Alonso was in his element, as was Sergio; in their Sunday best, they strutted their stuff in a very macho way. Maria knew her place and it was not with these two men. They politely invited her to join them in their regular bar before entering the *plaza*; she accepted but at once realised that as the only female she was completely out of place.

It was very much a male preserve, and Maria was finally quite relieved to be seated in the best seats in the *plaza* with other females for company. *El Don* had a private box with refreshments for guests.

Sergio, who had been keeping a close eye on her, approached.

'Maria, I'll keep you up to speed as we go along, but let me know if I get boring. There is a lot to understand if you want to really appreciate the finer points of the noble art of the corrida.'

'Sergio you just go ahead and I'll be listening, you can be sure, 'she replied.

The first lesson was the seating arrangements: the sun (*sol*) or the shade (*sobre*), the shade being the more expensive, for obvious reasons. Even the late-afternoon sun was bright and hot today.

Greetings were acknowledged all around; it was a social occasion going back many generations and Maria felt privileged to be passively included in the party.

The great buzz of the crowd suddenly silenced as a trumpet fanfare announced the start of the proceedings. The complete entourage paraded the arena, the matadors magnificent in their tight- fitting trousers and studded bolero jackets. Once the parade had ended the president then gave the signal to proceed by placing a hanky on the rail in front of him. The trumpet once again sounded.

The heavy wooden door, with years of thick red paint, burst open as the great black creature bounded into the arena. The sun temporarily blinded him; he snorted and menacingly pawed the sandy surface of the arena.

The crowd gasped; he was large, very heavy but super sharp and very alert, ready to cause trouble;-his jet-black body glistening from sweat, erect and motionless for a while, looking around for a target, ready to cause trouble. He bellowed and snorted, with his foaming tongue flopping around his mouth, the slightest movement causing him to turn his head in a split second;- he was ready to kill or be killed. This was what the aficionado's (the real fans) had paid their hard-earned cash to witness. Blood in the sand!

'Maria, I will explain what is going on if you would like that?' Sergio keenly asked.

'I would love that, Sergio, if it's not too much trouble.'

Sergio began;- 'The bull is allowed to freely run around as the *banderileros* attract his attention, waving the large capes, '*capos de brega*'. The bull charges and they run to take cover behind the barriers. This allows the matador to assess the way the bull moves. It's very important. He may hook to the left or to the right, and the matador needs to know at this stage.'

The president gave the signal for the *picadors* to enter the ring. Sergio continued his commentary.

'The *picadors* weaken the bull's neck muscles to enable the matador to perform his various moves. The trumpet sounds for the *picadors* to exit, and the matador enters. He is the only one who will kill the bull.'

Maria was filled with excited expectation as the matador entered the centre of the arena; magnificent in his gold silk studded *trace de luce,* (suit of light).

'The trousers are so tight, so that no folds could be hooked by the bull's horns.' Sergio explained.

Maria cast a glance at Sergio. Perched on the edge of his seat, he leaned forward as if he wanted to be down there in action.

'The matador makes a number of graceful passes with the *capo de brega*. He's totally in control now. He can do anything he wants, but as he demonstrates his skill with beautiful passes he must be very cautious. It can go wrong very quickly with tragic results. He's now exchanging the *brega* for the *muleta*, the small cape which hides the sword. Can you see that, Maria?'

She quietly, almost whispering said. 'Yes, I see it, Sergio.'

Maria could see it for sure;- she was totally in tune with the whole scene. She practically fell off her seat as the matador went in for a perfect kill.

The crowd went wild and cheered until the president awarded him one ear a symbol of recognition for a perfect kill. Sergio, in an excited gesture of surprise, put his arms around Maria, who reciprocated without hesitation.

'*Guapa, guapa, guapismo*' (Beautiful beautiful).' Sergio hollered in Maria's ear as the pair hugged in an excited, highly-charged emotional embrace.

Don Alonso Ramires looked on in surprise as the pair jumped up and down. For her, there was a sense of relief;- not only had she experienced the event but she had really enjoyed it. She caught a glimpse of *el don* who she imagined was unimpressed with their behaviour.

Afterwards, there was some drinking and tapas, which did not go on for too long, the group returning to the ranch in high spirits, for supper.

Maria met up with Montse to discuss a number of issues. Top in the order of preference was the proposed trip for the family she was supposed to be planning.

'Montse, when given this assignment, I was somewhat perplexed. Your family *has it all*. What could I possibly suggest that would seem in the slightest way, a treat? Having spent the last few days with you and your family and having seen how the family dynamics work, the only suggestion I might make would be as follows. Please, Montse, let me know right away if you think it's rubbish won't you?'

'Well it's very "left field" she began. 'The whole package is only for two weeks as I believe even that short period would be long enough for all of you.

'The first week would be a holiday in Benidorm staying in the Eldorado Bonanza Hotel on a half-board basis. That means you would have bed, breakfast and evening meal.' She checked for a reaction but only got ear-to-ear smiles.

'Now it gets even better. You don't have to worry about travel, as you will be collected in Palma del Rio and taken by bus to Benidorm. The hotel, classified three star, is well recommended in an English tabloid newspaper. There are a number of excursions available at an extra cost, however. You could visit the local farms, olive groves and vineyards and sample wine and cheese made locally. There's also a museum of bullfighting in Ronda, so there's plenty to do. There's bingo every night and quizzes most nights. Karaoke is high on the agenda. The list goes on and, oh, there's a heated pool.

'What do you think about that, Montse?, pretty good, eh?'

Montse was holding her sides from laughing.

'Well, it's certainly very different from anything the family have ever experienced, and are probably ever likely to entertain in the future. So in that respect alone it would be unique. Actually it's very clever and well considered, Maria. I'm having difficulty at present seeing *papa* on a coach with other passengers, let alone playing bingo, but of course, that's the point.'

'There's more,' Maria continued, the second week is in a Yurt.'

Montse exclaimed. 'A what? What on earth is a Yurt?'

Maria was quite surprised at Montse's reaction;- she thought Montse out of all the family would be the most likely to know about the glamping craze currently going on in Britain.

'Well Montse, a yurt is a very large tent, its' origins being in Mongolia. They have become all the rage in Britain as folks take to the latest craze of sophisticated camping known as glamping. Ringing any bells yet?'

'Vaguely, Maria but not too sure about this.' Montse replied.

Fortunately, she had taken along a well-illustrated brochure which explained the wholesome benefits of glamping. Clearly this had not been so well received, but then Maria herself had doubts about the venture; she thought she should formally present the proposals tonight after supper.

So far, Maria had skilfully avoided talking to Montse about the bull-fight, but as the men came into supper from the bar, Sergio approached. 'Maria, how did you enjoy your first *corrida*. Was it as you expected?'

'Well, Sergio, I have to say I surprised myself as to how much I actually enjoyed the whole thing. The sights sounds and smells of the event were very powerful and exciting.'

She glanced towards Montse, who nonchalantly looked away. 'I was extremely fortunate to have you alongside with an excellent commentary, enabling me to understand the intricacies of *la corrida*. There is a lot to learn, but the sensation, was one of intense excitement and expectation.

'Sorry to keep asking you questions, Sergio, but last night when we spoke, I asked you if you would ever consider the life of a *toreador*, and could a good living be made from bullfighting?'

Sergio opened up once more. 'Okay, so I still don't have an answer about me personally, I have yet to decide on my future. On the subject of earnings, a top matador can earn one hundred thousand dollars per fight, plus advertisements and endorsements. He could possibly have thirty to forty fights a year, out of which he would have to pay his *cuadrillo*, two *picadores* and three *bandererillos*.

'*la corrida's* popularity has waned in recent times so many matadors tend to move abroad to countries where it remains very popular indeed.' He ended.

'So I didn't realise it was so popular in other countries, Sergio.' Maria encouraged Sergio to tell more.

'Yes, top guys can get big money in Mexico, Peru and many other South American countries.'

'Wow, I hadn't realised that it was that popular these days, with animal rights issues very much to the fore.'

'I have one other thing that bothered me when I read about the severity of the beating that El Cordobes' took from the ranchers and the guards, then I promise I will let you get on with your life.'

The whole company laughed in a friendly way. She had got Sergio on a subject about which he had extensive knowledge and great passion. They knew that would open the door for Sergio to illuminate Maria at some length.

'*You have to understand, Maria, that the rancheros watch the bulls from birth. At the moment of birth, if the young bull goes towards its' mother, it's not a good sign. It will be too soft. But if it goes the other way from its mother then it is going to be tough and brave .They are only looking for the bravest bulls for the corrida.. Those bulls will be kept separate from all the others, so there can be no contamination from outside influences. Only the bravest bull will be selected for the bullring. They need to be wild enough to want to kill the man.'*

Maria reiterated her thanks to Sergio, and the whole family for their wonderful hospitality and the gracious manner in which they had welcomed her to spend time with their family.

They agreed that the proposals were interesting and would get back to her at a later date. With their permission. she would spend another night with them and leave in the morning.

Montse walked across the room to a sad-looking Maria and gave her a hug. They had become good friends and had shared a fair bit of emotional baggage together. The pair wandered very quietly back to their room.

'Montse I was curious as to how you would take my reaction to the bullfight. I know it's not your thing, but I have to be honest with myself and my feelings and I enjoyed it quite a lot. I've had such a good time with you here and learned a lot about myself.

'I believe that I may be on the cusp of making some changes, but I realise that I need to take a lot more effort around my self-honesty, people-pleasing and drinking.'

'Yeah, Maria, it's been a blast. I for one want to meet up again, really soon. As far as the *corrida* was concerned, it was your decision, and my life is not about control but acceptance.

'Why you enjoyed it, so much is simply that's the place you're at mentally and spiritually. That may or may not change as you make some effort, perhaps accepting that you can't do it all on your own.

'What would be of great benefit to you would be mixing with more spiritually inclined people, and I know that your life at present is heading in the opposite direction, so try and make some adjustments to that.

'You may find a power greater than yourself, a god of your understanding. There's a lot of good stuff out there, programmes to help relieve your tensions and anxieties instead of relying on alcohol. Take a look at some of the bits and pieces I gave you. Perhaps go on a retreat. Keep in touch. *Jai guru,*' Montse ended.

There had been an awful lot to process from that conversation, and Maria felt sad as she lay in bed waiting for her friend to shower. She began to prepare herself to accept leaving in the morning. The pair had grown very fond of each other and formed a strong bond.

Tomorrow she would be off again into uncharted territory, and was a little afraid; she had not made much progress on gaining serenity but she had made a start she thought.

As she waited for Montse to shower, she called Leanne.

'Leanne, baby, how's it going? Sorry I've not been in touch, so much going on. I've got very involved down here with this family. It's very complicated. I knew it would be tough but never expected to have to deal with so many issues. Still, I'm getting there and heading back tomorrow.' Maria said, but even as she spoke, she knew that was all a lie. She had been having a ball but could not admit it. Right away back into her old ways, being dishonest and she had not even left the ranch yet.

'So what sort of stuff are you talking about? I thought if it was too tricky we agreed to be in touch with one another? As I hadn't heard from you I naturally assumed all was well,' Leanne enquired.

'Yeah you're right, Leanne. I should have called but didn't want to bother you. You've got your own clients. How are they going? Well I hope.' Maria replied.

Leanne acknowledged with 'Not too bad actually. This job is a lot easier than I thought at first. A lot of silly people with too much time and money on their hands, if you ask me, but I wouldn't let the bosses hear that. Just sorry to hear it's got very complicated for you, baby.'

'We'll get over it, back tomorrow. Sorry I left you in the lurch with the move honey. How's that going? Not complicated as well, I hope. Can't wait to get back and see the place. Is it nice?' Maria asked said, trying to sound concerned and interested.

'Yeah, it's great. You'll love it, for sure. It's totally our kind of thing,' Leanne said.

'Haven't even really had the chance to contact Luis; only spoken once. I hope he's okay, nice guy, don't want to offend him. He's been very kind to me.

'Pity in some ways we're moving away from him but shouldn't be too much of a struggle with transport links as they are today, and I've got my shiny new car.'

Maria knew that her conversation was phoney making out that the job was difficult when in fact she had the time of her life, with enriching moments that she would never forget. She thought, *why do I have to lie all the time?'*

Leanne continued;- 'Personally, if it were me, I would pop down and see him before leaving for Barcelona. You could do that on your way home. Also I left that very expensive toaster in the kitchen. You could pick that up for us in the new place. It's looking cool the new apartment, you'll love it.'

Maria paused before responding;- it was moments like this that pulled her up sharply. Others' saw it but she did not; she snapped an angry response. 'There you go again, if you were me. You're not so forget it.' She hung up the phone.

Montse stood in her bathrobe and rubbed her hair with her towel; a picture of peace and beauty. Her slightly tanned firm body was the envy of Maria. Confused and angry, she shed a tear. 'Oh my love, what on earth is the matter? Is it something I can help you with?' asked Montse.

'I wish you or someone could as I don't have a clue these days. I seem to go from hot to cold and back all the time.

'Eventually people get fed up with me and move away. I foul up relationships and constantly move on to another, hoping things will improve but they don't. I'm not even drinking at the moment either.'

'Okay, here's what we're going to do. You have some information leaflets and brochures about prayer and meditation.

'You need to take time every day to sit quietly in a chair with your feet firmly planted on the floor, your spine erect and hands on your lap.

'Closing your eyes, you focus on the spot between the eyebrows and breathe in and hold the breath, out and hold, slowly, and repeat until you feel you're calming down.

'Then sit quietly and cast out all thoughts and relax for about twenty minutes. Now you have to be disciplined and do it every day. You need to call me every day so we can stay on track. It's a beginning. Please you have nothing to lose by trying.' Montse also suggested that it would be a very good idea if she called Leanne right back and apologised.

TWELVE

BARCELONA

Maria knew the quickest way back to Madrid and headed straight to the car showroom.

She surprised Luis, who fortunately had no customers so was able to spare the time to be with her. He immediately made coffee for them both and they shared the remnants of a box of croissants from Luis' breakfast earlier.

She dug deep into her bag and presented Luis with a small box, which he excitedly opened to find a miniature statue of a matador. He kissed her and the matador, which brought laughter from the lads in the showroom. He placed it on his desk, along with his pens and note-book.

'Firstly, Maria, how was the car? Meet your expectations, looks good apart from being covered in sand, been on the beach or what?' he joked.

Maria responded. 'No it's the dry, dusty Andalucían countryside, it's just like mid-summer down there. Quite a trip and the car was a dream. I love it to bits and Saint Christopher took great care of me. The lovely book you gave me was such a great idea. I refer to it constantly and even got to meet an aspiring matador in the family.

My concerns were totally unjustified as the Don as it turned out was a perfect gentleman. Not the monster I had made up in my imagination, in fact completely the opposite.

'A philanthropist who has given great sums of money to the community, building a hall and swimming pool, along with a medical clinic.

'They invited me into their home and family to celebrate the birthday of Sergio, their son,' she finished.

Luis was aware of Maria's high as she fairly bubbled with excitement of her story;- he just let her finish.

'Well, I would love to hear more about your little adventure. How about dinner tonight?'

That was like a dagger in her heart, but she knew she must be truthful. Unprepared, she knew she must be tactful and sensitive.

'Luis, I'm so sorry, I need to tell you something. I meant to tell you earlier but waited until the deal had been settled. Leanne and I have taken the lease to rent an apartment in Barcelona. Our office is based there and I'm driving there this afternoon.

'So, sadly, I can't do dinner tonight, but we must do it real soon and keep in touch every day. I'm very, very fond of you and really value your friendship so very much. I sincerely apologise for not telling you sooner, but we must keep our friendship warm and be in touch frequently as best of friends,' she finished.

She felt that she had handled a very delicate situation, that of letting down someone for whom she very much cared, in as truthful a way as possible. She really wanted to say that she loved him, but the words would simply not come out of her head and mouth.

Luis clearly very shocked and upset, tried his best not to show it as she reached across his desk and took his hand in hers and kissed it. The lads in the background pretended they had not heard the conversation but she knew they had.

She looked at the miniature matador and with a tear in her eye invited Luis to take her out to her car for some privacy. The midday sunshine burned their backs and Luis suggested she may be better closing the hood for protection, so close it they did.

They kissed and parted.

Maria checked around the apartment she found the toaster Leanne asked her to collect sitting on the marble worktop. There was nothing more to be done. She felt sad, not to be leaving the apartment, but to be leaving Luis. They vowed to keep in touch;- only time would tell.

*

The journey to Barcelona was pretty unremarkable, Maria's head was in turmoil; she knew that she was not keeping it simple, far from it. She was trying to deal with too many issues at once. She just ploughed on as if on auto-pilot

The latest episode with Luis had left her quite bereft, realising how strong her feelings were for him. She seriously doubted the wisdom in moving away from him to Barcelona.

'Am I being totally selfish and hurting yet another person in my life for my own pleasure? My God I sure know how to screw things up,' she said out loud.

She felt shattered and just set the sat-nav and let the car take her all the way right up to the new apartment building in a very smart district of Barcelona.

Eventually she pulled the car into the very swish car park with its red-painted very squeaky floor; she felt rather low, quite sad and very tired. She thought, *another swish apartment no doubt but so what?* Leanne was waiting for her, as she had the security details and keys and was super excited to show her the new place

They took the lift into the main hallway. Themed art deco with bi-coloured wood-panelled walls upon which were tinted and etched mirrors. Discreet wall lights and tables with a chestnut wood floor offered a beautiful reception area bound to impress the most demanding of clients.

'How about this place Maria? Bit special, eh?' she said.

Maria drew in her breath and let out a long sigh and could only manage to reply with,

'And how much is this lot going to cost them?' She loved it but not what it represented in her life. There was absolutely nothing to be done. It was all in place; just move in. Leanne had even taken care of Maria's personal belongings.

'Don't you just love it, Maria? What clever girls we are. What a team,' Leanne enthused.

The décor in the apartment reflected the reception area. A show apartment, the furnishings were very conveniently included in the deal.

'Well of course it's very special, and I'm a bit taken aback at the moment darling,' she said condescendingly.

Both were tired, and considered staying in with a pizza from the freezer and a bottle from the cooler.

The pair discussed the work aspect and concluded that all said and done, it was a great deal of money they were being paid, and the work was well within their capabilities.

As they finished the wine they sat and chuckled at the situation. Maria was at last warming to the new place as the wine infused her system. They agreed that never in their dreams would they have imagined that they would be living this lifestyle in such luxurious surroundings three months ago. All paid for by the firm;- it was the gift that kept on giving, they joked.

Leanne had also seen two clients; both were very satisfied with the proposals put forward to them for holiday trips. The amount of work involved was no more arduous than anything she had done in her previous job.

Neither of them had any further clients lined up at this juncture so they wondered what the next move would be from the bosses.

'Have you any concerns Leanne, about the whole operation? We've both dived in headlong carried away by the money and the prospect of being on the ground floor of a new enterprise that might have prospects for the future.'

'Well, Maria you're the one who's spent a few days in the company of the boss. What did you glean from that, any clues?'

'Okay, I would have to tell you at some point. Now is as good as any. I'm afraid I slipped back into my old behaviour while in the home of the Ramires family,' she confessed.

'Oh no, don't tell me you got drunk, and threw up everywhere.' Leanne guessed.

'Well, yeah that's par for the course it's almost expected from me by now. It's much more than that, though, and I can't sugar-coat it. Got drunk and ended up sleeping with the boss. How bad was that?' Maria giggled.

'Well, Maria, you've always been a bit of an old slapper, ever since I've known you, so really not exactly breaking news there girl. But even so, sleeping with the boss, that episode just about tops it. So how did that little lot wind up? Have you still got a job, or was there a promotion in it for you, dirty girl?'

'It's not funny, can you imagine how I felt the next few days after that? Probably everyone in the household knew about it, but nobody mentioned it. There was a fair bit of innuendo but nothing specific.

'I got on well with their daughter. She was a gem and helped me a great deal, trying to get me on a programme of self-help among other things.

'I know I need help but just can't figure out the right help. I know you've always done the best for me but I just self-destruct, mainly due to booze.' Maria ended.

'So you've had no contact since then, you don't know what they want you to do?' Leanne asked.

'I'll be honest, Leanne, having spent time with those people with serious money, I'm wondering firstly where it all comes from and what *our* guys' role is in all of it. Looks to me like money laundering;- Has that ever occurred to you, Leanne?'

The last piece of pizza sat in the box as Leanne took a swig of prosecco. She leaned forward holding the sides of her face with her sticky fingers.

'Oh my God what have we got ourselves into this time?' I have to admit that I had my suspicions, but now you've confirmed *your* doubts, I think we're both right.'

'Well, our choices are easy enough. It's just a question of deciding *if* we should act,' Maria said, with a degree of confidence.

'Let's say they are both involved in an illegal money laundering operation. Do we as a matter of conscience quit our jobs under some pretext and quietly disappear from their lives forever, pretending it never happened? Or, do we tell our concerns to the police? We would need to have more proof than we currently have, in that case. We would certainly not have a job after that;- or even worse, they might even put out a contract on us.

'Lastly, we just carry on as if we don't have any suspicions and see what the future brings. Playing the innocents.'

'What do you think? How does that sound, Leanne? Do you agree or do you have yet another scenario and proposal?'

'Pretty well nailed it, honey for options. We just need to agree the best-worst solution. Bearing in mind if we chose to knowingly remain, we would be complicit in the act and liable for the consequences of any resulting convictions. So it's at the moment up to us. We still have choices. As we say in black-jack, stick, twist, or bust. Pretty exciting if you can hold your nerve, honey.'

Maria, perverse as ever, completely changed the subject;-'I must phone Janet Higgingbotthom I might get some clarification from her. She's always been good at sorting complicated issues out. Yet another one of my closest friends I'm neglecting, and then feel guilty about afterwards,' Maria admitted.

'I don't think we're going to find a solution tonight but at least we're agreeing on the problem and not just getting paranoid about the situation. You also need to stop beating yourself up and act more positively. Cheer up, *chica*,' Leanne ended.

Maria pulled her lovely new art deco armchair nearer to the window overlooking the city, and sipped her vodka tonic. She thought, *this is the life for sure;-* top-quality apartment with stunning views as La Sagrada Familia came into her eyeline. Money in the bank, nice car, easy job; she questioned the wisdom of changing the status quo.

Janet eventually answered her phone after a long delay. 'Hi Mags, good to hear from you, been a while. I was beginning to worry about you, how's it going?'

'Well there's been a lot going on, lots of highs, lots of lows. You know me well enough, Jan. At the moment, just coming off a massive high, so expecting the low any day soon. Just so much stuff couldn't begin to tell you on the phone. But there's one really pressing issue. I'll email you on that one;- Where are you?' Maria enquired.

'Well at the moment I'm in the UK. If you remember I signed up for a counselling diploma course post-grad. Well, on completion all kinds of offers came flooding in so I'm working as a freelance consultant.

'Perfect for me, as I can work anywhere and have made great contacts here in the UK, and also in Spain. The next time I'm in Spain. I'll call. Perhaps we can meet up. Where are you right now?' Janet asked.

'Well, with my good friend Leanne, whom I've mentioned before. We've literally just moved to Barcelona from Madrid. However I've been travelling about a lot in my work. We must keep in touch.

'It's mainly the same old crap going on. Excessive mood swings screwing up relationships, all probably alcohol-related. People well-meaning offer help and then get fed up with my inability to sustain any period of sobriety, You must be sick and tired of hearing it too, Janet?'

'Not at all, Mags, it's just a question of you coming to me at some point when you've decided you want to get sober and stay sober. I would love to meet up with you and get busy with you on a programme of recovery. It sounds like the most likely opportunity would be when you are in the north, so whenever you can schedule that in your planner, we can get busy,' Janet finished.

'As soon as I can make time. I intend going north to see the folks, so who knows, we may even meet up then. Do you get back to see your folks much, Janet?'

'Yeah, do pretty good on that front. My office in Spain is in Santander.'

Maria had become a little emotional speaking with Janet. She felt guilty she knew she should be going home more frequently herself, but had neglected that, due to her work commitments, but also by simply having a good time. '*Hablar pronto, chica,*' Maria finished. (Speak soon, girl.)

They enjoyed the freedom from work issues;- neither one had been given another assignment as yet. But the main issue of the day pressed hard upon their minds. The decision for the moment was to stay quiet say nothing and wait for a call from head office.

The girls felt a little unsettled and decided the best option was to go out for a bit. Leanne had tried a couple of local restaurants made the choice.

Casa Dante was a very typical Spanish affair and one with which they both felt very comfortable. Straw-covered carafes hung from the ceiling;- the walls were hung with cheap prints of Spanish landscapes none could ever recall seeing in real life.

They both agreed that the red and yellow table-cloths took the Spanish theme too far; and were tacky. The food however was superb with calamari starter and veal cutlets with pasta to follow. Copious amounts of wine accompanied the meal.

Maria declared amnesty to abstinence and had well and truly fallen off the wagon. Fully sated and very tipsy, the pair attempted to hobble back to the apartment, but the combination of stiletto heels and uneven pavements beat them. They quit before someone got seriously injured and hailed a cab.

Back in the luxury of the apartment, they opened yet more wine. They fiddled around with the Sky box for a while. Neither could decide on a programme to view, and inevitably they drifted off into the arms of Morpheus. The TV was abandoned.

It was eight o'clock in the morning before she knew it. The smart TV, which clearly had a mind of its own, burst into life with the national news of a bomb attack in the Lebanon.

Completely disoriented, Maria awoke for the first time in her new apartment and wondered why she had slept on the settee and not in her new luxurious bed.

The old Maria was back, after a very short respite of moderate drinking. She hated herself. Still fully clothed, she made an attempt to to rise, but did not get very far before she slumped back down on the cushions.

The brilliant Catalonian sunshine was bursting through the half- drawn blinds right into Maria's eyes. She squinted with one eye, and saw an art deco ceiling light fitting.

'Where the hell am I? Silly cow, you've done it again.' Repeating those words to herself and feeling sick to her stomach was so familiar that, it made her even more angry.

'It's like you're playing a bloody broken record over and over again,' she said as she began weeping.

The Nokia waltz on her phone played. She scrambled as she tried to reach it before the voicemail kicked in. She didn't make it and only achieved knocking a couple of half-filled glasses from last night, flying across the room. The clatter of broken glass and puddles of stale wine did nothing to enhance the lovely polished wooden floor.

'What in the name of God is going on, Maria? You up to your old games again, causing havoc as per usual?' Leanne sarcastically said, standing in the open doorway, naked except for her panties, one arm on each of the door jambs.

'Oh, *callate boca grand*' (big mouth)'....I was trying to get to my phone if you must know. Now I've missed the call, and you're not helping, having a go at me' Maria spluttered.

'Well, I mean Maria, you're at it again, and only been back a few hours. When are you going to get yourself together, girl? Leave the mess, I'll clear it up. Go and check your phone and get your act together.'

'That's okay then, you don't take any responsibility, then it's all my fault is it? Funny that I only seem to be in trouble when I'm around you. Didn't have any problems for the last week although there was plenty of drink around,' Maria angrily blurted.

'Don't you dare put all that crap on me, Maria, Your drink problem is yours and only yours. I didn't see anyone holding you down and forcing the booze down your throat.'

Maria began clearing up the floor. Shakily she brushed the broken glass and wine into a dustpan;- a slushy mess made it worse.

'Come out of the way, Maria, it's getting to be like having a child around the place. Just leave it and sort your phone out.' Leanne shouted at her.

Maria left the mess to Leanne, and tried to retrieve the phone call but feeling sick, began retching. She dropped the phone, and almost made it to the toilet but threw up, making one more attempt to read the phone through tear-filled eyes, in her vomit-strewn blouse.

Leanne sat her down on the toilet, and wiped her face with a tissue. Checking and wiping down the phone, Leanne discovered that it had been Gregg who phoned.

'It was the boss, Holdsworth, who called. Why don't you send him a message that you're just about to shower and will call him right back?'

'Or better still, I'll do it while your shower.' Leanne helpfully bailed her out once again.

Sufficiently cleaned up and operational, Maria called the boss. 'Hi Maria, how are you? Looked as though you enjoyed that last assignment at *el rancho*. They spoke very highly of you and you obviously impressed them. I thought your idea was really wacky and very left field but highly original. They will talk it over between themselves and let us know.

'Your first job with the Kennedys went down well and I believe you already had good feedback from them. Very well done, Maria, top job.

'At the moment we don't have another client for you but don't be concerned as there are other initiatives we can organise for you. I'll explain all about that when you come in so look forward to meeting up later. I think it's exciting and hope you will feel the same way about it, so, later, Maria, *hasta pronto adios.*'

Leanne enquired, 'Maria, did Gregg mention anything about new assignments at all, because I've completed my last one and have nothing to follow up with at present?'

'No, he didn't Leanne, that's what we were talking about last night. How can we possibly be earning our keep operating in the way we do with no continuity of employment? We're agreed, aren't we, that we carry on and say nothing, take the money and run, eh?

'I'm really nervous about this guy Leanne, especially as he 'hit on me' at the ranch. It was so unprofessional. These guys, with all their money think they can get away with anything, and sadly they probably can.

'They know so many people at the highest level in business and politics, they're pretty-well fireproof. I get a sick feeling in my stomach most of the time and it increases as soon as he mentions another assignment.

'How about you come with me for a drive Leanne, in my new car or even drive it if you like, and disappear for an hour while I meet with Gregg? That way I've got a good cover story to leave his office when I need to meet with you'.

'Don't know what he's got in mind, but I've done quite a lot of work on Gregg and he's quite a guy for sure, I've typed up a resume of the man, which you might find interesting in the light of our recent conversations and our concerns regarding the integrity of the two men. I'll send it to your laptop. You can read it as we go or you can drive,' Maria suggested

'Send it, *chica*. I can drive any time but I gotta read this stuff.' Leanne said. She opened her laptop and read;

Greg was actually a senior airline captain for Global Pacific Airlines based in San Diego. His flying record was exemplary having been a highly decorated Top Gun Ace fighter pilot with the U.S. Airforce. After being discharged with full military honours from the Air Force, he was headhunted by foreign countries and numerous very reputable airlines, and had the pick of the best. The world was his oyster; he could demand his salary and get it without hesitation.

He made his home base in San Diego, an easy choice for him. Born in a suburb of San Diego, he graduated high school there and went on to graduate with a double first at Caltech. Highly educated both academically and practically, Gregg can fly anything. Most of his colleagues had similar qualifications and experience, but he was a man above all equals.

Whilst flying in the U.N. Peace Corps he met a number of men who would turn out to be very useful contacts in Civi Street. Most notable amongst them was a Mexican gentleman pilot named Snr. Gonzales, who could also fly anything. The location became a sort of a breeding ground for retired successful Top Gun Aces to enter the world of industry and commerce.

Snr Gonzales, a man of considerable wealth, ran a high-end travel business specialising in providing exclusive holiday packages for the great and good for not only of Southern California, but globally.

The two met on several occasions mainly of a masonic, or golfing nature, and it was not long before Gregg went into partnership in the company MexText. A formidable partnership between two men with the Midas touch, they went from strength to strength as their shares zoomed up in the market-place.

Gregg, also a man of substantial means, loved the high life and being a natural-born risk-taker was exciting to be around. Females in particular were extremely attracted to him. The fact that Gregg was married never seemed to present any difficulty to him living the playboy lifestyle.

Amongst his numerous and varied interests, Gregg owned a substantial five-bedroom house with tennis courts and swimming pools, where his ex-fashion model wife lived with their three gorgeous children.

Growing up in San Diego Gregg spoke Spanish from a very early age;- his Spanish language is word-perfect. Sailing at a very competitive level was second nature to Gregg, and his children were taught to handle boats, as well as take part in many other sports from early on. A member of the yacht club he moored a motor/sail yacht in the marina, along with a private aircraft in the local airfield which could be available at very short notice for his private use.

Well known in Rotary and Freemasonry, a great raconteur, he was a star attraction for after-dinner talks. His obvious success and lifestyle were in general admired by many but also resented by others.

Many questioned the mismatch between an airline pilot's' earnings and the extreme wealth that Gregg had no problems flaunting. He had the demeanour of a man who was indeed fireproof, an undercurrent of invincibility and total confidence in his own ability. The persona of a fearless Top Gun Ace. Who would have the nerve to challenge such a man?

Maria had, with incredible dedication, discovered an enormous amount about these two characters which she logged in her journal. El *testamento*, to be kept very secure. She had formed an overall picture and there was something about them that concerned her. It was 'gut feeling' intuitive emotion at this stage; completely unfounded but it was there.

'Well Maria, I'm so incredibly impressed with that I'll make sure it's kept locked on my laptop, well secured. You're such a talent when you're not drinking honey, you should really give yourself a chance. You could make a story around that guy alone but with the pair of those men of mystery, it could be a best-seller. That's a great piece you've collated there.

'Is Gonzales going to be at your meeting today?' Leanne enquired.

'Don't know for sure, wouldn't be surprised, hunting in pairs, always a good policy for these guys. I need to stay focused and not let him get into my head. So you can drive my new car, it's pretty cool. Park up and call me say, after about an hour, and I'll make my excuses to leave.'

Leanne loved the car and although envious as she had not herself been offered a car as yet, she jokingly reminded Maria of the many benefits of working for *The Firm*.

As she walked through the main body of the office, full of confidence, with a swagger in her step. The ladies huddled over their computers, noticing the difference in *this* Maria, who had timidly crept through to the boss's office just a few short weeks ago, for her interview. A lot had happened in the life of Maria' since then.

Gregg welcomed Maria with an offering of refreshment, but she declined, saying she had just had coffee a little earlier and was meeting with Leanne for dinner. He got straight to the point.

'Well, your work is exceptional, Maria. Your clients like you very much, as does your boss,' he sadly said with a smirk and a wink.

'I hope you now feel settled in with the company and ready to expand your CV with other activities on behalf of the company.

Maria responded. 'Yes, I must say I got into the swing of the job quite easily. I felt my confidence growing after the first client. This enabled me to work alongside the Ramires family in a smooth, controlled way.

'Yeah I must say I like the work and feel I will develop my own particular style as my repertoire expands. I have a few loose ends to tidy up with them but will be ready to take another client very soon. Have you got another client for me then, Gregg?'

Maria knew she was a different person from the one who had sat in this seat a few weeks ago. Her eyes scanned the office; it was the same but this time she noticed a picture of *el don,* and Gregg in Mexican outfits.

'Well you've got another assignment but not to assess a client. Something very different and I have every confidence that you'll be able to carry it off with your people skills *no problemo.*

'It requires interpersonal skills at a very high level. I believe that's something which you have *in spades.* We've already established that you can take care of yourself with the travelling;- You clearly enjoy it and as you don't have any ties are able to move at short notice.

'For your future assignments, you must always have your passport and any visas in order, ready to move quickly. It's useful if you have ready cash at short notice. That's the hall-mark for working with our clients; ready cash.

'You know the terms of your contract in as much as your salary will be paid into your account monthly and is not client dependent.

'However, bonuses' will be paid on an interim basis, which will be dependent on the success of a particular assignment. For long trips, you will get an extremely generous expense credit card allowance. Are you still with me, Maria?'

'Indeed I am Gregg, getting very excited already. I'm almost ahead of you. What's the next assignment then?'

'Have you ever been to Mexico, Maria?'

'No, why am I about to go to Mexico, Gregg? 'Not you but *we* are about to go to Mexico, the dream team. How does that sound?'

This particular revelation, even coming from Gregg, threw Maria a curve ball. Had it not been for the fact that she had uncovered a lot of information about Gregg, she would probably have thought it was so much baloney, but now, who knows?

'Wow, that's a fair bit to take in Gregg It's blown my mind a little. I need to think about that one… Mexico, like, it's not just down the road.'

'Of course, it's a surprise, Maria. That's why I needed you to come into the office today. Unfortunately, there's no time to lose. I will need an answer right away… It's a yes or no situation.

'If it's no, then I have to offer it to someone else. Our connection in Mexico City will only be there for a couple of days and I can't afford to lose him.' There's a lot at stake, Maria, this is *the big one*.'

'Maybe I'll take that coffee after all, Gregg.' Playing for time, she glanced at the clock. *Don't call now, Leanne*, she heard herself saying.

She also knew that should she refuse she almost certainly would be out of a job altogether. Leanne would be offered the assignment, and that would be unbearable.

'Not sure what my role in the job is exactly, Gregg?' she replied hesitantly, acutely aware of Gregg's previous behaviour towards her. She was very apprehensive.

'Well Maria, I can see your reticence, but let me try and reassure you. You will be expected to be my business partner on a professional basis throughout the visit.

'We'll be working together, but I will take the lead in all our dealings. Does that help? As I said, it's a yes or no tonight. Of course, I will tell you all about the job tomorrow, but I will need to book flights and make hotel reservations tonight. It's fiesta time in Mexico and the best hotels are filling fast. I will get my secretary on to the reservations right away.'

Maria sat back in her seat, head back, and scanned the room once again, encompassing Gregg this time. She placed her forefinger on her upper lip and closed her eyes, as she gave it serious thought.

'Okay, Gregg, I'm in, but no bloody monkey business.'

With impeccable timing, Maria's phone rang. Leanne was waiting downstairs in reception.

'Okay, Maria, if you're absolutely sure, I'll go ahead, and come back in tomorrow when we both have more time to spare. We'll go over the schedule and our plan. There's a lot you should know about, so I'll explain it to you tomorrow.

'Don't worry about the details tonight. I would emphasise the necessity for total discretion.' Gregg flipped back a framed painting of an old Spanish landscape on the wall, revealing a steel security grade wall safe.

Reaching in he pulled out some documents, a number of passports and packets of money sealed in plastic envelopes, in various denominations and countries of origin. Gregg gave Maria a substantive packet of new twenty-euro notes.

'Take this for now, and go and buy yourself some outfits and anything else you may need for the trip, Maria. Don't concern yourself with cost, buy really good stuff.

'We will need to impress. This is a very different client base, Maria. Be very discreet about whom you talk to about this trip.' He winked. Have a nice meal and give my regards to Leanne. *Hasta manana.*' (Until tomorrow.)

Stuffing the packet of money in her bag as she left Gregg's office, Maria could not resist a little hop, in the air, kicking her heels together, bringing a laugh of approval from the ladies in the office. '*Hasta la Vida*, baby,' she let out.

In the restaurant, the girls ordered their starters and aperitifs, Maria excitedly began telling Leanne about her meeting but stopped rather abruptly.

'What's going on, girl? You having a funny turn or what? Just pulled up in mid-sentence.'

'Oh sorry ... yeah, that's awkward Gregg's just told me not to discuss the trip with anyone and here am I with my best friend dying to tell you all about it but not supposed to. Oh bugger him, we're going to Mexico but for God's sake don't tell anyone.' She laughed.

'Oh, is that all? Going to Mexico, the pair of you, and you're not supposed to tell anyone. Does that not sound more than a bit fishy, girl?

'What's that all about? Has he proposed to you, Maria? After what we talked about last night, we're both in this together. They're both very tricky guys. I suppose we keep quiet, knowing they're up to something. Otherwise, there wouldn't be all this secrecy. We keep quiet and take the money, and you get to go to Mexico.'

'Well, I must admit he didn't give me too long to accept or turn it down. I knew he was pressuring me, but it was a generous offer. I know how clever he can be but then so can I be smart too. I figured it was a risk I was prepared to take. But I won't go along with total secrecy, like not letting you know. That would be plain irresponsible.' Maria concluded.

'Without giving too much away, Maria, I suggest that you tell Luis and your parents. They don't need to know any details. You're just on a business trip. Folks do it all the time. Whatever you do, Maria. keep me in the loop. I know the inside track and we need to make contact, especially if it starts to go pear-shaped.' Leanne advised.

'Well, Leanne it's great to have your support. I know the success of the trip will be based on my ability to keep off the booze. or at least keep it to a workable level.

'It's all going to take place so quickly so I need to keep off the booze. In the meantime, I'll finish my Martini and have *agua mineral* for the rest of the evening. *Salud, amiga, manana y otra manana.*' (Tomorrow is another day.)

Maria was dying to tell Leanne the best bit; she just had to tell. She dipped into her handbag and pulled out the packet of money, carefully hiding it under the tablecloth. Leanne grasped it.

'Holy mother, how much is in that?' and as if it was red hot, she quickly shoved it back towards Maria's open hands.

'Don't know, but it's all twenty-euro notes, a lot of them, and it's all for spending on clothes. Gregg insisted top quality as we need to impress. Want to come with me? Might swing something nice for you on my tab. Gregg won't be checking. I know that for sure.'

'Definitely, I'm up for that, Maria, got a free day tomorrow. By the way did Gregg mention my next assignment? Getting a little concerned that I might not be getting one. You seem to have landed on your feet with your little junket.' Leanne enviously enquired.

'No, it never came up, but I'll ask him tomorrow in our meeting. Sure it will be okay, though, don't worry. He'll come up with a plan for you, I'm sure.'

'Well, now we both feel a lot more comfortable with the deal, let's enjoy the benefits of it. You'll be fine. We both know you can do it, you've got great potential. This could be the making of you. This time next year, girl, we could all be millionaires. *Salud, chica.*' Maria toasted with her *agua mineral*.

They talked about recent events and how situations may have been managed differently. What were the most serious issues that had come up in the last few weeks?

Leanne was very aware of Maria's issues; alcohol the dominating factor, and as a major factor, it was very much a work in progress. Leanne for her part was coping with her assignments without any serious issues. As yet, she had not sorted out a new car. She was a little concerned that the firm had not given her the OK to organise that.

Leanne, undoubtedly the more stable of the two, had no *affaires de coeur*, except that her friend Ferdi, had been calling her from Madrid, wanting to arrange a date for a drink or a meal. However, she didn't want the distraction at the moment. Leanne admitted that she really was not too keen on Ferdi, but couldn't just tell him that outright.

Of the two, Leanne was the more soft-hearted and much more of a giver than a taker. That was her nature;- she naturally got along with people and would readily offer help to those more needy than she.

From time to time, without Maria's knowledge, she worked part-time in the local Oxfam charity shop, and on a couple of occasions she had helped out distributing food to the homeless, of which there were many in Barcelona.

The encounter in the restaurant as Maria handed her the wad of money, actually scared Leanne. It came out of the blue, with no idea of the amount or origins of its whereabouts; she almost threw it back to Maria.

Could this be the reason she wondered, that she was not getting some of the benefits that Maria appeared to be enjoying? *Am I just too soft for this job she asked herself.*

Maria, totally unaware of this side of Leanne, had been the beneficiary of her caring nature, indeed, when in her drunken states she often abused Leanne's hospitality.

Unfazed and totally non-judgemental, Leanne had cleared up many a mess, both physically and mentally, as a result of Maria's drinking. They were two diametrically opposed natures; it worked for them both, in very different ways.

*

The following morning Maria had a call from Gregg informing her that their meeting would be in the morning at 10.00. Maria was up and about by 7.30 so had plenty of time for a light breakfast.

With no hangover, she recalled the previous night with pleasure, and the planned shopping expedition in Barcelona. Very much the New Girl on the Block, she checked with Gregg's' personal secretary after their meeting for the best places to shop in Barcelona.

She wrote them down for Maria essentially the Passeig de Garcia Faria, and Placa de Sant Josep Oriol. Leanne would drive Maria's car, and park, whilst she had her meeting with Gregg, after which they would meet up and hit the town, shopping.

Gregg filled in a little more detail on the forthcoming trip, but nothing untoward was forthcoming. Maria knew what she had to do; she knew the importance of not only being sober but functioning at a very high level. Excited and in control, but always aware of Gregg's potential to change the agenda at very short notice, she could be formidable, but drinking she had the potential to be a disaster.

Gregg had already indicated that there may be a change in plan but did not elaborate. 'It will not affect you at all, so don't even think about it. You just do your stuff, Maria. Look good and stay sober.' That was his plan!

She was happy with that; she liked direct communication, even happy to take orders. She liked to have control and have others about her in control. Gregg, the master of that *modus operandi,* could change plans in an instant; after all, he had been an ace fighter pilot.

The ladies had a most wonderful shopping experience in their new surroundings, buying the most extravagant apparel between them.

Eventually, they capitulated, and on the recommendation of one of the shop assistants collapsed in the Roxy Bar. Their designer shopping bags littered the floor, until the friendly waiter put them behind the bar. The bar did not disappoint; the coffee and pastries were outstanding.

Back at base, they switched on the coffee machine and chilled.

Gregg left a message on the house phone. Unable to, get Maria on her shopping trip, he was very angry with he and scolded her fiercely.

He explained in no uncertain terms the necessity for her to be available twenty-four seven; that was the reason he was paying her a small fortune. He would collect her the following morning at five thirty to leave for Barcelona-El Prat Airport.

Maria realised her serious error in judgement and very angry with herself, asked Leanne to help her get ready for the early-morning departure. Fully expecting to be further admonished for her misdemeanour, she called Gregg.

'Hi Gregg, sorry I missed your call while out shopping with Leanne. Pretty noisy in the centre, it won't happen again. So I'm all packed and ready for the morning,' Maria got her bit in first.

'Hi Maria, yea well, we've got that sorted I hope. We can't have any mistakes no. It's really imperative that we are both on the same song sheet at all times. I will let you know when we can relax those rules, Maria.

'I got a call from Global the airline for whom I fly, and they are a man down sick, and asked me to step in, so I'll be flying tomorrow. I haven't drunk alcohol for twenty four hours so I'm good. This does not affect you one little bit. You have executive reservation. It's about twelve and a half hours trip, depending on weather.

'Okay Maria, I suggest we get two different phones, one for business, one for private calls, different colours, so there's no mixing them up. Leave that with me. See you early *manana. Buenas noche.* Maria.'

Realising she had not called Montse as promised, Maria guiltily called.

'Hi Maria really good to hear from you. How are things going for you at the moment? All good, I hope?'

'Well, yes, there's a fair bit going on. I'm sorry to say I haven't made much progress on the meditation but living in hope that I may find time soon. The big news is that I'm going on a trip, but I'm supposed to keep it secret. Leanne of course is aware, but I think I can trust her. She's always been there for me and my hope is that I've found a confidante in you; more of a mentor if possible.

'I'll get right to the point. Gregg and I are going to Mexico;- Yes I know how that sounds in the light of my recent experience with him at your place.'

'You're not wrong there, Maria. That does sound really weird. Please tell me more.' Montse sounded surprised.

'I'm sorry to say I've *sold my soul* in biblical terms, seduced by the excitement and possible thrills of first-class travel to exotic destinations with an exciting, if unpredictable man in uniform. He's actually flying the airliner to Mexico.'

'Oh, wow Maria I would never have predicted that. I hardly know quite how to respond to that. I'm really not going into a great dialogue on materialism and spiritualism, that's for another day, but on a practical level, just watch out for Gregg.

'I feel sure you've got his measure but he's been playing his games for a long time. You're the beginner. Instinctively, he knows you can handle him. It should be very interesting.

'Along with my father, he has many contacts in Mexico and we don't want to go into that. Just be aware, enjoy, and for goodness' sake, try and stay as sober as possible. Enjoy the experience and don't forget to keep up to date with El testament. God bless and Vamo con Dios cara Maria.'

No sooner had Maria hung up. Then her phone sounded with a text from Montse. It read;- *'And don't forget you can call, text or email any time day or night but remember, I think there's about seven hours difference between Mexico and Spain. XX'*

THIRTEEN

TO MEXICO

As Maria finished drinking her coffee in the apartment she could hardly contain her excitement, as she waited for Gregg to pick her up for the airport run. She could barely manage a slice of toast and marmalade.

As she looked out of the window across the Barcelona skyline, the sun was trying its best to appear, but it was very early as dawn was just about breaking. She felt cold as she threw the remnants of the toast in the swing bin, and rinsed her cup.

Not wishing to disturb Leanne, fast asleep in her room, she stealthily manoeuvred her suitcase and bags into the hallway. One last check for documents and money, she looked around and left a note for Leanne, along with the keys to her new car. She had arranged with Gregg to meet in the car park under the block.

The Janitor said good morning and opened the garage

doors just as Gregg pulled up. Perfect timing;- he would be impressed, she thought.

She, could not be any more impressed as Gregg in his airline captain's' outfit complete with gold-rimmed sunglasses, got out of the shiny black Mercedes to greet her with a peck on the cheek.

'*Hola beunas dias, Maria, comesta?*'

'*Muy b*uen, gracias,' she replied as they set off for the airport. They stowed the luggage and were off through the Barcelona streets just opening to the daily commuter intake. The journey was quiet with neither having much to say; it was too early even for small talk.

Gregg appeared more comfortable with these early-morning starts to the day than did Maria. The airport was just beginning to come to life as he summoned a porter to take care of the bags, with the exception of his flight bag, which he kept by his side at all times.

He made sure Maria knew how to access the VIP lounge and had her tickets and passport. Second nature to Gregg, he was nevertheless meticulous. He reminded her to keep a close eye on the departure board and stay awake, then disappeared to file the flight plans.

Maria, slightly bemused, sat and watched the cleaners sweep their enormous mops across the deserted tiled floor. The perfume shop ladies in their respective smart *livery* of their company, Dior, Versace, and so on uncovered their shiny-glistening shelves. Maria imagined them as Formula One racing teams in '*the pits*', preparing to compete with each other for customers.

Individually, the fragrances were pleasant enough but collectively the scent was overpowering, especially so early in the day. She was hungry but didn't want to go into the VIP lounge too soon; she bought coffee and a croissant.

She sat and looked out through the glass wall of the concourse and remembered the times with her family in airport lounges Papa would tell her 'they are taxiing,' or 'they're on the perimeter track getting lined-up for clearance.' *She became quite melancholy and emotional as a little tear ran down her cheek. She quite suddenly had strong pangs of emotion, and wondered what her parents would make of her now.*

Her memories were of rushing about in the early morning half-light, herded like cattle onto a bus and on occasion making the last- minute dash to the departure gate. *She was cheered by those memories of days gone by, although guilt always accompanied melancholy, which did not leave enough space for sheer joy.*

By comparison with family holidays, she was waiting for the cleaners to finish their work in the VIP lounge where she would wait for the word from Gregg, the captain. She required nothing from the stores, except perhaps some reading material.

Rather grandiosely, in a jokey way, the thought entered her head, '*I'll just stay out here with the peasants for a while' on the main concourse and get the VIP treatment later.* She could not resist such thoughts. *Leanne would never have such thoughts,* she admitted, but then, 'I'm not Leanne,' she said. Time to buy a magazine, a short story book, a book of quizzes and puzzles and a packet of mints.

VIP reception opened and checked her in, escorting her into the lounge.

'This is the life, for sure,' she said

The receptionist laughed and said,

'All this is for you' pointing to an array of delicious food and a free bar. Now she wished she had not bought food earlier. However, she ordered a *cafe con leche* and a Danish pastry.

An absolute Aladdin's cave to Maria, the bar was stocked with alcoholic delights from all over the globe; they glistened and sparkled in bottles of every shape and colour. It was magnetic to her. She gazed, almost transfixed, at the sight. As she cast her gaze from the bottles behind the bar to her cold coffee cup stained with Danish-pastry crumbs, her head said, *NO alcohol*, but inside she wanted the alcohol more than anything else.

A woman about the same age as her, probably thirty-something, who had been tidying-up the tables, stopped to speak with her, asking if she had finished.

'*Ha terminado, senora?*'

Maria looked and saw her name tag and responded.

'Yes, thanks, finished for now, Ginny.'

Maria's eyes flicked from the bottles to Ginny's eyes for a fraction of a second. A gold lapel badge of a camel glistened on Ginny's uniform. They were silent in that moment as she took away the cup and plate and went behind the bar.

She rinsed out the dishes and took a tall glass from the hooks along the front of the bar, and mixed a drink. Maria looked on, silent, almost in a trance-like state as Ginny expertly tossed a clean coaster with the flick of her wrist onto the table.

'*Ahi vas sin alcohol,*' as she offered Maria a *mocktail, no alcohol.*

Maria took up the glass and sniffed the contents, before sipping; it was delicious! Ginny went off to serve customers, but returned after a while to sit with her and explained that she, Ginny, was a recovering alcoholic and recognised Maria as needing help. For both, it was a significant moment, a spiritual moment.

'I thank you from the bottom of my heart, Ginny. Can you tell me how you do it?, I've tried many things yoga, health food, working out in the gym, they help but I'm right back at it again, then I'm out of control once more.'

'Well like you, Maria, I tried many things but eventually found a programme that works for me. Life got better very soon after that, as I daily work the programme, one day at a time. 'It works if you work it.' Ginny said.

'So may I ask Ginny, what is the camel badge about? Is that anything to do with your belief, is it a club thing?'

'No, Maria, it's not a club. It's a fellowship of men and women whose only wish is a desire to stop drinking. The camel is my personal thing. I used to work on cruise ships, and we have meetings on board most ships. The camel can go for many days, *one day at a time,* without drinking. An American lady in the fellowship gave it to me many years ago in Florida.'

Gregg phoned to tell Maria to get ready; they were going to start boarding soon. She left a twenty euro note on the table and went off to find the boarding gate with a distinct skip and a hop in her step.

Gregg had already organised her avoiding the queue for checking in; she simply walked to the front as bold as brass and told the check-in person she was with Gregg Holdsworth.

As if by magic, she was called through and shown to her seat right at the front of the plane. Not simply a seat but a bed. The steward, a very attractive Latino young woman, with a name tag of Rochelle, very obligingly took Maria's jacket and hand luggage. She had a great mid-Atlantic accent but with a strong hint of Española.

She demonstrated the wonders of the bed arrangement and offered refreshment. Maria ordered a non-alcoholic mocktail; she had really enjoyed that one she had in the VIP lounge.

She settled back with the in-flight magazine as Rochelle rapped her knuckles on the door to the flight deck; it swung open to reveal the man. With his gold-rimmed pilot Polaroid sunglasses and wearing a white shirt with gold epaulets and neck tie, Gregg was well and truly in his element in every sense of the word. Gregg, the man in charge, blew a kiss to her.

'Cabin crew to check doors for take-off,' he announced.

Once everyone was boarded and seated, Gregg's mellifluous tones came across the speakers, first in Spanish then in English;- *'Good morning everyone. Welcome aboard this Global Boeing treble seven two three six bound for Mexico Juarez Airport. As everyone boarded in good time, we have managed to get a take-off time a little earlier, so thank you for that.*

'Initially we will be climbing out to the left towards the Spanish coast and the Bay of Biscay, levelling out at 8000 metres. The weather is fine, so you should be able to get wonderful views of the sierras and the coastlines. There is a moderate headwind which will not affect our estimated time of arrival. My co-pilot is Captain Francisco Hernandes and he will keep you up to date with any news and interesting sights to be seen.'

Maria settled with her magazine and tried to plan her journey, very impressed with Gregg and feeling very privileged. Finishing her drink. she decided on a short nap. It had been an early start, with very little sleep last night.

As she dozed Maria's thoughts returned to the times she went on holiday with her parents. The early-morning rises from her comfortable bed. Despite the promise of an exciting holiday, she found it almost impossible to give it up in the dark of early morning.

Grumpily, moaning all the while, she would never come out of her mood until eventually she was sitting in the airport with *churros* and hot chocolate.

The crackle from the speaker broke Maria's sleep. Angry now, she had been forced to return to the real world. She felt guilty for not being more appreciative back in the day; her parents had saved hard to take the family on holidays. She felt bad.

Maria turned on her side, attempting to return to her dream. It did not work. It never worked. Here was she, club class, midway across the Atlantic Ocean with her boss as Captain, flying this magnificent Boeing. More memories flooded back... to the day her father, managed to get her onto the flight deck on her eleventh birthday. She still had a photograph somewhere of her wearing the captain's cap.

Confused and still tired, she wanted a proper drink, but determined, she resisted and asked for coffee and her bag from the overhead compartment.

Taking out her journal, she opened it and realised she had not made an entry for quite a while, and remembered that she was always with Bunny by her side. She looked through the in-flight mag for a fluffy toy, a bunny but all she could find was Pancho, a Mexican boy in a sombrero. She bought him and thought he looked sad, and he certainly did not offer comfort to Maria; he could never be Bunny.

'Hello, everyone Francisco here. I hope you are having a pleasant flight. We are now cruising at an altitude of 35,000 feet. The weather is clear all the way, but we may experience some small amount of turbulence as we cross the mountains much later, so sit back and relax. There's a great selection of films available so you should find one to your taste. Just ask the cabin crew for anything you need. We'll get back with any news.'

As she opened her journal with the intention of updating it from her rough notes. Small shorthand notebooks littered the bottom of her bag so she made that her first task; to get the rough notes transcribed into the journal.

Enjoying the sensation of handling her gold-plated propelling pencil, she thought of *Abuela,* who had gifted the pencil many years ago when she started high school; it was an old Eversharp. She preferred to use pencil in favour of any other medium, for sentimental reasons.

She just loved to hold the hexagonal-shaped barrel and to feel the pencil moving across the paper. *Abuela*, she believed, was guiding her hand.

The process of recording was another journey of discovery for Maria, bringing up a lot of buried memories, both good and not so good. She spent a little over an hour collating and recording material for the journal. Eventually, needing a break, she closed the books and fell into a deep sleep.

With no idea how long she had slept, Maria was awakened by Gregg emerging from the flight deck to stretch his legs. He walked the length of the plane end to end.

'How's the journey, Maria?, coping with it all right?' Gregg enquired as he sat on the edge of her bed.

She responded as best she could, arousing herself from her slumbers. 'Yeah, it's all right-ish, don't know how you manage this on a regular basis. I'm already dreading having to repeat it all again on our return.'

'Not far now and we'll be making a gradual descent before approaching the field. We get used to it over time. There's no flying actually involved, these things fly themselves, but we just have to monitor the controls. Once we've landed and cleared customs and emigration, I have transport laid on and it's no distance to the apartment.' Gregg said. 'Apartment, Gregg? Thought you said hotel.' Maria snapped back at him.

'Don't get so excited, Maria, Benjamin and I have a penthouse condo in Mexico City. great spot, you'll love it.

•

Nothing to do, got your own chef and maid, life of Riley. Better than any hotel,' he concluded, going back to the flight deck.

'We're Just making our final descent and will be on the ground in twenty minutes. Hope you have enjoyed your flight with Global and look forward to seeing you again. Have a safe and comfortable onward journey.'

Looking out of the windows, Maria took in the vast expanse of the city of the Mexico sprawl. It went on for miles, but other thoughts occupied her mind. They were about Gregg, who seemed to duck and dive in all of his affairs, and she wondered if he was actually capable of being straightforward and truthful at all.

Maria knew nothing about her and Gregg's plans on this trip; he had only given her some very vague guidelines. Coupled with the concerns she had about the degree to which he could be honest, she felt rather uneasy. Far from home and unfamiliar with the city, realising that the only information she had about Mexico was from what she had watched on TV and the movies. Excited but apprehensive, she hoped that she could rely on Gregg, but she had reservations. She had no other choice, she had to trust him.

Once Gregg had debriefed and cleared to go landside, Maria met with him. He was greeted by officials like an old friend, who had returned home. He moved through officialdom with the ease usually afforded to the diplomatic corps, as they boarded their black Toyota Land-Cruiser with blacked out windows, baggage and all.

The intense heat and unique smell of Mexico City, hit Maria. All new destinations, she thought, had unique smells but this place also had a sound;- a noise of traffic and loud voices mixed with ever-present music. Truly a cacophony she had never experienced elsewhere in her travels.

Fortunately, the air conditioning in the vehicle masked both to a great degree, so the short journey to the condominium was not too unpleasant. Maria, however, felt nervous, and was thankful that she was not driving herself;- a strange journey, mostly in silence, which disconcerted her. She felt it was like a secret military operation; the shiny black car with tinted windows, another person in the car, who had not been introduced. She felt tense.

They drew up at the front of the condo. and were met by attendants. Two men in uniform of the company, who looked as though they were maintenance men, whisked the baggage away the moment the car came to a stop.

Gregg jumped out first, along with his unknown friend. Maria, wishing to give an impression of strength, tried to jump out too but found herself more in uncoiling mode. Recovering from the very long flight, she forced herself upright and wondered who the mystery man was?

Eventually, as the lift whisked them up to the penthouse, Gregg said, 'Jose, this is Maria;- Maria this is Jose.'

She thought that was rude and so angrily retorted. 'Can someone get me some water? I'm dying of thirst here.' Gregg responded by asking Jose to fetch water. 'You should have said, Maria. There were plenty of drinks in the car.' Maria struggled with the whole situation, trying to make sense of it. She felt she had to assert her position. Tired and thirsty, she had to establish her identity right away. He was busying himself having low-volume conversations with Jose the mystery man, which further infuriated her.

Perhaps, she reasoned, this was Gregg's way of debriefing from the action of flying for so long, although he was very dismissive by earlier saying 'these things fly themselves,' Maria knew that was not the case. It would bear little resemblance to military operations, when the stakes were considerably higher, flying top gun jet fighters in hostile situations. Or perhaps he was just being bloody rude; either way, she needed a proper drink, and soon.

FOURTEEN

THE CONDOMINIUM

Maria, sipped the iced water with a slice of lemon and decided to sit quietly and observe. Jose was helping Gregg to unpack and put away his clothes in a room which she took to be his bedroom. Her own baggage remained where it had been placed by the condo staff, just inside the front door. She just sat and waited for the next move.

She did not have to wait very long before the door buzzer sounded and Jose bounding across what was clearly a very expensive carpet, answered the door for Consuela.

'*Hola Consuela comesta? Adelante.*' (Come in.') Consuela quickly introduced herself to Maria, explaining that she was the maid who would be available for all domestic duties for the duration of the stay.

She promptly signalled for Maria to follow her as she wheeled her baggage into another room.

Consuela, a pretty forty-something year old with a very strong Mexican accent, was politeness itself. She asked Maria a few questions about her clothes and suggested that she shower whilst *she,* put away Maria's clothes.

'Consuela, thank you for that, and yes, I will take a shower. That was a very long journey. I will probably have an early night to catch up on sleep,' Maria confided.

'You come from very far *senora*?' Consuela asked. Maria immediately realised that Consuela probably knew very little or nothing about Gregg's private life. Obviously somewhat guarded she nevertheless would have preferred Consuela to be something of a confidante. She would have to play the situation by ear. 'Yes, far enough, Consuela. Has *senor* Gregg left any message for me?' Maria asked.

'No, senora I no see message and he no tell nothing, so sorry for that,' she apologised.

The bathroom was straight out of *Homes and Gardens,* immaculate and so very much in vogue. It was stunning. She showered in a magnificent wet-room;- the tiling was very special, with built-in benches to rest upon.

Wrapped in her super-soft white robe, she went in search of Gregg, who was not to be found. He had, however, left a message with Jose that he would be retiring to bed and would see her on waking. She was fine with that, she understood that she was in Gregg's domain and would do well to remember the rules. She also went to bed; in her wonderful spacious bed, she slept soundly.

On waking, Consuela was by her side at once.

'You sleep real good *senora*. You very tired, no?' she asked.

'*Si, si Consuela, muy buen, gracias,*' Maria replied in Spanish, and ordered breakfast. She had some difficulty with the local dialect but enjoyed learning new Mexican phrases.

Maria threw back the bedclothes and attempted to open the blinds, unsuccessfully. She called to Consuela to discover that they were electrically operated, as indeed was most of the apartment. She switched on her cell phone and eventually got a connection, to find out the time was two fifteen in the afternoon.

Consuela arrived with the food and they shared a joke together, as Maria imagined it would be breakfast time. She ate at a small table in her bedroom as music played quietly in the background; the coffee and croissant hit the spot.

On her second coffee Maria wandered over to the window and gazed out.

What she saw took her breath away. She had no idea how high they were in the penthouse. It felt as if she was still airborne; the penthouse was so high, she looked down on the fantastic view of the dense sprawl of Mexico City.

Venturing onto the vast expanse of the lounge carpet, she admired the whiteness of everything. The leather settees and armchairs, the dining chairs and the carpet; it was immaculate.

Jose appeared, and introduced himself apologising for not greeting her properly on arrival. He enquired as to her sleep, and added a welcome to Mexico City. Maria had never been in such luxurious surrounding ever in her life. Original oil and water-colour paintings adorned the wall, as did enormous gold-framed mirrors. There was even an open-fire grate with a log cage full of logs. She was impressed.

The main man himself was nowhere to be seen, but Jose gave Gregg's' apologies, saying he had a meeting, adding that he intended being back for dinner. As Maria well knew dinner (*cena*) could be nine o'clock at night; she had to play according to Gregg's rules, which was fine, as she would use the opportunity in his absence to get to know Jose and Consuela.

Acutely aware that she would need to be totally discrete and let nothing out of the bag, she wanted to get the class issue out of the way. She suggested they drop the senora address and call her Maria.

But they both stated that Gregg would not agree to that; they knew their place in life. That rather upset Maria but once more, she knew she would have to play according to his rules.

Maria started by telling them this was her first visit to Mexico City and hoped they could fill her in with a little detail about the place. Jose enjoyed telling Maria all he knew about his city. warts and all.

'I have love-hate relationship with my city. It's tough place to live for ordinary folk, life is hard, too hard. But we get by. My old man, he was good cook. He work in some of best restaurants in city.

'He taught me all I know, so I got good job. Then some guys came in restaurant one day. They was well loaded with cash, they had some idea about they want to have their own restaurant. So they say you want come work with us. Of course I say yeah, you bet. They was Snr. Gregg and Snr Gonzales. So here am I, thanks be to God.' He crossed himself.

'Mexico City was always called F.D. (Federal District). All old guys called it that. Then somebody decide to call it CDMX. Who know why? We don't get asked 'bout nothin'. Big Shots make the rules."

He puffed on a cigarette, which he was smoking out on the balcony.

'This condo is Palo Alto, on Avenida Homero, Polanco, pretty nice place for sure, eh?' Maria noticed a slight shift in his usual formal tone. She asked once more if they could exchange cell phone numbers, but again they would need to get approval from Gregg.

Both were more than happy to disclose general information that was available to tourists but were considerably more reticent in indulging in more open dialogue.

They both, however, warned about the high levels of crime, especially with tourists being robbed, but if she was in a group all would be well.

'I would love to see some of the Aztec ruins and learn more of their culture, and I believe there are some magnificent cathedrals to visit. Obviously, I imagine Snr. Gregg would be able to take me, but it would also be nice if you could show me around.'

'Yes, there's many good things to see in Mexico but Snr. Gregg, he no allow that, for sure. You stay close to Snr Gregg, it best that way. You never go out at night alone, for sure.'

She enjoyed talking with Jose and Consuela, picking up local phrases and tips, to help her blend in more easily.

Neither one would consider taking Maria out of the condo. They both lived far away from the district of Polanco, known for luxurious shopping, five-star hotels, high-net-worth individuals, Michelin Star restaurants and diplomatic embassies; very exclusive, and about as far away from their respective lifestyles as could be imagined, they explained.

Jose's role was one of a personal aide to Gregg, but he was actually a highly rated *chef de cuisine* working in the local Polancon restaurant, owned by Gregg and Benjamin.

Jose would come and work for Gregg whenever he was in town. Maria knew that neither of them would ever dream of using such personal terms as their forenames.

Consuela was much more forthcoming and spoke freely about her home life and the conditions for the poor in the city. She had a long bus journey from one of the poorest districts in the city, Neza Chalcoltza.

She had three children and lived in very modest conditions. Born there, like so many, she had very few opportunities to escape the extreme poverty. Juan her husband drove a bus so he had regular money coming in, but there was no security; if he was sick there was no sick pay.

Consuela worked wherever she could. This was, she said, the best job she ever had and she could not believe her good fortune. She said she was blessed to have this job. Gregg paid her exceptional money and even when he was not using the condo himself, he paid her.

On very rare occasions, Gregg's wife would visit with her children but Consuela did not speak very favourably about her, clearly not wishing to comment at all.

'But Snr. Gregg, well, this man is saint, Santa Gregorio,' she finished, hesitatingly, afraid she may have said too much.

'Maria almost felt duty-bound to disclose about her personal life and how she came to be working for MexTex. She gave it some thought but then remembered, how little, Gregg, had told Consuela about her and decided that she would not disclose too much personal information.

She talked in general terms about growing up in northern Spain and how she was researching her family history. On no account would she divulge the slightest information about Gregg, but Maria would be very interested to hear more on Santa Gregorio.

She soon discovered there were many common interests between them but also significant differences. Maria wanted to understand more about Consuela, without prying in any way. She felt that the right approach would be caring, in a professional way. Acutely aware of her surroundings, she would need to be very cautious. They spoke about similarities in language but with different nuances; between Spanish and Mexican Spanish.

Maria shrewdly devised a strategy for getting alongside Consuela in a general manner, non-specific; how children learn differently depending on their environment. It was a successful ploy.

Consuela opened up to describe life at home, and how making time for children was difficult. Just getting food, clothes and fresh water was the priority. She told Maria that she would love to simply sit down with the children and read from a book, but it was difficult to find even a short time in the day.

Maria could only listen, with no direct experience of poverty herself, and not having raised children herself, she felt it was quite disingenuous to talk about such matters. Language was very similar, the culture not so similar and social values very dissimilar. She acknowledged poverty levels could not compare with European levels, and there was a massive disparity in social welfare, which, in essence, did not exist.

Consuela clearly enjoyed the conversation and showed a great deal of interest. The relationship had changed, with much more informal talk and sharing.

'There no social care, the poor get by best they can. Buy stuff, sell stuff, maybe do gardens or paint houses for rich people. My man real lucky, he drive bus. He get sick, he don get paid. I'm lucky one, now you see? But we have God and the saints to protect us.

'My *mama* and *papa*, they die real young. They no have good life. The bosses get fat and rich, we just die young. It no fair no fair for sure.' Crossing herself, she held her rosary between her skinny fingers with a single very thin gold wedding ring; there was no spare flesh on Consuela.

She wore fairly standard apparel for women in service; a white blouse with a black skirt and flat back shoes. Her long jet-black hair had some grey streaks, which she had made no attempt to conceal and was swept back and held by a simple clasp.

Consuela had the ability to move around in a very efficient way, very attentive but not pushy; she was naturally helpful.

The morning bore fruit for Maria's verbal *fishing expedition;* she felt pretty well informed about the two people that she may be spending quite a bit of time with, if today was anything to go by.

Eventually, her phone lit up and rang. It was Gregg, informing her of his impending arrival. She struggled a little with his behaviour and *modus operandi,* she was still learning how he worked and how she could best deal with it to her advantage.

She knew she had better get used to it or the whole deal would be off; where he had been and with whom she would leave alone. Uncomfortable, it was alien to her normal way of working. She liked to be integrated and connected, with lots of dialogue going on, but it was difficult with Gregg; he needed to keep all the balls in his court.

He turned up wearing designer smart casual apparel, a cream linen jacket with cotton shirt and tie, pale blue linen trousers and dark tan leather loafers. He promptly informed Maria that he had made initial contact with the group with whom he intended doing business.

'We had a working breakfast at the golf club and it went very well,' he said.

'Maria I've been neglecting you somewhat. Let me make it up to you and take you for a drive to a local attraction. It's a wonderful park, not very far. You'll love it.

'Jose, bring the car around to the front. We're going to Bosque de Chapultepec. Ten minutes, Maria come as you are, smart casual, It's only a park and maybe a little lunch. There's a nice bistro in there.'

Jose, a man in his late forties, was tall and very slim and always wore the same clothes: a navy blue suit with black casual shoes and a white unbuttoned shirt. He was quite gaunt in appearance with a scrawny neck and a cough of a very heavy smoker. He also had the look of a man who could handle himself in a tight corner. With a scar on his left cheek, it later transpired that he had a black belt in karate from many years ago.

The car was available within minutes.

Maria was just glad to be out for the first time. Excited, she had always enjoyed new experiences and all of this was right up there. In the car with the blacked-out windows, she turned to Gregg and jokingly whispered, this car's like a hearse. 'I feel like a mafiosa moll in this beast of a car.'

'Well, after you get to see a bit more of the place, you'll feel different and far more reassured travelling like this. You'll need a while to acclimatise, but once you get the hang of it, you'll see what a great place it is. Very edgy but as long as you know how it works here, you'll be fine,' Gregg reassured her. Gregg drove the car and parked in secure parking at the Bosque.

The atmosphere in the park was special, and being a Saturday it was pretty busy with folk enjoying the fresh air, well, at least fresher than downtown. They strutted their stuff in a Spanish way but with high Mexican influences. They knew how to do it; their clothes, especially the women's and children's' were especially colourful, very fashionable and flamboyant. They strolled around the lake, and she realised that although similar to Spain, it was essentially Mexican. Maria slowly absorbed the ambiance, enjoying every minute of it. She was in her element.

'There's a museum housed in that beautiful building over there. It's worth a visit at some time if we can arrange that. Mexico has many examples of Aztec cultural sites. But first let's get something to eat, the bistro's over there. Are you hungry?' Gregg asked as he pointed it out to her.

Maria was keen to find out his schedule but knew him well enough by now not to ask. She decided that she would let him take the lead in everything; this was his territory.

'*Hola senor Gregg, comesta?*' the man behind the bar called out. Maria had the sense that wherever they went, someone would know Gregg. The men chatted as enchiladas and a couple of beers were brought to the table.

'Do you play golf here, Gregg? The climate looks perfect for golf,' Maria asked.

'Yeah, you bet, there's great golf here, and all year round, although it can get relatively cold in winter. I may try and get a round in this trip. I was up there this morning on a bit of business, but no golf.

'What I would like you to do, Maria, is to come with me for dinner tonight and meet a couple of men that may be very useful business connections. I will introduce you as my business partner. They will like that. You are the travel consultancy partner, expert in providing high-end exclusive travel plans for high-net-worth individuals and groups, of which there are many around Polanco. What do you say, Maria?'

'Sounds like me for sure. As long as I don't have to get involved in your other side of the business of which I know absolutely nothing, I'll be fine,' she replied.

'Got it in one, Maria.' They finished their snacks and slowly strolled through the park back to the car.

Gregg drove through the Saturday evening traffic as the locals began hurrying home, hectic but not beyond Gregg, by any means. He went on to tell Maria about the restaurant he and Benjamin owned locally in Polanco. She didn't let on that she already knew about it; instead, she invited Gregg to tell her more about the food.

He however made it very clear that this was a very important meeting, which she and he needed to get just right. Once this went according to plan, then they were free to do whatever suited the pair of them.

He instructed her to act as if she knew all about Gregg's business affairs; smile and nod in the right places but not to get drawn into details. For the first time, he confirmed, her role was as a front, but she needed to pretend that she was a partner in his business.

'Once we get this meeting out of the way, Maria, it's all a question of how long we intend staying. It's really such a wonderful place with so much to see and do.'

'Well, it's your call, Gregg, I'm working.' They both laughed wholeheartedly at that statement.

'It would be a shame to miss some of the sights, of which there are many, Maria. Perhaps when we get through the business we could take in Aztec stuff and cathedrals. They are well worth-while, and on another day maybe we could check out a beach. I know you've spent a lot of time around Spanish beaches but the atmosphere on Mexican beaches is different.'

'I'm up for anything at all. That plan sounds perfect, Gregg, and as for going home, I'll leave that to your discretion, boss.' Maria replied cheekily.

'I could drive to the nearest beach, Tecolutla, but at about two hundred and fifty miles, it's a long drive probably three hours or so depending on traffic. The other thing is, I could fly us there?' Gregg posed a question.

Laughing, she replied, 'Oh yeah, of course we could fly.'

'I love working with you, Maria. You're always funny, totally unimpressed by all the wealth we guys have. You're happy to fit in with the life-style. In fact, you embrace it, take it while you can.'

'Yeah, you bet, it all could disappear tomorrow. I love it while it lasts. I keep a journal and each time I write up something like that. Someday I will share it with my parents but right now I don't want to tempt fate and blow it.' She confessed.

'Good for you, girl, that's why you're here. We do however need to discuss the Elephant in the room.' Gregg admitted.

'If I'm on your wave-length, Gregg, we're talking about San Diego?' Maria asked.

'Yep, can't really come all this way across the globe without visiting home. That may involve asking you to amuse yourself for a couple of days while I take care of that.'

'Well I know you like me to take the initiative Gregg, and looking at the local maps and your flying charts, San Diego is close to Encinitas, a place I would love to visit.'

Gregg tried to pretend that he was not curious but really deep down he had an enormous crisis of control and letting go. She had never shared Encinitas with him and he resented that enormously.

As the pair walked through the door to the apartment and collapsed onto the settee, Consuella immediately arrived with drinks.

'Jose, I know that you are going to the restaurant to prepare for tonight's dinner and as I will not be requiring the car, please feel free to take it as long as someone can come and pick us up and drive us home after dinner.' Gregg said.

Maria had worked out this episode very skilfully without giving away any clues; she felt quite smug and clever. She realised that she had drawn a little power from Gregg but was aware of the need for caution. She knew that her best ploy would be sharing the power; he had shared how *he* saw Maria but *she* dared not reciprocate.

'Thanks for that little glimpse of the area, Gregg. Certainly got the taste for venturing further afield. In the meantime, what time do I have to start preparing for our dinner date?'

Gregg, was a little slow in responding; she sensed that he was trying to figure out who she might have known in Encinitas and cross that she had worked out a plan in advance. She was determined to milk this situation for all it was worth.

'Erm… oh, I don't know. Dinner at eight. Can you be ready for seven thirty? I'll call El Iguaden later to check progress. Jose has just left for there.'

'Great, looking forward to it, should be cool from what you tell me. How's the business side going? Is it making money? I presume so, not likely to lose money if you've got anything to do with it. Gregg.' Maria asked, knowing she was taking an enormous risk into unfamiliar territory. Gregg's other businesses.

'Yeah we're good. In the black. Oh by the way it's called El Iguaden.'

They spent the rest of the afternoon just lounging in relaxing conversation about no particular subjects.

Maria loved her luxurious spacious bedroom. She invited Consuella to sit with her in one of the two armchairs she had there. Consuella proudly shared a photograph of her family dressed up in their "Sunday best," a lovely picture which Maria took to her heart.

They played around with jewellery as Consuella tried on various earrings and bangles that belonged to Maria. A lovely girly session with both sharing, ending with Consuella receiving a pair of earrings as a keep-sake. Throwing caution to the wind, obviously feeling safe with Maria, she gave her an enormous hug.

*

The restaurant was superb, candle-lit throughout with starched linen table coverings, white linen napkins, silver cutlery and crystal glasses. Practically perfect in every way.

Maria, in her dark blue satin cocktail dress, looked stunning. She had toyed with the idea of wearing the

St Christopher that Luis gave her, but vanity won over sentiment.

She favoured a single string of imitation pearls. She reasoned no one would know the difference in the dimly-lit surroundings. She had been checked over by Gregg prior to leaving the apartment, and with the strict warning, *do not get drunk,* she passed muster.

The food was as expected; superb. Maria started with crayfish and went onto Lobster, followed by Dover sole; all very convivial and cordon bleu, Michelin-rated. The men were most agreeable gentlemen, who made her very welcome.

She carried off the charade with grace and elegance as was befitting a company director in a high-end international travel company. Two of the men invited Gregg, with the permission of the ladies, to join them for cigars on the patio.

Sofia the wife of one of the business-men, sat with Maria and introduced herself. The pair chatted about the wonderful designer shops in Polanco. Sofia was a woman of around late forties, heavily made up and overloaded with designer everything; clothes, shoes, and jewellery.

Maria discreetly observed Sofia and thought that she had never met, close up, anyone quite like her. She was like a character in a TV soap such as *Dynasty*. She said she had met Ignacio, her husband, when she was an aspiring actress in her late twenties, making TV commercials for hair products. She produced yet another photo of her back then.

Ignacio had known Gregg for many years, always played at least one round of golf when Gregg was in town.

Sofia had absolutely no idea what line of business her husband was involved in, and cared not. They owned a stunning house, pictures of which she proudly showed to Maria, in a gated community with private armed security guards.

'You simply must come over We don't get to see much of Gregg these days and he's such good company. We're having a swimming party next weekend that would be a good time to come over, Maria, darling,' she said. 'The youngsters will be back from boarding school so you can get to meet them too.'

Maria diplomatically suggested that Gregg had a very busy schedule but she hoped he could fit that into his plans. She imagined he would not wish to accept.

The meal finished and the business satisfactorily concluded, Maria through the window, spotted Gregg in the car park. He collected a small hand holdall from Ignacio and placed it in the trunk of the car.

'*Adios*' all around as they all made their way through the car park. Maria was taken by surprise as they all climbed aboard their respective cars to drive home, after consuming a lot of alcohol.

The wine at table had been flowing freely throughout the evening; but there was an air of invincibility about them, they were so well connected. Minor inconveniences, such as traffic violations seemed to be of no concern, she reasoned, and there was always plenty of "folding money" around. Gregg made his way to find Jose before leaving, and gave him a sizeable gratuity for the evening.

FIFTEEN

THE BEACH

'Maria, my initial thought about the beach trip is that it might be too far for a day. We would need to stay overnight in order for us to enjoy it at its' best. The alternative could be I fly us down there. How are you in light aircraft?'

'I really don't know. I've never been in a light plane. Would that be safe? Sorry, silly question, but I might be scared is what I mean,' she sheepishly replied.

'Tell you what, first thing tomorrow we'll go to the airfield. I'll take you up, I'm sure you'll love it, if okay then. we're on for a flight to the coast at Tecolutla.

'If all goes well, we could follow up with a trip to San Diego another day and you could visit Encinitas. First things first, up early six o'clock tomorrow morning, check the plane, short test flight for you. All being well, then pack some bags, swimwear and off to the coast.'

Maria loved the way he took charge; that was him at his best in full flight mode. She thought he had never really left his military training behind, an expert in his field. She would follow this man, trust him implicitly. At least as an aviator.

'Maria, I'm off to bed. I suggest you do so also and we'll be up fresh in the morning, fresh and raring to go. Nite nite.'

Maria was stunned. Gregg never even made a move on her for the bedroom. She sat and scratched the back of her head in total amazement, and with some disappointment. After that lovely meal and a few glasses of excellent wine, she felt in the mood for a little love-making. She would have put money on Gregg being in a similar frame of mind, but alas not tonight, Josephine.

She swilled her last drop from the glass and went into the shower. Pleased with her day, she checked herself in the mirror whilst she dried herself with a huge white Turkish towel. 'Oh, for goodness' sake,' she said, 'that's big enough to dry two people. Shame it's only for one. Your loss tonight, big boy.' She slipped into the enormous soft, welcoming bed and felt very alone.

She slept very heavily and woke feeling great, with no hangover; she was ready for the day. '*Hola, buenas dia, Consella.* Where is Snr. Gregg? is he still in bed?'

'No, no, *senora*. *Senor* Gregg he up for ages ago and gone to *aerodromo* to get plane ready. He no liking hanging about, is normal for him, early start. He used to him fly off someplace, regular stuff. He love flying. I got you light breakfast cereal and coffee, *es Buena, si?*'

It was not long before Gregg returned full of energy

and eager to get going. Maria had never seen him in this mode, seriously turned on and ready to go.

'Ah, great, Maria. Glad you're up. Just prepped the kite ready, all gassed up and checked over. As soon as you're ready, we're off. Jose will take us so he can have use of the car in my absence. *Vamanos.*' (let's go.')

She got the gist and just assumed it was some sort of pilot banter, for getting the plane ready and all fuelled up. They climbed into the *Hearse* and about thirty minutes later they were loading into the plane. She was very keen to understand about private flying and knew that would please Gregg.

'Tell me about the plane and where we're going, Gregg. It's all a completely new world of adventure for me. I don't know one end of a plane from the other. I can see there are two propellers, Is that right?'

Gregg loved that, and explained the fundamentals of flight to her as they walked around doing pre-flight inspections of the airframe and wheels. To her surprise, she soon became an eager listener; she hung on his every word.

'You've probably heard that flying is the safest way to travel in the world?'

'Erm... no, actually Gregg, I haven't heard that,' she replied.

'Well, I'm here to tell you Maria, that it is, and once you see how your world becomes expanded by the freedom brought about from flying, you'll be a convert... I hope.' They completed the pre-flight external checks and boarded. Gregg gave her earphones with a mic and called up the control tower with the aircraft identification. They knew Gregg; he had been in earlier to file the flight plan, and was a regular anyway. Gregg, ever the professional, wore his white shirt with epaulets but omitted the neck tie; the pilot sunglasses were obligatory.

After a perfect take-off on the grass runway, they climbed out to 1000 feet and called the tower, requesting permission to climb to 3000 feet, left the circuit and set their course. She heard the talk through her head-set, and looked at Gregg with admiration. He showed her how to operate the mic and she bubbled with excitement as she watched Gregg fiddle with some knobs and switches but thought it wise not to distract him.

'Well Maria, what do you think? Are we having fun yet?' Gregg crackled through the head-set.

'Wow, I'll say; this is super cool, Gregg, I've never seen the view from the driver's seat before. It's so spectacular. I love it, Captain H.'

'A little info about the aircraft… You've already spotted it's a twin-engine petrol engine made by the American company Cessna, been making planes for many years. Very safe and with a good reputation.

'This particular plane is a rental. Many sport professionals, golfers, formula-one drivers and the like use rental companies to travel around the globe. Some have their own planes and are licenced to fly. This plane has limited range due to refuelling capabilities, but it's a great plane, entirely suitable for trips like this one.

'Our company, MexTex, has an account with this rental firm and Benjamin also uses the facility when required.

He's a great pilot, covered my back a few times in Iraq. Would you like to fly it yourself Maria?'

'Me? You've got to be kidding, No way, Gregg, it's way too scary.'

'Okay' said Gregg, 'Just put your hands on the controls and get a feel of the plane making gentle turns left then right. Now pull back on the stick and you're climbing. Push and you're going down then back to centre. There you go you're flying the aircraft.'

'Oh my gosh, that was really special, Gregg. I really loved that. What a feeling! I can't believe I just did that. Thank you sooo much Gregg.'

'There you go, girl flying at three thousand feet at almost two hundred-miles per hour. You were brilliant.

What is nice for me is sharing moments like that with someone like you, full of enthusiasm. I have another plane a Piper Cub which is an amazing thing to fly; it's real flying. The big stuff holds no thrill at all. It's like driving a bus. We'll be making our final approach soon so watch and listen but don't switch on your mic please.'

Once back on *'terra firma'* they secured the plane and jumped in a cab. '*Vamos la playa amigo,*' (the beach friend), Gregg instructed the cabbie.

'*Si, senor la playa.*' They headed for the beach.

Gregg had a favourite place where he knew the family well, and had been a regular for many years, which guaranteed the very best traditional Mexican food prepared by authentic Mexican *artisanos*.

Right on the beach; Manuelitos. It had a rustic familiar charm and never failed to delight. The local house-wine was produced by the owner, Manuel, from his own vineyard, the vegetables farmed by him, whilst Matais, his brother, supplied locally caught fish.

The atmosphere reminded Maria of home; comfortable inner warmth radiated here. They ate outside; the tables on wooden decking set in the sand; the fish grilled right in front of them just a few metres from the gentle ocean lapping the shore. Manuel would fill a bucket with salt water scooped from the sea, in which he cooked the vegetables; the potatoes had a special quality cooked that way. Manuel's family and friends seemed to come and go at intervals throughout the day, helping themselves to food and playing on the beach.

Manuel clipped the ear of the youngest with 'keep out of the kitchen, very dangerous, lot of hot stuff.' Maria just loved the place; she felt quite at home.

She ate calamari and fish (*corvina*) *a la plancha* and finished with a local fruit *tarta de la casa* with fresh cream and ice cream.

Coffee and brandy followed the meal, and for Gregg and Manuel. They both delighted in lighting up Havana cigars together. Gregg slowly reclined his chair He said to Manuel, I'm in heaven. Wonderful meal in fantastic surroundings, a beautiful young woman by my side, top-quality cigar with my good friend, and wife couple of hundred miles away.' They all laughed out loud at that. Maria, for her part, having consumed a fair share of the house wine, turned her attention to Cuarente Y Tres, a very sweet liqueur, and having demolished several glasses, dozed off. The afternoon had gently slipped soporifically away, and was finally interrupted by strumming *mariachi* guitars, but they were waved on by Manuel.

'Hey Manuel do you still have the bed and breakfast deal going, buddy? Looks like we might be needing that. Time's getting on and so is Maria. I quite fancy making a night of it. Haven't had a good old drink-up for quite a while, too much flying and business stuff. What do you think, amigo? Fancy joining me or what?' Gregg suggested.

'Yeah, I could go for that, Gregg. As you say been a while. I'll get the girls to sort out the room for the night. What you going to do about Filipo, the guy you have to meet?'

'Yeah, I'll call him and bring it forward before we get into the drinking.' He was straight on the phone to Filipo and invited him round and perhaps have a drink and play some cards later.

That arranged, Gregg put a blanket over Maria, fast asleep in the chair. The sun was going down and the breeze off the ocean was getting very fresh; folk began packing up lilos, beach chairs, towels and other beach gear and were making their way to their cars to head home. He thought he would just leave her there and wake her after his meeting with his new contact Filipo.

He arrived wearing a very crumpled cream linen suit, with an equally crumpled panama hat. He wore a black silk eye patch over his right eye. As he stretched out his arm to greet Gregg, his jacket fell open, exposing a leather shoulder gun holster. He parked his white Mercedes car on the sandy road behind the restaurant. They spoke briefly and he accepted the offer of a drink and card game but signalled to go out back first. He handed Gregg a small hand-sized holdall. Manuel took charge of it immediately and swiftly took it indoors.

Maria awoke, shivered in the cool evening air, and stretched her arms over her head, exhaling a massive yawn.

'You're awake, baby. Have a nice sleep, Maria? Bet you'd love a nice coffee, eh?' Gregg said.

'Well, no, honey. I'd sooner have a nice brandy, old boy, if it's all the same to you,' she said.

Gregg, somewhat reluctantly, obliged; he could tell that Maria was still pretty drunk and he knew from previous experience how volatile she could be in this state. He cautiously offered her some calming words of advice as he explained his plan with his pals for a game of cards later.

'Are you feeling hungry at all, Maria, or do you just want to sit quietly sipping your brandy?'

'Actually, Gregg, I feel pretty rough and don't fancy that flight back at all. Could I just sit here for a while? I may want to chuck up at any moment... sorry.' Maria somehow got the words out from the back of her throat.

'Listen, don't you feel bad about it. just hang on Lori (Manuel's wife) will give you a bowl if you feel sick. She's used to that running a beach side café, for goodness' sake, comes with the job. It's really not a problem, we'll take care of it,' he re-assured her.

'I'll have a word with her and see if she has by any chance a bed for the night. I don't really want to fly tonight, I'm well over the legal limit myself, so don't worry.' Gregg cleverly reframed the whole scene to his advantage.

'Would you do that for me, Gregg? You're such an angel.'

Lorita came in dressed in a blue-grey flowery dress, wearing a white apron and carrying a bowl, towel and words of comfort, just in case Maria wanted to be sick.

'Maria, why don you come upstairs and get nice warm bed? You feel much better real soon, *chica*.'

Lorita was quite portly and a really comforting *mamacita*, married to Manuel for more than twenty years, raising two boys and a girl.

With a fair-sized vineyard and farm, they produced sufficient food for their own needs, but also derived a fair income at market.

Located about a mile from the coast, the farmhouse was a typical *finca* built around a yard, complete with a well in the centre. A profusion of colourful dahlias and local sun-loving plants in pots surrounded the yard. The *aljibe* (well) had clear fresh drinking water, accessible with rope and bucket. In authentic fashion, the rooms all accessed the yard. The family were very comfortably off and were to some extent the envy of their neighbours; farming in these parts was not considered in general a high-income business.

The restaurant was located right on the beach with two others in close proximity; an old rustic building made from timber with multiple layers of red and green paint applied over many years to protect it and keep it looking smart. Upstairs were two bedrooms with showers and a shared bathroom, which were rented out in the season. Manuel drove a smart pick-up truck and the boys shared a car, and a motorbike.

'Come on, Maria, get you cosied up for the night. You be fine in this room, I sleep here when me and Mani we fight over something or other. It's real quiet when the sun gone down and folks all go home.

'We don't let kids down here after dark. Mani and pals making sure of that,' she reassured Maria, and placing a carafe of fresh water and a glass on the bedside table, she switched on the small table lamp, and left. Maria was asleep almost before Lorita had reached downstairs.

Lorita laid on an assortment of rich spicy snacks for the men to enjoy whilst playing cards. She loved to see her man doing the *man thing* with his pals. Although a common event, the scene always evoked the same feelings for her.

Manuel would at times stray from the straight and narrow but always came home. She had settled for that many years ago. She quietly whispered, 'He's my man, he's my Mani. God bless him keep him safe, *gracias a Dios*.'

The men played poker, drank all manner of alcohol but mainly 'Jack Daniel's' and smoked cigars as was the custom amongst serious poker players the world over.

Late into the night and just as the first rays of the sun appeared on the eastern horizon, Gregg decided to call it a night, and grabbing a handful of crumpled-up twenty-*peso* notes he stuffed them in his pocket with a '*Buenas noches, amigos*' He tiptoed into the bedroom and slipped very gently into the bed cuddling up to Marias soft, warm inviting buttocks. She was fast asleep, so he left her alone.

*

Maria walked though her village in Cantabria, the sun warm on her back. Mama and papa *were sitting out front of the café and she wondered why they were not in the café working. Pedro was landing an enormous catch, of all manner of fish, so much that the boat was listing to starboard. Her good friend Janet, suddenly appeared from around the corner of the café, shouted 'Hola' but continued running, calling for Maria to follow, but trying as hard as she could she failed, unable to run. Mama never got up to greet her, which scared Maria; calling for 'Abuela, Abuela,' afraid and confused, all the while calling out, but as she tried to run to her house, her legs wouldn't work. Desperate, she cried out, 'abuela,' over and over, but she couldn't move. Out of nowhere, the skies darkened as a massive squall broke out, with the wind and rain in torrents washing through the streets, practically engulfing Pedro's boat. A very strange surge of emotion and passion filled Maria, frightening and out of control. With pressure crushing her chest, she panicked.*

Then suddenly she was awake in a cold sweat; Gregg was on top of her. She hollered at him, and with both hands she smacked his broad shoulders with a thump. '*Get off, get off*' and pushed his shoulders but he did not move. '*For God's sake, what the hell are you doing man?*' She never recognised Gregg.

'What's up with me? What's up with you? You were writhing all over the place in ecstasy moments ago … What's with the *man* stuff? Don't you even know where you are?' He angrily slipped off Maria and rolled onto his back, sighing in disbelief. 'Jeeze, Maria.'

They were both in shock; Mani and Lori sleeping in the next room heard them but tried to ignore the scene.

'Gregg, I just had the most horrible nightmare of my life. I was back in my village trying to get home to *abuela* but couldn't make it. It was so scary and realistic. I was right there. A massive pressure was on my chest holding me down. Then I woke with you on top of me. I felt that I was dying. I'm so sorry, Gregg.'

Gregg checked the time; it was five o'clock. He tried to placate her but somehow couldn't get the right words out. He was shocked and frustrated.

'Maybe you should get yourself together and phone home and speak with the family. It may make you feel better. With the time difference now would be a good time to call. Here, use my satellite phone. You'll be sure to get through on that.'

Maria called and she told them she was worried about *abuela*.

'Maria, it's so good to hear from you. How are you? Where are you darling?' m*ama i*s asked.

'I'm fine, *mama i*s everyone well there?'

'Yeah, we're okay but *abuela*'s not so good. She was found on her kitchen floor, couldn't move. They think she may have had a stroke and broken her hip with the fall.

'She's been taken to hospital to be checked all over. She's conscious but doesn't know what happened, whether she slipped or fainted, but she's doing well. We just got back from Santander, the big hospital there. Pedro ran us to the hospital. He's a blessing, that man.

'He had just landed the most enormous catch. He had to get help from the other fishermen to unload as an enormous storm broke loose and flooded the streets down to the harbour.

'That's a great hospital. She'll get the best of care there, so don't you worry. Strange you should call at this time. Where are you?'

'Well just thought it was time for a catch up. I'm in Mexico with my boss on a business trip. You've got to be thinking ahead to stay in the travel business these days. Glad you're well. Give my love to *papa* and Pedro and of course big love, kisses and hugs to *abuela*. Will try and get to see you on my return. *Adios, hasta pronto.*'

Gregg had been listening to the conversation and looked at her, shrugging his shoulders. Slightly bruised from the earlier beating, he smiled and suggested they go for an early skinny dip and forget this scene. The ocean looked inviting and the beach was still deserted.

They grabbed a couple of beach towels and arm in arm they ran kicking the sand, up to the water's' edge. Naked, they plunged headlong into the cooling fresh waters of the Gulf of Mexico. With very little surf and absolutely no one in sight, it was the perfect antidote to the earlier stressful encounter in the bedroom.

After fooling about in the warm sea for a while, they returned to the house for breakfast. She had fresh fruit and juice whilst Gregg took something more substantial, traditional Mexican.

'Hey, Gregg that's one fine *chica* you got yourself there, man.' Mani had seen the pair of them skinny dipping.

'Yeah, caught you ogling, you dirty ol' hombre. Jealous, *amigo*? Saw the sun glinting on your binoculars, Mani.' They laughed.

'Mani, does your lad still have that Lambretta scooter?,

If so, do you think he would lend it to me for a short ride along the coast to show Maria the beauty of the place?' Gregg enquired.

'Well, he's away at college right now. I call him and ask. But I paid for it so no problem, but I call anyway, for sure, right to ask.'

After breakfast they set off on the bike. She grabbed him with all her might.

'I've never been on the back of a motorbike before, Gregg. She said her voice a little shaky.'

'Well first thing, you don't have to hold too tightly. I have to be able to breathe. Relax and go with the flow. Remember to lean when I lean and don't move about.

'Nothing to it, easy as flying, and you can do that now, can't you?'

Both were relaxed again and were determined to put the morning situation behind them. The beach from Tecolutla, to Vera Cruz was approximately twelve miles long with plenty of stopping-off places en route.

Dressed only in tee-shirts and shorts, their departure had been rather spontaneous, lacking any preparation, so Gregg with his weather-eye scanned the road ahead.

'You okay on the back there, Maria, warm enough?' he shouted above the sound of the two-stroke engine.

'Yeah, great, it's such fun, a real feeling of freedom. Wonder why I never tried this before. Could manage a comfort break, though at some point, but don't worry too much, can always go behind a gorse bush… with great care.' They laughed together.

They spotted beach umbrellas ahead, and pulled the

bike over to the side of the road, onto the beach. The café was nothing more than a wooden shack with no electricity. It had bottled gas.

The barman looked as if he could do with a good shave and definitely could do with a shower. The toilet would be condemned by public health if there was such an authority.

However, Maria thought she had seen worse, so, provided she did not actually touch anything, she should be safe. She always had a packet of anti-bacterial wipes in her pocket wherever she travelled. She considered that an essential basic requirement.

They decided this would do for a quick snack. Both were very surprised when the owner cooked up fabulous fish on the griddle and served it with fresh bread and *pimientos de Padron* peppers. It was exactly right for the scene. Gregg had a *cerveza* (beer), whist she, deciding to have an alcohol-free day, had a Coke.

They sat at a rusty old table and chairs; the meal was delightful. The owner, Carlo smelling of cigars, brandy, garlic and body sweat, chewed on the short stubby remnant of a cigar. He somehow conjured up a quality brandy and Havana cigar for Gregg, who sat back in what was left of a reclining chair, sipped his brandy and puffed on his cigar.

'You know, I've eaten in some of the best restaurants all over the world, but I can honestly say this is one of the most memorable meals I've ever eaten. What say you, Maria?'

'Absolutely, Gregg, from a very shaky start, we certainly made up for it with this lovely little trip. I'm loving it for sure. Don't want to leave but guess we should be thinking about it, eh?' she enquired.

'Give it twenty minutes, then we'll be off.'

As they were saying their farewells to Carlo, he pointed to the skies changing rapidly from blue to very ominous grey-black, with flashes of lightning mixed in for good measure.

Turning to Maria, '*Venga aqui,*' (come here) he took her by the hand and escorted her to the back of the café. A wheelie bin was full of discarded sweat-shirts, cagoules and all manner of clothing, including wetsuit tops. Carlo said, 'Help yourself.'

'Gregg, get back here and help yourself, buddy. It's a free yard sale.' She picked a quite smart hooded sweatshirt, whilst Gregg found a well-worn cagoule. Grateful they thanked him kindly as the rain began to fall. '*Hasta pronto,*' and they were off.

They found an optimum speed that was comfortable enough in the rain. Neither one of them wore a crash helmet, but at least Maria had a hood for protection from the rain. The weather progressively deteriorated to the point where they eventually had to pull over for a break; under a small copse of trees, up a dirt track.

As they cuddled up for warmth, she joyfully announced, 'I feel like a teenager.'

Happy and full of life, Gregg, dripping from head to foot, gratefully acknowledged they had seen 'The best of the weather earlier in the day.'

The ground had been so dry that the water gushed over the surface in torrents. Maria went very quiet; she was a little disturbed by recent events, and felt it was too much of a coincidence the dream seemed to be coming true. Even the rain washing down the road disturbed her.

Gregg very much the pragmatist, never prone to flights of fancy did his best to reassure her. It was, in his opinion, pure coincidence. They cuddled and kissed.

'Sorry about this morning, it was so scary, but I'll make it up to you later, Gregg,' she said.

'Don't worry about it, one of those things. Bit weird but we're still good. We'll need to take it slowly. These roads will be very greasy after the rain.'

The rain abated, allowing them to continue unhindered as the sun came out once again. The intense heat made the roads steam so they finished in warm sunshine once more. They hugged again as they put the scooter away.

Once back at the café, Manuel was pleased to see them back safe and sound; it had been quite a storm. It transpired that Manuel knew Juan Carlo at the shack.

'Quite a character Carlo, knows all the local hippies and surfers, miserable-looking guy, but a load of fun when you get to know him. Don't wanna play him at cards tho' bro, skin you alive. What plans you guys got then? Another night or what?' asked Mani.

'Not too sure, she had a bad night with a fearsome dream. Don't know if she fancies another night. No disrespect, Mani.'

'*No problema*, Gregg. Totally get it. We couldn't help hear the noise this morning, man. It's up to you, man. Just tell Lori if you want. You welcome any time, Gregg.'

They discussed the overnight plan; she favoured going back to the city and the condo. She said, 'I need to get grounded again. Good night's' sleep alone and perhaps in the morning I'll be able to process my feelings. Feel I've got a lot of stuff to work on emotionally.

'I hope you won't be disappointed by going back to the city. I'm having a great time and absolutely love it, a great place and very lovely folks, but I need to get a change of clothes and get my head together. I mean, look at me, wearing other people's throw-away clothes. Just one thing I would really like to do while I'm here, can't let the chance go by.'

'Just say the word, kiddo, and it's yours,' he said.

'Do you think I could have a try at riding the Lambretta?' she asked.

They all loved that suggestion and just fell about laughing, perhaps expecting a more demanding request. They all went to the rear of the cafe and on the dirt road after a few simple instructions she was off. She zoomed up and down the trail. 'Just as I expected, kiddo, you're a natural,' he complimented her.

The family all ate together and shared a traditional Mexican meal. Maria loved the meal and the family; a feeling that was apparently mutual.

'What plan you guys got? There's a whole lot of stuff going on in our wonderful country.' Lorita asked. 'Good to have plan, but Gregg know his way around for sure.'

'We haven't really planned anything other than this trip. You're right, of course, Lori, can't come all this way and miss the tourist traps, even if they now get very overcrowded.' He looked across the table to Maria.

'Well, we could do the Inca stuff and the cathedrals

tomorrow if we have the energy, and maybe the other thing the next day or two.'

Lorita asked, 'What other thing?' somewhat indiscreetly and then wished she had not.

Gregg picked up the thread and simply said, 'Need to visit family in San Diego. That means another flight, but that's not a problem.

'Maria may have some business she needs to attend to near there, so maybe overnight and back to the condo the following day. Pretty flexible, eh, baby?' Gregg exclaimed.

Lorita came back in: 'Sorry Gregg, for that nosey parker me.'

'No worries, Lori, you're good. We're all friends here. We sure can trust one another after all the stuff we've been through together over the years. Well, I think you guys know well enough, things are not great in San Diego, but hey!' Gregg finished.

*

Manuel insisted on taking them to the airstrip. Lorita went along too; she liked to see Gregg flying his own plane. She felt proud to know such a man. They loaded their luggage and Manuel pulled Gregg to one side and surreptitiously handed him a package. He stowed it away separately from the other luggage.

'Okay Maria, over to you for checks.'

She called out the checks as she went around the aircraft; of the ailerons, elevators, rudder, olio on the nose wheel. All checked satisfactorily, Captain.'

They climbed aboard and fitted their headsets and mics as Gregg carried out pre take-off checks and called the tower. Everything all clear, they waved goodbye, lined up, took off and climbed away.

She watched him with great interest. She could never have imagined that this could be something for her; flying. He realised this, and was more than happy to explain in more detail.

He had an instructor's licence, but these days had little time for the extra work. He was certainly keen for her to handle the aircraft through simple manoeuvres. She loved that about him, and these moments of powerful emotional feelings of togetherness increased that sense of bonding.

Soon enough, they were approaching the *aerodromo* in Mexico City and as he contacted the tower, he allowed her to handle the aircraft for a while until the final approach. Maria had great peripheral vision and a cool head under pressure; he knew that she would be a great pilot and urged her to get involved with a flying school. 'I have control.' She knew to take her hands and feet off the controls. He landed the plane and she taxied to the stand and turned the master switch to off. The pair stared straight ahead through the windshield and laughed out loud. She was ecstatic but calm and for a brief moment imagined that she was falling for him in a big way. But she was very wary of him.

SIXTEEN

CALIFORNIA

They had much to discuss as they processed the last few days at the beach. They agreed the trip had been a success. Greg had conducted his business, they had fun, explored a little, became teenage-like all over again as they sheltered from the rain whilst out on the bike. Maria was truly excited about learning how to ride a scooter and fly a twin-engine airplane. Deeper issues were open for debate, those of an emotional nature which could not be denied. By mutual consent, they agreed that a little *quid pro quo* might be the way forward.

Gregg agreed to begin. 'Well, for me, I have to be brutally frank and say that I am very fond of you and love working with you. However there's a very big But.

'Quite simply, it's obvious that you have a problem with alcohol or at least the excess of it. You are a quite wonderful person to be around when you are not drinking

You are sharp, alert and very creative. When you drink a little, you become more relaxed and less inhibited, but still great company.

'The next phase is more problematic, that is when you drink to excess and then your mood and actions become totally unpredictable. Anything can and probably will happen to cause concern.

'Frankly beyond that point, you're a nightmare. I just wonder how your body copes with the abuse you give it and what the future may hold for you if you continue on that road.'

By general agreement they agreed not to respond to feedback but to simply listen passively and internalise.

Maria's turn; she said, 'Gregg, my issue is not so personal but no less irritating. I suppose it's more of how I regard our relationship. I have no illusions about the fact that I am an employee in your firm.

'I am very happy and extremely grateful for that and enjoy the many benefits that brings about, not least of which is the very generous pay cheque each month, the car and travel expenses.

'Clearly, what is now emerging is a difference in my role and job description. I suppose what I'm really talking about is my feelings of self-esteem or indeed lack of it. We both understand that I am accompanying you purely as a glamorous accessory. I am not working in my capacity as an employee in any way. We have no illusions about that.'

'Well Maria, if you ...'

'Uh uh, no, Gregg, we agreed no answering back. Be quiet and listen passively.' she interrupted.

'We are both sensible enough to know that I must be aware of clandestine activities being carried out. Now that for me is scary, and up until now I've tried to pretend it wasn't going on; head in the sand stuff, I could play the innocent foil. But the situation has escalated in the last few weeks and now I find I am an accessory to what must surely be illegal.

'Putting it into straight-forward language, Gregg, I think we've both been getting away with it up until now, where I could possibly plead the naïve, innocent party. I suppose what I need to know is how much more is going on from this point forward?'

'Wow, okay Maria, I'm actually pleased you're able to bring that out at this time. I am increasingly aware of the change in our relationship, and wondering exactly how to proceed myself. You're absolutely right, of course, it needs to be sorted and quickly. We've both got a lot to think about, for sure. Perhaps we should have a drink, not get drunk, sleep on it and sort it in the morning. How does that sound, Maria?'

'Well, Gregg, I think that's a start, part of the deal. But what about the big issue? Let's cut to the chase. Are there any more drops?'

'Oh, you're handing this so well, and let me try and reassure you. Our business is concluded on this trip. We can just enjoy being tourists from this point forward and have fun.

'What will you drink, honey? I'm having a large Jack and that will do me. I'm tired anyway.'

'Large vodka tonic, ice and a slice. I can't get drunk on the amount either.'

'*Saludos, todos.*' (Cheers, everyone.)

*

The following morning, Maria awoke really early; she needed to be up and about before he surfaced. Last night's' confessional was pretty thorough and certainly very thought-provoking, but she thought unconvincing.

She needed to update her journal, as she had got a little behind with entries. The pair had agreed last night not to give immediate feedback, but Maria had already used her 'testamento' as a confessional, with great effect.

Her thoughts and experiences would never be disclosed to Gregg. She wrote:

'*A man of many talents, not least of which is his ability to create an astonishing number of social and business contacts in every part of the globe.*

She intended these notes would remain secret in her journal forever.

Maria continued:

A well-connected and influential man, cultured, with an engaging personality, a guest on many an "A list". However, there was another side to Gregg that was mysterious and a little sinister.

This is the side of Gregg able to present the amiable, handsome bon-viveur and generous. "'man about town'" whilst having numerous, clandestine affairs de coeur.

As she sat and considered these notes, she realised that she would be better served by writing about how all this affected *her* life, and not focusing on Gregg's character defects.

She knew only two people in her life who would be even remotely interested in her feelings: Janet and Montserrat

(Montse). Of these, Janet, the pragmatist, would be the one most able to offer professional advice, but she was always very busy and not as available as Montse.

She called both but neither one was available; she would try again later.

As Maria was enjoying a light breakfast. Gregg burst onto the scene. 'Hola Buenas dias comesta chica.' He very chirpily announced his arrival; as if last night's episode had never existed at all.

'Oh, morning, Gregg. I'm just enjoying breakfast. Are you not joining me?'

'Just looked over the balcony and there's no one on the tennis court. Why don't we give it a go then, after breakfast, a short drive? I have got to meet someone not far away. Up for that, Maria?'

She looked up from her breakfast sighed, and agreed about the tennis but told him she wanted to finish her food first, then she would be fine for tennis.

There was always someone to meet and Maria had learned never to enquire. A system that worked better for him than for her, but that was the deal. She reasoned that at least with tennis it would not take up too much of the day, whereas golf took four or five hours and on occasion, depending on the company he was in, perhaps the entire day. She had, however, serious doubts about the meeting; was he really keeping his word about *No More Drops*?

Tennis was fun and they laughed a lot, Gregg letting Maria win lots of points. He could be very generous in that way; he was a very good player but had nothing to prove. She knew that he always worked out the odds in everything he did. It may all look spontaneous, but very little was left to chance with Gregg.

Between them, they could be formidable She had the ability to visually take in a whole scene and remember the most insignificant detail; he could assess the risk and reward in any given situation. He realised their potential together but wondered how best it could be harnessed.

The condo pool beckoned, and they cheerfully obliged. Plunging in together, they raced to the far end. She was almost as powerful as him, having grown up by the sea. Swimming could be a matter of survival not simply a leisure activity. He was very heavily built and she was slight.

After a few mock races up and down the pool, it was time to relax in the warm sunshine. She splashed on sun protection; Gregg never bothered, his Californian tan never really disappeared, even in winter. The waiter approached and they ordered soft mocktails.

'This is the odd thing about your drinking. You can go days without touching alcohol then wham, you blitz it, weird. Have you ever taken advice on that aspect?' Gregg asked.

'No, not that aspect on its own, Gregg, but various people have suggested Alcoholics Anonymous, but I don't think I'm an alcoholic,' she replied, sadness in her voice.

His phone jangled, and he took the call in the lobby, out of earshot. She sipped her drink, fearing another deal was pending. She laid back when a young handsome man approached. Maria recognised him as someone who was staying on the condo. She had seen him with an extremely attractive woman, whom she also recognised from a TV programme but could not recall her name.

He greeted her '*Hola, senorita comesta?*'

She replied, '*Hola*' whilst out of the corner of her eye she spotted Gregg paying close attention from the lobby. He hurriedly finished his call and was by her side. She had sort of got used to the idea she was never very often alone. Somehow she was being protected; an odd feeling but very real.

Many times, Maria had been approached by good-looking young men looking to 'chat her up' only for them to discover that she was '"private property"'; she knew not how, but they never came back.

Gregg recognised the man: Diego Morales, a young professional golfer. They chatted a while mainly, unsurprisingly, about golf. He explained that he was going to the club directly to do a little business. The woman with him was his girlfriend, Conchitta. It was all very convivial and pleasant.

However Maria was cross about how little control she had in certain situations, and how Gregg hijacked many of her conversations. He ordered a further round of drinks as they talked about golf.

'I am sorry, I know your face from TV but can't recall your name,' Maria apologetically enquired of the lady. 'I'm shocking with names but faces I do recognise very well.'

'I'm Conchitta.' She spoke about her recent TV release which was in Spanish but subtitled and dubbed, a system about which she had doubts. She was of the opinion that dubbing was the way forward, but the studio had their own methods of marketing and she was powerless in the decision-making. Maria empathised with that but naturally said nothing.

'Now I've got you,' Maria said. 'So sorry, Conchitta Ramires from the TV series *Los Sierras*. That was great, watched whenever I got free time but always so busy with work and travel. I do apologise. You're not related to the Ramires family in the south of Spain, are you, by any chance?'

'Not that I'm aware, but it's a very common name as I'm sure you know,' Conchitta said. 'We're making a lot of films nowadays for TV, very good business, *'telenovellas'* they call them.'

She asked, 'So what brings you to Mexico? Holiday or business? The pair of you look as though you're on vacation. Is he your man?'

'Oh no, Gregg's my business partner. We have another partner who is Mexican who currently lives in Barcelona. We're here to extend our travel business into the Mexican market.'

'Looks like we're on the move. He's shaking hands with Diego. Think we're off to the golf club to meet someone. I would love to spend more time talking with you, Conchitta, but I'm afraid that's how it goes. We're off.'

'*Adios, Maria, Buena suerta,*' (good luck) Conchitta ended.

Gregg quickly changed into smart casual but not forgetting the neck tie; standard attire for golf clubs the world over. Maria in skirt and blouse with silk scarf around her shoulders. The golf club restaurant overlooked the eighteenth hole, very smart, with an excellent menu, so they decided to eat there, but first Gregg had business he had to deal with.

Maria drew one of the brown leather armchairs nearer to the large patio doors in order to get a full view of the course. She would not be sitting around waiting for him; she ordered a sweet Martini on his tab.

As she relaxed with her drink, she truly realised how fortunate she was, but she was beginning to resent waiting around for Gregg, being at his behest all the time. She felt it was time for her to address these issues, but timing would be crucial.

There was still no sign of him when into the restaurant walked the couple from earlier at the condo pool. He asked Maria if she would like a drink but she declined, explaining that she was waiting for Gregg and they were going to eat there.

She did, however, suggest that they sit together for a drink. She knew from experience that Gregg would not approve of her inviting them to lunch together. She was in her element as she fully engaged with this interesting couple, professionals from the world of sport and entertainment. Diego insisted on buying another drink to enhance the scene. Maria thought they were refreshing company.

Eventually, Gregg arrived and looked around, a little confused, as Maria was in company. He appeared rather resentful and had difficulty concealing the fact.

'Oh, I see you've got new friends,' he said rather awkwardly. He had not recognised the couple from earlier.

'What a nice surprise! Are you eating lunch here also?' he enquired, desperately trying to cover up his *faux pas*.

'Well, we had given it some thought,' said Diego. 'I need to meet with the club professional to discuss a tournament. But I can do that later. He's on the course at the moment, coaching.'

'Settled then, let's get a table for four.' Gregg forcibly took control. Maria seethed inside but said nothing.

Lunch was always a simple affair, the very best of food; steaks, fish, lobster, langoustine but in very moderate portions, always with attention to separating carbs from protein, and always accompanied by the very best wines.

They both kept themselves in good shape; careful about food and taking exercise, mainly daily gym sessions. She was a fair golfer and on occasion Gregg would take her to one of the many clubs of which he was a member. She never went alone anywhere. When with Gregg, she had no real friends, only acquaintances, something which she resented.

Lunch went well, and in Gregg's familiar custom he finished with a Cuban cigar and the finest brandy and coffee. Maria had the coffee, as did the other two.

'You wouldn't be able to smoke in a European golf club, Gregg.' Diego remarked. Gregg's face was like thunder but he said nothing; he could barely contain his anger. There followed a very awkward silence before the couple broke up the party.

'Nice to have met you. Perhaps we will meet up again somewhere,' said Conchitta, but they all knew that would not be happening.

They returned to the condo, as there was still some warmth in the early-evening sunshine. They reclined on the loungers.

'The bloody cheek of that young whippersnapper. He won't be winning any tournaments any time soon. Insulting me like that! Who does he think he is? I've got his number.' Gregg said, clearly still hurt, but the fact that he knew so many figures of authority was scary to Maria.

Maria was aware of the faint sound of Mexican music playing through the speakers around the pool; she did not respond but snuggled down to let the wine do the rest. She dozed off.

'Are you asleep, Maria?' Gregg said some time later.

'Not now, Gregg… thanks. Why?'

His next question puzzled her. 'Have you ever visited the Canary Islands, Maria?' It took her a while to wake up and another while to understand the question.

'What are you on about, Gregg? I was fast asleep.'

'I was wondering if you have been to the Canaries, that's all.'

'Think my parents took me there when I was very young. Why are are you asking about the Canaries? Are you not satisfied with Mexico?'

'Yeah, it's great here. You love it here, don't you, *chica*?' he responded.

'No, it's just that I get an allocation of free flights from my airline company each year and, it's use them or lose them time.'

Maria by now had him figured. He was up to

something, for sure, and as usual was spinning a very plausible line of horse feathers.

Lovely, as they surely were, she thought the Canaries could not compare with this experience of living in a luxury condominium in Mexico City. *Canary Islands, what's up his sleeve this time?* However, she knew not to question him and his decisions too closely.

She played the game. 'Nice there, is it then, Gregg?' she tamely asked.

'Well it depends where. There are a few different islands there and I've got a little business thing coming up; thought you might like to see another part of the globe.'

'Yeah, Gregg, you know me well enough, I'm up for that, somewhere different. When do you have in mind?'

'Yes, that's one of the best things about you, always ready to go whatever, whenever,' he replied, then got, up, dived into the pool and splashed up and down at great speed for four lengths. He stood there dripping wet in his tight black Speedo swimmers. She checked him up and down and approved unconditionally. He brushed his slightly greying hair back from his dripping wet face.

'Going up for a bit, Maria. You coming up now? We don't need dinner so we can relax for the rest of the day and check out Fuerteventura?'

Maria didn't need to be asked twice; she was up for it. She joined him in their beach robes and cuddled in the cold air-conditioned lift up to the penthouse.

Much later, after their exertions of sustained love-making, they made light snacks together. English Somerset cheese, cream cracker biscuits and sweet onion chutney pickles, and with cups of tea, watched a little TV.

Maria set up her laptop to Google the Canary Islands and looked at maps, and tourist notes of the Canary Islands online. As they checked out the various islands, she remembered that her parents knew people from home who had moved to Lanzarote about fifteen years ago, and thought it might be nice to contact them.

Having run it by him, that idea didn't appeal. He seemed to have preference for Fuerteventura, and it was no surprise to Maria to hear that he knew people on both islands and indeed also in Tenerife.

He knew a golf professional who more or less ran the club in the south of the island of Lanzarote and he would contact him.

They both agreed on one thing; the islands looked attractive and all that was required was to set aside some time in Gregg's busy schedule. She could go at the drop of a hat, which perfectly suited him.

'We can sort out the details for the Canarian trip once we're back in Barcelona. What we really need to focus on, Maria, is our trip around town and our trip to California. Okay here's what we're going to do. Tomorrow, we're taking a guided tour by bus around the city and the local sights. That way, you get to see the place more thoroughly.

'I get to rest up before flying to California the following day, with possibly an overnight stop-over. Does that work for you honey?' One of Gregg's now famous rhetorical questions.

'Okay, sounds like fun, can't wait. Just give me the

timings when you have more details. Will I need to book a room somewhere for the overnight?'

'Don't worry about the details, Maria. Just let me work it all out. You may get another flying lesson as a bonus, and I can take a nap.'

'I'll be looking for an official uniform soon, buddy. I really loved taking the controls and I know there's a lot more to flying than that, but I do believe it's something I could be good at. Shame we've not got more time but who knows?'

*

The weather the following day was blisteringly hot as the pair set off to join the guided tour of the city. The bus was air conditioned, which helped a little, but the heavy mix of aromas was too much for Maria; aftershave, aerosols, cigars and something she could not identify filled the bus. But Maria, uncomplaining stiff-upper-lip coped somehow. It would be ungrateful to complain, she thought.

However, Gregg, who had paid for the trip, had no such inhibitions and moaned 'big time'. The first stop was the marketplace, and stepping out of the air-con into the heat of the Mexican midday sun was excruciating. They had a full day ahead so they'd better get 'into the whole thing, or get out, Maria reasoned.

Finding a friendly bar, they left the group and *dos cervezas* (couple of beers) later, they found the energy to regroup. The rest of the day was spent at all the well-known tourist' sights; the Zocalo, Templo Mayor, Great Pyramid of Tenochtitlan finally ending up at the Metropolitan Cathedral. The entire bus was filled with passengers who sang songs and laughed all the way around. They made a day of it, for sure.

Everyone had a ball, including Gregg and Maria. Hot, tired and hungry, the refuge of the condo came into sight just at the right moment.

Exhausted, they collapsed on sun loungers by the pool. Gregg in his black Calvin Klein underpants just plunged right in, but no such luck for Maria. She soon rectified that by quickly going up to the apartment for her swimmers and was back in no time to join Gregg in the cool, refreshing water of the pool. They agreed it had been a great day.

Up at dawn, Gregg and Maria ate a fulsome breakfast, as they had a long flight ahead. Maria was happy in the knowledge that she would not be troubled with travel sickness in the light aircraft.

*

As she remembered the pre-flight external checks, she carried them out and gave the OK to Captain Gregg. Safely aboard and wired for sound, Gregg had already filed a flight plan, and waited for the Tower to give take-off instructions.

Gregg was aware that the journey time would be around four hours, a long time without comfort breaks. They were careful not to drink too much before departure, but they needed to take on water whilst flying to avoid dehydration. Gregg had removed two of the rear seats and fitted a chemical toilet in case of emergencies, so at least they had some peace of mind in that way.

Gregg could see that Maria was tiring even with the autopilot set, so he took over the controls to give her a break.

'Okay, I have the controls,' he confirmed.

Maria listened intently to the telecom as they approached the border between the USA and Mexico. All was okay. They proceeded to San Diego, and Gregg allowed Maria to take the controls once again for a spell.

'Whatever else I may do with the rest of my life Gregg, I will never ever forget that experience. I would never in a million years have believed that I would be in that position in my life, flying an aircraft. Who is ever going to believe me? I can't wait to tell *mama* and *papa*. Thank you from the bottom of my heart, Gregg.'

'You're a natural Maria. You should follow up and get trained. You'd sail through training. Believe me, I've seen plenty of guys who could not do what you've just done after hours of training. Go for it, gal.'

Maria was curious about the arrangements at the airport; Gregg had not specified the procedure on landing. He taxied behind the '"Follow Me Jeep"' and parked in a designated bay. They knew Gregg and escorted him to the Tower to fill out the paperwork. She was still airside, waiting in a lounge area. Gregg eventually appeared from behind a smoked glass screen with a cheery 'Come on, Maria.'

As they were about to leave the lounge, an immigration officer approached requesting Maria's passport and any other identification papers she may have. Gregg intervened, but this officer was new and unfamiliar to him.

He asked Gregg to step back into the other room, as he had some questions he needed to ask him. Gregg was clearly put out by this and asked to see another officer, Murphy, but he was denied on the grounds that Officer Murphy was not on duty. Maria had never seen Gregg looking so awkward, ever.

The situation escalated when this officer, Ryman, asked them to escort him out to the aircraft. The luggage was checked, the aircraft and the hold; he even banged a couple of panels for good measure to check nothing was concealed behind them.

Finding nothing untoward, Officer Ryman cleared them through. As they crossed the car lot Murphy, arrived for his shift. He called. 'Hey, Gregg, howya doin?' All good, buddy?' Here for a while?'

'Hi Murph, good to see you. No, not for long, couple of days maybe. Got a little issue, will call you later.' Gregg replied still wearing his best poker face he'd put on earlier for his confrontation with the officer.

Gregg, behind the wheel, enquired of Maria where she wanted to be dropped. The one issue they had not discussed was avoiding contact between her and his wife. Delving into the depths of her old faithful brown leather handbag, she recovered a card Montserrat had given her about the retreat building in Encinitas.

'Got a number here Gregg, for the ashram place I wanted to visit.'

'Ashram? You never mentioned anything about an ashram.' Gregg eventually broke his stony silence, for the first time since the issue with Officer Ryman.

'Well, you never asked, didn't think you were particularly interested.' 'Sorry, bit distracted, but back with you now. Call them,' he said.

The reception at the retreat was brilliant, so friendly and welcoming. They even suggested Maria could stay overnight and discover the benefit of the retreat programme.

He had a rough idea of the address. He dropped Maria off outside the main gate on the understanding that they would maintain contact by text; phones were not permitted in the retreat proper.

The main feature of the centre was one of peace and harmony; from the moment she was greeted at the entrance, she felt at ease and at peace within herself. The men and women (brothers and sisters) dressed in orange robes moved about quietly but not in silence. They were quick to welcome her with the traditional greeting of the clasped palms (*pranaam*).

The daily programme was outlined for Maria with meals and meditation, and individual counselling was available if required.

Her room sufficient for her needs, she unpacked and placed her St Christopher gift from Luis on her side table. She showered and, wearing loose-fitting clothes, walked around the gardens. On top of the bluffs overlooking the Pacific Ocean, the gardens were a natural complement to the peace and serenity that Maria was experiencing. Ornamental ponds with golden carp, waterfalls and flowers were filled all manner of tropical plants. Maria sat on a bench and breathed the air of serenity.

'Am I dreaming this?' she softly said. 'Oh my God, I feel so blessed.' Suddenly she felt that she must go back to her room and fetch her St Christopher pendant; and clutching it between her fingers, she returned to the bench.

The only sound of which she was aware were soft musical birdsong and the crashing Pacific surf far beneath the cliffs (bluffs). She remembered Montse showing her a meditative posture; she assumed that pose, and stilled her mind as best she could.

She softly called Montse to mind far away, thousands of miles, over land and ocean. Comfortable in that mind-state, she had no idea for how long she sat there, but the cool evening air off the ocean and the faint angelic sound of voices chanting somewhere caused her to explore.

The singing came from the temple; the door was ajar so she dared to enter and join them. She immediately became immersed with the experience; she felt it was otherworldly.

*

The Holdsworth family were enjoying Dad at home on one of his rare family visits. He was playing hoops with the ball against the garage door, with one of the boys, the sound of which had always infuriated Mom. She, a brilliant former high school swimming champion, swan-like, glided up and down the lengths of their pretty substantial pool with effortless style.

Their home in a leafy suburb of San Diego befitted the style of a typical affluent American family. In this seemingly idyllic setting, he figured he could probably manage perhaps a couple of days of this before the boredom struck and he would be off again. He clearly had got his nose put out of joint by the incident at the airport.

In the main, he was fireproof with his numerous connections worldwide. However, he always sensed danger and decided to let this one with Officer Ryman pass by.

More importantly his skills with the BBQ were required. Large steaks and crayfish to be cooked. The second full day of family passed, with the possibility of another overnight stay, was beginning to unsettle Gregg.

More restless than usual, he did not even want to play golf; something that concerned his wife more than he himself. The relationship had not been good for many years, but they remained together, as many do without really understanding why.

They got along fine and provided they did not ask each other difficult questions, life went on in a sort of charade. Even the kids knew the way to play the game.

They all firmly believed that Gregg was the source of this detached way of living together. Possibly due to the high-adventure life he formally experienced as an ace fighter pilot in the US Air Force, dicing with death on a daily basis. Civilian life without an edge was a serious challenge for Gregg.

Then it was over in a flash, as his phone registered a text from Maria saying she would like to meet, as she was leaving the ashram. For Gregg, it was as simple as that. As per usual, he packed a bag, said his farewells and left.

Gregg jumped into action just like a fighter pilot who had been waiting for the signal to scramble. The bell rang; it would be another sortie.

As Maria waited outside the main gates to the ashram, the strong sunlight combined with traffic noise felt harsh to her senses. The sudden shock from the tranquillity she had been experiencing for the last few days was shattered.

Simply watching the cars passing, waiting for Gregg, she could not even remember the colour of the hire car. It was all too much effort, and she would simply have loved to turn around and go back into the retreat.

Conversation was difficult, as each was on a different mental wave-length; Gregg super-high and Maria so calm, she felt as though she was on a different planet.

'Hi, Maria, how did you get on? I didn't get any messages from you so naturally assumed all was well. Had a close shave just now as Cynth offered to drive me, but fortunately I have to take the hire car back.'

This added further to Maria's confused state; she assumed Cynth was short for Cynthia, presumably his wife. Gregg had never actually referred to his wife by name.

As Gregg negotiated the heavy traffic enroute to the airport, he casually enquired if Maria needed anything for the trip, but she said she was fine. She was finding it difficult to communicate and deal with material reality as she moved from the esoteric world of the ashram.

Once in the airport, Gregg met with officer Murphy. 'That was a short trip. Everything okay at home, buddy? We never seem to get together much these days, not even for a round of golf… busy man?'

'Yeah, were all good. Just never seems to be enough hours in the day. 'So what's with this Officer Ryman guy giving me a hard time, stripping out the plane and body-searching us?'

'Not too sure, Gregg. He suddenly appeared saying he had been requested by his commander to check a number of people making regular flights between the States and Mexico, and you were on his lists. Good job you were clean, eh, Gregg?'

'Yeah, Murph, perhaps you can give me the heads-up in future, just to be extra sure. We're coming through bound for CDMX today, and then sometime next week probably back to Barcelona, Spain.'

They filed the flight plan and refuelled the plane, but Maria was less enthusiastic about taking the controls as before.

Gregg was fine with that; he took off, got into the cruise and switched on autopilot, with the bare minimum of conversation. This time, the flight charts had been replaced by a couple of small books Maria had been given in the retreat.

The flight was pretty unremarkable and took place in a very subdued manner; neither one of them had much to say. She had hoped that he might divulge a little more about his family but it was not to be. The family would remain secret; she would have to content herself with the status quo. Maria had given no thought to alcohol for two days so perhaps something was happening for her, she thought.

'So what did you make of the retreat?' Gregg finally asked. 'Did you find the answer to the meaning of life and the origins of the universe Maria?'

'Well I wasn't looking for that. In fact, I don't know what I was looking for. Montse Ramires is a member of that fellowship and she has something I wouldn't mind having: peace and serenity.'

'Did anyone think they might be able to help you with your drinking, Maria?'

'We didn't talk about that. No, nobody tried to offer advice. It's very much a programme of self-discovery and self-realisation with God,' said Maria.'

The return flight took almost exactly the same time as the outbound but just seemed to go on forever. They were both tired and relieved when they landed and it would not be long before they were luxuriating in the comfort of their condo. Too tired to even have a swim, they had cake and hot chocolate and turned in for an early night.

Gregg was off to sleep as soon as his head hit the pillow, but Maria's head was working overtime. She left her bedside light on and read literature from the retreat. As she performed the breathing techniques, she realised she had not consumed any alcohol for two days. *Perhaps something is working for me here and I must really try and get on with it.* She thought.

SEVENTEEN

MEXICO

Back in the condo, they both agreed they needed time to recoup and rest a while.

The previous few weeks had been pretty full on with a lot of travelling, and now it was time to be still if only for a while, as Gregg clearly had plans for another trip.

Maria paused and as she looked from the penthouse balcony, she could at a glance take in the city landscape and way beyond towards distant mountains. This place had grown on her and she felt comfortable and secure here at least in the condo.

She could not imagine it ever feeling homely; it was like a showroom, furnished with very expensive items. In contrast to Manuel and Lorita's place on the beach, which was the complete opposite. Homely and untidy with utility furnishings.

She loved their place. *I could live in that place with a*

man I loved and raise kids there right on the beach.

Both felt it was time to rest up whilst preparing for the next trip back to base in Barcelona. They ate breakfast together with fresh brioche, croissant and scrambled eggs. The local Mexican coffee, strength five, slipped down a treat.

'How about a short trip later, nothing strenuous, say, to the golf club, a little tennis and swim? Maybe eat and drink but easy does it. What say you Maria?'

'Yeah need to rest up a while but keep loose. That sounds about right, Gregg.'

Jose and Consuella had a pretty quiet time of it in Gregg's absence, so he called for them to come over for around noon.

Whilst they were waiting, Maria updated her journal and Gregg spent a lot of time playing on his ephone and making calls on his satellite phone. They just hung out for a while reading, and in Maria's case writing.

Maria phoned Leanne in Barcelona to check that she was okay. She was fine but missing her; that was mutual.

Consuella arrived and asked Maria, 'How you like your trip, *senorita?* You like to see our country, *es muy buen no?*'

'*Si Consuella es muy buen y Hermosa.* (very nice and beautiful). We've had a wonderful time. There's so much to see and do. We're pretty well exhausted, but happy.'

Consuella laughed. 'Maybe I get you nice tortilla supper with fresh corn salad?'

'Sounds perfect but Snr. Gregg has plans to visit the club so you had better check with him, Consuella.'

'Why yes, that sounds wonderful. Consuella's tortillas are world- beaters and not to be missed,' he said.

He suggested they go to the club, have a game of tennis and return for tortillas; that made her day. Maria rather fancied the tortilla without the tennis but went along with the arrangement.

The tennis was a very leisurely affair with neither one especially interested, but they agreed it was necessary for a little light exercise. The pool was not a patch on the condo pool, with too many swimmers and not enough privacy for their liking.

After tennis, as they put their gear back in the car, Maria noticed a bag with a book sticking halfway out of the zip. In a second of forgetfulness, she almost pulled it out of the bag before Gregg barked at her, 'ER, THAT'S NOT YOURS.' Shocked by the suddenness and ferocity of Gregg's voice, Maria dropped it like a hot potato.

She physically recoiled and shook a little, but not before she had noticed a Nazi swastika on the cover of the ring binder. She had never seen him react in such a forceful manner towards her.

'Sorry, old girl, that's private. You know better than that.' He deliberately lowered his voice and almost in a whisper, very quietly, apologised for shouting at her. She said no more; it was clearly a very sensitive subject.

She felt small and disrespected; she processed her feelings; *he had embarrassed himself and she would take it no further.*

They swam and made small talk but a change had occurred, and Maria was unsure about how she should continue. She had gained in confidence around Gregg considerably in recent weeks and did not like being reprimanded.

She called the waiter and ordered herself a very large vodka tonic. Lounging by the poolside, Maria tried to figure out the significance of the swastika on the book cover. Could Gregg be involved in some clandestine neo-Nazi organisation?

She rather wished to dwell on happier recent moments, such as the retreat, and not on Gregg's overreaction to somehow being discovered to be up to something, *being found out.*

He wandered off to talk with his golfing buddies, and vaguely aware of loud guffawing in the background, she drifted off to solace in an alcohol-induced sleep.

Returning to the reality of wakefulness, she languorously stretched her long, slim arms over her head and yawned.

Gregg suggested they make a start for home. The trip in the 'Hearse' was less than twenty minutes.

Returning by road through countryside dotted with small holdings and some larger farms, the pair made small talk about their earlier tennis game and swim. In reality, Maria just wanted to put the other nonsense behind her and move on.

She opened the chat by reiterating how much she had enjoyed their stay at the beach in Mexico and how the atmosphere reminded her of home

'Yeah, I'm glad you feel that way about it. I can tell you enjoyed it. You never talk much about home,' Gregg said.

She did not reply but thought, *that's rich, coming from you, as your home and family exist in another world altogether, a world of which I will never be a part.*

As Jose drove them home, Maria reflected on the day: how tenuous was her situation. She was at Gregg's' beck and call for sure; she anxiously awaited instructions regarding the proposed Canarian expedition.

All she had so far was a half invitation to accompany him there on a business trip. This was how life was for her with him. She reflected that was how it had been since the get-go. There would always be this degree of separation.

She pondered and questioned her future, or indeed even if she had one; how would it end? Perhaps he even had another "'bit on the side.'" Her status felt that fragile. Her status was not even that of 'an "official mistress"' in the traditionally accepted manner; having her own apartment and income without having to work for it. Gregg's deal was to utilise her assets in a professional way and occasionally throw her tit-bits of goodies.

Once back in the condo, with all this rubbish going on, she headed straight for the drinks cabinet. She put together a sort of Martini cocktail but honestly realised that any alcohol would do to stop her mind racing.

The drink certainly took the edge off her troubles for a while, but she continued in a negative frame of mind. Why does he never put music on his sound systems in the car or the apartment? On the occasions when she was alone (unsupervised), she may play music, but he would turn it off when he came into the room.

Gregg appeared, having showered. Wearing a silk bathrobe, and smelling of something very expensive, he looked the part, but she did not fancy *that* again today.

They sat at the breakfast bar and ate their delicious tortilla prepared by Consuela. They both agreed that the tortilla was the best they ever tasted and graciously thanked her.

Gregg told the pair of them to take the rest of the day off, but be back with the car for the evening which they gratefully accepted.

Maria needed to write home but was feeling tired so collapsed on the settee exhaling a great yawn.

Gregg slipped alongside her on the white leather settee, almost knocking her drink flying. She had learned very early on in their relationship that it was unwise to resist in these situations.

Soon he was making love to her, or rather molesting her; Unwilling, she hated that, another of his behaviours with which she had become increasingly uncomfortable.

Later, Gregg poured himself a Jack Daniel's and switched on the TV to watch baseball. Maria decided she would attempt to write a letter to her mother.

Maria struggled with writing home. She could not even manage a sentence that would convey what she was feeling and thinking. It was impossible to share with her mother how she felt.

Sometimes, everything was perfect; she loved the travel and the luxurious lifestyle, but it came with this strange undercurrent of tension which caused her to feel used and unappreciated. She could not even hint at that in a letter to *mama,* who would always sense danger for her family; she seemed to have a sixth sense.

Confused, her head had too much going on, and alcohol compounded the issue. *How do I learn to keep it simple? I try and fail day after day.*

She abandoned the letter and screwed up yet another sheet of paper into the waste-basket. In desperation she called out loud; 'Dear lord give me understanding , show me what I must do to keep my life more simple.'

Gregg was half watching and dozing in front of the TV.

'Did you say something Maria?'

She knew it was of no use talking to him about her feeling. She was smart enough to understand that this way of life in general was not conducive to a simple life style

'I'm fed up sitting here, so going for a walk,' she announced.

Without looking up, Gregg said, 'Going for a walk? Where the hell do you think you're going to walk around here?'

Maria decided to take the risk anyway; she just needed to get out of the apartment. She grabbed her phone and headed for the lift.

She simply needed some space away from him for a while; she didn't want or need to walk far, just get away and have her own space for a while. She thought of home and how best to deal with these issues. She ordered a drink and pushed a sun lounger out of the shade and into the fading sunlight.

She was able to have a few moments of contemplation whilst away from Gregg; even so, she felt his presence in her head.

They had been moving in all the 'right circles', mixing with celebrities, sports personalities for quite some time, in that rarefied 'A' list atmosphere.

On occasion, Maria had overheard gossip suggesting an airline captain's salary would not afford the luxurious lifestyle Gregg enjoyed.

But she chose to ignore those comments; no one would, she reasoned, ever question his integrity.

The best tables in the top restaurants, drinking the finest wines was the norm and, she fully enjoyed those benefits.

There had also been rumours that she was a gold digger reaping the benefits of the "'kept woman'" which hurt, but as they were but rumours, she was able to put that, aside and move on.

She had sufficient strength of character to tolerate such innuendo and was more concerned about her own issues with Gregg.

In the full knowledge that she had willingly been seduced into this lifestyle, she remained resolved not to go down the road of using hard drugs, which were freely available.

There was always a supply of the "'white stuff'" (cocaine) available, with which she experimented but rejected on the grounds that she found alcohol more convenient. He used on occasion, but neither of them could be described as "'users.'"

Vodka in hand, she called Montserrat.

'Hi Montse, sorry I've not been in touch but life has been a bit of a roller coaster with Gregg and his many adventures. How are you, darling?'

'Well, Maria. *Namaste*, so good to hear from you and glad you're still in one piece. One never knows with your highs and lows. How did you enjoy Mexico?'

'Oh, you didn't realise, we're still in Mexico, but wow we've had a wonderful time for sure. On the whole the trip was amazing. I saw and did amazing things. I went to the ashram in Encinitas and stayed for a couple of days, which was amazing.' Maria gushed.

'Oh my gosh how wonderful was that, Maria? That is so cool. I'm very envious. I would love to have done that with you. Are you giving any thought to becoming a member?'

'I'm certainly giving it some thought. The people there were truly awesome. I could have stayed longer and maybe one day I shall.

'I need to get back to Barcelona and get grounded again. I'm still drinking too much with the same results, the same old merry-go-round. I could really do with sitting down with someone, probably professional, to help me sort myself out. I'm hanging on to Gregg's coat-tails, enjoying the ride but paying for it in terms of my own self-esteem.

'In fact, I could just do with staying in one place for a while. It's all very well, all the free travel with perks, and I love the travel, but I never expected this amount. Plus the fact that it's all about Gregg. I don't have any say in any of it.'

'Oh, poor you, Maria. Well listen, when you get back we must meet up together and get you on a programme to deal with your drinking problem and remember it's a three fold problem. It's mental, physical and spiritual; we need to work together to find a solution for you Maria.

Please call me when you're back in Spain. Sorry, but have to go, I've got someone coming to the door. But please, please Maria keep in touch. It's so important. *Hasta pronto ve con Dios.*' (Go with God) She hung up.

Meanwhile, Gregg, unable to get through to Maria asked the waiter to give her a message. She was furious and decided not to respond. She wanted to process her talk with Montse and continue the positive vibe she gave off; she adopted the yoga pose and closed her eyes.

Minutes later, Gregg was by her side clutching a handful of brochures about the Canary Islands.

'Hey, Maria thought we might take a look at these, as we're clearly both bored at present.' He pulled a sunbed close to Maria.

Somehow she had this strange feeling that he was a little boy and wanted to show his mother something he had discovered; she was being his mother; but mother was very cross indeed.

'Actually, Gregg, I was meditating, having just spoken with Montse.'

'Oh, is she well?' He disinterestedly enquired, without the hint of an apology.

'Yeah, she's fine, getting on with her programme and getting a lot of enquiries online for group meditation. She's using the Limoneria at present but is looking to expand as numbers grow.'

'Well, got a meeting early next week so need to be back for that. I've not got the *gig* for flying back so I'll use some of my ticket allocation for the return to Spain.

She felt the very life being sucked out of her by this behaviour. She took a while to answer feeling once again that she really did not have any real input she was being coerced all the time.

All she could manage was; 'Whatever.'

'That's okay, we'll travel executive class honey. I'll sort that out tomorrow and we can be back in Barca in a couple of days' time. Is that okay with you?'

A little astonished, almost amused at the repetitive nature of these rhetorical questions. Maria simply said; 'That's fine.'

He didn't really want her opinion; it was a *fait accompli.*

She wished she could be more gracious; but she was very angry and sadly still suspicious; could this be a change of heart or a change in strategy? She knew Gregg well enough to understand how his mind worked in his world of intrigue and deception.

She was also aware that she was behaving in a similar fashion. Thinking she would try to keep one step ahead of him she asked 'So where do you want to go first, Gregg? Fuerteventura or Lanzarote?'

'Well, I know the golf professional… and…' Her mind wandered off before he had even finished his sentence. *Here we go again,* she thought, *wherever we go, he has a contact. Name it, and he knows someone there.*

It would be Lanzarote first, but that was all she needed to know. There was some mention of golf, but she drifted away before any details may have been forthcoming.

Later, they enjoyed an excellent meal in El Iguardon, Gregg and Benjamin Gonzales' restaurant in Polanco. Very uncharacteristic of him, he invited staff for a farewell supper.

Consuela and Jose sat at table, a very strange move, as he always maintained very strict social boundaries between staff and himself.

Unsurprisingly, they looked very ill-at-ease and uncomfortable, and Maria herself wondered what he was up to but she dared not ask.

Consuela sidled up alongside Maria.

'The boss, he fire us, no? The boss, he gonna fire us all. We think business is good, but maybe no?' she repeatedly asked Maria.

'*Por favour, Dios,* don let him fire us.' Sadly, Maria could not offer assurances one way or the other. She knew he could be unpredictable and this was another one of his surprises.

'No, don't worry, everything is all right. Snr. Holdsworth just wants to thank you all for your hard work,' she unconvincingly tried to reassure them, and herself. Consuela looked around for guidance on which silverware to use; she was baffled by the array.

'I wash so many these knives and forks but still don' know what is for,' she whispered to Maria.

'Don't worry, just use what you're comfortable with. Have another glass of wine,' she replied.

'*Gracias, pero no, no senora es sufficiente, gracias nada mas.*' (No more wine for her; she had enough), but she did a discreet double-take on Maria's consumption.

As the meal drew to a close, Gregg got to his feet and rattling the side of a wine glass with a fork to get attention, he made an announcement.

'Well everyone, I hope you have had a pleasant evening. The meal as usual prepared with the same loving care we have come to expect from the excellent staff we are fortunate enough to have at our restaurant. I want to thank Jose and Consuella for their hard work and efforts to maintain MexTex's presence in Mexico.

'I understand that some of you here tonight were concerned about your future with the company. I don't know from where the rumours were initiated, but let me reassure everyone here tonight that you may all look forward to many happy years ahead with our company. So on that note, let's be upstanding and raise a glass to the company. *Saludas a la empressa.*'

At that, Consuela threw her arms around Maria and gave her one enormous hug and kiss on the cheek. '*Gracias, senora Maria, gracias, Dios.*'

Maria, now very tipsy just managed to get to her feet to embrace Consuela, almost knocking her off balance. They laughed as she responded, wishing Consuela and her family God's blessing.

Maria saw that Gregg and '"the boys"' were going to have a bit of a session, so she staggered across the restaurant floor and asked if Jose would run her home.

Gregg looked her up and down and clearly annoyed, agreed that it would be a very good idea for her to go home.

He turned to Jose 'Try and get her to go to bed and

sleep it off. No more drink tonight, if you can convince her, it would be great. *Gracias, hombre*.'

Back in the condo Jose had his work cut out trying to convince Maria to go to bed; in fact, she angrily pushed him aside, picked up the phone and attempted to make a call, but she was so drunk she dropped the phone.

'*Senora* may I be of some assistance to you?' Jose politely asked.

'No, you bloody well can't be of assistance, Who do you think you are? How dare you? You're nothing to me. You're just Superman's little lackey. I'm phoning my mother if you must know. She understands me, nobody else does. You don't, he doesn't.'

Jose discreetly stepped back with his hands behind his back, as she tried once again and failed. Completely unaware of the time difference, she failed to contact her mother then collapsed onto the settee.

Realising that discretion was the better part of valour. Jose cautiously took a blanket from the bedroom and lovingly draped it over her. She fell into a deep sleep, and Jose positioned himself where he could keep an eye on her, but out of sight.

Later, when Gregg arrived, they had a brief discussion as to what should happen to Maria.

'I think it best to leave the *senora* sleeping there, no ? where she is. If we try to move, she wake and get real mad, it scares me,' Jose said.

'I agree, and I don't want another scene tonight. It's getting too frequent now. It's the drink, always the drink. She's a different person when she doesn't drink,' he said, but stopped abruptly as he realised that he had breached yet another wall between that master-servant relationship.

He showered and re-emerged in his bathrobe ready for bed, but mindful of Maria's condition he looked to Jose and shrugged his shoulders. Jose shrewd as ever, picked up on the body language and immediately offered.

'That's all right, boss I keep eye on the *senora* and sit in the armchair.' Jose had been a loyal and trusted member of the household who had stepped into the breach on many such occasions, smoothing over the most challenging situations, especially when Gregg's wife was in town.

Watching her as she slept in a deep alcoholic stupor, Jose had every right to be very angry and resentful towards her, but somehow he managed to contain such emotions. He did wonder, however, what Gregg would have made of the earlier outburst. Instead he prayed asking for help 'from above' for her.

The following morning, Maria was totally unaware of her behaviour the previous night and spoke to Jose as if nothing adverse had occurred at all. As far as she was concerned, it was a normal morning; breakfast was being prepared. Jose said nothing but with love in his heart he wondered; perhaps his prayers had been answered.

EIGHTEEN

ADIOS, MEXICO

There was a general consensus of opinion that it was time for all concerned in the Mexican adventure to return to the Iberian Peninsula. Well, at least that was how Maria would have preferred it to be, but the reality was that Gregg had decided to go and she would agree.

They did, however, agree that it had been a wonderful experience sharing their lives together in unforeseen ways. They had had fun and discovered new people and places. As far as she was concerned, she had discovered more of what made her tick; her pleasures, her pains, including her deepest demons aroused by drinking to excess.

She had spent a great deal of time and energy on soul-searching, with mixed results. In particular, she had come to the conclusion that she would seek help with some of her behavioural issues, with an emphasis on the inevitable destructive behaviour that ensued in the drastic aftermath of her drinking.

It was impossible to have any idea what effect, if any, the trip had on Gregg. The pragmatist to the end, he did not give anything away about himself, which truly puzzled her. She had never met such a closed person emotionally. She tried to rationalise his callousing on the grounds that it was his military training. He remained the same closed, secret man all throughout the trip. She never once saw an emotional proverbial tear in the eye of Gregg.

Everything in place for the next leg of the trip, they said their farewells to all in Polanco. Consuela was tearful as she said goodbye to Maria; they had got along well together and bonded. Jose also thanked Maria for her kindness and consideration and hoped they would meet again at some time in the future.

Gregg, as usual, handled the travel arrangements which on this particular occasion meant that he would hand the reins over to another senior captain of the airline. He needed to use his allocation of complimentary air travel tickets from the airline.

Maria had eventually managed to pen a few words on paper and sent off a letter to *mama*, but she sensed it may have been rather inadequate, so using Gregg's satellite phone, she called her and regaled her with adventures around Mexico and the USA.

Papa joined in the conference mode on the phone so the three shared the conversation; he was very envious, and hoped she had made the most of her wonderful opportunity to see that part of the world.

'Well done my darling daughter. What a wonderful trip! You're very brave, so now perhaps you can make a little time to visit us soon?'

As she sat with Gregg in the main concourse of the airport Maria felt nothing of the sense of excitement she had experienced on the outward leg of her adventure. Quite the opposite; she wondered how people adjusted to the constant time changes differences and zones, the weather patterns and different languages.

She decided that this extreme way of life was not for her and felt pleased to be returning home. She also felt guilty about not visiting her folks more often and planned on rectifying that soon. She felt very homesick.

Throwing a glance in Gregg's' direction, she was curious about how he dealt with this mundane aspect of his world of adventure. He had his head firmly buried in a book. *Man's' Adventures in the Arctic Region*; the trials and tribulations in the frozen North, trying to forge a way through the ice to open the Northwest Passage.

'Don't you ever get fed up with airports, planes, passengers and the tedium of sitting around airport lounges, Gregg?' she asked.

There was a delayed reaction but then Gregg lifted his eyes from the printed page with,

'Erm… sorry, what was that?' She knew his sarcastic ways and gave him a playful slap on the head with the free newspaper she'd picked up in the lounge. It was time for them to stroll over to the VIP lounge, and get busy on the free drinks and food.

Gregg helped himself to coffee and a *jamon boccadillo*,

(ham sandwich) whilst she had a large vodka tonic with ice and a slice and *manchego* cheese on rye bread. As they sat the waitress came over and sternly addressed them. They should not have helped themselves but should have waited to be served.

The lounge was busy with the low hum of muted conversation, although a group of particularly noisy Mexican business-type gentlemen, quite rotund, in smart suits and wearing Stetsons, had begun to annoy Gregg. He very slowly and deliberately strolled over to the group and said something.

She could not quite hear but whatever it was, they immediately became quiet, to the obvious delight of two very smart elderly women, who mockingly gave a quiet hand-clap in appreciation. All was still once more.

As the novelty of the VIP lounge wore off, so Maria's boredom returned. She did not feel the usual high, she normally experienced from travel; even the VIP lounge was not working for her.

Drifting towards an emotional low, she felt afraid, as she had recently become aware of the consequences of her emotional lows. They would inevitably lead her to drinking. This was the latest revelation she had acquired from Janet; the problem was, she needed to put preventive measures in place to prevent ensuing problems.

She had several vodka tonics and although Gregg had been reading all the while, she knew that he was keeping a check on her. This thought only served to increase her uncomfortable feelings of low self-esteem. Being spied upon!

Throwing caution to the wind,

'Gregg, I'm having a vodka tonic. Do you want anything?' she boldly announced.

'No, thanks, girl. Time to ease up maybe?' he rhetorically replied.

Ignoring that remark she went ahead and ordered her vodka tonic. He shrugged his shoulders.

She had been reading through her journal and wanted to clean up the random entries into a more cohesive package.

Sensing that Gregg was watching keeping an eye on her, she decided to wait until they were on board. She then remembered a piece she had done earlier on him having saved it on her laptop.

Janet had spoken about a fourth step, a personal inventory on the programme but she didn't fully understand the meaning of it.

She thought this piece she had put together on Gregg might be part of the process.

Eventually the flight was called; they boarded and were on their way.

The flight was totally unremarkable, apart from a serious amount of clear-air turbulence over the mountains. Gregg read books, conversed with the captain, spent time on the flight deck and chatted up the cabin crew. Maria tidied up her journal, read a little and sent the email attachment to Janet.

I would have to admit I was caught in his mysterious web. I know my lack of self control was brought about by my drinking. Warning signs had been flashing for quite some time. It was just a matter of time before my drinking would lead me into more complicated situations. Like a broken record I hear myself repeating the same old phrase; if only I could drink like normal people. For some reason, I don't seem able to put in place the controls to restrict my excessive behaviour, including my drinking. I know I like the risky nature of drinking and using drugs, so I need something to replace my desire for risk but can't find that. Montserrat Ramires was great. She showed me some techniques to help me. I was more self-assured around Montse.

I love her and will definitely get back in touch. I'm sick and tired of repeating myself and feeling so bad. Walking back down that same well-trodden pathway.

Unless and until I can find a way of keeping my emotions under control I will continue to make the same inappropriate decisions. Quite happily, I made a decision to go along for the ride with Gregg, in the full knowledge that he would cast me aside when he grew tired of me. Complicit in the subterfuge, Gregg was aware of his marital problems. Of course, my agenda was to collude with the deception and capitalise in the best way to serve my needs. I have no room to complain, I plotted as much as did Gregg. Now we have cleared the air, I wonder if he will keep his word or will there be further deceptions that I may stumble across, to which I must be party. I must wait and see!

Maria sent the attachment then watched a number of films on and off through sleeping eyes. She was bored, and would be glad to get back to Barcelona and eventually up north to *mama* and *papa*. Then she remembered Gregg had plans for a trip to the Canaries. *'Oh no, can I take another trip with this guy?* ; she asked herself.

Janet read the email and acknowledged that it was a very good start on her personal moral inventory, but it was all about Gregg; she needed to make a start on her issues, not Gregg's.

*

After what seemed like an eternity, they landed back in Barcelona. The airport was heaving with holiday-makers as well as regular passengers making business trips.

Gregg, now as an ordinary passenger, found himself in unfamiliar territory He tried to swing it by getting in the flight crew group, but that failed, as the customs officer called him out of line to check his, and Maria's bags. She had never seen Gregg looking so uncomfortable. Something had changed, and even he, the *fireproof* Gregg, seemed to lack his normal confidence. All checked out okay, nothing to declare and nothing about which they should be concerned. Except that he no longer appeared to be the carefree guy with whom she had become familiar, his whole demeanour seemed to have changed.

NINETEEN

BARCELONA

Gregg drove straight to the office. There was something which needed his attention right away, but Maria was not party to that information. He immediately arranged a car to take her to the apartment.

She practically threw herself into the rear seats in the very new white Prius cab, with a tremendous sense of relief. She was desperate to share her adventures and attempted to chat with the cabbie, but he showed not a bit of interest, so she gave up on that idea.

Home at last, she called Leanne from the cab and was deliriously happy to find her at home in the apartment.

'Hey, Maria great to hear from you. Where are you, *chica*?'

'Not far; in a cab, I'll be with you real soon, darling. Can't 't wait to tell you about my adventures.'

She waited in high expectation by the door for Maria. As she arrived, she threw her bags through the doorway and jumped on Leanne, kissing and hugging her, plastering her face with kisses.

'So good to have you back. Seems like you've been away for months, baby girl. How the heck are you?'

'I can't begin to tell you how much I've missed you, Leanne, and how great it feels to be back home. Yeah, you're right, it does feel like months. Going to take a while to re-adjust, I can tell you. Just so much been going on.'

She opened her bag and gave Leanne a little *mariachi* toy man, complete with guitar and sombrero. She loved it; they embraced and kissed again.

'I've also got you such a great tee-shirt in my bag. I'll get it out later,' she said.

'I don't expect you to catch up on everything today, but what was your overall impression of the trip?' Leanne asked.

'Well, the truth is, I really don't know how best to explain, but in short it seemed to me throughout that I was just something of a decoy for clandestine operations about which I had no idea.

'I've had my suspicions for some time, and by the way all of this is very hush-hush. We both know he is a very tricky customer and not to be crossed. He's also untrustworthy, but I've almost got the hang of him, although nobody ever figures out guys like him. It's sort of like a continuous war of attrition catch-as-catch-can.

Having said that we've had some truly memorable and fabulous times together, but that's for another day. You won't believe some of the things we did.'

'What have you been up to, Leanne?'

'Not very much at all if the truth be known. Silly bits and pieces of work but nothing even remotely justifying the money I'm earning. I think we we're right about these guys, Maria. Where does all the money come from?'

'Sounds like we already know now.' Leanne replied.

'What do you think we should do? Play dumb, as we said before, take the money and play innocent or get out? I tell you now that getting out would be fraught with danger. That's not going to be so easy now.

'I've had the advantage of observing Gregg at close quarters. He's a very shrewd, clever and cunning guy, capable of manipulating people in high places. I've probably learned more than I should on this trip, and certainly feel very vulnerable now,' she explained.

'Okay so what's the bottom line, Maria? As you say, you've seen him operating close up, you must have got some clues?'

'Drugs and money laundering, Leanne.' There was a long pause.

'Yeah, sounds like it. We thought that was the story and now you're pretty well convinced,' Leanne agreed.

'Pretty serious amounts judging by the size of some of the parcels I've seen moving around, supposedly undercover.

'You see, he's got so many contacts wherever he goes, and with having a private aircraft capable of flying long distances and cars at his disposal, it's quite an operation.

'My immediate personal concern is that he's got another job lined up in the Canaries and he needs me to go with him. When I confronted him telling him I knew he was up to something he promised me there would be no more drops. All I really want to do is go and see my family up north and forget all this crap.'

'Crikey, you took some chance confronting him like that. You're lucky to still be here by the sound of it.' Leanne replied.

'I suppose you could do this Canary thing, whatever it is, and then just hand in your notice and give him your word that you would never divulge your suspicions. At the moment, that's all they are. You never actually saw money or drugs, did you, or did you?

'Tell him you've had enough and want out and return to your family life in the north for a quiet life,' Leanne suggested.

'No. I've never seen anything other than grey plastic packages taped up with gaffer tape. There's another issue and that is I think they may be onto him. The net might be closing. He got a pull in California and also at Barca Airport. He's normally untouchable, just walks through security and customs, but I sense a change going on,' Maria confided.

'So he had urgent business calling him into the office when you landed?' Leanne asked.

'Exactly, Leanne, he needed me out of the way.'

'Okay, that's enough about him, Maria. I've got absolutely nothing to report, been doing some really Mickey Mouse crap jobs in your absence and still picking up huge pay cheques.

Your pal Luis has been asking for you. Have you not been in touch with him; and where do you want to eat? In or out tonight?'

'I'm so tired, honey, could we just eat in? Don't want to put you to any trouble.'

'No trouble, Maria, I'm on it. Take a look at the Chinese menu. Dinner's on me.'

As they sat and gossiped, Maria could not have been happier. Back with her very close friend they awaited the Chinese delivery. She felt felt secure at last in her own apartment.

Aware that she had neglected some of her friends and family, she felt guilty and was desperate to make amends to them all at once. Fortunately, Janet was able to come to her aid on that one. Easy does it, she had advised. However, she vowed to work through it, starting tomorrow. Out came her Journal and she made notes on that conversation.

She mentioned the message she had sent to Janet about the fourth step, which just confused Leanne; so they let that go.

Leanne laid up a couple of places at the table with glasses, candles, chop-sticks and the table warmer in readiness for the Chinese meal.

Of course there was a very cold bottle of Chardonnay.

The meal they shared together again after a long break, was great and they agreed that the rest of the evening would be spent talking about food, clothes, shoes and other boyfriends they had known, loved and left behind; plus a little time discussing the beloved Barca F.C. Leanne reminded them that they had complimentary tickets for the Camp Nou of which they had not taken advantage and which they should put to rights at the earliest opportunity.

Then Leanne came right out of left field with a ground-shattering piece of information; 'Did you know that people from Barcelona abbreviate the name to Barna and that Barca is only used when referring to Barcelona F.C.?'

The silence was deafening; then the girls fell about the place, laughing and giggling.

Maria for the first time in a very long time, felt totally relaxed. 'Breaking news Leanne, eh? Well I didn't know that' she said.

They decided no more mention of Gregg and they declared it had been a wonderful reunion for them as they confirmed their deep friendship for one another. They would leave the clearing up until the morning as each prepared for an early night, feeling totally relaxed.

'Do you know what I'm thinking, Leanne? My life is on a conveyor belt. I go from one assignment to the next without any breaks. I have no friends, apart from the people I am working with or their associates. I have no family contact, apart from virtual electronic contact by phone or computer. Can't go on like that indefinitely without a bit more forward planning.'

Leanne replied, 'Well, I don't have the same degree of commitment to my role as you do and certainly don't have your pressures. However I get the same sense of where's it all going and for how long? I'm sorry, that I keep repeating the mantra take the money and run. Not an ideal way to live at all.'

Maria's cell phone sprang into life with flashing and ringing breaking the peace and tranquillity.

'Hi, Maria how are you? okay I hope. Sorry I had to dash back to the office, Something urgent cropped up and had to sort it with *Snr* Gonzales,' he said.

The girls together made eye contact in disbelief.

'All sorted now but we need to make preparations for our trip to Lanzarote. Should be a nice, easy assignment, that one. Give me a couple of days to make travel arrangements. Work on the assumption that we will be flying out in three days from now.

'May need you to come into the office but will let you know in advance so you can spend some time with Leanne. Give her my regards. *Buenas noches*, Maria.'

'Yeah ok Gregg just call when you've got some details. Adios.'

'Everything okay, Maria? Bloody cheek, that Gregg. Can't believe he would call at this hour.' Leanne grumbled.

'Yeah. That's how he is all the time I'm at his beck and call, the Lanzarote trip is on three days' time. He sends his regards Leanne.'

'That's nice of him. Come on, get into my bed for a cuddle of friendship to celebrate your return to me. I'll leave the bedside lamp on. You'll probably be getting up in the night after all that wine. Nite nite.'

As she began to doze she reflected on Leanne's statement, '… all that wine.' Maria did not consider she had, had nearly enough and that was fundamentally her drink issue right there. She did not know what the cut-off point for her drinking was. She put her arm across Leanne and kissed her on the forehead. '*Noches*' baby girl.'

*

Morning saw Leanne up and about early; the weather was superb and she didn't want to waste the day in bed. They at the moment had a rare, free day ahead.

She loved living here; the apartment was exquisite and furthermore there was a *pasteleria* just about a five-minute walk away. She bought fresh *rollos de pan and croissants,* which were still warm when she put them in a wicker basket lined with a blue check cloth on the breakfast bar.

Seville oranges, were quietly juiced so as not to disturb Maria. A very faint voice from the bedroom called, *'Hola Leanne, estas ahi?* (are you there?)

Leanne replied, *'Si, si, buenas dias, desayuno esta aqui'* (Good day, breakfast is ready.) That was the signal to make the fresh coffee, the aroma of which filled the whole apartment seductively wafting into the bedroom.

Maria appeared wearing only a tee shirt. As she rubbed her eyes and winced at the brilliant sunlight streaming through the windows she realised she had not given Leanne the tee-shirt she promised her last night. She left it for later as she did not wish to spoil Leanne's surprise breakfast treat. Leanne had also bought cheese and Iberico ham with a speciality soft goats cheese queso blanco; a big favourite in Lanzarote.

The pair sat at the breakfast bar; the juice, rolls, tomatoes, cheese, ham and coffee awaited them. Maria hugged Leanne and they took turns to feed one another, whilst giggling a little.

She presented the tee-shirt to Leanne, who immediately put it on. 'Give me a twirl girl. You've got great legs; well fit.' The design, a contemporary take on traditional Aztec designs, was stunning and Leanne loved it.

Getting down from the breakfast bar the pair, dressed only in tee-shirts, cuddled up on the settee. They joked about with fake tickling for a while. The kissing and cuddling began to take on a more intimate level. This was for both a new experience; they began to explore each other's body. The sensations became more intense, more passionate, with a fervour that was unstoppable, legs and arms entwined in an erotic dance, until finally they shuddered in ecstasy.

They lay still for while, held hands and gazed into each other's' eyes, amazed and a little confused. They concurred that these feelings must have been latent, but certainly they would never have thought of each other in a sexual way, ever. It had been a totally random and impromptu act of love and passion.

Once the breakfast things had been cleared away, they had a free day, with the proviso that the bosses would not call. Whilst the pair carried out a little lightweight tidying up of the apartment Maria received a call from Luis. They shared how life was working out for each of them respectively, and agreed how sad it was that they had not met up for a while.

Luis went on to ask what plans she had for the day.

'Well it's amazing, but unusually we both are free from all work commitments for the day. We're both thinking we should get out while we still have the chance before the boss calls us to work,' Maria said.

'That's a coincidence as the showroom is closed for refurbishment for a couple of days and that works out well for Felix and I who have tickets for the match at Camp Nou. It's the big one Madrid and Barca and we wondered how near your apartment is to the stadium. There might be a possibility that we could meet up.' Luis said.

'Oh wow! what a great surprise this is. I'm so glad you called. I miss you so much Luis and feel really bad that I've allowed work to dominate my life to such an extent. Now here's the thing; we actually have season tickets for Barca which we have not even used so far. Would they be eligible for that match?' she asked.

'Of course they are good for the match. That's outrageous you've never used them; their like gold- dust those tickets. We're actually coming over right now on the supporters bus, but we could ask the driver to drop us off anywhere you like. We could all go together, that would be 'hoot' for sure. The kick off is not until 20.00 so there's plenty of time for a meal somewhere; have you got any suggestions?' he asked.

'Well obviously the bus will be on main roads so give us a while and well sort out a suitable place within easy reach of the stadium and give you the coordinates for your phone. How does that sound Luis darling?'

'That sounds perfect darling Maria. I cant wait I'm super excited' Luis replied amid the noise of the supporters chanting in the background. Leanne took the initiative in tracking down a suitable restaurant close to the stadium.

She offered to do the driving as she had become very familiar with the environs of Barcelona whereas Maria had spent most of her time away from the area. She was also very efficient with the technology required to find coordinates and so on.

The girls had great fun playing with the internet looking up football players from both teams.

'Come here Maria and just take a look at some of the properties these guys own all in various parts of the globe. They are quite amazing; these guys are among the super-rich in society over the world. Their cars and boats are so expensive; some of them have private aircraft even.'

'I know we spoke about these issues when a was at the Ranchero with young Sergio and Montse. And please never get involved with Janet on this stuff; she will get really angry at the disparity of such things. She struggles with the whole state of the world economics. Actually I have to say I was quite surprised when Sergio told me how much money bull-fighters can earn in a year.' Maria said.

I would have imagined in these times of political correctness and animal welfare rights that would have been outlawed throughout the world. However that's not the case; its big money both here in Spain and abroad, especially in south America.' She ended.

Something we could discuss with the lads when we meet up later; perhaps not, lets just go out and have fun.' Leanne said. 'Right I've tracked down a couple of restaurants and narrowed it down; La Gaviota not far from the stadium and just off the main road so the driver wont get held up be the lads getting off. We can meet them and drive a little, then walk; so its flat shoes and cagoules girl. Need to get a Barca scarf off a street seller…this is gonna be fun chica.' She was well up for it.

After the quick meal they made it in plenty of time to their seats which were in different parts of the enormous stadium. The girls were blown away with the whole scene; they had never seen or experienced anything remotely resembling it. The noise, the colour the smoke from flares and the atmosphere was other-worldly to the girls, who had seats with refreshments in the hospitality boxes. It was a truly memorable and enjoyable night. With no chance of meeting the lads after the match, they made their separate ways home.

Back at the apartment the girls relaxed with hot drinks. The lads had a long bus-drive home, but after the amount of beer they drank they slept most of the way. Maria made a quick call to Luis, promising to call him before leaving on her next assignment.

They all agreed it was a great night…Barca won 3-1.

TWENTY

THE CANARIES

An early start Gregg called maria into the office; they drank coffee and ate croissants over the paperwork on the coffee table in his office.

They spoke casually about the location of the Canarian group of islands and their close proximity to the African coast. Although unfamiliar personally with any of the islands, Maria knew her parents had friends living in Lanzarote and that the climate was very beneficial health-wise for their arthritis.

On a much more ghastly subject, she noted that there was an almost daily toll of bodies of fleeing refugees being washed up on Canarian shores.

Lanzarote was only seventy miles from the Saharan coastline and Gregg knew that stretch of water was extremely perilous, with huge waves and tidal currents.

He added that as each island independently ran their affairs, although the problem was a global humanitarian crisis, he feared that self-interest in the tourist trade appeared to be a priority to some.

At that point, Maria could not believe her ears; this was an aspect of Gregg that was hitherto unseen. She silently processed this and remained quite still.

After a respectful pause, Gregg came in with, 'I think Lanzarote is the preference for the initial visit, then on to Fuerteventura. What say you Maria?'

As this was one of Gregg's rhetorical questions, they both smiled and she nodded, saying, 'Well yes Gregg I couldn't agree more. Excellent choice.' The reality was that she had never been consulted in any matters of business the whole time she had known Gregg.

'There's something I want to talk over with you, Gregg. It's a delicate matter but I'm now considering what my options might be for the foreseeable future. I am at the point where I need to take some action about my drinking and that's clear, and that's for me to decide.

'What really bothers me, though, Gregg is the risky business that you're undertaking. As we are in such close proximity a great deal of our time, I feel I'm in a position to comment and dare I say, advise.

'The problem as I see it is that I'm pretty certain about what's going on and I don't want to know any more. I'm deliberately choosing my words carefully, but what I'm really getting at is I don't believe I'm the only one who suspects, and for that reason I feel after this trip to the Canaries I would like to move on.'

After a considerable silence, Gregg eventually commented.

'I suppose you're referring to the two incidents with customs officers?'

'Exactly so, Gregg, a close call if you ask me. I mean, do you think it's worth taking a further risk with this Canaries trip?' she asked.

'Maria, I'm grateful for your comments and advice on how you see the situation. I've got really good friends on this trip with excellent intel, so I'm happy to proceed. But if you feel you want to pull out now, please do so. Needless to say, I would prefer you to stay, I think we make a great team; but at least let's do one more trip and we can talk on our return.'

'Okay on the basis that we're clear that I will be looking to leave the organisation I'm in for the ride on this trip. What's the plan Gregg?'

'Okay, one of my oldest friends, Dieter Muller, is our man in Lanzarote. I've known him for some time, very reliable and very methodical in all his arrangements and forward planning. He's been in the past a golf professional, and we've had some good rounds together on first-class courses in different parts of the globe, but that was long ago,' Gregg opened with.

'I've never come across that name before. I used to follow quite keenly at home in the North. but have lost touch with the game recently. So what are the courses like there, any good?' she asked.

'In truth Maria, I have no idea, but Dieter bought a long lease on a course from the local *ayuntamiento* (town hall) in the south of Lanzarote. We could head there and make it our base.'

'Are you taking your clubs Gregg?'

'Erm… no, Maria, but thanks for suggesting, I fear my days of carting my clubs around the globe are long gone. I can always get hire sets, some of which are top quality, but not this trip Maria.'

'Would you like me to help out with the travel and accommodation arrangements, Gregg? I've not got much on at the moment.

'No, thanks all the same, but I'll call Dieter this morning and we'll sort it out, but thanks. The free air tickets are sorted and we get priority boarding, which will give us the opportunity to assess how much interest the officials show in us. See you in the morning, and don't get anxious; that will only make matters worse, be cool.' He finished with.

Maria pleased that she had dealt with the burning question, said good-bye to Gregg.

Relieved but still nervous, she returned to her apartment to sort out her affairs before the trip, got her personal business together and said her farewells to those who mattered; Luis in particular, who she thought was somewhat subdued the other night. She told them she expected to be away no longer than a week.

*

It was another early start at Barcelona Airport. The flight time was 8.30 a.m. and the duration would be approximately three and a quarter hours.

Compared with their recent trips, this was pretty mundane and totally uninteresting, Maria thought. She read, wrote a little and ate a lot of rubbish snacks. She was bored, a fact that she couldn't conceal from Gregg. He teased her, saying that many people would be visiting Lanzarote for their main annual holiday.

Dieter a tall very slim and elegant man, probably early sixties in years, met them at Arrecife airport. He had the skin tone of someone who had spent a lot of time in the tropics; light tan with creases and cracks throughout. He wore a crumpled grey designer shirt with matching trousers, with sockless espadrilles on his feet. She thought he looked "designer scruffy." He was, however, sporting very expensive looking real tortoiseshell sunglasses.

His rather old Mercedes estate had the appearance of a car which had also spent most of its life in tropical sunlight. It was old and faded, with an interior to match. Well-worn leather seats, possibly cream in colour, it was a masterpiece of German ancient craftsmanship. It smelled of fuel and leather and Maria loved it.

Dieter was the opposite to old and faded; old but full of vim and vigour. He very warmly greeted Gregg like a long-lost brother might and turned to Maria.

He stretched out a thin, sinewy brown hand and picking up Maria's hand kissed it all in one movement; there was a faint hint of very expensive aftershave, which she couldn't identify. He greeted her: '*Encantado,* Maria.' (Pleased to meet you.) This man, she thought, was the real deal; world-travelled, probably in and out of scrapes in different banana republics around the globe, sorted away a fair bit of money and living out his twilight days in the subtropical paradise of Lanzarote; bought himself a golf club. She liked him very much; he definitely intrigued her. She found no record of any golfing history on this guy.

'You guys ever been here before?' he asked, and both in unison, they answered, 'No, never', although she had visited with her parents many years previously.

'Well, I've been here fifteen years and love it, would never leave now. If we get the time, Gregg, when we have completed our business, I would be happy to show you the island. Meanwhile, I've booked you into the Crystal Paradise Hotel, yeah, I know, bit pretentious but great location in Puerta Caldera, a beautiful marina not too touristy,' he said.

The car windows open Maria struggled to hear but the heat was getting to her. He noticed and pulled off the road. 'Sorry, Maria, not far to go, but take off some layers, It's only twenty-six degrees but a big difference from Barcelona.'

He drove on and pointed out the golf club as they passed the turn-off, and then they were at the hotel. You guys get freshened up and I'll be back down for you later for dinner at the hotel, if that suits.'

Maria looked to Gregg, who had dozed off with the heat. 'Gregg' she nudged him.

Embarrassed, he answered, 'Sorry, I missed that,' but Dieter was out of the car and grabbing the bags.

'Buddy, so sorry about that…' Gregg started but Dieter simply said, 'Don't worry *amigo, hasta pronto*' and was gone.

Maria's first thought was *where are the staff?* She had been spoiled in her travels with Gregg; first-class service everywhere and lots of help but suddenly there was nobody to carry her luggage.

Gregg was on it; they made for the bar for a cold lager as the bags were taken to their room.

The hotel was great; they had a swim and rested awhile then strolled around the marina. In his element, Gregg checked out the boats from the smallest to the grandest. He knew most of the models, run-of-the-mill stock. However, the designer yachts, all custom built to the owners' individual specifications, were more interesting to him.

The whole place was immaculate; even the large bollards for tying up were polished brass. There was not a cigarette stub or sweet wrapper in sight. The marina staff saw to that. Plentiful fish in the crystal-clear water of the marina swam around, attracting Gregg's attention. The gardens were amazing with hibiscus, various cacti and omnipresent bougainvillea set amongst the black volcanic ash, *picon*.

Gregg remarked that he had never seen a smarter marina than this one. He had his own yacht in San Diego so he felt right at home here, but it was all new to Maria. A few cafes and restaurants lined one side of the marina in a very understated way. She grabbed a seat in El Sardinero.

'Gregg, want a drink? I'm heading for the shade. Its way too hot.'

'Yeah, okay, right there, Maria. *'Una cerveza por favor.'* He called. She thought she would also have a cold beer.

They sat together relaxing; with a *salud, (cheers)* they toasted themselves as if congratulating each other. Totally, in their natural environment, but then she had the sudden realisation that she never actually had any money with her. She never carried pocket money; he had always picked up the tab one way or the other.

Engaging the waiter in small talk, Gregg casually enquired about the ownership of one of the larger boats in the marina. Maria silently chuckled. He was on a '"fishing trip"' for information; this was his MO. (*modus operandi*).

'Oh, that one belongs to a very rich Asian gentleman, who is said to be a multi-millionaire. He came here twenty-five years ago with very little money, and opened a small electrical shop which was successful and eventually he branched out with the family becoming involved in the business he diversified. He owns a number of Asian and Italian restaurants on the island and many other businesses.'

'Does he come down and take the boat out very often?' Gregg asked.

'Very rarely, he uses it mainly to show off to friends, and when they leave the marina he has a skipper who takes the boat when required. His restaurant is just along from here.'

Maria had already put two and two together with Gregg's questions to the waiter. The Asian gentleman multi-millionaire was the contact Gregg needed to make. Sipping her beer, living *el buena vida* she was having second thoughts about breaking with Gregg.

She had adapted well to being around the super-rich; that was not a problem, but Gregg's dubious activities were giving her nervous tension almost all of the time when on assignment.

He had wandered off presumably to check out the Indian restaurant owned by his new contact but was now back to join her for a drink.

The waiter came with drinks, so Maria made the most of the situation. 'So do you know the name of the owner of that lovely boat?'

The waiter answered, 'Oh yes his name is Kamlish. That's all I know. It's never a good idea for people like me to ask questions about such people, they're very private.'

Gregg threw back the ice-cold beer. 'Jeeze, that was cold, got brain freeze. Just been talking with the manager of The Bengal Cuisine, nice guy. It's owned by the guy who owns this big yacht. He knows Dieter. Who knows? May even get an outing on his yacht. How about that, Maria?' She resented being taken for a fool; she wished she could respond with an honest heart but she could not. She instinctively knew it was all wrong and really wanted no further part in this scene, but for now she would have to keep up the pretence; there was no bailing-out now.

Gregg asked her again, 'Don't you feel excited about that prospect, Maria? Might even get to go across to Fuerteventura. Now that would be a trip.

'Don't know about that, Gregg, could be very sick-making. Just look at the waves outside the harbour;' she eventually managed to reply.

The old Mercedes pulled up and out jumped Dieter, full of energy; perhaps, Maria thought a little too much energy for a man of his years, perhaps some chemical energy thing going on, but she said nothing.

He and Gregg wandered off to look at the boat. It was an impressive outfit bristling with antennae and very long heavy-duty fishing rods. Clearly a deep-sea vessel suitable for big game fish such as marling and shark.

'Come, take a look, Maria. Quite a serious bit of kit.' Gregg suggested; and dutifully she obeyed. She had seen plenty of fishing boats in her home town, so she feigned showing interest to placate them.

'What do you guys want to do about dinner?' Dieter asked. If you prefer to eat out I can take you to a perfect spot where we can watch the sun going down and I can promise you, Maria, a sunset to remember. Just put on a jacket or something as it's very breezy but stunning.'

Maria's first instinct was; *another control freak* but of course she went with it.

The old Merc was testament to good old German technology and ran as quietly as a sewing machine. It would certainly have done thousands of miles.

Gregg made a sarcastic remark about getting a workout with the wind-up windows; they all laughed. In fact, the car was very comfortable and strangely reassuring.

The evening air was cooling as they climbed high in a mountain range to a very small hamlet, Femes, perched on the very edge. They parked by a small church, typical of the region. The terrain, inhospitable in appearance, magically supported a handful of small-holders growing crops, mainly potatoes and onions.

The local goat's cheese, *queso blanco*, was loved by locals and visitors alike. They stopped to admire the view.

It was stunning, offering an amazing uninterrupted vista right across the southernmost part of the island, across the sea to Fuerteventura and beyond. In a half-hearted attempt to be sociable, she let out; 'Wow, that really is something, that view. It's like flying eh. Gregg?'

'Thought you would like that Maria,' said Dieter, just wait till you see the sunset from the restaurant later. You'll love that.'

Maria stood to one side away from the others, feeding her soul on the silence to be experienced there; the only sound was the wind blowing across the plateau.

A revelation to Maria, she felt a strong emotional connection there. She could smell the goats and other animal smells which she did not recognise.

She later discovered they had camels stabled here for the tourist trade these days; once used for ploughing and carrying water and general farm duties similar to workhorses.

The silence was all too soon broken as the others decided it was time to move on. Perhaps, she thought, she could return here one day on her own; she felt a very definite deep sense of peace.

The descent was steep down a scary serpentine road to the plateau below; her ears popped with the sudden change in air pressure. The road took them across a rock and boulder-strewn valley, passing the old salt flats towards Los Hervideros, (the boiling pots,) A rugged volcanic coastline with under-water caves of solidified lava.

Once more Dieter was kind enough to stop and let them experience this place of wonder.

'Known for the crashing Atlantic waves hitting the rocks and causing weird and wonderful sounds,' Dieter explained. Gregg was never one to routinely stop and stare; he said nothing. The strong southern wind carried warm fresh air from the Azores, further south in the Atlantic Ocean.

Maria was totally in tune with this place. Turning to Dieter, she said, 'Thank you so much for bringing us here, It's truly magical and so invigorating. I absolutely love it, Dieter.'

The sun was lowering in the western sky as they passed the green lagoon and on to El Golfo a small genuine working fishing village. Dieter took them to his favourite restaurant; it would be his treat.

'Whatever else you choose, you really must try *la vieja*, a speciality. Parrot fish is not widely available in many seafood restaurants. Also, *lapas*... ' (limpets) ... ' taken off the rocks right in front of the restaurant.'

On checking the menu, Maria called the waiter. 'You have *pimientos de Padron* on the menu. Are they genuinely from Padron?'

He answered her in a very assured manner. He then went on to say that they came from Padron in Galicia and that name was protected, so they were genuine.

Maria thanked him, saying she was from Galicia herself so she loved them and also the *lapas* were a favourite of hers.

Gregg intervened. 'She's from Galicia and she's also protected.' They enjoyed the joke together. The meal was superb. They all tried the *vieja*, remembering to eat the bit behind the eyes; that was considered the best part.

'I can't believe I've never been to Lanzarote before now. It's such a great place. Thank you, Dieter for bringing us here, El Golfo, what a place, what a meal. and it's only three hours from Barca.'

Gregg called for cigars and brandies all round but Maria declined the brandy. Dieter was right about the weather; it was cooling fast with a stiff breeze off the Atlantic Ocean.

There was nothing between them and America except open water. The sun was turning the sky and sea from a golden hue to an astonishing vibrant deep red.

The men pulled on their cigars and sipped their brandies; it was times like these that Maria missed the company of Leanne. She vowed to bring her to this place one day soon.

Darkness came upon the scene, candles were ignited and the house lights came on as the evening clientele began to arrive. Gregg grabbed the bill from the waiter; he knew it would be an expensive meal. It was expensive.

'Dieter would you like me to drive?' Maria asked, out of politeness. 'Erm…well, no, thank you, Maria. I know the roads.' Clearly quite shocked at her offer he continued.

'We'll be returning by another more direct route and the roads can be tricky at night. Generally locals drive too fast here. Accidents are frequent, and often fatal. Don't worry I know the hot spots and the police know me. I was the mayor a couple of years ago and know all the officers this side of the island.

'But thank you Maria,' He kissed the back of her hand. As they drove through the moonlit Lanzarote landscape,

Maria was relieved that Dieter had turned down her offer to drive; with the glare of the oncoming cars' headlights and the unfamiliar roads, it was hazardous.

*

The following morning after breakfast, they met with Kamlish; the man with the boat. Maria was up early and had a little stroll around the marina. Set in amongst the rocky landscape, the marina was already very hot. It was like a burning cauldron. She had thought about taking a short walk but the road out was up a very steep hill and the sun was so hot she though better of it.

Some of the cafes were opening up but there were very few people around; mainly those who were preparing their boats for sea. Looking over the harbour wall Maria noted that some pretty large breakers were crashing about causing smaller craft to return to safety. It was awhile since she sailed and wondered how her sea-legs and stomach would cope.

TWENTY ONE

FUERTEVENTURA

The men met at the boat and made preparations for departure; Kam, as he was known, had deckhands to crew, so it would seem that he did not do a lot of hands-on work himself. Gregg had a lot of experience with boats as well as planes. He used to skipper boats off the southern Californian coast.

Maria had sailed a fair bit with her Uncle Pedro back home, so all in all everything should be 'plain sailing'.

Dieter admitted that his first choice would be to fly, but he was game for the trip and apparently had to rendezvous in Fuerteventura.

Roughly a two-and-a-half-hour trip depending on tides, they would be there for lunch; the weather was set fair-ish. The boat was essentially a motor-sailer and was well capable of coping with the weather, so they had the option to use the sails. That would be a matter of personal choice, dependant on many factors but most likely, speed was of the essence.

Maria strategically positioned herself close by Dieter; he would be her guide she reasoned. She always enjoyed learning from informed sources. They left the quite extreme heat of the marina and soon the cooling breeze tempted Gregg to offer the possibility of sailing; but Kam declined in favour of motoring.

'Passing Playa Quemada towards the headland at Papagayo, the well-known nudist beach. To starboard we have a good line of sight to the Fred Olsen ferry leaving Playa Blanca Harbour bound for Coralleco on Fuerteventura.' Dieter knew the waters well and was happy to oblige. The sea roughened up some but the boat was more than capable of coping with that. He continued as tour guide.

'We're approaching Isla de Lobos, inhabited only by seals (*lobos*), then we head straight to Coralleco.' However, as they made their approach Gregg and Kam for some reason had a change of plan and decided to put into Caleta de Fustes, a smaller port further down the coast. It would be necessary to go ashore by the inflatable tender.

Kam knew the owner of a great restaurant right on the seafront in Caleta, where they dined regally. Gregg naturally would accept nothing less; he never roughed it wherever he went with his friends. She loved that bit about him.

The afternoon was slowly melting into early evening; the men had yet another plan which involved leaving her at the restaurant whilst they disappeared to go elsewhere;

buttock-clenching time for her once again. It had never been discussed openly so was a total surprise to her.

She had firmly planted herself on a sun-lounger with an inexhaustible supply of liquor and had no intention of moving in any event.

'Maria. so sorry but we have to go and meet some people on some really boring business deal. You know how it is by now don't you? But we won't be gone too long.' Gregg explained.

'Yeah Gregg you're cool, I'll just sit and write and read. Probably have a doze,' she replied.

'Make sure you've got good sunscreen on. The sun here is very strong and with wind it's even stronger than Mexico and California.' They left; she felt quite relieved as inwardly she laughed at his apparent interest in her welfare. He was an expert at re-framing conversation to his advantage.

She had long since resigned herself to the fact that she was an accessory; that was not going to change, no matter how much she resented it. She was part of the fixtures and fittings would be her fate and she had to accept that. He had not denied that was the case.

As she sat alone without the presence of Gregg, she gave free range to her emotions; she wanted to formulate a plan not just to move on and escape from Gregg, but a plan of how best she could manage her affairs without him. There was a great deal more to this man than she was able to discover on her own.

The discovery of the book which had caused Gregg to fly into a rage only served to make her more curious. The book with a Nazi swastika on the binder. She had done some homework on the Canary Islands and in particular the Island's' wartime involvement and association with Nazi- high-ranking officers.

The waitress approached. 'Can I get you anything, *senorita*?'

'Actually, yes. My name is Maria. What's your name?' she asked, as she went on her own fishing expedition. She had learned at the feet of the master, Gregg.

'My name is Eloise but I prefer to known as Ellie,' she replied.

'Ellie tell me have you always lived here or are you from the mainland as so many seem to be?' she asked.

'My family go back three generations on this island. My father knows everything about the island,' she continued.

'I've been researching stories from World War Two for some time, especially about the occupation by Germans here at that time. I know that the German submarines used to come into the Canaries to replenish their stores and I believe munitions,' Maria said enquiringly.

Ellie came in. 'Yes, my father is the one you should speak with, he knows a lot of that stuff. Hitler financed the Spanish Revolution under Franco and created chaos in the Peninsula, but also had quite an influence in our affairs here.

'German high command used to come here and have wild parties in a big house down in Gandia. A German guy built a house there, you can find a book about that.

'The area was, and still is, full of mystery. It was

rumoured that experimentation on humans took place, but it was impossible to check.

'Security was tough and there was a fence right across Gandia to stop the locals passing, right up until 1950. It's still a strange and mysterious place even today. My father won't go anywhere near there.' She finished and returned to work; the boss had been watching her.

The men returned from their private rendezvous quite animated and not giving any clue as to where they had been.

Maria felt rather smug, as she had managed to elicit quite a lot of information about the secret side of the island from Ellie, and she felt no inclination to share her discovery with anyone.

Unless her imagination had got the better of her, Maria believed she saw Gregg give a Nazi salute to the man who picked them up earlier. Not a full stand-up *Heil Hitler'* salute, but that raising the forearm at a right angle, palm facing out salute; Hitler style. 'Weird lot for sure, you and your secret pals, Gregg,' she muttered.'

As she was totally unaware of their next move and having consumed a considerable amount of alcohol throughout the day, she grabbed the initiative and quite aggressively enquired.

'Does anyone have any idea about where we are going now?' Ashore or sleeping on board would be a start.'

Clearly somewhat taken aback by this remark, Gregg gave her a look of disapproval and, in an attempt to redress the balance of power amongst his cronies, said in a patronising tone. 'All in good time, my dear. You'll be told where you're going.'

Totally uninhibited by the amount of alcohol she had put away through the afternoon, that remark was going to be challenged. She came right out with it. She let him have it with both barrels.

'Screw you, Holdsworth, you patronising jerk. Who the hell do you think you are? don't you ever talk to me like that. EVER.' The silence was intense, as people shuffled about uncomfortably until Kam suggested they go back on board and discuss plans.

Crossing the stretch of water in the inflatable in the dark, Maria actually feared for her life, especially as Gregg reached out to help her aboard. The pair found a space to be alone just as his satellite phone sprung into life.

It was his wife, Cynth, calling from San Diego. 'Gregg, it's Cynth. Got some really bad news. Ricky has been involved in a multiple car crash on the freeway.'

'Oh my God, what happened? How is he? Where is he?' Gregg responded in shock.

'We don't know all the details but he's been seriously injured and been taken to the military hospital in San Diego.' Cynth replied.

'The military hospital! Is it *that* serious? What the hell happened to him?' Gregg was puzzled.

'It appears that he was taking his new girlfriend to the base to show her where you were once based, and a truck carrying fruit up from Mexico overturned spilling it's load all across the freeway, causing a whole bunch of cars to collide with one another and Rick was caught up in the mayhem,' Cynth explained.

'So what are they saying about his injuries?' Gregg nervously asked.

'His legs are damaged, but he has lost consciousness. That's their main concern. The paramedics from the base recognised him as our boy and got him straight into their hospital right away,' she said with gratitude.

'Okay look, I'm in the Canaries right now but I'll get a flight from somewhere to get right back immediately. Would you let Ben Gonzales know right away? Try and stay positive and be there for the kids. Love you, babe. We'll get him safe, please God.'

Gregg finished and immediately went into rescue mode, phoning his contacts to find the most accessible flights back to the USA, and his influential medical contacts to ensure the best possible care would be available. He knew that scheduled flights from Fuerteventura would not be an option, and although Barcelona to San Diego would be possible, it would take up valuable time.

Taking him to one side, Maria apologised for her outburst and suggested he concentrate on getting back home and she would do likewise. She wished the family well and said she would pray for his son. They kissed and sort of made up, with Gregg giving her the company credit card, and sharing a cab to El Matorral Airport, Puerto del Rosario, where she got a scheduled flight, whilst Gregg made arrangements for a private flight to San Diego.

TWENTY-TWO

BARCA BUST-UP

Maria now felt quite at home in Barcelona; she liked the locals and their strong sense of solidarity and Catalan identity. She believed that they had a proud tradition of solidarity. The Catalan language, culture and their outlook on life was unique.

She felt the city growing on her, but she still needed to get her life on an even keel. The extraordinary events of recent weeks had left her in a state of confusion; she seriously needed to re-evaluate her life in general.

After the drama of the accident with Gregg's son in San Diego, he managed to get back and help to organise Rick's treatment and subsequent recovery plan. Although concerned for Gregg's family, Maria had fun organising her own trip back to base in Barcelona; It was good to spend some time away from Gregg and re-affirm some sense of independence.

Sharing the apartment worked well for both she and Leanne; they enjoyed each other's' company. They rarely met in the office and their roles were quite dissimilar.

Leanne's clients' were of a more domestic nature, not requiring travel out of the Spanish mainland.

As they lunched together, Maria picked up a slice of hand- carved Iberico ham to accompany yet another glass of prosecco. She told Leanne about the latest episode, culminating in Gregg flying home to be with his family.

'Leanne, I don't know about you but I'm tired of the job, the subterfuge and secrecy. The worry that we'll get a knock on the door some night and it will be the FBI or CIA, or even the local police.

'Is it just me or do you worry too?'

'Yeah, could be.'

'What's that supposed to mean, Leanne? *Yeah, could be?*'

'Well, we've both been getting a bit tetchy lately and perhaps were getting near a time for moving on?' Leanne suggested.

'Do you mean moving on together or separately?'

'Maria, you know I can't stand confrontations. They make me deeply uncomfortable and your irrational outbursts are becoming even more frequent. Look at this latest spat you had with Gregg. It was crazy. Not only was it rude but it was potentially dangerous. We neither one of us know of what these people are capable.

'It's about your drinking, Maria, which has increased so much in the last few months. We're not having fun anymore. Your mood and behaviour change so quickly and you get so angry and aggressive. It's very scary.'

She paused again for another swig.

'There, I've said it. I've been quite afraid to even discuss the subject but now we're facing facts, it seems the timing is right.'

'Well, Leanne, I think most of my *true* friends know I like a drink. It's in my culture, I'm Spanish, it comes with the territory. I suppose the question is what constitutes too much?'

Leanne sensing that the situation was escalating tried to soften the things a little. 'Don't you notice any change in yourself. You're starting to miss appointments at work and that's definitely not like you.' Leanne realised she had said the wrong thing.

At that, Maria flew into a rage and banged her glass on the coffee table. The glass shattered making a terrible noise. Screaming and crying, she tried to run to the kitchen for something to wipe up the mess but fell. The door bell sounded; no one had ever rung the door bell.

'Oh, hello, I'm from next door, Is everything all right? We heard an almighty crash and screams. Are you sure you're alright.'

'Yes, we're fine. Everything is under control, just a little too much wine, but we appreciate your concern. Thank you and please accept our apology,' Leanne said.

Calm eventually restored, Leanne, embarrassed by the neighbour's attention, sat for a while with realisation that the situation had deteriorated and needed action. She went to her bed and left Maria on the couch with the remnants of a bottle of wine.

*

The early-morning silence was broken by the sound of Maria vomiting in the bathroom. Leanne simply checked that she was all right and hastily prepared for work without a word being shared between them.

A lovely sun-filled morning, warm enough to wear summer clothes. Leanne made her way to the office. There was an energy in the streets, busy with locals and tourists going about their business.

Metal roller blinds noisily opened shops; road traffic was on the move. The "'bendy bus'" was gradually filling up with passengers as it slinked its' way through the city like giant caterpillar.

The tree-lined boulevards offered the prospect of a pleasant day's' shopping; alas, not for Leanne today. There was, she hoped, much work to be done especially if Maria was off sick.

Leanne was deeply uncomfortable carrying a sick feeling deep in her, worried and concerned for Maria, and their future together

Leanne's favourite café in la Ramblas was, as usual, very crowded and vibrant as customers eagerly awaited their fresh baked bread, croissant and coffee breakfast.

It was pure theatre; the grinding of the beans and, the hissing of the espresso machine combined with aromas was a total turn-on for Leanne, who could hardly wait to grab her goodies. She picked up her usual; *café con leche* and croissant, wishing she could tarry awhile. She knew it would be a difficult morning at work and was dreading it.

'*Buenas dias*' left and right to the girls in the office as she ran the gauntlet to the sanctuary of her desk. Quickly, she closed the door and composed herself. There was no sign of Maria in the office.

Snr. Gonzales wished her '*buena dia*.'

'I would like to have a word with you and Maria'

Leanne shuffled some paperwork and files around on her desk.

'Maria,?' he repeated.

'Erm… sorry, *senor* Gonzales, Maria has not arrived yet.'

He was a fair-minded man who was no stranger to conflict; his military background bore testament to that. Realising that Leanne was compromised, he tactfully withdrew.

'The moment Maria comes in, I want to see you both in my office, please.'

Leanne responded. '*Si senor.*'

Maria eventually turned up for work about an hour late. She looked very much the 'worse for wear' especially as she had also just experienced the noxious ride in the lift, nursing a hangover. She could barely hold her coffee in her shaking hand. They met with the boss.

'Ladies, I've been brought up to speed with your social situation, and want to move it on quickly. We all have issues. That's the nature of life, but I'm running a business and need full cooperation, a total commitment and efficiency.' They shuffled around uncomfortably, but were clearly relieved that he had not fired them on the spot.

'Maria, without going into detail, and I'm certainly not in the business of offering counselling, I believe at this moment you would possibly benefit from a short break from work, and perhaps take time to visit your family in Santander.

'I believe there are a number of issues you need to address before returning to work. We will monitor your progress as we go along, so don't worry about your pay. We will cover that for a period of three weeks so if you feel that's insufficient then you will have to finance an extension from your own resources.'

Pausing for a sip on his *café cortado,* and a puff of Havana cigar, he turned his attention to Leanne.

'Leanne, I would like you to take over Maria's clients until she returns and hopefully we can get back on track quickly. Take a little time this afternoon to make preparations. That's all. Thank you and God bless you, Maria.'

Relieved at the shortness and directness of the meeting, they were aware that the rest of the staff were enjoying the show at the pair's' expense.

After a little time to compose themselves they realised they must make the best of the chance to put matters right.

Maria took the initiative and politely addressed the boss. '*Senor* Gonzales, would you mind if we took a little time out in the cafe downstairs?'

'Certainly, that would be acceptable,' he agreed.

Taking him at his word, they left the office and were soon ensconced in the warmth and comfort of the café, away from the giggling girls in the main office.

Leanne looked through Maria's case files, only to discover that she had no new clients on her books. She had been away with Gregg for so long there had not been time to even discuss new clients. They both wondered how much or how little, *senor* Gonzales knew about Gregg's' activities. He never mentioned the Canarian fracas.

There were no new clients; it was the end of the month and neither of them had received their pay cheques. Since returning from the Canaries trip, Maria had not had any form of contact with Gregg.

The last she had heard from him was that he had to go home to deal with the family issue and she knew enough to leave well alone.

Neither of them was entirely sure about their next move.

As far as Maria was concerned, the trip north to her home was probably an opportunity not to be missed. She would need warm clothes for the north, a light suitcase and just go for it. Leanne would probably make herself available as usual, with very little actual work to carry out. Keeping a low profile would be her best policy.

They returned to the apartment after eating out, having made no progress on a plan. So another bottle was opened, and the pair just got very drunk. Maria was not so skilfully avoiding the real issue; her drinking!

'Tonight, I really do not wish to discuss my drinking issues but I need to contact my boss for some money to go north, and be at home with my lovely family.' She flounced around the apartment, bottle in one hand, glass in the other. Very drunk, very arrogant, and as Leanne knew;

very dangerous. She found Gregg's mobile number in her notebook and called. There was a long delay.

'Hi, Gregg long time no see; Everything good with you my handsome fly boy?' There was another pause; she could hear someone else's voice.

'For crying out loud, Maria, are you crazy? It's three in the morning. I'm in bed at home, you're on the wrong damn phone, crazy woman.'

'AAARGH, shit,' she screamed. 'I've really screwed up big time. Gregg's in bed with his wife in San Diego. I got the time wrong and used the wrong damn phone too. I'm really in the doggy doos. Better get moving before he puts out a contract on me,' she said to Leanne, half-jokingly.

She was upset, not only at Gregg hanging up on her but, that she had got the timing all wrong. Meticulously careful to keep their movements secret, she had probably blown their cover.

She was still mad at him an hour later. Drinking in her apartment, with little money. Totally stressed and paranoid she now imagined all kinds of scenarios the worst case being Gregg putting a contract out on her. Maria attempted to make plans to visit her parents. Too embarrassed to ask Leanne and too afraid to call Gregg, she realised her vulnerability, and was very afraid. She wondered if she would even get her monthly cheque after her recent drunken blunders.

All that had been decided was that she would leave work for three weeks and perhaps travel home, but she had not contacted home to check if that would be convenient.

But that had suddenly all changed with the blunder. She felt she needed to get out of town and go north.

Stuck between a rock and a hard place, she literally did not know which way to turn. The one constant for Maria was that she was in total denial of the fact that she had to quit drinking ; full stop. She sat and carried on drinking. Three days had elapsed since the meeting and still drinking she had been incapable of making a firm plan of action. She felt lonely and deserted.

Baffled at her own inability to get it together, she plucked up courage to call Gonzales for an advance of one week of her wages, which he agreed to without question.

She called home but there was no answer, and in her paranoid state she left a message and hung up. She called Leanne at work.

'Hello, Leanne. How's things going back at the ranch?' Maria joked.

'Hi, good to hear from you. How are you doing?' Leanne replied anxiously. She closed down her laptop; she wanted to try and help her friend, but was as puzzled as everyone else around her.

Maria, I'm very worried about you. Where are you now? What are you up to? The boss suggested I call you, which is odd but nice, I suppose,'

'Well I'm home in the apartment but planning to go north. I've just left a message with *mama* to see if it's okay to visit. Thought I might surprise her but then I changed my mind. Do a lot of that nowadays, can't make my mind up and then make the wrong decisions when I do.'

'Now, Maria listen to me,' Leanne responded, angrily. 'You promised everyone that you would address your drinking problem, but it seems you haven't even started.

'The boss has given you a lot of slack here and you'd be a mug not to grasp it. It's now three days and you're actually drinking more, rather than trying to cut down. The problem is getting worse and people who care about you want to help, but feeling useless they step back.'

'Everyone's getting on to me having a go at me. They don't understand how I feel. It's horrible and not fair, you don't know what it's like. I've tried to cut down and even managed to stop, but it doesn't last.'

'Okay' said Leanne, let's look at it now. Are you admitting that you need to stop drinking completely as an initial step forward? It's important.

'What you need to do is find another interest away from alcohol, which dominates your thoughts every day. You're sounding pretty drunk right now.'

'Oh yeah that sounds so easy. You say you understand but you don't have a clue. Drink is the only thing that takes away my pain and despair.'

'Maria, you're never going to move forward as long as you're so full of self-pity. Stop feeling sorry for yourself and be positive... hello, are you there?'

Maria hung up the phone, packed her bag and walked out, slamming the door. She bought a bottle of vodka, wrapped it in a brown paper bag, and said aloud, 'I'm not an alcoholic. I can quit anytime.'

Very worried for her, Leanne immediately drove back at speed to the apartment in a vain attempt to prevent her getting into further trouble. She was too late; Maria had gone and nobody knew to where.

She had no plan, very little money and her mental state was fragile. In her present state, she was placing herself at considerable risk of exploitation, and at the very worst, personal physical harm; but she recklessly ploughed on, determined to make the journey home to the north, with the odds of success pretty slim. It was Maria at her very worst; irrational, impetuous and compulsive; a recipe for disaster.

The one rational move she made at that point was the decision not to take her car out of the garage. It would be easy, she reasoned, to travel by public transport and save on her dwindling financial reserves. She made for the bus stop adjacent to the apartment block.

TWENTY-THREE

HEADING NORTH

She boarded the bus outside the apartment but had no idea how the system worked. She fumbled with money and a variety of debit cards, dropping several items from her bag onto the bus platform.

An elderly lady passenger sitting in the reserved seat got up to help her and eventually she managed to buy a ticket to the bus station in Barcelona, not before the lady passenger muttered as she smelled Maria's breath, '*Un poco temprano para beber*' (it's a little early for drinking.)

The journey started off well as Maria happily enjoyed the sights of the city for a while. Fortunately for Maria, her bus stop was the end of the line. She dozed off but the lady in the front seat aroused Maria with ' *Dios ayuda,*' *(*God help you.)

There was a tapas bar at the bus terminal, which Maria spotted the instant she alighted from the bus. As she headed straight towards it. She looked around and felt ashamed that she had come to this. A serious drop in her standards; she felt she was hitting a new low in her self-esteem.

She made straight for the toilet, which was grim, causing her to retch but not quite vomit.

'What am I doing in this dump?' she muttered. It was smoky, and dirty from screwed-up tissues thrown on the floor by tapas-eaters earlier in the day. The tables were in need of a good wipe-down; she felt unclean and ashamed.

A woman and two small children were eating their breakfast. Maria greeted them but they were unresponsive. The woman begrudgingly said hello but clearly did not encourage the children to speak with her; that gesture hurt her very much. The only other people were a couple of back-packers, who finished their drinks and dashed to make their bus in time. She was totally out of her comfort zone in this place; she shed a tear.

The scruffy barman in a greasy (once white) apron approached to ask Maria if she wanted to buy a drink. She looked at the blackboard behind the bar for guidance, but it was out of focus. He walked off, muttering obscenities before she could reply.

He swept some tissues as he went, so she called to him for a glass of house red wine, which he thumped down on the greasy table with a '*dos euros.*'

She asked him about times of buses, to be told he was 'nothing to do with the buses.'

The whole place depressed her, as she tried to read bus destinations and times from the TV screen hanging up behind the bar. She could not make it out; her eyes were blurred with tears. Spying an official-looking man in a bus station uniform. she got up to make enquiries, only to learn she had missed the early bus to Burgos. The journey time was eight hours. There she would need to change for Santander, another three-hours journey.

She thanked the official, and with her head spinning she had been quite unable to cope, she turned to be met by the grumpy barman shouting in her face. '*DOS EUROS POR FAVOR.*'

'*This is a bloody nightmare and I've hit a brick wall before I even get started, I may have to kill that rude, scruffy joke of a barman.*' She paid the two euros and sat bewildered.

Her head in turmoil, she glanced around mulling over the recent events that had led to being in this situation. She blamed herself for the flare-up in the Canaries, but she also reasoned that the fallout from that was not her fault.

Gregg had to return home and that was his problem. She decided that this venue and her state of mind were not helping her to resolve the immediate issue of, '"to bus or not to bus."'

Being a '"kept woman"' had suited her; the benefits were incredible. The lifestyle had been exciting and very luxurious. Perhaps, she pondered, it was all over; had she thrown it all away?' She felt foolish.

Gregg had hurt her when he hung up the phone on her, but it had been a defining moment. She could easily have played the needy woman, but drunk as she was, she realised that she would be back on the old merry-go-round again.

'No more lies and deception,' she he said out loud as the barman shrugged his shoulders.

The journey north would be complicated. So far, she had not even made preliminary enquiries about the times and duration of the bus journeys.

Tempting as it was to return to the apartment, which on the face of it would be the simplest option, she said NO. With tremendous determination coming from way down inside her, she said NO.

'I'm not letting him get away with that anymore, I'm going to just walk away from that life. I'll find the solution once I get back to my roots in the north, that's where my strength lays. I will find the right pathway with renewed purpose I'll find a way.' she muttered.

Forever the opportunist, Maria also knew that this fine-looking man who had just entered the bar might just offer another option. He approached and asked if the seat by her was free. 'That was music to her ear.'

She had always used her special ability to assess situations very clearly (when sober). The problem was that drink had befuddled her, so she needed to work a little harder on her intuitive skills.

She knew that he would have spotted her bag under the seat and put that into his strategic plan. She would only be in the bus station for one reason. Maria decided to take the initiative.

'Yes, the seat's free, I'm just trying to make a decision about travelling by bus; It's not something I would normally do, so I'm pretty confused.'

He accepted the invitation and took the seat.

'Hi, my name is Juan Carlos, but please call me Juan or JC. I just popped in for a quick *cortado (coffee)*. Perhaps I may be able to assist you?' he asked.

'Pleased to meet you, Juan. I'm Maria. Confused, indecisive and getting more fed up by the minute. Only got myself to blame, had a row with my boyfriend and stormed out in a rage and now dealing with the consequences, or not dealing with them would be more appropriate,' she blurted out in one drunken breath; he knew right away that she was drunk.

They laughed, as they were both aware of how that sounded. The pair made small-talk; it was not complicated.

He ordered wine for her and an apple juice mineral water for himself. She declined the offer of food but gratefully accepted the wine. She intellectually understood what was going on and knew where it may lead; she had always loved the journey into the unknown. The problem for Maria was that although very astute when sober when drunk her fail-safe filters malfunctioned. She knew to open up to an extent, but maintain a background story that there was a powerful man with many contacts, who could at any moment intervene and rescue her.

This journey would be different. She knew to be cautious.

The decision to walk away slipped away as fast as did the wine; she seemed incapable of resisting and helping herself out of the hole she had been digging.

It was old behaviour and she was nervous with it, going on for years, long before she had even met Gregg. Perversely, she continued drinking in the full knowledge that trouble may be lurking around the corner. She reasoned she would treat this man with caution but at the same time see what he had to offer.

'So, Maria, where are you trying to get to and what seems to be the problem getting there if I may ask?'

'Well, my folks live in a village not very far from Santander, but that's a long way from here and as far as I can make out, I would have to change at Burgos. It's going to take forever, so I'm doubting the whole idea now. It's far too complicated,' she admitted.

'Do you visit home frequently or is this just a one-off arrangement?' Juan enquired.

Feeing suspicious Maria replied, 'Yes, we keep in touch all the time. I visit frequently, usually with my friend. Unfortunately he can't make it today, business reasons hence my reason for being here on my own. I always keep in touch all the way by phone calls and texts.'

Maria tried to impress Juan by pretending she understood the information screen on the wall. She stood, head cranked, scanning the screen, and sat down again.

'I missed the early bus and now I've got an interminable wait for the next one,' she said, rather unconvincingly.

'Well I may be too presumptuous, so please tell me if I am. I'm driving to Burgos delivering a car to a client, so I'm suggesting that I could take you there, but you would still need to make your own way from there.

'I'll tell you more about myself, unless you say no to the whole idea. Just to let you know, I don't normally hang around bus stations trying to pick up girls,' Juan said.

'That sounds great, Juan. Tell me more, then I'll let you know who I am.' Maria agreed.' She liked the idea of a fresh adventure.

I'm Juan Carlos, thirty-nine years old, single, living in Madrid. I'm a freelance professional driver with my own businesses. I dabble somewhat in the stock market. However, my main business is helping very well-off clients, acquire bespoke, exclusive fine cars. I handle the finances and personally deliver the cars. Mainly, my business is within Europe but occasionally I have clients from the USA and the Emirates.'

Maria accepted this story as feasible. 'Wow, Juan, that's a bit like my job in many ways, providing bespoke personal services to well- off clients.'

'Well, today, I'm taking a very nice car to a client in Burgos. I could take you partway if you fancied that I'm driving a '"top-end"' Mercedes sports saloon. Perhaps we could travel together.'

Maria was doing her best to process all this, but the wine had slowed her faculties. Undecided, she struggled, but she knew that with another glass or two, the decision would be easy. She would go. Playing for time, she asked him. May I ask how much have you had to drink today?'

'Did you not notice? I have only been mineral water and fruit juice I can't afford to touch any alcohol in my line of business.' Juan explained.

'That's not a problem for me. I'm making these journeys all the time. It's my business, that's what I do,' Juan reiterated. 'The only downside for you is unfortunately you would have to make your own way from Burgos to

Santander. I have another car to take from Burgos to St Moritz in Switzerland.'

Maria loved the very sound of that. Adventure beckoned; she was beginning to experience similar feelings of arousal to those Gregg had always stirred in her.

A good-looking man, fancy car, driving through the night. What's not to like? She felt adventure, and she had always been a seeker.

Her alcohol-induced dream-like state of adventure was suddenly broken as Juan suddenly jumped to his feet.

'If you fancy it, I'll get a couple of *bocadillos* (rolls) and coffees for the journey. Do you eat ham?'

Taken by surprise, her head not working with the heart too well, Maria blurted out, '*Erm…si, senor, es perfecto, sin mostaza, (no mustard) por favor.*' She didn't like mustard with her ham.

Juan slapped a fifty euro note on the bar and made for the car, parked safely nearby in a secure garage.

'Wait here for me. I'll be back in front in ten minutes,' Juan said.

With the perfect opportunity, Maria quickly grabbed another drink. Calling to the grubby waiter, she ordered another drink. '*Camarer, un cognac doble por favor*' *(double brandy please)*. She loved barking that command at him/to him.

The Grumpy, scruffy waiter begrudgingly shuffled through the half-swept screwed-up tapas papers, littering the floor, and banged the cognac on the table.

Nonchalantly, he picked up a broom, swept the floor and muttered an abuse. He had witnessed this scene many times; usually, hookers and drug addicts playing-out the role.

Maria looked around the bar; she was the only customer. Nervously she looked at the TV monitor in the pretence that she was in control but she had trouble focusing and could not comprehend the information. Maria fully realised what she was doing. Knowing the risk she was unable to check and stop herself.

She felt very alone and exposed once more. The TV, the only concession to modernity in the place, did nothing to comfort her. She felt the grumpy *camarero*'s eyes burning through her.

'I'll go to the toilet and break this awful atmosphere,' but once in there she wished she had not bothered; it was grim. The silence was suddenly broken by the sound of a loud car horn.

'Thank God,' she blurted out. She grabbed the remnants in the bottle and headed for the car.

'I don't think so, Maria.' Juan said. Embarrassed, she sheepishly took the bottle back to the table and ran to Juan in the car, with a quick, '*hasta luego*' (see you) to the grumpy waiter. She had no idea if the fifty euros covered the bill, and could not have cared less.

Juan was not kidding about the car; it was *exclusive* and then some.

The trunk opened automatically; she threw her bag in and jumped in the passenger seat like an excited teenager. Scarcely had she buckled up when she felt her back being pressed into the super luxurious passenger seat, as they took off to the roar of the seven-litre Mercedes sports engine. Maria's sense of relief was palpable as she escaped from the oppression of the bar.

Juan knew the backstreets, alleyways and roads by heart; in no time at all, they were out of the cobble-stoned streets and onto the main highway.

Maria was no stranger to speed. With style, many of her ex-"'boyfriends,'" had driven high-end classy cars at speed to try and impress her. She admitted that it did work for her to an extent. Gregg had a number of expensive toys; Lamborghini, Aston Martin, and Jaguars, but this car and this man driving, was in a different class.

She knew he was not trying to impress, but she was impressed anyway. Negotiating the traffic at speed in the city was really cool, and she wondered if he possibly had police driving connections.

Leaving the city, they were soon on the Autopista AP-2 via Zaragoza, just as the last rays of sunshine of the beautiful autumnal evening faded from view over the Sierras.

The sun was behind them as they left the urban outskirts of the city; it lit up a quite wonderful panorama across the Mediterranean. They turned northwards as Maria took a sideways glance to check out the vista and get a closer look at Juan.

She had not really taken him in before in her nervous state back in the bar. Behind his very expensive sunglasses. he was a good- looking man; she began to relax.

The Merc. at around 120 miles per hour, purred like a soft well-upholstered tiger just waiting to pounce. She had no real interest in cars, but she knew class when she saw it, and this was "'way up there.'"

Soft classical music played over the sound system; the experience was unique. The appearance of speed was minimised to such an extent, that she felt as if she could just open the door and step out.

The sunshine had completely gone; the sky ahead towards the mountains was black, foreboding and ominous.

Maria had been dozing in and out of sleep for possibly the best part of an hour; she awoke. 'So, Juan, what's the verdict on this car, Will it do?' she said, laughingly.

'Well, I have to tell you, this is as good as it gets,' he replied.

The coffee was all gone but they had the sandwiches to eat.

'Are you hungry yet, Maria? I'm starving.' Juan asked.

'Well, I have to admit I am, but didn't want to suggest we eat the *boccadillos* for fear of messing up the car, it's so pristine,' she replied.

'Don't worry about that. It'll be professionally valeted before it's presented to the client. Get the sandwiches out of the bag behind your seat. There's a couple of napkins in there too.'

There was just about enough room for the bag. as this car was only really designed for two.

'We'll press-on as we're making good time, and eat when we get there,' he said. The *boccadillos* were great and just in time. Maria, however, could really do with a comfort break; she had not had one since the grotty bar by the bus station but was hesitant in asking him to stop.

The black, ominous-looking clouds decided to dump thousands of litres of water combined with hail-stones in a matter of minutes. It was so loud they could not hear themselves speak but it did not last.

'You okay Maria bit of a squall blew in there? Juan asked. She took a while to reply as she was visibly quite shaken by the suddenness of the squall.

'Don't know how you managed to see where you were going in that, it was truly scary,' she said

'Oh, I was relying on you for the directions. I couldn't see a thing in front of me. I didn't have a clue, Maria.' They laughed together.

'No, seriously, that's very, very impressive. Well done, you hardly deviated at all.' she said.

'Well, the windscreen wipers on this piece of kit are the same as they use for Jumbo jets from Boeing. Just one single wiper right in the centre gets rid of water, hail snow. Brilliant design, are you interested in cars?' He asked. Maria was feeling much more relaxed with Juan now. 'Well, I understand what you're telling me. I really appreciate the aesthetic quality of fine workmanship, but I've never felt the need to own an expensive car.

'However, I did have a company car in Barcelona which was very nice, I loved that, for sure. I have to say, however, certain aspects of this car and... ' (she nodded to Juan) ... 'the driver intrigue me. On the *autopista*, you're clearly using cruise control. That much I do know, but there's something else going on when the car changes speed every so often.'

'Ah, well-spotted, Maria. That's the radar detection system which automatically slows the car when it picks up police radar from approximately half a kilometre out. It's an option if you want it, and as many of these roads have radar control It's quite useful.'

Maria was impressed with his choice of words, avoiding the term '"speed traps."' *smart guy this JC.*

'Juan I'm really sorry to ask as I know you're on a mission but I really need a comfort break.'

'Maria, thought you'd never ask. Breaking my neck for a pee. Next service area, we'll pull over.'

Maria suspected that Juan probably had a comprehensive knowledge of the Spanish road system, as he slowed to pull off the motorway into a service area.

She made a dash for the toilet, to be confronted by a massive queue of seniors who had arrived by coach, having made an unscheduled stop due to the road ahead being flooded.

'Oh my gosh, I'm going to wet myself if I can't jump this queue, Juan. I'm that desperate.'

'Don't worry and get stressed. I know the manager, Domingo, here. I'll have a word. I'm sure he will help us.' Not entirely surprised at this, Maria seemed to have acquired another man of similar capabilities to Gregg, very resourceful when required.

Sure enough, within minutes, Maria found herself comfortably sitting in the managers' loo, quietly singing, 'It's not what you know, but who you know in life, that gets you by.'

Meeting up in the main concourse, lots of senior folk milled around and waited for instructions, dependent on traffic reports ahead.

'Maria why don't you get some coffee and anything else you want while I have a little business chat with Dom the manager? Won't be long, then we can get back on the road. It's clear ahead now.'

Maria was relieved, but felt unsure of their plans at this point. She picked up the drinks and as she paid, received a rather knowing look from the woman on the till. Her hands were shaking uncontrollably and she felt really embarrassed. She was aware that this tremor had been going on for some time; she was in withdrawals and had been noticed. It made her feel really sad.

With prior knowledge that the cure is topping up with alcohol of any description, Maria hurried to the gift shop, which thankfully was crowd-free. She bought a small bottle of vodka, in the mistaken belief that the smell of vodka could not be detected. She paid on her debit card so Juan Carlos would not know.

She scurried back to her table and bought a glass of brandy to authenticate the smell of alcohol as Juan returned. He drank the cold coffee and gulped down the Danish pastry with a 'let's do a final comfort call and get this show back on the road before the coach sets off.'

The Merc was soon purring along towards Burgos.

What sort of music do you like, Maria, Classical, jazz, pop, mainstream, country? Got it all on the system, you name the tune, we got it down.'

As she tried to come up with an answer to the simple question, Maria was miles away with a hundred and one thoughts going around in her head. She expected the question to be coming from Gregg; this other voice had her totally confused.

'Classical piano, please... Juan.' She had to think hard to remember the new man in her life's name.

She felt a moment of sadness as she missed Gregg. The pair had shared many an adventure together and been in similar situations to this one; *perhaps she would never see him again.*

After a while, as Chopin's *Nocturnes* softly filled the Merc, Maria exclaimed. 'Oh my gosh, I've never heard such high-quality sound in a car's system. It's like a live performance.' The car's' engine was so quiet, and the road noise was so negligible; they just purred along to Chopin. Nothing was said as the kilometres drifted by.

'Well, you know what they say. You get what you pay for. People pay a lot of money to get a car like this, and the sounds have to be perfect. It's been fun having you along for the trip, Maria. Wondering what plans, if any, you've got for your on-going journey to Santander ?' Juan asked.

Hesitating, she had to work that one out, and wondered how to reply. She was in withdrawals and needed to face reality soon.

Maria eventually replied, in a somewhat incoherent non-committal manner; Juan turned off the sounds to hear her reply.

'Erm... I'm not altogether sure, to be honest. I suppose I've been very foolish.' She paused.

'There's a lot going on for me. I don't want to give you a lot of boring detail. Things have not been going well for me in Barcelona and I just wanted to get out of there and go home to *mama*.'

She turned her head to one side, away from Juan, quietly sobbing into her handkerchief.

They travelled on in silence for a while until the silence became unbearable for both of them; Juan turned on the radio once more to break the silence.

He sympathised with Maria but had no solution to offer. Part of him wished he had not even asked her along, but, then he also liked her a lot and wanted to help. He hated the fact that she was clearly an alcoholic and needed help. He knew she would have to reach her own rock bottom.

Foremost in Juan Carlos' mind was the car being delivered in pristine condition, given the horrendous amount of rain through which it had been driven, quite a challenge. His usual facility had never let him down before, but he had never handed them such a dirty car in the past; it had to be in the best possible condition.

The car had one previous owner; thus, it would save the new buyer thousands of euros. It had ridiculously low mileage and was only being sold so the owner could purchase the new model with all the latest updates installed.

'The news and weather will be coming on the radio in a minute.' Juan eventually said. It was the best he could offer at the time. He needed a little time to try and work something out for Maria.

The main item on the news was about disturbances in the Basque region, the stock market figures and how the director of a well-known travel company in Barcelona had been arrested in the United States on drug smuggling charges, and un-American activities. The weather forecast for the region tomorrow stated it would be fine and sunny, with no rain forecast.

'Hear that, Maria? Weather for tomorrow, fine and sunny, no rain,' Juan thankfully said. 'I'll take the car to be valeted first thing and deliver it to the client.'

Juan Carlos had an arrangement with the *Hotel Tres Coronas*, Burgos; a smart four-star hotel close to the centre of town, the food and wine cellar were both very acceptable. Juan had been using it for years and they more or less guaranteed him a room. His car delivery operation included two other drivers in Spain and several in other countries. *The Tres Coronas* Hotel was used as an unofficial midway office-rendezvous; the system worked well.

Juan made a phone call on ear buds for some privacy,

'*Hola*, Miguel it's Juan Carlos, the car man, I hope you are well and have a room for me for tonight' he asked.

'Well, hello Juan. Good to hear from you. Business must be good, back again so soon. Yes, you're in luck. We have one room left. There's a fiesta going on for a couple of days so we're really busy but you can have your usual room. I held it back just in case.' Miguel confirmed.

'Maria, I've just booked a room for tonight in a place I always use when in the Burgos area, good accommodation and excellent food. I've got to get the car valeted early in the morning so need an early night. Miguel's a great guy, very congenial,' Juan explained.

Maria was slowly taking in the situation. She really needed another drink but she was unable to get at the vodka in her bag, without Juan spotting her.

The numbing effect of the earlier brandy was wearing off. She now realised her dependence on the substance to keep body and mind together. Drinking had no longer any social pleasure; it had become a necessity. Her hands shook as she fumbled around in her handbag and Juan spotted this.

'That's not so good, looks like you need another belt,' Juan said. 'Maria felt mortified as the situation had become so apparent. She once again wept into her handkerchief.

'I know, I feel terrible and don't know how to handle it. I've been covering it up for so long now, I'm tired of it. I don't know which way to turn.'

There was a long silence.

Eventually, Maria asked. 'Do you think Miguel would have a room for me? I've got myself into this situation mainly through my drinking. I've got nowhere to go. I never planned anything. Now I'm asking for help. What does he charge? I mean, can't blame it all on alcohol but my behaviour…'

Her voice was incoherent and gradually petered out.

Juan came in with, 'Maria, just stop talking for a while. I'll pull over. There's layby up ahead. We can talk then.'

They drove on in silence through flooded areas of the motorway, splashing through enormous puddles with a *whoosh,* hardly slowing at all, and eventually pulled into the lay-by. Juan turned off the engine. 'Maria, put your seat in the upright position.' Juan asked of her. 'Let's have a little chat, he said.

Pulling her seat upright, Maria sheepishly looked up from staring into her lap. She started. 'Juan, I really want… '

'No, please just listen for a minute' Juan interrupted. 'I'm not stupid, and I hope not insensitive, so I know what's going on. We're both playing a game here, both looking for fun and a little adventure?

'I'm as guilty as you are of being complicit in the act, but right now without looking at the bigger picture, your alcoholism, we need to address the accommodation issue.'

At that, Maria burst into floods of tears and sobbed uncontrollably. 'I'm not a bloody alcoholic. *How dare you! You… you don't even know me. How dare you!*'

There was another long period of silence after which, Juan considered, a discrete length of time he spoke.

'Right, Maria, two things. First, you're in withdrawal. My father was an alcoholic, so I know about that, and it will help you temporarily if you take some alcohol. As a short-term relief, take a shot or two from that bottle you've hidden in your bag. At least it will stop the shaky hands, but in the long term you need professional help.' he concluded. 'Believe me!'

'What bottle are you talking about?' Maria came back at him.

'Oh, come on now, Maria, The game's up. You need to own up to the problem, I've seen the bottle in your bag.'

Maria slowly opened the bag, unscrewed the lid and took a slug. The car was permeated with the smell of vodka.

'Yes, Maria, vodka does smell, so top yourself up and put it away. I don't need the smell of it in the car. Secondly with regard to the hotel, I'm happy to share with you. There's a bed settee in the room. I'll take that and promise you no *hanky-panky,* on my honour.' That's the offer on the table.'

Maria, angry initially, was astute enough to see the offer of hospitality could not be turned down; she needed a bed for the night. She decided to share a little more of herself. as she reasoned it might be useful for him to understand her concerns. Having taken a drink, she was once again more confident, and less shaky.

'Thank you, Juan. I gratefully accept that offer. However, I think it's only fair that I say a little more about my concerns. This current situation, unfortunately, is a pattern of old destructive behaviour of mine. Get myself drunk and end up in bed with someone. Regret it the next day, and after feeling sick and throwing up, look for another drink to steady myself, mentally and physically.

'It's a dreadful merry-go-around, and while I'm sick and tired of it, I've not found a solution. I would dearly like tonight not to be another one of those nights, Juan.'

Nothing was said; He fired up the Merc and it was soon purring as Juan swept-back onto the minor roads towards the lights of the city and *El Tres Coronas.*

'Maria, all I can say is this. If you want me to sleep on the sofa bed, I am more than willing to do so. Just say the word. I have never in all my life taken advantage of anyone with regards to imposing my will upon them and am not about to start today on that path.' Juan said as he skilfully steered the car towards Burgos.

The car radio came on as Juan switched on the ignition and she sort of half-recalled a news item she had heard earlier. She asked Juan if they could hear the news again when it came back on air. Juan agreed and said.

'How are you feeling now, Maria? You seem to have settled down considerably, the drink obviously working for the nervous system, shaking practically stopped. Sadly, I've seen it all before. As I said earlier, my *papa* was a chronic alcoholic, so *mama* and I lived with that for many years.'

'That's so sad, Juan. Did he manage to get it under control?' Maria enquired.

'No, sadly, he never accepted the fact that he could not quit on his own and needed help. Despite the best efforts of his doctor, he relapsed time and again and became so ill with liver, kidney, heart issues and claudication in his legs. He was a walking dead man. He passed away aged forty, still drinking up to his final moments. A total waste of a life, and a tragedy.

'Some would say I should not have allowed you to drink, as that makes me an enabler. So although I wanted to stop you from shaking, I would urge you to seek proper treatment and not go down the same road.' Juan finally paused as the news came on the radio.

Maria listened more intently this time to hear that, *"… the CEO of a Barcelona-based travel company, MexTex, has been arrested by the FBI in San Diego California, on drugs charges. Spanish detectives are keen to interview the two business partners and anyone else who may have had dealings with the company."*

Maria shuddered at the news statement and temporarily froze up quite unable to speak; her head was in total chaos. Juan had been speaking to her, but with no response whatsoever he drove on. Maria, you are clearly very upset at the news item. Is there anything I can do to help you?' Juan enquired.

'*Dios omnipotente*' (God almighty) she replied. Juan decided not to press the issue; they continued in an uncomfortable silence to the hotel. 'God Almighty! ' she repeated.

TWENTY-FOUR

BURGOS

Miguel was on reception at *Los Tres Coronas* and warmly greeted them as he handed them the key to room twenty-three. 'Dinner at eight, Juan, and of course for you also *senorita…?*' 'Maria', she answered.

The hotel was centuries-old; sandstone walls and low timber beams. The hall and lounge featured an open log fire, whilst glistening suits of armour guarded the building. Their room faced the busy main square where folk were enjoying the stalls selling all manner of goods; food, souvenirs, religious items, tee-shirts and general clothes.

Room twenty-three was adequate for two, with ensuite and just enough space; She threw her holdall on the bed and flopped on top of the duvet.

'Maria, I'll take the first shower, if that's okay with you. We can get changed for dinner. I did have an idea, which I'll run by you if you're feeling up to it later.'

'That's cool JC, I'm just going to call my friend Leanne to let her know I'm safe.' She threw in the familiar term JC for fun. He didn't appear to notice.

Leanne answered the phone and was shocked that Maria had left town so suddenly.

'I'm okay just needed to get away from everything for a while Leanne, have you heard the news?'

'Maria, you're priceless. You disappear off the map, everyone's worried for your safety and you casually phone up about the news. Yes, of course I've heard the news. Has anyone contacted you yet?'

'No, not yet Leanne. Do you think they will contact us then?'

'Wouldn't be surprised, you'd better make sure you've got your story right, and don't give anything away. Just remember what we discussed previously, plead ignorance. We've never been privy to the inner sanctum. Where the hell are you, girl?'

'We're in Burgos. I'm making my way back home to see my folks by road.' Maria explained.

'Oh no... who's the *WE*?' Leanne joked.

'Tell you later, must go. The shower is free.'

'You know what you are *chica... perra sucia* (a dirty bitch).'

They both laughed out loud.

'Shower's free, Maria,' Juan called out.

After they had showered and dressed, they had a drink in the lounge. Juan came up with a pre-dinner plan. Santo Domingo de Silos, a stunning medieval village was less than half an hour away. He suggested they could make it there and back in time for dinner. She thought that was a great idea.

She had heard of the monastery from her school days, remembering that the architecture was admired the world over.

Named after an eleventh-century saint, Dominic de Silos, the original was about seventh century. She especially remembered as she was due to visit with her school in her final year but was unwell and missed the trip.

It did not disappoint, and as they wandered around, Maria had many happy memories of her school days; her faith, she believed, had sustained her despite her shortcomings.

Sitting in the church, they eagerly awaited the entrance of the Benedictine monks; dressed in black cowelled robes, they processed through the body of the church, illuminated solely by candlelight.

Singing Gregorian chants in the spine-tingling atmosphere of this historic and venerable old building, they were loath to leave; but dinner was at eight and Juan had reserved trout, which was apparently in short supply.

As they returned to the car, an English couple was checking it out making well informed comments; Juan clicked the doors open with the remote control, surprising the gentleman.

'Oh, is that your car? very nice too. Expensive bit of kit there eh?' he asked.

Juan replied, 'No it's not mine, a bit out of my league, I'm afraid. I'm delivering it in the morning to the new owner. Are you a motor enthusiast, sir?'

'Well, yes, to a point. I have a vintage Saab convertible, that one over there. My wife and I have been touring Spain for the last three weeks and are on the last leg of our epic tour.

'The Saab never missed a beat, all the way, three thousand and five hundred miles so far. We're catching the ferry from Santander to Plymouth tomorrow, then back to Kent. Truly wonderful trip.'

'Sounds fabulous. Take it you're retired, or as we say in Spain, *jubilados?* Much nicer word than retired.'

'*Si, senor somos jubilados*' (we're retired) he said eager to show off his Spanish.

'Bravo, very good *caballero.* see you back at the hotel, saw your car there.' Juan said over his shoulder as they turned to leave.

The hotel was fully booked and a multitude of different accents filled the air of the dining room; the most pronounced of which was the English accent of the two from the car park; the Saab man and wife.

'Hello again, fancy meeting you here. Do you come here often? By the way, my name is Guy and my wife is Sylvie,' he said, and Juan responded, 'Juan and Maria,' and smiled across to the English couple in response. Guy was trying to impress the waiter with his obvious knowledge of wines of Spain and in particular the fact that tomorrow they would be visiting a local *bodega*, which carried some *excellent Rioja.*

'So we'll have a bottle of the local house wine as it will obviously be Rioja; and for the main course, we'll have the local river trout,' Guy said to the waiter.

'Of course, *senor,* the Rioja is fine, but unfortunately we have no trout tonight. It has been so popular.'

'Maria managed a smile, which had been missing since seeing a picture of Gregg as a wanted man on the TV news.

'Did you want to talk about the news item, Maria? It clearly shocked you considerably.' Juan asked.

'It's really difficult. It's a long story and I don't wish to bore you with the details, but confidentially I will tell you that the man on the TV news in trouble with the FBI and the Spanish CNI, is my boss at that firm, MexTex,' she whispered.

Dinner was superb; Juan had secured the last two trout prior to their little excursion to the monastery. Prepared and served to perfection.

Retiring to the bar for a nightcap, they had hoped for a quiet drink. Maria had finished off the wine and would welcome a liquor or two in the bar. They had scarcely settled into their seats when Guy and Sylvie entered.

'Hello again, can I get you a drink, folks?' Juan checked with Maria, who reluctantly declined; she was not in the habit of turning down the offer of a drink under any circumstances.

'Do you mind if we join you?' Guy asked.

Being the perfect gentleman, Juan said, 'Why not?'

Inside maria shuddered; she dreaded the idea of making small talk with complete strangers. They were bound to ask tricky questions. She knew she would have to come up with a cover story, and all she really wanted to do was have a good drink and go to bed.

'Well, you beat us to the trout for dinner. It looked very nice.' Guy said.

'*Perfecto, como siempre,*' (As always) Juan replied knowing that Guy liked to speak Spanish.

Guy started the conversation. 'We've been coming to Spain for holidays since the sixties, when the kids were small.

'Always to the Costas, then the Canaries in winter. I always admired the bathroom fittings in the hotels and as I had a plumbing business in the UK I started importing Spanish bathroom and toiletware.

'It's now a thriving business which I've handed on to my son, Gary, so he's doing very well now.'

At that point, Sylvie decided to join the conversation.

'I'm sure these folks don't want to hear about your toilet stories, Guy,' she said in jest.

'Not at all,' said Juan. 'It's interesting that you saw an opportunity and went for it, good for you. Similar to myself in some ways. I've not exactly cornered the market but carved out a niche market in providing bespoke high-end cars for very well-off clients.'

Sylvie sidled up to Maria and had a quiet chat; inebriated as she was, she managed to manipulate the conversation to her advantage.

Juan did his best to show interest in bathrooms and toilets, but the conversation had very limited prospects. However he could see out of the corner of his eye that Maria was making progress with Sylvie, who was embracing her in a motherly fashion.

"Guy, we have a plan for tomorrow. After we've been to the *bodega*, we'll come back here for a bit of lunch and take Maria with us in our car to Santander. Are you okay with that, Guy?'

'What about Juan? What's will he be doing?'

'Well, he'll be busy with his car transfer tomorrow after he has it valeted. Maria's going to visit her folks near Santander. We've got plenty of time. We don't sail till much later tomorrow night,' said Sylvie.

Maria felt very pleased with her day; everything seemed to be working out as they made their way to the room.

There were snippets of conversation about the TV news flying around, but Maria chose to ignore them. Essentially, it seemed that the police were asking anyone involved with the company to contact them. Following her telephone conversation with Leanne, they agreed to keep quiet; "'*que sera sera*'".

It had been a very busy and interesting day for both as they decided on a night cap.

'Nighty-night then Maria.' Juan said as he prepared to make up the sofa bed.

'Come here you. Get your butt in this bed. I'm not sleeping alone tonight I need a good cuddle,' she said.

'Well, I'm sure I'll be able to manage that.' They stripped off and naked, fell into each other's' arms.

TWENTY-FIVE

SANTANDER

Morning brought a fresh breeze with crystal clear blue skies and wall-to-wall sunshine. The village square was still quiet with just the odd person strolling by. Maria and Juan Carlos slowly emerged from the cocoon of the duvet yawning and stretching. They both took a few seconds to focus on where they were, and with whom. Maria was first to make a move, she held her hand in front of her mouth and checked her stale breath. In horror she quickly made to the bathroom and furiously scrubbed her teeth.

'Maria would you like some tea?' asked Juan, she replied through a mouthful of toothpaste that she would.

Juan asked for a pot of tea for two. As they waited; with a little squeeze, they managed to shower together. The tea, was cold by the time they'd showered, but they didn't care. She thought, *well, I can always get another pot of tea, but...?*

Breakfast for Maria had never been a particularly enjoyable time, as she was frequently hung-over. Today, however, would be an exception, so she managed freshly squeezed Seville orange juice, a little muesli and coffee with toasted bread. Juan started with the traditional sliced salted tomato with olive oil on freshly baked bread with coffee. Juan however, in recent years, associating with English workmen, had been seduced by the wonders of the full *English breakfast*. But not for today.

Guy and Sylvie had not as yet surfaced , so Maria said *adios* to Juan, who gave her his business card.

'You never know, our paths may cross again sometime in the future.' They kissed and he left, with a roar from the Merc.

It was another one-night stand; a conquest of sorts, and whilst she had enjoyed the experience, it nevertheless left Maria feeling empty and guilty once more. She called Leanne to give her an update on the latest news.

'*Hola*, Leanne, had a wonderful trip with "Juan-Juan Mercedes Man". He was a real fun guy. He's gone off to get the car valeted and I'm waiting for my English friends to surface for breakfast before they are taking me to Santander. What you up to, girl?'

'Well, could not get hold of Gonzales. He's unavailable to the world at present. No one has any knowledge of his whereabouts. My money had been paid into the bank so I decided to get away from Barca and go home to my parents in Gibraltar. They were over the moon to see me and are spoiling me rotten. Have you heard anything about Gregg?' Leanne replied.

'Well the last contact I had with him was when he left Fuerteventura to fly back to his injured son in a San Diego hospital.

'I just get the sense that the brown smelly stuff has hit the fan at last, Leanne. Have you heard from Luis at all?'

'Had a chat with him before setting off and he sends his love. So it's all very weird without you here at present. What's your take on it, Maria, with the un-American activities and all, you were pretty tight with him, kiddo?'

'I don't think we should discuss these matters over the phone. We have nothing to hide, as we're simply employees, but you can bet your bottom dollar this phone call is being tapped. As I say, I don't care, got nothing to hide. And now my "'ride'" has just come down for breakfast, so I'll call you later baby *'hasta pronto.'*

'Morning, Guy, How are you this morning? On your own?' Maria enquired.

'Morning, Maria, yes. Sylvie takes a little longer to get started in the morning nowadays, but she gets there, that's the main thing. Have you eaten your breakfast don't see Juan?'

'Yes, we were up early. It was such a gorgeous morning, we had an early breakfast. Juan has taken the car to be valeted before delivering it to his client later today. Fortunately, it's a nice dry day so the car will look its' best for his client.'

'Ah, here comes Sylvie, all bright-eyed and bushy-tailed,' Guy chuckled. 'She's so looking forward to you travelling with us, bit of company for her.'

'Yeah, I am too. It'll be nice. I'll catch up with you two after you've had your breakfast. *Bon appetit.'*

Maria took herself off to see the news on the bar TV, which was now saying they were '...*trying to locate senor Benjamin Gonzales in Barcelona, to help them with their enquiries ...*'

There was no further news on Gregg. As she sat in the lounge, she opened her journal and ordered another coffee. She felt cross, as she had neglected recent entries; she felt that was disrespectful.

After breakfast, Guy loaded up the car and paid his bill, declaring to Miguel that he had the most wonderful time and, every intention of revisiting at the earliest opportunity.

As it was a stunningly beautiful day of warm sunshine, they all agreed to start the journey with the top down in the Saab.

There had been a change of plan.

First stop would be the *bodega* for Guy to collect his case of Rioja, and then, they would set off for Santander.

Maria had seen enough *bodegas* in her lifetime of drinking, so she was disinclined to have a tour of bottles of wine to which she had no access. Likewise, free tasting had absolutely no appeal whatsoever. She politely suggested she would wait in the car, as she wanted to catch up on her emails.

The journey time would be around two and a half hours, with a break for food. When she called Janet before they got underway, her parents answered to explain that Janet was in England but they expected her back in Spain the following day and hoped they could all meet up then.

Maria, wishing to make an unannounced visit to her parents, called her uncle (tio) Pedro and luckily caught him working on his boat.

'Hi, uncle, it's Maria Cabrera. How are you?'

He was fitting a new radio in the boat's wheelhouse and practically dropped the phone in surprise.

She explained the situation to him updating him on her recent adventures; he was greatly relieved to hear good news.

She had always been his favourite; they got along so well. She grew up in a fishing community in which he had always played a major part, and she loved going out in his boat; unsurprisingly named *Maria*.

The tough nature of sea fishing, she believed, had to a great extent been a factor in building Maria's character. They went out together in all weathers, forming a strong independent bond. In short, it made her tough enough to face anything that was thrown at her.

'I'm travelling with a lovely English couple, so let me find out where they will drop me off and I'll call back. Would that be okay uncle?' she said.

'That's fine and it's probably time you dropped the uncle stuff, don't you think, at your age?'

'*Nunca*... (never), tio Pedro... you'll always be; *tio Pedro,* call you later. *hasta pronto*.'

Sitting in the back of the Saab, the air decidedly chilly, she reminisced about those freezing cold days at sea; days with him had been a major influence in her life. She believed he gave her the inner strength which she needed to tap into once more, to help her tackle the drink problem. He had been the main person to encourage her to 'fly the nest' and discover the world beyond Cantabria. She was so excited to be going home and meeting up with these people she loved and missed so much.

She jumped out of the car, full of renewed energy as the couple tottered back, laden with cases of Rioja.

'Sorry to have left you alone for so long. Are you okay Maria.?' Sylvie enquired.

'I'm fine, let me get my bag out of the boot and put it on the passenger seat. We'll be in Santander in a few hours, 'Maria excitedly said. 'Two hours, forty minutes,' Guy chipped in, obviously having worked out the journey in advance. *I like that in a man, well some men anyway* she thought.

'Think we'll need to put up the hood. It's getting quite chilly here in the mountains. Very beautiful country but considerably cooler than the warm south. Plus, it will give us more space in the boot. The hood takes up quite a bit of space, as it stows itself away in the boot,' Guy said.

The countryside was full of wild flowers, yellow gorse and bracken amongst craggy outcrops of rock. They were fortunate enough to spot wild deer and Guy excitedly pulled over at one stage to point out a bird, high over the rocky valley.

'Look, it's a griffon Vulture,' he shouted very excitedly. In truth, Maria had difficulty spotting the bird but happily joined in the moment with great excitement. It was a quite wonderful drive which all three enjoyed immensely. She felt the love these new friends exuded and realised that was a large part of her life that had been missing for a long while. She wished for more of the same.

Having made good time with no delays, they had a light lunch. They stumbled across a small café off the beaten track. It was simple homemade fresh food, superbly prepared by local folk. As they finished the meal with coffee all around, they spread out a detailed map of the area for one final check and picked out and agreed upon a suitable place for the drop-off. On the understanding that there would probably not be a lot of time to say their farewells in the layby en route, they bid each other *adieu*, shedding a tear, and set off towards Santander. Calling Pedro and arranged the rendezvous spot; a layby at the side of the main road to Santander.

TWENTY-SIX

THE LAY-BY

Their journey through the picturesque countryside sadly drew to a close. The aromas of the fresh countryside had now been replaced by the acrid smell of diesel fumes; sounds replaced by the roar of traffic thundering along the hard road surfaces. They were on the main highway to Santander.

Traffic of all shapes and sizes, from cars towing caravans to heavy-duty trucks, and even a procession of vintage Bentley's on their annual club run from the U.K. heading for the Santander to Plymouth ferry.

Guy pulled the car off the road and into the layby. As they waited, Maria closed her eyes and thought about the journey she had been on and how fortunate she was to be returning to the bosom of her family with their roots in Cantabria. Even the very noisy traffic sounds could not disturb her train of thought, until the car horn blasted her back to reality.

Maria could hardly contain her excitement any longer. She strained her neck around looking out of the rear window for tio Pedro. She spotted him and, like a teenager, jumped with a great leap out of the car.

SWOOOOOOSH… CRAAAASH… BAANG

Stunned silence.

Maria lay on the gravel road motionless; unconscious.

Everyone in the layby shrieked in horror with one accord. Guy, and Sylvie froze, quite unable to move. They were rooted momentarily to the spot.

Further along in the layby, a young man dressed in a black leather jacket, jeans and cowboy boots also lay unconscious on top of the parked car into which he had just ploughed the motorbike.

Pedro sprung into life and immediately rushed to Maria's lifeless body. He checked for her breathing and pulse and his relief was obvious and visible.

'She's alive,' he shouted. 'Get moving, anyone call an ambulance. Quickly, c'mon, get moving, get phoning. Get an ambulance *NOW*.' Pedro shouted at the top of his voice.

He very gently tried to revive her but got no immediate response. He quietly prayed, '*Santo Madre de Dios, por favor no le dejos morir.*' (Holy Mother please don't let her die.)

Totally in shock, Sylvie, sat in the front seat of the car with the door still open, was incapable of moving.

Guy, however, was phoning and reassuringly informed all concerned that help was on the way. Pedro wanted to hold Maria's head in his arms but understood from his training that it was not the thing to do; he must wait for the professionals, and not move her head. He had witnessed many serious accidents at sea and knew the importance of staying calmly active.

Meanwhile, at the other end of the lay-by, a tremendous commotion had been taking place, with a great deal of shouting and screaming going on.

The *brigade de bomberos,* (the fire service) were first to arrive in their shiny red truck equipped with ladders, hoses and all manner of life-saving devices. They immediately took command and politely but firmly ushered Pedro to one side. Very quickly, they put Maria's neck in a brace and administered oxygen; everyone was asked to step back. Unable to actually see what was going on, standing in silence, they feared the worst.

The senior officer who had taken charge calmly and efficiently went about his business, removed his bulky helmet and pronounced.

'SHE WILL LIVE.'

Paramedics and police arrived in numbers as Maria was stretchered into an ambulance; forced to reverse owing to the congestion and confusion at the far end of the layby, had difficulty getting back onto the highway as traffic had built up with 'rubber- neckers' attracted by the flashing blue and amber lights. It finally sped along the main highway towards the hospital.

Pedro managed enough composure to introduce himself to Guy and Sylvie. A strange and bizarre way for anyone to meet up for the first time; they automatically embraced each other. Pedro enthusiastically praised

Guy for his prompt and decisive action on calling the emergency services. They tried to comfort Sylvie, who remained frozen in a state of shock. No one had any idea as to where Maria had been taken.

The police eventually approached, saying they needed to take statements to try and work out what had occurred. Together with other witnesses in the layby, they explained what they believed had happened; the motorbike, being driven at high speed, had swept into the layby and caught Maria's arm, spinning her around in a circle, knocking her to the ground.

What happened next they didn't actually see but assumed that the bike had careered on, eventually colliding with the parked car at the far end of the layby.

The police officer noted their version of events and their relationship with the victim of the accident. Satisfied with their accounts and statements. He thanked them and joined the other officers who were erecting a screen around the crash scene.

All the while, Pedro was fingering his rosary and uttering prayers under his breath, giving thanks to the Holy Mother for saving Maria's life.

It would be some while before they would be leaving the layby. Pedro called his wife Alicia, who immediately went to pieces at the news. She had no doubt about what she should do and was heading straight for church to pray for Maria.

'Alicia, whatever you do, don't let Maria's folks know what's going on. Keep it absolutely secret, the shock would kill them,' Pedro advised.

'I must pray for her safe deliverance, Pedro, so must you. Dear God, keep her with us, She's such a sweet soul. I'll go quietly to the church to light a candle.' she said, sobbing.

Pedro had given all the necessary details to the paramedics, including his cell phone number, but Maria's phone was still in her jacket pocket. They told him she was going to be admitted to the Marques de Valdecilla hospital in Santander.

He had got his act together quickly and was back in operational mode, with an idea to assist the English couple. Seeing they were clearly traumatised he made a suggestion. '*Senor* Guy, we are all in a terrible shock and I am sure you do not want to drive to the port in this condition, is that not so?'

'*Senor* Pedro, thank you for taking charge. We're both, as you say, extremely traumatised and I for one do not want to continue our trip.'

'So what time is the ship due to sail?' Pedro asked.

Guy replied. 'We're not due to depart until eleven thirty tonight. What are you thinking Pedro?'

'Buena. Why don't you come with me to my house and recover with some hot drinks and a little food, and when you feel confident to travel you can get back on the road. In the meantime, we may have some good news from the hospital. They have my number.'

'Of course, if it is not too much trouble that would be a very nice thing to do. Many thanks,' Guy replied as Sylvie, who had not said a word since the accident, quietly nodded her head in approval.

He was a man of considerable experience in dealing with difficult situations, a skipper of a deep-sea fishing vessel and a volunteer for the lifeboat rescue team; he handled the situation with consummate ease, inspiring confidence in the others.

He was thinking ahead to come up with the next move. He could take them in his car, locking up the Saab, in the hope that it would be secure in the layby. The second choice would be for Guy to follow him back to his home in his own car.

There was yet another more pressing issue; that of the lad on the bike who had caused the accident. No one knew of his status; it was possible that the three of them would possibly be called as witnesses.

Guy decided to follow Pedro to his home; testing his ability to drive safely. Alicia warmly welcomed them with tea and scones. She well knew form her English friends that they liked afternoon tea.   She was more than happy to oblige.

Their home; a traditional Spanish house with a large back garden full of vegetables of all descriptions and the front garden a floral treat, dominated in the main by Dahlias the size of dinner plates. The scones Alicia had baked to order were magnificent. Having managed to get into the village without Maria's parents' spotting them, they relaxed comfortably with the afternoon tea.

Pedro's phone jangled; every one stopped talking. It was not the hospital as was expected, but Maria's friend Janet.

'Hi, Pedro, how are you? I got a voice message from Maria but I called her and she's not picking up.'

'Maria has been involved in an accident and unfortunately has been admitted to hospital,' he explained.

'Oh my God, is it serious?' Janet asked calmly.

'Yeah, pretty serious, she was still unconscious when they took her away. Please don't call her folks, whatever you do,' he pleaded.

She came back. 'Of course not but please tell me right away if there are any developments. My God, I'm so sorry for that girl. Trouble seems to follow her. I love her so much. I'm in Kent in England right now but coming back to Spain tomorrow, as I've got several meetings in Santander. Let's hope she is able to come home soon. God bless. Adios Pedro, bless her.'

Alicia did her best to entertain her guests, as her grandchildren played in and out of the garden.

Sylvie had loosened up somewhat, conversing at least, albeit a little incoherently. She realised she had never been in a Spanish household before now. She watched and gave a little giggle. 'We're really all the same under the skin, Guy,' she said. 'Lovely families. Don't know why I thought they would be different.' With a knowing gesture to each other, the men shrugged; she was in shock.

The afternoon dragged on as Alicia offered food to pass the time, but nobody had an appetite; the atmosphere was oppressive and foreboding as they tried to make small talk. Under normal circumstances, Alicia would prepare *cena* (dinner) for nine o'clock but today was far from normal.

'Come, Sylvie, do you like gardening? Come and I'll show you my vegetable garden,' said Alicia.

THE LAY-BY

Sylvie very slowly got to her feet; the emotion of the last few hours had drained her energy. Guy looked worried, as she was in no fit state to consider a twenty-two-hour boat journey to Plymouth. They tottered out to the garden, Alicia holding Sylvie by the arm. As they were admiring the magnificent enormous cauliflowers, Pedro's phone jangled once more.

It was the doctor from the hospital. 'Hello, am I speaking with senor Pedro Garcia ?' Pedro confirmed his identity. *'Si senor correcto.'*

'Well, first of all, I have good news and not so good news. Maria has just gained consciousness and is sitting up drinking water. She has sustained a broken wrist and, as far as I can tell, no further injuries, but we need to do further tests. She will experience bruising in various areas of her body over the coming day and weeks even.

She is concussed and so we're keeping her overnight to be on the safe side. Her bloods are fine, although she seems to have fairly high levels of alcohol. We feel she would be free to leave in the morning unless there are further complications overnight. So that's good news too. The police are still here and would like to talk with you.'

Pedro could not wait for the police before giving the news to all concerned. 'Maria is sitting up drinking water,' he shouted to them, 'she's doing okay.'

He could not thank the doctor enough and practically broke down in relief but quickly restored his composure as the police officer filled him in with the details of the crash. He read the following statement:

The lad who had been riding the motorbike was actually in a high-speed chase with the police. He swerved into the layby to try and avoid capture by the police. He had stolen the bike, but was actually on bail for far more serious offences about which the police were not at liberty to divulge information. Tests had shown there were large quantities of cocaine and alcohol in his blood. The lad, aged fourteen, had sustained considerable serious injuries including a broken leg and arm and was also concussed. Senor P. Cabrera would be required to give evidence as a witness but there was no need for the English couple to be further involve. They were free to return to the UK.

The relief was palpable; it was as if a great blockage had been cleared. Great excitement ensued, and also some weeping of relief and joy accompanied a ripple of applause.

The children, too young to really understand, screeched with joy just to join in clapping and cheering with the grown-ups. Pedro immediately reached for the Rioja, but also for a local more expensive Xentia Juan Carrillo.

Alicia was already in the kitchen with pots and pans clattering to accompany the CD playing Cantabrian contemporary cross-over music by a local band, which they proudly supported.

The mood was electric as Sylvie became more animated, the colour restored to her cheeks, which had previously become ashen-looking with the stress.

'Alicia, can I help you?' she asked as she went into the kitchen.

'Of course you can, slice some of those peppers for me, I'm making a fish stew with peppers and potatoes and fresh bread. Go get a couple of glasses of the good stuff before Pedro gets to it.' she joked.

'Pedro, take Guy and the kids to the *panaderia* and get bread. I'm sure he would like to see the village, and the kids need to get out for a break, but take care to avoid Maria's parents.'

The aromas from Alicia's stew were stupendous; the fresh garlic and herbs, fresh from the garden, combined with the seafood selection, gladdened Sylvie's heart with joy. She felt privileged to be working alongside Alicia, whom she had never met before, on this very old wooden table.

They had a very large outside fridge-freezer room in the back garden where Pedro stored his catch, ready for distribution to his customers, guaranteeing fresh produce. Alicia showed her the selection of seafood all caught by Pedro.

'What do you fancy for the stew Sylvie?; Lobster, pulpos, hake, corvina?' A rhetorical question; Sylvie clasped placed her hands around her face. 'Are you kidding me? She said laughing.

Sylvie and Guy had a very nice home in Kent. Four bedrooms, detached, they had worked hard to achieve a very good standard of life.

With a smart house, a very pretty garden and a lovely family, they had all the attributes of a successful marriage. However, standing in this house was like a dream; like something she had seen in the movies, a seemingly idyllic way of life.

These folks, she thought, had everything. They were up to date with modernity in terms of technology but somehow not affected by it.

The house was warm, old and friendly, with few references to modernity. Sylvie loved it and knew her daughter would feel the same way about the place. Perhaps she mused, she may return one day and stay in the village. Alicia had promised her a mini-tour after dinner.

There was, of course, the matter of Maria's plight, which took priority, but, all seemed to be in order in that department. There was nothing she could do except pray for her. As they awaited the boys returning with the bread, Alicia suggested that anyone who wished to could use the altar in her bedroom for prayer.

The room was large, with very large old furniture, probably inherited. The scent of lavender, filled the space, possibly from the votive burning there. Pictures of various saints were on display; all very peaceful and serene but possibly a little too Catholic for Sylvie, who admitted to being a weddings, baptisms and funerals sort of worshipper.

She did, however, kneel before the alter and offer a silent prayer; in a way she admired those with a strong belief or faith and wished it was something she might attain, but had never bothered to advance the subject.

The boys returned with the bread and lots of pastries; their excuse being, *'perhaps abuela would like those for dessert.'*

Meanwhile, Pedro tried once more to contact Janet; 'Hi, Janet. Great news. Maria has gained consciousness and has been sitting up drinking water. We're all so relieved and so grateful to the Good Lord for bringing her back to us.

'She had been out for quite a while so we're having a sort of celebratory *cena* with Guy and Sylvie, with whom she had been travelling. Would you like to come over and join us? You'd be very welcome and we'd love to see you.'

She reminded him. 'I would love to but I'm still in England at the moment. Maybe catch you tomorrow. I have a meeting to attend with the health services in Santander, so I'll be around once they are dealt with. Please let me know if there are any further developments. Can I call her?'

'Well, we can't call, as her phone is either off or lost in the confusion, but we'll look forward to seeing you perhaps sometime tomorrow.' he concluded.

The meal was a tremendous affair, enjoyed immensely by one and all. They sat back with coffee and liquors, totally relaxed at last.

'Guy, do you like football at all?' Pedro asked.

'Very much indeed. I'm a lifelong supporter of Chelsea and both of us have season tickets at Stamford Bridge. Why do you ask?'

'Well, our club Racing Club Santander are playing tonight and I had planned to watch it on TV. We could do that together if you would like to?'

'Don't forget we're leaving tonight, Pedro,' Guy replied.

'Well, are you sure you're up to the journey Guy? You could stay here tonight and catch the ferry tomorrow?'

That way, you get to see Maria and wish her well. Please God they discharge her tomorrow.'

'Not sure if they'll honour my ticket if I cancel just like that. What do you think?' Pedro answered, 'They get cancellations all the time on that route, bad weather, and breakdown, passengers arriving late. I've been involved with the Maritime Marine Association for years, was president once. Let me make a call.'

'Sylvie are you okay about staying the night here, love?' Guy asked. 'Of course, if it's not too much trouble for Alicia, it would be wonderful.' Pedro was soon back after making his call.

'All sorted Guy. Get the TV on. Do you want a brandy or a beer? I'm having a brandy and cigar. It's my only vice these days, join me if you will.'

'That's brilliant Pedro thanks for that; get your baby doll nightie out the bag, Sylv, we're staying the night.' Guy wisecracked as the wine was began to relax him.

The ladies took the boys out to the village for a walk; they were getting an extended play time before bed. Sylvie was so thrilled to be shown around the stunning village and harbour; a few locals were messing about in boats but the big stuff was all secure for the night.

Tomorrow, Pedro would be sailing; he had crew who needed to earn money, and this posed the question about picking up Maria in the event she would be discharged in the morning.

'I can't drive his truck, it's manual and horrible to drive.' Alicia announced. 'Maria's phone is still out of action, and I'm struggling with who else I could ask without alerting her folks.' On checking her own phone she called Pablo she called Pablo a lovely lad who had been very keen on Maria, but it went to answerphone.

'You have it all here, Alicia. What a place to live! It's pretty well idyllic,' Sylvie said.

'Well it's like anywhere else. We have our share of problems but certainly not heavy stuff. We all tend to look out for each other, generational thing going back many years,' said Alicia. The day was drawing to a close, but a few restaurants remained open. The sun was slowly sinking in a golden haze in the western sky.

'Let's get these little fellows back and ready for bed.' Alicia suggested. The six-year-old twin boys Max and Josh were Alicia's son's' children. their mother Karen, an English-woman, worked in Santander so Alicia shared in their care.

Back at the house, Sylvie helped Alicia get the boys showered and ready for bed; but prayers had to be offered before they both jumped noisily into their bunk beds.

The ladies joined the men; but they were still engrossed in the match, so the ladies had tea in the kitchen and talked about life with growing families, childcare and balancing the family budgets.

Suddenly Alicia remembered to call Pablo Lopez; fortunately, he was at home so she apprised him of Maria's situation. He was so emotional and very upset, suggesting, he would come over at short notice and help in any way required.

'Just tell me when she is being discharged and I'll be over right away. Is there anything you need to do tonight that I could help with? I saw the news showing an accident, but didn't know it was Maria; they didn't make clear who was involved, I didn't pay much attention, but I know the spot where it occurred. I'll go over there and look around in case her phone is lying on the ground. I'll definitely collect her if you ask me to.'

Alicia spoke; 'It's very late, Pablo, and it'll be dark soon, so don't worry yourself tonight, really, we'll check it out tomorrow. Take care. God bless you. Pablo, you're a good man.'

'I can't help myself. I love that girl, and have done so for many years. You know, I'd marry her tomorrow if she would have me,' he said. 'We all know that, Pablo. Say hello to your *mama* and *papa* from us.' Alicia hung up.

*

Daybreak brought a full blue sky with a light breeze, boding well for Pedro as he prepared to sail into the Bay of Biscay in search of fish. In the main, the sea had been good to him. With years of experience, he rarely used electronic fish-seeking devices; he generally knew where the fish were. Local knowledge of different times of the year coupled with his innate ability to work with the tides had enabled him to be successful most of the time.

A quiet rap on the bedroom door got Sylvie's attention. '*Hola*, I thought you might like some tea and biscuits in bed. It's another English thing, *no es asi?* (is it not?), Alicia asked as she brought the tray to their bed and sat on a stool. 'Did you sleep well, *mi amigos*?'

Guy stirred at that point and propped himself up on the pillows. 'Very nice too, never had a better sleep anywhere. It was so quiet last night, it was really beautiful.' he replied.

A ship's' whistle interrupted the chat; curious, Guy slipped out of bed to look out of the window overlooking the harbour. Pedro was vigorously waving, bidding farewell; the good ship *Maria* sailed out of port, ocean-bound for Biscay. Alicia enquired if they wanted English or continental breakfast. She knew Guy like to practise Spanish, she asked if they wanted English breakfast or continental?

'*Ahora amigos para desayuno, Ingles ou continental?*'

'*Inglis por favor*' replied Guy. He always preferred a full English breakfast.

As Alicia cleared breakfast away, she called the hospital, only to be told the doctors had not completed their ward rounds. However, there was some good news. Pablo turned up, having scoured the layby in the dark last night, by the light of his cell phone. He had found Maria's phone amid the dirt and grime of the layby. It was still intact and appeared to be working, but out of respect he had not tried it out.

Alicia thanked him profusely and taking possession of it she discovered that it was full of unanswered messages which she left well alone.

Maria lay in her hospital bed, under strict orders not to make any calls and to avoid too much stimulus until the specialist had seen her.

'So what's the delay, doctor? I'm feeling fine. When can I go home?' she enquired. Well, it's good that you're feeling fine but with head injuries, we don't like to take chances. You may get a delayed reaction at any time. We scanned the brain and all looked perfectly in order, so the chances of you being discharged are good. Doctor Stein is a very experienced neuro-surgeon so you're in very good hands.' the doctor explained.

Maria lay there with the events of the last few days, weeks and months going around in her head; she couldn't relax, try as she might. She vaguely recalled the English couple but could not remember their names.

Gazing around the ward, she felt very depressed. She had never been very good at being ill. This, she thought, was worse than the worst hangover she had ever had.

Lunch was brought round and she managed to eat something, but it was her lack of recall that troubled her.

'What's the name of this hospital?' she asked one of the orderlies, not wanting to appear vacant in front of the specialist. The orderly answered but Maria quizzed her further. 'Where are we then?' So this little game continued until the nurse came and interrupted the chat. Desperate to get out of the hospital, she knew she needed to present as lucid and alert to have any chance of being discharged.

Looking at her plastered arm in a full sling, it was obvious to her that there had been an accident or incident but she knew not where or when. That worried her, as her inability to recall could jeopardise her chance of escaping, she reasoned. She just wanted to get out of the hospital.

Senor Stein eventually appeared on the scene, discussed her injuries and how best to proceed with any further treatment and self-care issues.

'You were very fortunate, Maria that the motorbike did not actually hit you but caught the sleeve of your jacket and spun you around with great force, throwing you to the ground where you banged your head on the gravel road of the layby. Your wrist took the impact of hitting the road, causing it to fracture. That will heal very quickly. But your head injury will need to be monitored to avoid blood clots. No driving for a while and no violent actions such as sports for a while. You can get someone to collect you this afternoon but take things really easy for a while, plenty of rest among friends and family.'

'Thank you so much. Doctor I suddenly feel so much better.' she said as the doctor smiled knowingly at her, but as she swung her legs, attempting to jump off the bed she felt dizzy. But he spotted that.

'You really need to take it easy. Don't rush and think you're back to normal.' She tried to walk across the ward but he noticed her stumble. 'Let me make a call for you to be collected and I can explain, your need to be careful.' Alicia took the call and immediately understood the need for Maria to be cautious. She explained everything to Pablo, who set off accompanied by Sylvie, who felt the need to help.

As the pair collected her from the hospital reception, Maria had trouble remembering who they were. Pablo explained the situation. He was very shocked to see her like this; she could not remember the crash. He realised her struggle so tried to help her with gentle reminders of recent events; but she just focussed on the here and now.

'Has anyone got my phone? I seem to have mislaid it.' she asked. Pablo told her to take a look in the glove compartment, and as she did, she shrieked with excitement, throwing her arms around his neck, practically causing another car crash.

The phone worked and had enough charge; she phoned Alicia. The call lasted almost the entire journey from the hospital back home.

As they pulled into the village car park, Pablo took the opportunity to express his love to Maria; he was very emotional and pleaded with her to at least give him another chance to take her out on dates. It was clearly not the right time for that as she was too confused.

'Of course, Pablo, you know I think the world of you. You've been the one who stood by me when others deserted me. It's just that I don't want firm commitments. I like to be free and wander, but maybe that is coming to an end, who knows.'

'My first priority right now is to see *mama*, *papa* and *abuela* and see what happens after that.' Pablo carried her bag as they walked arm in arm to Pedro's house. Sylvie just looked on with love in her heart.

There was joy and laughter as everyone welcomed Maria back into the fold. Alicia called Maria's mother. 'Benita, it's Alicia. I have wonderful news. A surprise visit from Maria She's home and in our house. Come on over and I'll explain everything. Her parents practically collapsed in shock at the news; she was in the village without letting them know.

Beni, who had been working in the restaurant, ripped off her apron and was about to leave when Claudio announced he was joining her. They hastily left the staff in charge and dashed over to Pedro's.

'Oh, my baby girl, what on earth has happened to you?' Beni exclaimed as she saw Maria's arm in a plaster cast and sling.

'*Oh es nada mama yo buen;*' (oh it nothing mama how are you) she answered dismissively, as *papa* was all over her too. The English couple had been in the background; they stood up and made to leave as the time was fast approaching for them to catch the ferry. Alicia apologised profusely and introduced them.

Maria stood right in front of them, and stretching out her hands she clasped their hands and simply stared at them, speechless. Desperately trying to locate them in her memory, this carried on for a while, motionless; it was painful for all three of them.

Then, from behind her somewhere in the room, glasses chinking and the sound and smell of wine being poured, sparked something in Maria's head; Rioja… *bodega*…the English couple; the names escaped her for the moment, but it was a start. They hugged and shed a tear.

Beni and Claudio were baffled but said nothing; all very mysterious, they thought. Guy and Sylvie said their farewells, on the understanding that they would always be welcome. 'You are practically family,' said Alicia. They felt saddened in that although there had been some recognition, Maria was unable to totally recall them to mind.

Pablo sat right close by Maria, occasionally holding her hand, but she felt somewhat oppressed and needed her space. She remembered him well enough.

'Pablo, I don't want to offend you, as you're giving me a lot of love, but I really need to go back home to mama's and rest.' *Papa* got to his feet and with her mother, politely ushered her towards the door.

Maria gushed out her gratitude for all the help everyone had given. 'Alicia, thank you so much for keeping everything together and not letting on to them. What a surprise they had. I'll go home and rest for the remainder of the day and be in touch tomorrow. I hope by tomorrow my memory will begin to improve with rest, *muchas gracias.*'

As she walked back home through the village and by the harbour-side the fresh salt-permeated air was never more refreshing. Back in her familiar surroundings the screeching of the gulls, which could at times irritate, were as music to her ears. Her mind began to clear. Pausing awhile by the harbour-side she prayed. She felt that she never wanted to leave this haven of peace again. Feeling deep gratitude and love for her higher power, she knew she must change her life forever without further delay. Without question, she had been given another chance, and must take action to save herself.

TWENTY-SEVEN

ABUELA

The next morning brought so many calls to her voicemail. She sat up in her familiar homely bed and decided to ignore the calls and just recover. *Mama* brought her a light breakfast, which she savoured with great delight and an overwhelming feeling of love.

As she tried to assimilate the last few days' events; she struggled; The accident had had a greater affect on her than she had realised. She looked about her for reassurance. Her mind was still somewhat fragmented. She was back home. Mama was sitting at the foot of the bed having served her breakfast, but inside something was nagging away at her.

Abuela; she had still not seen *abuela*.

'**Oh my God mother.**' she exclaimed, 'I haven't seen or heard about *abuela;* where is *abuela* how is she mama?' she pushed her breakfast tray away but her mother stopped her.

First things first Maria finish your breakfast.

'I'm afraid *abuela*'s health is very poor.' Mother explained as Maria sat bolt upright in trepidation.

'What does that mean, very poor, *mama*?' There was no easy way for her mother to explain; she needed to be honest but gentle. She knew how close Maria held *abuela* in her heart.

Maria, you need to get rest and take things easy. Obviously, you can't drive at present but you don't need to go anywhere. We will get you back to full health in good time.

'Finish your breakfast, Maria .You need to eat and rest. We can see *abuela* later.'

'No, *mama*, you have to tell me all about *abuela* first.'

'Well, okay; *abuela*'s heart is very weak. She has had several minor heart attacks which have compromised her body and mental health. In short, she doesn't want to go on much longer.'

'Oh my God. Mother, we have to get her well. I can't live without *abuela*. Take me to her, *mama*,' she sobbed.

'She had a stroke recently which left her without speech for a while. Remarkably, she regained some speech, but she's very weak. The truth is, Maria, she could go at any time,' *mama* managed to get out amidst tears and sobbing.

Maria could not move; she sat on her bed weeping aloud and physically aching with pangs of guilt. *I should have come sooner why did I not come home sooner? I hate myself I've been so selfish, my darling abuela I let you down so badly. How will you ever forgive me abuela?*.

'I need to go to her right now *mama*. Is she still in her house?' she asked, sobbing her heart-out her reddened face saturated in tears

'No, we could not leave her there. We had the downstairs back bedroom adapted for her so we could keep an eye on her throughout the day and night. She should be awake by now. I'll take her a little food which she probably will refuse but I'll give her medication and you can surprise her.'

Maria asked, 'So how is *abuelo* (granddad) coping? Is he in his own in the house?'

Mama replied, 'He's coping well. You know him, no fuss and nonsense. They are from that generation, Maria. Seen so much hardship in their lives, they just dig deeper into their emotional reserves.

'There's always someone popping round, and although they have deep love for each other, they are somehow able to detach. They're both very independent in that way.'

Abuelo had decorated the room in a style befitting a small child's room; bright yellow, brilliant red and blue flowers. Maria loved the room and felt the love that had been instilled through *abuelo*'s workmanship in decorating it for her.

Abuela was sitting ready to receive Benita, but on seeing Maria, she visibly shook with excitement.

'*Dios mio, no puedo creer lo que veo,*' (My God, I can't believe my eyes.) She wept as she pushed both arms forward to embrace Maria, who almost fell on top of her in her joy.

Beni gave *abuela* her medication in the realisation that it really would have little *or no* benefit at this stage.

She knew that *abuela* was close to leaving, although she defiantly resisted. 'Whatever is the matter with you darling Maria your face is so blotchy and wet? come and tell me all about your travels my darling baby girl.'

As she shared the tale of her Trans-Spanish-Mexican epic journey, Maria felt that somehow *abuela* was sharing the journey with her. Areas in the south and on the roads northward where she would have walked for days in a vain attempt to flee horrors of the civil wars.

Eventually abuela, who had been gripping Marias hand tightly said.

'*Este hombre Gregg es un buen hombre si ou no?* (Is this man Gregg a good man or not?). A question that Maria found astonishing given *abuela's* state of health. She answered as softly as possible. Sometimes good and other times not. *Abuela* smiled.

All the while Maria related the tale of her life's journey, *abuela's* grey watery eyes never moved from gazing into Maria's. *Abuela* herself was making the journey, with Maria. It was quite wonderful and deeply spiritual, she thought. Both were transfixed; but as they both sat in silence, with mama sitting in the chair in the corner, something else was taking place. Maria said very softly without changing her gaze, mama go and fetch *abuelo* now.' He arrived, worried and looking very sad, he joined them. All three somehow managed to sit on the bed embracing one another. Prayers were uttered and words were whispered as they embraced this wonderful, tranquil and serene experience. *Abuela* lay back on the pillow and departed to the afterlife. Maria bravely stretched forward and gently closed abuela's eyelids and kissed her on her lips. *Abuela* had gone.

Father Francisco was summoned and performed the last rites.

Maria chose to spend as much time as possible with her parents and all of the extended family for as long as it would take for the arrangements to be made. Later that evening, the bell tolled in the church tower. Folk arrived and, with Maria and the rest of the family, made their way to church and to celebrate mass.

A small sincere group contributed to the respectful ending of a wonderful, much-loved member of the village community. A real Espanola in every sense. Afterwards, there was a gathering of locals in the Café El Reunion, a fitting reflection of the community spirit. Father Francisco happily joined in the proceedings and would be making the necessary arrangements. He had officiated at all their family's church affairs for years.

The following week was one in which Maria did a lot of catching up with family in the main. Folk came from far and wide to offer their respects and Maria was happy to receive them.

Her arm being in a sling presented considerable challenges, mainly as she could not drive anywhere, but ever-faithful Pablo would appear at the drop of a hat to bid her will.

Maria sought solace by simply being within the community; she realised how important were the simple things in life. She helped in the garden and visited Alicia and Pedro, who wanted to take her out on the boat, but she was slightly nervous about the limitations of her injury.

During this unplanned extended period of reflection, Maria experienced many diverse thoughts. In recent times, aware of the benefits from "'time out'", she always managed to sabotage her own efforts. Maybe this period would be just the thing. she thought, for a little spiritual harmony; she remembered how it had worked for her in Encinitas, California.

After what Maria decided was a suitable period of reflection, she became more energised and got in touch with many of her former contacts in the north.

Principally, she wanted to meet up with Janet and called her to meet up at El Reunion for a meal and chat. Although *mama* and *papa* had little to do with the day-to-day running of the café these days, Maria loved the atmosphere of the café, and the food was always very good. They spent some time on general chit-chat before getting "down to business" as Janet would say.

'Mags, I can't tell you how nice it really is to have you back. I truly believed that you would be a *goner* by now. Some of the antics you've got up are quite unbelievable. Perhaps now is the time to reappraise your life and make some adjustments.

'Don't get me wrong. I envy you in many ways and full credit, You've shown a lot of commitment to getting drunk and staying drunk over the years; that's hard work. Now if you could apply a fraction of that dedication to staying sober, it'll be a breeze.'

'Well, don't hold back, Jan. Why don't you tell it how

you see it?' They both laughed 'So, Jan, what are you proposing? Do you have some sort of plan in mind?' Maria asked.

'As a recovering alcoholic myself, I know where you're coming from, and without sounding all know-it-all, you know me well enough to understand my level of expertise with working with addiction. To that end, I've landed a plum job, as head of addictions services.

'To me that means nothing if I can't get my best friend on to a programme of living that could save her life, because I know deep- down that if you carry on your days are numbered. I've seen your medical records. Your system is failing. How you're getting away with it is a testament to sheer will-power, Maria'

'So what do you want me to do? Obviously, you have a comprehensive knowledge about substance misuse and I believe you when you say my days are numbered. So am I a helpless case? Am I a lost cause, Jan?'

'No, Mags, I don't believe you are, but you need to take immediate action and get on a programme of living free from drugs and alcohol. You came to my graduation and since then I got a Masters Degree opening up all sorts of opportunities, so I've studied about every treatment plan known to man. The simplest is based on the Minnesota model of twelve steps to recovery.'

'People have been calling me an alcoholic for years but I don't think I am, and I hate the whole idea of being given that label, an alcoholic. I'm not one of those people. I can stop any time,' Maria stuttered out as tears began to form and her voice began to choke.

'That's where we've got to start, Mags; acceptance. I'll be round tomorrow and well get started. Meanwhile get thinking about our conversation and consider '"quitting one day at a time"'. Just one day at a time, not the rest of your life but one day only."

'Thanks for coming over. Jan, been a while, so let's get something going if you can spare the time. You're obviously very busy in your new position. Hope that works out for you. You've worked really hard to get where you are, Jan. Tomorrow then.'

Maria had plenty to think about as she waited for her parents to finish off in the café. It was only a short walk home and Maria had been getting used to walking around the village, but *papa* had the car; they always had something to carry so the car was necessary.

'Maria, if you need me to take you anywhere, just ask. It must be awful for you not being able to drive.' She did want to take advantage of their hospitality but she needed to visit Janet's house tomorrow and get started.

'Thanks, *papa*, that's fine, I'm fine. I appreciate all that everyone is doing for me. It's really nice just hanging out with you both. Maybe tomorrow if you're not busy. We need to support one another, as *abuela*'s funeral is going to be tough. I can't begin to tell you how much it meant for me to come home and see *abuela* for the last time.'

Papa did not understand the extent of Maria's alcohol problem and the subsequent situation with MexTex, but he and *mama* had already decided that whatever it cost, they would pay for her treatment.

In the car, she explained to *papa* about the dream she had had in Mexico about *abuela*; he pulled the car over and stopped.

'You know, on her death-bed while I waited for *mama* to fetch *abuelo*, she very softly whispered in my ear, *"I prayed for you every night and knew you were listening. When I had a fall in the kitchen, I knew you were there for me, Maria, I knew you were coming home so I hung on and waited for you, and here you are. Bless you, darling."*'

All three sat in the car by the side of the road and wept, then carried on to Janet's home.

*

The days rolled by with Maria now in the bosom of her family, getting used to the inactivity up to a point. It was relaxing; watching TV, visiting friends and generally chilling out. The arm was healing and the doctors said another week and she could have the plaster cast removed.

Abuela's funeral was a wonderful event as they celebrated the dear old lady's long and interesting life. There were eulogies a-plenty and anecdotal treats. Maria scribbled notes on the order of service sheets; it was too good an opportunity to miss out on material for her journal.

For Maria, the service, a mass, was far too long and unable to cope she tippled away at vodka throughout the day. The wake was appropriately held in the Fishermen's Union Hall, which was a touching idea but totally inadequate, as so many turned up to honour the occasion.

Most of the activities took place on the lawns overlooking the harbour.

Folks came from far and wide. The furthermost point was Vancouver Island, Canada; another fisherman in the tradition of the family, a wealthy man owning a large fishing and processing business.

Relatives and friends meeting after a long absence renewed friendships, vowing to 'keep in touch.'

Maria had any amount of job offers but she was not really in the market to come home just yet. She felt the love and the genuine desire from others to rekindle old friendships, but she still had a strong fascination with the world outside the confines of village life; she knew not where, but that was the point of adventure.

'*What's round the next bend on the road?*' she thought. Possibly a trip to the ashram in Encinatas. California had been thrilling and thought-provoking, as was the wonderful time she spent with Montse in Andalucia. She called Leanne.

'Thank God you're there Leanne. How are you, babe?' There was a rumbling sound from Leanne's phone.

'Hello, are you there, Leanne? Maria repeated.

'Yeah, sorry, can't hear too well windows open in the car bit noisy. You good or what?' Leanne replied.

'Well I've got so much news, I don't know where to start, but the crux of the matter is how are we going to get together and sort out *you know what?*'

'Well I was trying to surprise you with an unannounced visit, but that's blown now so here's my story. You know I went home to Gibraltar? Well these two soldiers, a captain and his wife in the Royal Marine band were stationed on the Rock but have been posted back to the U.K. as the woman is pregnant. The long and the short of it is we're all travelling by car to… Santander. We should be there by tomorrow night.'

'Shutuuup, I don't believe you, Leanne.'

'Honest, no kidding, that's the truth. Be with you *manana*, honey.'

*

The sunrise over the Cantabrian mountains was stunning as Maria ventured out alone into the fresh, invigorating salty air.

'I love this place so much, I'm never going to leave. I've got love and family here. Why should I wander?' she asked *mama*.

'I for one, darling, would love that more than anything else in the world, but I can't really believe you would stay after your adventures,' *mama* replied.

Leanne arrived, full of fun. She had tacky souvenirs of Gibraltar for Maria and her parents. Beni had never met Leanne before, and as she saw them together, she understood the mutual attraction. They were so happy together.

'Those two are as crazy as each other, No wonder they get into scrapes together, like a pair of teenagers,' *Mama* said to *papa* as they finished their lunch in *mama*'s café.

'Just look at the way they polished off that bottle of red. You would think it was fruit juice. They're not even tipsy.' Despite his advancing years, *papa* was very young in his outlook and attitude to life. Self-aware, confident and comfortable, his faith was very important to him, but he never pushed it onto others. Maria had always 'done her own thing.'

He simply shrugged in a very non-judgemental manner; worldly-wise with vast life experiences, which included severe deprivation and crippling hardship. He had lived 'one day at a time' with gratitude. 'Let them enjoy it while they can. They're blessed to have one another,' he said.

Papa had many friends not only in the village but in the wider world. He maintained his links with like-minded people. Maria's friend Janet and he were very close; she had a similar philosophy for life, which included living one day at a time.

He never had the privilege of a formal academic education, but his intuition and ability to assess situations and people was very sharp. He was instinctively aware that Maria and Leanne had serious issues which needed to be addressed but he said nothing.

Janet had to attend business meetings in Santander with the health service but as promised, she met Maria for a brief session to offer suggestions, which included going to a meeting that night. She left but not before giving Maria another catch-phrase; '*Rigorous honesty in all your affairs*'.

Conscious, that they could be overheard in the café the pair withdrew to the house where they spoke freely about the pressing issue of MexTex and in particular, Gregg Holdsworth.

The discussions went on most of the afternoon, mostly re-living the good times and how much fun and excitement they both had, but most especially Maria's experience of living a movie-star existence, if only for a short while. The trade-off, being a kept woman with Gregg calling all the shots, she now realised, that was totally dishonest.

Having spent enough time on the fun stuff, they thought they had better get down to business. Their predicament was that they had managed to keep everything secret, so there was no one around to try and help them resolve matters. Cool, calm and collected they sat and wrote down their present situation in the hope that they would find solutions to their dilemmas;

1. They had a very expensive apartment which was unoccupied as far as they were aware. Should they remove their personal items and simply abandon the place?

2. They both had lovely new cars, with registration documents of ownership. What should they do about them?

3. Their salaries had been on standing orders, paid into their respective banks, but now there was no recent payment.

4. They both had unlimited access to credit cards through the company. What should they do about that?

Probably the most important item on the agenda was:

5. Should they come forward to the FBI and CNI, and declare their interest?

After a couple of hours, with the distraction of many and varied alcoholic beverages, no solution had been found. Indeed, all that had been achieved was the oblivion of sleep.

Their trip into the arms of Morpheus' was only disturbed by the sound of the front door slamming as Beni, Claudio and Janet entered the house.

'What the heck's going on in here?' Janet exclaimed as she saw the pair knocked-out on the settee, surrounded by empty bottles and dirty glasses.

Genuinely very shocked, Beni could not believe what she was seeing as she began tidying up the mess. She was angry and felt quite let-down by Maria.

'You and I are going to have some serious words, *senorita*.' said Janet. 'I'll make coffee' said Claudio.

'I had intended to collect you for a meeting tonight as I was returning from Santander, but there's a change of plan. I'll go home and freshen up and be back around seven and we'll go to the meeting once you've sobered up a little.' Janet said, and departed. She was familiar with clients letting themselves down especially in the early stages of recovery.

TWENTY-EIGHT

ARRIONDAS

The day arrived for Maria to try out her arm with driving the car. She arose early and with Leanne ate breakfast on the patio out front of El Reunion; her parents were doing a shift at the restaurant, as it was apparent that they were doing to have a busy day.

'What do you fancy doing today then. Leanne? Drive maybe?' Maria asked.

'Well, if you're okay to drive with your arm and all, yeah, that would be cool. We could get off the patch for a bit. Nice as it is, I find it gets a bit claustrophobic after a while,' Leanne admitted.

'I'm bound to say I agree with you, There's only so much serenity I can handle at the moment.' Maria agreed.

'Yeah, so how did that meeting go last night? Any good, Maria?'

There was a slight pause before Maria answered; she was unsure exactly how to answer that question. She didn't want to dismiss it out of hand, but she didn't agree with it either. 'Interesting, quite a mixed bunch. They all identified themselves as alcoholic.

'Didn't know what to expect really. They were just ordinary folk admitting they were alcohol dependent. "I'm Carlo, I'm alcoholic," that stuff you see in the movies. There was a doctor, a surgeon actually, which I thought was a bit dodgy; a priest, but not in uniform; a mum with three kids, not with her, thank God; a professional footballer; bit of everything going, to be honest, Leanne.'

'Going to go back, kid?' Leanne asked.

'Janet is putting me on her programme. She said she will give me one last chance to get straight. It's time I got honest with my life and the damage alcohol is doing to my mind, body and spirit, and to others.'

It will mean moving away for a bit and she wants total abstinence. Nothing else will do. I've run out of options. This programme could save my life. It's as serious as that.

'She knows me well enough. Residential rehabs, did not work in the past. They were a waste of time and money. This is a concerted effort. My part is to not take a drink one day at a time and get to ninety meetings in ninety days.'

'Bloody hell, Maria. That sounds really tough. Where on earth are you even going to find ninety meetings around here? You'll never do that, *chica*!' Leanne told Maria, unconvinced.

'That's exactly why she wants me to move away. I must have positive people around me or I've got no chance. Sadly,

Leanne, we need to get stuff sorted before I leave. Come on, let's drive down the coast a little and maybe visit Janet at her parent's' home. It's quite beautiful there,' she suggested.

As they drove westward along the coastal route, with the sun high in the cloudless blue sky, Maria thought it was paradise. She wished she had her lovely convertible car, but that was somewhere she knew not where down in Barcelona. Leanne had gone very quiet, clearly upset that her friend appeared to be abandoning her.

'We'll pull over for a coffee. There's a great village, San Vicente, just off to the side on the bay.' It was so quiet and peaceful; the fishing boats had put to sea and the café's were not yet busy.

They picked out a café right on the quayside, but Leanne complained that it smelled of fish.

'What do you expect?' Maria said, 'It's a fishing village. Are you going to be difficult or can we have a sensible conversation? We've got a lot to sort out and we've put it off for too long. We made a list and then got drunk before we even attempted to tackle it.'

'Oh, so you've been to one meeting and suddenly you know everything. The first thing is to get rid of me, who's seen you through most of your terrible times, embarrassing and frightening times.'

'No, of course not, darling. You've always been there for me through thick and thin. I know that, but that was a different time. We had lots of fun and got through some dodgy stuff together. That will never be forgotten but we were living in cloud cuckoo land, working for a couple of very tricky guys.

'They are deep in the poo and will probably be going away for a very long time. We've got to save our sorry asses and clear ourselves. The word for me is that if I don't get straight, I have no future at all. It's literally do or die. Let's go and see Janet.'

Janet's parents were English. Gwen and Albert (Bert) had two other daughters, Laura and Kelly, and a son, Andrew. The extended family lived in England but loved to get together, especially on special occasions like Christmas. They made sure that was a priority, praying for snow which although infrequent, would transform the landscape into a winter wonderland. An agrarian bonanza of plants trees, flora and fauna of every description. The summer air, scented with natural fragrances, was intoxicating; it permeated the entire area, accompanied by the amazing variety of birdsong.

Their house, a converted Hermitage, dated back about 300 years. It had been restyled in a sympathetic manner reflecting their love for the origins of the property. There was also an outbuilding (*almacen*), which was used for parties and extra guests when required.

Set amongst the foothills of the Picos Europa, the property lay on a hillside sloping gently away to the valley below. There was a goat grazing, along with hens and geese and a very old black Labrador dog. With impaired vision, it sadly bumped into everything.

The house had been run very successfully for many years as a *posada*. They had a regular returning clientele of folk of all nationalities most of whom enjoyed walking the trails which Bert had compiled over time. He had printed maps for the use of the clients.

As they pulled up on the drive, the only bit of level ground. Gwen came out to greet them with hugs and kisses. Her guests had all gone walking, giving her time to offer tea and scones before preparing lunch.

Basking in the warm sunshine, Leanne could see the attraction of this lifestyle and wondered if this would suit her in the future; but not for today she thought.

'Where's Dad, Ma?' Janet hollered out. 'We're going to walk down to the village with Maria, and Laura.' Maria thought Laura had a very similar disposition to her friend Montse in Andalucía; calm, serene and deeply spiritual. She had just completed her yoga session and suggested a walk.

'Oh, your father's down at the bottom of the garden, chipping golf balls into a net, I imagine, and he won't make that walk these days with his knee problems. I'll give him a shout. See him when you get back from your walk,' Gwen said.

Leanne took one look down the valley. 'It looks simple enough going down but I honestly can't see me getting back up that hill, girls. I'm not as fit as you Yoga types.'

'Ah, that's where we have a surprise for you, Leanne, we get a cab back up. The cabbies know us well and as we give them business, we get special rates,' Laura explained.

They set off down a fairly steep sloping hill, through an area abounding with scented plants and butterflies, The peace and serenity only broken by the occasional backyard dog growling to ward-off intruders.

As Janet walked with Maria, they ran over some of the more pressing issues, but the big issue was her silence in avoiding the authorities. Should she come forward? she asked Janet. As far as Janet was concerned, there was no doubt in her mind. She must come forward and face the consequences, if she really wanted to get sober and stay sober, Janet emphasised very strongly.

'It's about rigorous honesty in all your affairs. All means all,' she repeated. The walk finished in the heart of Arriondas, known for its *siderias* (cider bars). The whole place smelled of cider that had been splashed around by waiters attempting to get some bubbles into the flat, very strong cider. Maria coped with the strange situation very well; she resisted, whilst the others managed half a glass, at most.

They got the cab back up and had tea on the terrace with Gwen, and the serious worry had been broached. Janet offered to take the girls to the police station in Santander and face the music.

Intuitively, she had concerns about the police station visit. She did not wish to take her car but rather opted to be driven by Maria, who had not had a drink for some time, and was beginning to get quite jittery. They stopped en route for something to eat; Janet anticipated a long night at the police station.

On arrival, the desk sergeant was out of his depth with the information coming across his desk from the girls, so he called for help from one of the detectives.

They were escorted into an ante-room, at which point Janet was asked to leave. Telephone calls, text messages, emails, photocopies of Gregg and Gonzales; it was a techno nightmare. The girls became increasingly afraid, as they felt quite helpless and unable to get across their version of events. The police were clearly very angry at their slowness at coming forward earlier. A senior detective inspector, D.I Martinez, arrived.

'We don't really believe your stories, and while you play innocent, you were clearly complicit in the company conspiracy. For that reason, while you're not actually under arrest, we want you to remain here overnight while we get instructions from a higher authority and further details of the company's activities.'

Janet left the police station feeling very uncomfortable, having second thoughts about the advice she had given; she felt really bad about them being detained.

She took Maria's car and driving back home, she phoned a good friend, a top barrister, Massimo. She discussed the basic details of the situation, and his view was that although they should have come forward earlier, that in itself could be excused.

The police would never be able to offer a case to prove the girls' involvement with Gregg's clandestine operations. Massimo would be happy to take the case and have them released first thing in the morning. He finished with an invitation to Janet.

'Would you like to join me? I'm going to a meeting tonight in Santander? We could have a little supper after.' Janet was more than happy with that result all round. Massimo would get in touch with the police and let the girls know the good news.

Massimo called in at the police station to explain that he would be handling the case and was clear that at no time did the women ever actually see any money-handling or indeed any drugs at all. In his opinion, they had no case to answer, and as soon as the superintendent detective could be summoned they should be released under his cognisance.

Meanwhile, in separate cells, they tried to settle down as best they could. Maria was cold and hungry, with a single blanket. She called for the guard to bring her another blanket but could get no response. Leanne called out from somewhere in the depths of the underground cell block.

'Hey, whoever you girls are shut up. We're trying to get some sleep.' Came through the air from another cell.

Maria knew the guards were trying to punish them for not coming forward earlier with information and for trying to get away with it.

Cold, hungry and very angry, the girls kept each other company, calling out and ignoring the other prisoner's plea for silence. Just when they thought it couldn't get any worse, the guards turned out the single light in the cell. They knew that the guards were being particularly vindictive because they believed the girls were guilty.

*

Morning couldn't come soon enough as handcuffed the pair were led up the cold stone staircase to the custody suite.

Massimo had worked a minor miracle. The girls would have to stay in the area and not attempt to leave until the judiciary felt it was appropriate, but they were free to leave the police station.

Maria had the most overwhelming sense of dread as she looked at the custody sergeant; an enormous man, quite expressionless. She thought all that was missing was the shiny black hat of the dreaded sinister *Guardia Civil* of old.

Massimo and Janet whisked the pair away for breakfast in a local café which they demolished with great relish. Full English with all the trimmings.

Janet wasted no time at all and arranged for Maria to have a medical examination later in the day to confirm the necessity for her to enter a rehabilitation programme in London for treatment for her alcohol addiction.

They attended the local magistrate's' court after breakfast; the magistrate somewhat reluctantly agreed with that proposal and made the necessary arrangements for Maria's release on Janet's cognisance. However, Leanne's case was more complicated due to her legal status. They could not make up their minds if she was Spanish or English, necessitating further enquiries, but she was released on Massimo's cognisance.

'Her release would be conditional on the understanding that she, Leanne, remained in Spain, until some resolution could be found. I certainly don't believe the prosecution service would want to risk wasting public tax payer's' money on a case as flimsy as this one. They have got the big guys and they will of course, engage a top defence council, which could protract the whole affair out considerably. She must surrender her passport,' Massimo explained.

She had planned on going home to Gibraltar. That posed a massive problem; that would mean leaving Spain.

Massimo would have to work on that issue; otherwise, she would not be able to go home and get support from her family at this very emotionally trying time.

Maria, very confused and full of guilt, amid a whole range of other emotions, called Luis. She had a moment of realisation that he was the one consistent part of her life that had not been contaminated by the ring of deception and corruption in which she had been living for some time.

'*Hola Luis es Maria, Comesta?* Hope you're well, and sorry I've not been in touch for a little while. There's been so much going on. I don't know where to start to tell you about it all.' she said.

'How about at the beginning? That might be a good place, *cara mia*,' he replied.

'Well, it's far too complicated, but I'll tell you I've been released from police custody in Santander and I'm missing you very much. If you have the time later…I'll tell you more, she said.

Sitting in a bar close by the magistrates' court in Santander. Maria was overwhelmed with emotion following the call to Luis.

Maria, Leanne, Massimo and Janet were all delighted with the outcome of the hearing; albeit there was work to be done on behalf of Leanne.

Driving back to Maria's parents,' café for lunch Massimo outlined his strategy for each of them. They needed to show a serious commitment and strong resolve to the judiciary, and to comply with the order with immediate effect.

They enjoyed a seafood platter to share with no alcohol for Maria. The days were getting shorter as winter was fast approaching, but it was unseasonably very warm as small, puffy white clouds reflected out of the clear blue sky on the water in the harbour.

Maria's phone jangled into life with a very excited Luis telling her that he had booked a flight from Madrid to Santander and would be arriving later in the day. Massimo asked for the phone and spoke with Luis, advising him under no circumstances to go near Maria's apartment, and to leave the car wherever it was. He impressed upon them the importance of not delaying in implementing the plan.

Tio Pedro, with Maria, collected Luis from the airport later that day. A moving and joyful reunion; they ate at Beni's house and chatted late into the night. Luis the gentleman that he was, opted for sleeping in the spare room out of respect for the situation. *Mama* commented. 'He's a rare man you have there. Maria, You should hang on to that one, *cara mia*.'

*

Morning brought another exceptionally sunny and warm day, with Maria cooking Luis breakfast, which they ate on the patio. Realising they were on a time-limited day. Maria asked *papa* if she could borrow his car, just to show Luis a little of the village and the surrounding countryside where she had grown up.

He loved the place and as she drove into the hills, they could still see Santa Maria del Mar below. She excitedly pointed out places where family and friends lived, her old school and the church by the sea where she had her first communion. They took a blanket from the car and lay out in the fresh, warm air of Cantabria.

She was aware that the only two men in her life who loved her for who she was were Luis and Pablo. Neither of them had made any sexual advance towards her.

She slowly moved her head across to place it in Luis' lap and as he caressed her hair, he bent down and kissed her. It was the kiss of a man who was giving her his love. She raised herself up and grasped his neck, pulling him down on her. There was a simmering passion within and around them, that neither of them had ever felt before. Maria wanted the love of this man, the passion of this man; a gentle loving sensation which he seemed to exude as they gradually became intertwined and became as one. The sensation just went on and on until they finally just lay there embraced. *I love this man with every fibre of my being I just want have this mans children this is the way I must go. At last I understand true love. I want this to last forever*

They lay there afterwards, neither wanting to spoil the moment both wanting it to go on forever.

Luis was the first to speak, 'Maria, I need to tell you that I'm totally in love with you and have been so since first we met. I know the timing is not great, as you're about to be whisked off to England for some time so we'll be separated, but...' and he stood up at that point and then knelt back down again on one knee, producing a ring from his pocket ... erm'... would you do me the great honour of considering me in marriage?' he asked.

She scrambled herself together and grabbing him around the neck, smothered him all over his face with kisses.

'I will, I will, I will… I definitely will. I'll make you a wife to be proud of Luis. I'm the happiest woman in Spain, no, in the whole world right now. I dreamed of this day ever since you gave me the St Christopher in Madrid to guide me on my journey to La Mancha. You sure got organised since our phone call yesterday morning. Where did you get the ring? It's so beautiful.'

'The ring I've had for quite a while. My mother gave it to me ages ago. It belonged to my *abuela*. It's been waiting patiently for the right moment with the right person. Now it has happened, the right person is in my life.' Luis said with great sincerity and no small amount of pride in his voice.

Maria replied, 'I will wear it with pride and dignity and can't wait to show *mama*. She really likes you and now she will love you, as will all the family in their own way. But now we need to get back home, as Janet will be taking me to the airport tonight, bound for London Gatwick.'

Mama was absolutely delighted and immediately instructed Maria on getting busy on the baby front; she had been desperate for Maria to produce grandchildren for most of her adult life and now she had possibilities.

Janet arrived and wishing to minimise the pain of separation, organised everyone in a very matter-of-fact manner. She promised Maria's return in approximately six weeks' time. The farewells were sad and tearful but she pressed on with her official 'social care hat on,' and soon they were on their way to the airport.

TWENTY-NINE

THE LAST CHANCE

ULTIMO OPERTUNIDAD

The cheap, budget-jet airliner circled London Gatwick at 3000 feet as the flight attendant checked that all was secure in the cabin. Maria felt some excitement, mixed with apprehension as she opened her window blind; all she could see was grey mist, so she closed the blind again. Janet, sitting in the next seat, laughed.

The flight attendant wished everyone a safe onward journey and reminded them that the time was 6 am October 25th 2015. It was far too early for jokes, Maria thought.

'Welcome to London, Maria. You'll be all right. You've got plenty of warm clothes and you're starting the first day of your new life.'

Leaving the aircraft, the covered link walkway seemed to go on forever, adding to Maria's already depressed state. The grey mist thickened and Janet worried that they may not be able to make the road journey to South London through the fog.

Quick to pick up the mood, Janet said, 'Fancy a coffee and croissant here, or get going straight home, Mags?' Without a moment's' hesitation, she opted for the here and now option.

They cleared customs and headed to Starbucks. As they sipped their café lattes, Maria felt sad deep inside and admitted to Janet she was desperate for a drink.

'These first few days are going to be really tough, Maria, and I'm not going to sugar-coat it at all. I'm not going to "'therap'" your whole life either, but I will hand you many useful tips along the way, so just get used to it. That's my style. It has a proven track record for most cases. I'll go the extra mile for you, Maria, but you must give one hundred per cent of yourself.'

'There a good example right there and you didn't even notice.'

'What's that, Jan?'

'Well, you opted for the drink of coffee rather than go on with the journey. That was the smart move. If you're hungry or thirsty, eat and drink. Simple as that, but of course, no alcohol.

'Always have some water with you. Keep your journal going, write stuff down no matter how trivial it may seem. It may come in useful at some point, believe me.

'A little very useful acronym for you, Mags. It's proved to be invaluable over the years. HALT; hungry, angry, lonely, tired. Any one of those feelings can be a trigger; get all four together then it get very dangerous for the alcoholic.

'I can see how addicted you are and how your dependence has increased since last I saw you. What I'm proposing, now I've had the chance to observe you, is a very short stay in a detox and rehab facility, to which I have access.

'We'll go back to the flat first, get settled and I'll make a couple of calls. Don't worry, *chica*. All will be well, eventually, but this is the real world now no messing.'

'Janet, I feel so bad. Can I have a little drink? That always works for me, just to take the edge off things and stop the hands from shaking... I, f... f... feel sick and r... really ill.' She stuttered.

'Absolutely not, Maria, No alcohol within a mile for you.' Janet stressed.

They arrived at the flat and in the half-light of the rainy, foggy day, it looked pretty grim. Maria shuddered once more and on the verge of tears said.

'Is that it? Have you brought me all this way to stay in a bloody squat? Can't believe you, Janet.'

The lights from the shop below the flat were the only sign of light and human warmth, Maria thought, as she stood shivering on the door-step.

Jan pushed the shop door open with a '*Ping*' and called, 'Hello, Arv, are you there? It's Spanish Jan, and my friend Maria, just back from Spain.'

Arv came running to the door and grabbed the pair of them, 'Come in, come in, for goodness' sake, out of the rain.' He welcomed them with a cheery smile. The shop was bright and warm with an inviting aroma of Indian food, mingled with sandalwood incense burning somewhere in the back.

'I hope you're staying for a while, Janet.' Arv said.

'Yeah, we've got some business to attend to, which means we will be staying for a while until that is completed. This is my good friend Maria, who will be moving in for a while, but we'll get upstairs now and catch up later. Good to see you. Love to Meera.

'Bye for now, mate.' Janet said as they opened the door and climbed the stairs to the flat above.

Entering the flat, Maria was quite shocked; it was clean, dry and warm, but that was about all she could see in its favour. Basic did not begin to describe it. She felt even more miserable than before she'd opened the door.

'Well here we are, Maria. You're beginning the first day of your new life. I can see it's a shock to you but it's adequate for your needs. You will start to work out your own priorities and they, along with the programme, will enable you to think more clearly about which way you want your life to proceed.' Janet laid it on the line.

'I've sent a message to a doctor friend of mine who will give you something to take the edge off the withdrawals. There will be a little "'cold turkey'" involved but we will manage that between us. You have to let go and trust us on that one,' Janet continued.

Janet had managed to convince her colleagues in the residential rehabilitation centre for substance misuse services to accept Maria on a short period of treatment.

It would be a short fairly sharp detoxification under supervised medical care followed by a day programme and a compulsory period of attendance at the meetings.

It was a no-nonsense tried and tested method which had worked for many over the years.

The treatment plan would be supervised by Janet, who agreed to act as her sponsor to guarantee her attendance for forty meetings in forty days.

Janet went on to explain to her. 'This, of course sounds a very draconian measure, and I would normally not try and coerce a patient into treatment. However, because I care so much for you, I want to push you hard to save yourself. All other options, in my opinion, were almost bound to fail.

'I'm really worried about you, Maria and believe you have one last chance, (*el ultimo opertunidad*). If after this you go back to your old behaviour, you will die. and I don't want that, and neither do you. Believe me when I say I've seen it all too often, *chica*. I'll be your sponsor and we'll get through this one day at a time.'

Maria could do no more than listen to Janet and take everything on trust; she could barely understand most of it anyway her mind just craving drink.

The prescription for the drugs to ease withdrawals arrived and she was able to start self-medicating right away under Janet's supervision.

'Well it's going to be a long haul Maria to get you through some difficult times, but I know together we can do it. It's going to be an emotional roller coaster at times with lessons to be learned along the way. But I know you can do it, Maria, if you apply the tenacity of which we both know you're capable.

'The hardest part through the initial stages will be in the UK, when it's going to be very much one day at a time. Don't worry, before you know it, you'll be back in your homeland with friends and family in your beloved Cantabria,' she promised.

'Hi, ladies good to see you and we would love for you to come and eat with us to welcome you. The children are super excited and Meera has prepared a lovely vegetarian Indian treat for all of us. So as soon as you like, come down.' Arv *pranaamed* and went downstairs.

'Well, that's a brilliant start to the first day of your new life. Mags. Janet prayed;*'Mags, Jan and the Higher Power together we can make it.'*

> "Look to this day
> For it is life
> The very life of life
> In its brief course lies all
> The realities and verities of existence
> The bliss of growth
> The splendour of action,
> The glory of power
>
> For yesterday is but a dream
> And tomorrow is only a vision
> But today, well lived,
> Makes every yesterday a dream of happiness
> And every tomorrow a vision of hope.
> Look well, therefore, to this day."
>
> ***Sanskrit proverb***

EPILOGUE

Totally abstinent from alcohol and other mind-altering substances, Maria set up a regular meeting in the village for those visiting from abroad and locals alike. Inspired by Ginny, the waitress in the VIP airport lounge in Barcelona, back in her bad old days, the meeting proved a great success. The sign over the door to the meeting room reads *CARPE DIEM* (seize the day).

She left the travel business behind her and devoted her new life to raising her new baby girl, who they named Arcoiris (rainbow) as it symbolised the perfect ending to Maria's amazing journey; her Odyssey.

Abuela, left a considerable legacy of a very large parcel of farmland not far from the village. Maria used her share to open a motor franchise with Luis in Santander, promoting and selling hybrid and all-electric cars.

The pair undertook a complete renovation of *abuela*'s old house, including an architecturally sensitive extension built with local sandstone block work. With their two children Arcoiris and Ignacio, they settled right back where Maria started; in Santa Maria del Mar, close by her parents and extended family in Cantabria. However her prize possession was *abuela*'s rosary beads which upon her deathbed, she had pressed into Maria's hand and with her last breath, had whispered, *Dios lo bendiga.*' (God bless you.) An episode that Maria kept private, feeling it was too precious to share.

Janet became the director of a children's services organisation in Spain and had a roving commission to oversee substance misuse services in England.

She was awarded an OBE by the British Government for her services in the field of substance misuse.

Leanne returned to La Linea, southern Spain, where she became the primary carer for her disabled and widowed father.

She never married and frequently visited Maria's family, often holidaying with them in their villa on the Canary island of Lanzarote.

The directors of MexTex, Mr.Gregg Holdsworth and Snr. Benjamin Gonzales, were tried in their respective countries and found guilty of dealing in illegal drugs and money laundering.

Summing up for sentencing, the judge said. 'The convictions for drug dealing and money laundering are clear and evident. The charges of un-American activities by Gregg Holdsworth are inconclusive and acknowledge that while there was insufficient evidence for a conviction, the whole affair is distasteful, especially for a man who served his country in the airforce with such distinction. As a role model for future generations he has a great deal for which to answer.'

Both men were handed down very severe sentences and were currently serving extremely lengthy custodial sentences in their respective countries. All of their assets had been confiscated.

Both Maria and Leanne made comprehensive statements, witnessed by their solicitor in Santander, of their respective roles within the company MexTex. The high court judiciary agreed that those statements made under oath and witnessed by the appropriate authorities were sufficient and as neither of them had actually personally seen drugs or illegal monies. they had no evidence to offer and as such would not be required to appear in court.

Neither Maria nor Leanne ever had any further contact with their former employers. They both lost their apartment and cars but retained their liberty. They frequently shared their good fortune with each other holding fast to the serenity prayer;

"God grant me the serenity
To accept the things I cannot change
The courage to change the things I can
And the wisdom to know the difference".

ACKNOWLEDGEMENTS

This book is a work of fiction. All characters, organisations and events portrayed in this novel are products of the author's imagination or are used fictitiously.

The book most likely would never have seen the light of day had it not been for the global pandemic, the deadly virus Covid 19. As we were classified by the Government as clinically extremely vulnerable, it meant we had to stay at home. For everyone life changed, forever possibly.

So firstly I acknowledge gratitude for all those who brought in food and medication throughout that period. Gardening became a life saver along with jigsaw and crosswords puzzles. Exercise was limited to indoor cycling. Golf was forbidden. Inspired by the Scottish Makar (Laureate) Jackie Kay I began writing poetry; so big thanks to Jackie, love your work.

Brian Sparks a published author and professional golf coach encouraged me at that point to write a novel. 'Write what you know about.' He gave me great tips and hard feedback on my early attempts, and warned that writing the book was only part of the process. Publishing could be fraught with difficulty. Brian you were right. Fortunately help was at hand from Kay Moriarty, and John Ayerrs published authors and Laura Erb. They enabled me to steer a path through the world of publishing. Thank you all.

A big thank you for the really tough job of proof reading to Gwen Nairn Brian Sparks and Laura Erb.

With the great cover design and artwork by Allan Nairn, Arnelle Dow and Rick Wiley, Maria is brought to life visually. Many thanks for that; great job

Photography by grandchildren Millie Barr and Dan Nairn. Many thanks to you both.

To Troubador the publishers many thanks for getting Maria in print. Great looking book. Special thanks to Emily, and Fern for their patience, and Ann-Marie screen editing with great sensitivity accompanying Maria on her journey. Lastly to you dear reader, many thanks for taking the time to join Maria on her Odyssey. I hope you believe in her as much as I do.

Carpe Diem.

BIBLIOGRAPHY

Collins and Lapierre *Or I'll Dress You in Mourning* (Weidenfield and Nicholson, 8 Winsley Street, London W.1, 1968)

Mellody Pia, *Facing Codependence* (Harper, San Francisco ,1989)

Perls, Hefferline, Goodman, *Gestalt Therapy* (Souvenir Press, London, 1986)

AUTHORS NOTE

Born to Scottish parents in London at the outbreak of w.w.2. Sonny spent his early years between London and Glasgow. His father serving at sea in the North Atlantic and his mother raising him and his sister Kitty avoiding bombs in each of those cities, he soon became aware of danger, risk and protection issues in order to survive. This not only enabled him to enjoy the rich benefits of multiculturism, but also to experience the negative aspects of racism, In common with other immigrant families he found it necessary to make an extra effort to get on in life in London. Brother Allan Brian would arrive post-war. Sonny's career pathway was threefold, from structural design engineering, through entrepreneurship with Gwen in the health food business, eventually blossoming into the world of psychology and social care. Practicing both privately and in the public sector, with a double degree in European social work he specialised in the field of substance misuse. Having found his true vocation he practiced way beyond retirement age. Married for 60 years with Gwen by his side, he proudly claims ***that,*** along with his loving, caring, extensive and ever-expanding multicultural family, is his finest achievement.

Maria's Odyssey, a work of fiction is the authors first novel.

Matador

For exclusive discounts on Matador titles,
sign up to our occasional newsletter at
troubador.co.uk/bookshop